THE REVOLUTIONS OF STAGE DESIGN IN THE 20th CENTURY

1. F. Depero, *I miei balli plastici,* a panorama of all of Depero's plastic ballets conceived for the Piccoli Theater, 1918. Detailed. Mattioli Coll. Photo. M. Perotti.

DENIS BABLET

THE REVOLUTIONS OF STAGE DESIGN
IN THE 20th CENTURY

Original Lithographs by
JOAN MIRO

Book design by
Jacques Dopagne

LEON AMIEL • PUBLISHER
PARIS - NEW YORK

FERNALD LIBRARY
COLBY-SAWYER COLLEGE
NEW LONDON, N.H. 03257

PN
2091
S8
B25

11/88 Barnett 59.95

In preparing this work we required, among other things, serious research and documentation. We could not have accomplished these tasks without the cooperation of many people and organizations.

We gratefully acknowledge the contribution of the artists and the assistance of collectors, libraries and museums whose documents we were able to reproduce in this work.

I would like to express my personal gratitude to Maiten Bouisset for her great aid in assembling the illustrations; to Nadege Mayet for valuable work done in compiling the book. I think especially of Jacques Dopagne who so well understood the work which I undertook, and solved all the necessary aesthetic and didactic problems.

I certainly cannot forget two men without whom this work would have never seen the light of day. My heartfelt thanks go to Leon Amiel whose tenacity and dedication made the realization of this book possible and to Gualtieri San Lazzaro who did not live to see the work completed.

And finally I must express my great respect and admiration for Joan Miro whose two beautiful, original lithographs illustrate this book. My profoundest thanks to all.

D.B.

88271

© 1977 BY LEON AMIEL • PUBLISHER
ISBN 0-8148-0652-X
Printed in France

Introduction

List of abbreviations: See page 386

The transformation in the arts that has taken place since the end of the nineteenth century is in every respect comparable to the economic, scientific and social upheavals that have had such a profound effect upon our civilization. It has been an epoch of crisis similar to Renaissance times. One world has been gradually disappearing while new forms have been created out of the extraordinary confrontation between experience and ideas as the present is shaped from the explosive encounter between the past and the future. The theater has also been going through a period of reevaluation and questioning. This is the scope of my concern here. Specifically, I shall try to analyze the evolution of stage design from 1880 until the present, from the academicism of the romantic period to more recent theatrical productions.

The problems of stage design are central to the important issues concerning the theater and art in general. It has been said that the theater is the mirror of man, but it might be asked — what mirror and of which man? Is it enough for the theater to offer a simple and faithful image, or should it attempt to introduce a new universe that will give us a better understanding of the real world? Can theater be called creation or is its role merely one of imitation?

Some people have said that the theater should be like a rite. But what sort of rite do they mean? A form of light entertainment that can be viewed dispassionately and that provides simply a pleasant escape from life's daily cares? Or should it be a vital spiritual ritual to be celebrated in communal fashion?

Everyone, of course, has his own ideas about what structures and means of expression are essential to the theater. For some the text is king; for others the actor is everything. Some even assert that the theater is the highest form of art because it brings together and synthesizes many different arts. Others argue, however, that to see the theater as a synthesis of other forms is to deny its autonomy.

The diversity of opinion leads one to doubt that there is an "essence" to the theater; in fact, the theater has no fixed and eternal essence. It is an art that at each stage of its evolution is defined by its aims and means of expression and by its ways of addressing its audience. This has been true from the beginning of its long history and is particularly the case in our century which has seen the birth of so many different and conflicting theatrical ideologies.

The evolution of stage design is not simply the result of development in the other arts. And it would be futile to deny the original role played by its creators. But, it would be equally wrong to isolate scenography from the context of the other arts or to abstract it from its much larger historical environment. Although each art affirms itself in its uniqueness, there is no intangible barrier between them, and in fact they mutually interact with each other. Stage design participates in the evolution of the plastic arts generally, in that of the mass media, television and the movies, and at the same time reflects some of their methods and means through imitation or some kind of reaction. Stage design takes advantage of the discovery of new inventions (think of the determinant effect that electricity had on the theater) or else systematically rejects them out of a desire for purity; (from Copeau to Grotowski the list of supporters for a "poor" theater is long!). Nor is theater immune from the influences of political events which it reflects both directly and indirectly as it does the political leaders of the time. Finally, the theater is dependent upon the economy; if poverty is a virtue, the theater is often compelled to be virtuous!

The study of stage design thus implies a twofold recognition, namely, of the essential role of its creators, and of the equally basic role played by the civilization that more or less conditioned their activity. The present work was undertaken with this perspective in mind. It does not aim to furnish an exhaustive history, replete with the names of men and countries, and is not intended to be either an encyclopedia or a dictionary. What it does attempt is to understand and clarify the living process of history, to explain its movements by selecting examples from the most vital currents of the modern theater and to place the accent on new ventures without being afraid to sacrifice whatever pertains to vulgarization or bears witness to forms surviving from the past.

Stage design is an organized space, that is filled with signs and symbols, and is alive with shapes and objects, colors and materials. Out of this arrangement comes a world that captures the spectator's attention and acts as a revelation. The setting is more than just a visual experience. Like a book, it demands to be read and deciphered while it stimulates the emotions of the viewers. The spectator grasps its meaning, but he also becomes its captive. The tension created by this interaction defines the modes of action as well as the functions of stage design. Moreover, the setting tends to illuminate the dramatic action and facilitate its development. What I am particularly interested in, is to present the important movements and significant productions in recent theatrical history and to clarify the role of the decor with regard to the dramatic work, the actor and the audience.

JOAN MIRO. Original Lithograph executed especially for this volume.

The End of an Illusion

2

2. Author unknown, sketch for V. Hugo's *Hernani*, Paris, Comedie-Francaise, 1879, Bibl. Comedie-Francaise, Paris. An admirer of Viollet-le-Duc, knowledgeable in archeology and geography, and clever at imitation, the designer copied various styles and filled the stage with ornamental details.

3. Ph. Chaperon, *Hamlet,* an opera by A. Thomas, Paris Opera, 1895. Bibl. de l'Opera, Paris. End of the 19th century designer, a master of perspective and *trompe l'oeil.*

3

11

In 1880 the Italian or illusionist theater reigned and its structures seemed eternal. The theater was made up of two conflicting worlds separated by the magic curtain or the invisible "fourth wall." On one side was the omnipresent auditorium in which the audience sat and looked at the play or at each other. On the other, was the stage, a sort of all-purpose box on which after each curtain drop the sets, which framed the action and constituted the background, were changed.

ACADEMICISM AND CONTRADICTIONS

Suppose a set designer were given the task of "decorating" *Hamlet.* Did he take time to think of Shakespeare's work, of its structure, dominant ideas, poetic qualities, or the imaginary world it evokes? What mattered to him above all was the "places" where the action occurred. It made no difference whether a tragedy was written by Shakespeare or Victorien Sardou, for this heir of the Romantics had not forgotten the *Preface of Cromwell* in which Hugo stated that the exact locale is one of the first elements of

reality; the place becomes an indispensable witness to the action. The designer's efforts at that time were therefore directed towards the reconstitution of the appropriate scenery. An admirer of Viollet-le-Duc, versed in the archaeological and geographical sciences, a facile imitator, our typical designer copied styles and filled the stage with ornamental details. What did it matter if they suffocated the drama? Unaware of the central currents of a civilization, he focused on the anecdote and its literal translation. At a time when photography was being developed, his work was not an act of creation but of reproduction, and more often than not, consisted of arbitrarily arranged objects. In short, he was a restorer who worked with staff and stucco.

These "master painters" at the end of the nineteenth century worked within the framework of an illusionist perspective that since the Renaissance had been as important to the development of the theater as it had been to painting. What was at stake, more than ever, was to convince the spectator that the universe of the stage was real, a mirage more convincing than our own world. To achieve this, traditional techniques of academic painting were used. For a long time

tors would divide the sets for the same opera among their colleagues according to the 'specialty' of each; one would do the fortified castle, the other, the moonlit grotto...! That the designer might be sensitive to a musical form or dramatic atmosphere was an idea completely alien to a period in which theater was governed by the tricks of the craft.

It is not surprising that the majority of spectators and critics were for the most part satisfied with this situation which catered to their taste for history and exoticism. What the bourgeois public wanted from the theater was the pleasure of escape and they found it in the false images of reality. No room was left for the imagination. Passivity was the rule and academicism, although growing old, had not yet lost its seductive power.

THE CRISIS

In fact, a crisis was approaching which would be overwhelming. Traditional stage design was in its dying spasms, caught in its own trap and unable to renew itself. It would certainly survive for some time, but attacks against it were increasing. Furthermore, the plastic arts had already experienced an upheaval. What relationship could there be between a picture by Manet or Monet and the awful reproductions of Amable, between a living art and one whose death warrant had already been signed?

In the middle of the nineteenth century the dual revolt that was initiated against the aesthetic status of the theater inevitably led to its total redefinition. Here and there a few men had begun to anticipate a renewal of theatrical art, thus heralding the fundamental reevaluation that would take place around the turn of the century. The first current of opposition did not know how to become liberated from its visions and tastes; as for the second, while scarcely anybody paid any attention to it, its principles were not lost.

Richard Wagner inaugurated the Festspielhaus of Bayreuth in 1876. It was a magnificent building representing a compromise between the Italian style theater and the Greco-Roman amphitheater, and fulfilled the Master's desire for illusion and for the spirit of communion among a large number of people. For the first time the lights in the auditorium were turned out during the performance so that the entire attention of the audience was concentrated on the stage. Unfortunately, the scenery did not harmonize with the music and did not have the same quality as the text it was meant to serve. Richard Wagner's stage directions were certainly followed, but the sketches by Josef Hoffmann and Paul von Joucovsky, the painters Wagner had called upon to decorate the sets, were strictly in the tradition of romantic academic painting and could hardly be distinguished from the models and realizations of Max Bruckner: the same literalness, decorative excesses and descriptive abuses.

Wagner provides us with a typical example of an artist who was incapable of fully carrying out his great theoretical dream because he remained a prisoner of the styles of representation of his time. Yet, his dream is of major importance for the modern theater. As early as 1850, Wagner envisaged a *Gesamtkunstwerk* — an artistic synthesis embracing music, poetry, mime, architecture and "landscape painting"; the latter was meant to give the drama a sense of plastic expression. One of the key concepts that emerged from German romanticism, it implied the union of all the elements that compose the spectacle and presumed their perfect harmony. Although this theory was opposed by those who refused to see the theater as a fusion of the arts, it nevertheless influenced all artists who in one way or another advocated a *total theater* founded on the simultaneous action of the plastic, gestual and musical elements.

In 1869 Theodore de Banville, a poet somewhat forgotten today, was one of the first in France to understand Wagner's conception of "the lyrical drama as a harmonious ensemble in which all the arts ... form an essential part of the drama and work together to control and captivate the soul of the viewer and listener by making a deep and lasting impression upon him." Banville appreciated the significance of this theory but did not believe in it himself. His own ideas, although more modest, were equally important for the future.

During the nineteenth century voices were heard, Goethe, De Bonald, Leon Halevy, Delacroix, protesting against scenic luxury as a sign of decadence that was suffocating the theater and deceiving the public. The successive encroachments of the spectacle were denounced. But Banville was the only one who synthesized the various ideas that were in the air and proposed a constructive, intelligent concept for the reform of theatrical production.

With great vigor the poet opposed the excessive use of stage effects and properties, and the pretentious quality of the com-

8

7-10. Richard Wagner at the Festspielhaus in Bayreuth during the last quarter of the 19th century. M. Bruckner, *Lohengrin,* 1894. Inst. Th. Coll., Cologne, Cf. Color reproduction. fig. 19. **8.** J. Hoffmann, *The Valkyrie,* 1876. Doc. Th. Mus. Munich. **9.** J. Hoffmann, *The Rhinegold,* 1876. Doc. R. Wagner Archives, Bayreuth. **10.** M. Bruckner, *Tristan and Isolde,* 1886 Th. Mus. Coll. Munich.

9

7 10

plex dioramic-like sets whose installation required that the curtain remain lowered for lengthy periods of time. Banville was hardly concerned with local color, advocating simple decors that would be "precise, spiritual and not too emphatic." He also urged that the curtain not be lowered to conceal the changes in scenery. By affirming the priority of theatrical convention and the persuasive force that would grow out of the continuity of the performance, he increased the spectator's awareness of the unity of the work.

In an age dominated by historicism, Banville spoke in the name of poetry. Rather than on illusion, he based the power of the performance on a communion between the actor and the public. "Every dramatic performance," he wrote in 1878, "is a joint effort of the poet, actor and public. From a theatrical point of view, what is good and profitable is that which establishes a direct communion between the actor and the spectator; what is bad and fatal are the obstacles to this communion." To our ears today this text has an astonishingly modern ring, announcing the desires of the Symbolists and the theories of Copeau.

Wagner and Banville can be regarded then as representing two basic movements. On the one hand, a complex art form founded on the synthesis of all of its elements, on the other, an emphasis on theatrical convention, the priority of language and acting. These two main orientations remained throughout the century despite the diversity of styles and the variety of options available.

At the end of the last century the crisis concerned not only the theater's aesthetic status but its ultimate aims as well. In 1887 Antoine's Theatre Libre was created, and three years later, Paul Fort's Theatre d'Art. Both existed independently, outside of the official circuits, but differed greatly in their ideals. The first quickly became the center of scenic naturalism in which man was viewed as a social individual within the context of his history and his environment. The second, devoted to the cult of beauty, was the ardent exponent of Symbolist doctrine which spoke of the eternal nature of man. This breakdown may be a little too contrived but it is essentially accurate, and clearly illustrates the two opposing tendencies of the modern theater. One is concerned with depicting reality which it seeks to explain and control; the other attempts to flee from reality in order to affirm the superior world of Art. However paradoxical it may seem, exchanges between the two trends were not only possible but actually occurred.

THE NATURALIST STAGE

Like Banville, Zola denounced the evils of traditional theatrical decoration. But the arguments he used in *Naturalism in the Theater* (1881) and the goals he hoped to achieve were different from those of the poet. The accusers were not involved in the same struggle. Whereas Banville's aesthetic idealism had to wait for the Symbolist breakthrough before it could be realized, the naturalist vision was intrinsic to the productions of Antoine in France, and finally attained world recognition in Stanislavsky's works.

It would be a mistake to think that the naturalist vision was created *ex nihilo*. Indeed it formed part of one of the major currents of a century which was preoccupied with analytical precision. What did Zola want? That the experimental and scientific spirit of the century should transform the theater as it already had the sciences, the pictorial arts and the novel. What did Zola desire? "The real drama of modern society . . . . living the double life of the characters and their surroundings." Metaphysical man was to be replaced by the physiological and social individual who was rooted in the real world. No more papier mache palaces! The decor of modern life became the bourgeois apartment and places pulsating with daily activity like the market place, the railroad station or the factory. Enough "conventional braggadocio"! "A work of art is only a battle against conventions, and its greatness can be measured by the extent of its victory."

The stage sets could no longer remain simply "witnesses" to the action. They now had to depict the "environment in which the characters were born, lived and died," and became as important to the theater as narrative description to the novel. It was up to the spectator to perceive their constant interrelationship with the dramatic action, and their influence on the characters as portrayed by the actors. In addition, the props and realistic atmosphere gave the actor the support necessary for him to enter completely into his role.

To continue our analysis of the naturalist stage, we must look at the productions of Antoine and Stanislavsky (who in 1898 founded the Moscow Art Theater). Even though there are slight differences between them, their work cannot be considered within the narrow framework of the naturalist style since in various ways they both helped to undermine it.

11. Georg II of Meiningen, *Fiesco,* by F. Schiller; dir. L. Chronegk. Meiningen, 1874. Niessen Coll. Inst. Th. Cologne. Though the historical realism of his productions place Georg II of Meiningen in the 19th century, his sense of space and movement rank him among the first of modern directors.

11

Never before had the concern with precise documentation of an historical or contemporary milieu been pushed so far. Georg II, Duke of Saxe-Meiningen, director of the famed Meininger Company, had been a precursor of this tendency at a time when the historical paintings of Pilety and Makart were triumphant in Germany. Under the Meininger influence Antoine and Stanislavsky became the greatest exponents of realism. In their sets they tried to portray real life with meticulous precision "according to the observable fact." For *The Lower Depths* Stanislavsky and his decorator Simov went to the Khitrov market and studied the lives of the inhabitants of the flophouses. Similarly, Antoine found the ideal setting for *Tom Thumb* in the London laundries.

12. *The Wild Duck* by H. Ibsen, dir. A. Antoine, Paris. Th. Antoine, 1906. Rondel Coll. Bibl. Arsenal, Paris. His concern as a naturalist for authenticity led to the construction of the garret in *The Wild Duck* out of Norwegian pine.

17

12

But this descriptive truth was not enough. The stage had to become a place one could live in; and the decor had to be a space in which the actor could perform as if he were not being observed by the spectators. The stage, as Antoine stated, is a "closed space in which something happens." And Jean Julien added: "The curtain must function like a fourth wall, that is, transparent for the public and opaque for the actor." In other words, the audience was meant to look at the play as if through a key hole while the actors played out the drama as though it were a slice of real life.

This explains the elaborate, detailed work that went into the stage sets of the time. It explains why Simov built complete apartments on the stage even though the spectators only saw one of the reconstituted rooms through a half-open door. For Antoine the topography of the scenery directly conditioned the actors' movements; for Simov it shed light on the internal movement of the drama as it was realized by the actors in their relationship with the objects and places on stage. For both, however, the scenic illusion grew out of a harmony between the decor and the actor, and was based on the dynamic exchange that animated them.

In the course of this identification of the drama with real life, there is a great temptation to substitute the object for its representation. Neither Antoine nor Stanislavsky could resist. Of course, no one reproached them for preferring visible beams and real ceilings and windows to the flabby painted canvases of traditional decoration. But was it necessary to carry their concern for authenticity so far as to build the garret in *The Wild Duck* out of Norwegian pine or to have the roofs made of real straw in *The Power of*

13. V. A. Simov, *The Lower Depths,* by M. Gorky, dir. C. Stanislavsky, Moscow Art Th., 1902. Doc. Th. Lib., Moscow. In preparing this production Stanislavsky and Simov went to the famous Khitrov market and visited the flophouses. In *My Life in Art* the director recalled: "After that famous excursion into the lower depths of life, I found it easy to design a stage decor; I felt as though I were an inhabitant of those underground cellars."

14. Menessier, *Earth (La Terre)* by E. Zola; dir. A. Antoine, Paris, Th. Antoine, 1902. In *Le Theatre,* 1902. Real hens clucked on stage. **15.** Lemeunier, *L'Assommoir* (*Drink* in the English stage version); dir. L. Guitry, Paris, Th. de la Porte Saint-Martin, 1900. In *Le Theatre,* 1900. The production blends social realism and naturalism. **16.** V. A. Simov, *Tsar Fyodor* by A. Tolstoy, dir. C. Stanislavsky, Moscow Art Th., 1898. In N. N. Tchouchkin's *The Moscow Art Theater,* 1955.

14

15

19

16

17. V.A. Simov, *When We Dead Awaken* by H. Ibsen, dir. Nemirovich-Danchenko, Moscow Art Theater, 1900. Doc. Th. Lib. Moscow. 18. V.A. Simov, *The Cherry Orchard* by A. Chekhov, dir. C. Stanislavsky and Nemirovich-Danchenko, Moscow Art Theater, 1904. Doc. Th. Lib. Moscow.

17

18

Darkness? In the sets for *The Butchers* Antoine hung up real quarters of beef, and at the Moscow Art Theater, Stanislavsky had a stream ten feet wide flowing on the stage for *When We Dead Awaken*. Lucien Guitry had a real public "assommoir" built for the sets of the theatrical adaptation of Zola's novel *L'Assommoir* (staged in an English version as *Drink*). The play was mounted in 1900 at the Theatre de la Porte Saint-Martin.

Antoine and Stanislavsky were certainly justified in trying to show man in his historical context or the individual as part of society, and to make the unity of the spectacle the basis for its dramatic effectiveness. However, the photographic reproduction they imposed on the viewer, with its complete picture free of synthesis and selection, implicitly rejected the collaboration of the viewer's intelligence and imagination. The limits of their achievements were clear. That is, it was impossible to go any further in the creation of scenic illusion without substituting reality itself for its image, which would be tantamount to denying it. Never had there been such concern for concretizing the dramatic universe, nor had there ever been such a radical separation between the play and the audience; and never had the proscenium arch defined such a sharp barrier between the stage platform and the auditorium. Realism had attained the highest degree of illusionist perfection. And, just as in the other arts, the moment had come for a revolt against the very structures that permitted its development. This did not mean that all realism was condemned. What was necessary was the creation of a new realism, that far from denying theatricality, would use it to its own advantage. Future aesthetic revolutions had to put an end to illusionist structures and the integral imitation of appearances.

**The Revolt Against
Illusionist Realism**

19

19. M. Bruckner, *Lohengrin* by R. Wagner, dir. A. Fuchs, Bayreuth, Festspielhaus, 1894. Inst. Th. Coll. Cologne. Perspective, *trompe l'oeil*, decorative excesses, accumulation of archeological and pseudo-historical details, virtuosity in rendering appearances — thus four centuries of courting scenic illusion are completed. Designers and directors alike rebelled against these practices and the theater of illusion, in their search for an imaginative, evocative theater that would still observe theatrical conventions. The development of the theater parallels that of the other arts.

For a long time academicism survived. While assimilating certain elements of Naturalism, it also profitted from technical progress by installing equipment that could handle more elaborate and cumbersome scenery. In 1896 Karl Lautenschlager inaugurated the first European model of the revolving stage at the Residenztheater in Munich. There was no question then of using it for any purpose other than to create a purely illusionist perspective.

But, in 1896, the revolt against illusionist realism had already been going on for six years at the Theatre d'Art in Paris under the leadership of the young poet Paul Fort. The rebellion soon spread even though its manifestations were scattered and took place over long intervals, and even though theory sometimes prevailed over the practical aspects of production. Adolphe Appia, a French-speaking Swiss artist, was the main advocate in Switzerland as was Edward Gordon Craig in England. In Russia, Stanislavsky was an active participant. But it was one of Stanislavsky's actors, Vsevolod Meyerhold, who soon played a major role. These different personalities were united in their opposition to the status quo, although they did not always agree on the methods and solutions to remedy the situation.

The question for them was how to react to the apparent triumph of academicism and the naturalist offensive. It seemed that the theater was becoming the victim of a dangerous degeneration. Should they condemn every style and form of presentation that failed to arouse strong emotions in the audience? Or, like Mallarme perhaps, should they dream of an "ideal" theater that would have neither actors nor stage sets, a spiritual phenomenon, or "holy of holies, but mental" delighting the solitary reader. Mallarme's solution was obviously too extreme to those for whom the essence of the theater resided in the effective encounter between the actor and the public. To them it was of great importance that the theater participate in the

general evolution of the arts and reacquire those characteristics that had made it a powerful form of artistic expression in the past. Theater, like all of the arts, implies a set of conventions. Whether it serves as a pretext for escape or as an acting exercise, a festival or a celebration, the theater must demand the active involvement of the spectator, now complacently accustomed to a passive role. From this imprecise ideal choices had to be made. The new forms for restoration still had to be defined, and the spirit in which they would become manifest, would condition the role and forms of future stage design.

CALLING UPON THE PAINTER
THE FIRST PERIOD

At the end of the nineteenth century there was a general rebellion against illusionist realism. Artists were looking for the original purity and autonomy of their respective arts. It was not by chance that Paul Fort founded the Theatre d'Art in the same year that Maurice Denis proposed his famous definition of painting: "Keep in mind that a picture, before representing a battle horse, a nude woman or some kind of anecdote, is essentially a flat surface covered with colors that are arranged in a certain order." But at the very moment that an attempt was being made to restore to each art form its true aesthetic status, the idea of an association of the arts along the lines of the Wagnerian Gesamtkunstwerk was in the air. It was in this context that the painter was called upon. Paul Fort was the first to enlist his help, followed shortly thereafter by Lugne-Poe, Meyerhold, Stanislavsky and Reinhardt. Fifteen years later, Serge Diaghilev and the Ballets Russes successfully developed and popularized an artistic formula that was put into practice on the stages of avant garde theaters.

From Paul Fort's Theatre d'Art to Lugne-Poe's Theatre de Oeuvre

All of Paul Fort's energies, his vision of man, the theatrical forms and scenic means he employed, were directed against naturalism. The Symbolists, whose ideas he shared, explored the world of the soul, the mystery of beings and things; they evoked the ineffable and intended their theater as a "pretext for dreams." Instead of presenting an accurate image of our everyday world, they fled from a technologically-oriented civilization and strived to create refined aesthetic enjoyments that would raise the spiritual individual above the vulgar realities of the material world.

The new theater that they envisaged required new settings. Pierre Quillard, author of *The Girl with the Severed Hands* which was staged at the Theatre d'Art in 1891, concisely described Paul Fort's conception of the decor, which rested on a total belief in the power of language: "Language creates the decor as it does the rest." There was no longer any question of description or reproduction, or of sacrifices to matters of perspective and *trompe l'oeil*. "The decor ought to be a pure ornamental fiction that com-

pletes the illusion by color and lines analogous with the drama. Usually a background and a few movable curtains will be enough to give the impression of the infinite multiplicity of time and place."

There is no doubt that Paul Fort's experiments were not to be found in the customary theatrical circuits, but this eliminated his dependence on the master designers and their technical knowledge. Besides, their knowledge would not have been of any help even if he had called upon them, since they could not create that imprecise evocation which was dependent on sensibility alone and not on mechanical processes and the tricks of the trade. Naturally then, he looked for painters who thought in ways similar to his dramatists, and asked Serusier, Bonnard, Ibels and Maurice Denis to create the "artistic decor" or "the pictorial part" of his productions. Unfortunately, we must base our knowledge of what they did on the illustrations that appeared in the reviews of the Theatre d'Art and on descriptions written by critics.

It is not surprising that those who professed this conception of the stage were attracted to the theory of correspondences between ideas, colors and moods, and that they thought of presenting pictures on the stage accompanied by music and perfumes. Indeed, at the end of 1891, Paul Fort even tried to put together a synthesis of the arts for Solomon's *Song of Songs*, orchestrating simultaneously language, music, color and fragrance. The setting was purely symbolic, and for each scene the projected lights changed color and new perfumes were wafted over the stage and into the auditorium. The experience was unique and had a certain hermetic quality, but in spite of the primitive nature of the techniques used, a creative theater emerged that spoke to the intellect as well as to the senses of the spectator. It was a form of total theater halfway between the Wagnerian Gesamtkunstwerk and Kandinsky's "sounds".

In 1892 Lugne-Poe took over the Theatre d'Art from Paul Fort and renamed it the Theatre de l'Oeuvre. He was very friendly with Bonnard, Maurice Denis and Vuillard whose "disdain of vulgar naturalism" and "love of poetic syntheses" he greatly appreciated. Of course, he asked them as well as Dethomas, Munch, Valtat, Serusier and Toulouse-Lautrec to design the sets and costumes for his productions.

The first play that he staged, *Pelleas and Melisande* (1892) by Maeterlinck, set the tone. Instead of the nineteen settings appar-

20. H. de Toulouse-Lautrec, program for *Raphael* by R. Coolus and *Salome* by O. Wilde; dir. Lugne-Poe, Th. de l'Oeuvre, 1896. On the left, R. Coolus; on the right, O. Wilde. Doc. Bibl. Arsenal, Paris. **21.** E. Munch, program for *Peer Gynt* by H. Ibsen, dir. Lugne-Poe, Th. de l'Oeuvre, 1896. Bibl. Arsenal, Paris. In the absence of sketches of the decor or photos of the sets, the programs of the theater, which were illustrated by the painters who collaborated on the decors, are the only visual documents which can help us imagine the style of the different productions.

20

21

ently demanded by the play, Lugne-Poe used only two imprecise decors by the painter Vogler, two kinds of backdrops that provided a vaguely ornamental framework without local color, properties, or a skillful *trompe l'oeil* persepctive. The harmony of their misty tones and dull shading of the costumes reflected the mystery and melancholy of the drama.

Undoubtedly, critics are not always enthusiastic. Jules Lemaitre hardly appreciated Vuillard's set for *La Gardienne* by H. de Regnier (1894), in which he thought he recognized an "imitation fresco of Puvis de Chavannes by the wavering hand of a newborn child afflicted with daltonism." However, who knows whether or not Jules Lemaitre was a strong admirer of Meissonnier...

In his early years at the Theatre de l'Oeuvre Lugne-Poe further developed the experiments of Paul Fort. He encouraged the same revolt against illusionist realism and decorative excesses in favor of an art based on discrete evocations and synthetic simplification. But, there was one play in particular whose deliberate incoherence both destroyed and extended the frontiers of symbolism. It denied the logic inherent in the traditional spectacle, and mocked illusionist realism. The theater poked fun at the theater in a single setting created by Bonnard and Serusier with the assistance of Vuillard, Toulouse-Lautrec and Ranson. On the left was a bed, at the foot, a chamber pot; on the right, a palm tree, a view of the sea, trees and a hill; in the rear of the center, a fireplace through which the hero and other characters trooped in and out. At the end of each scene a ghostly-looking old man would come and hang up a placard on the proscenium arch, which was full of intentional spelling errors and announced the place of the action. This play was none other than *Ubu Roi* whose author Alfred Jarry proclaimed "the uselessness of the theater in the theater." But in the enormous buffoonery of the farce he rediscovered the origins and pleasures associated with the theater. *Ubu Roi* in 1896 anticipated *Parade, The Bride and Groom of the Eiffel Tower,* Dada and the Surrealist plays. If the theater seemed to be disintegrating, it was only in order to renew itself.

26

22

22. A. Jarry, *Ubu Roi,* "A true portrait of Monsieur Ubu," wood engraving published in 1896, dir. Lugne-Poe, Nouveau Th. de l'Oeuvre, Paris, 1896.

23. A. Jarry, *Ubu Roi* by A. Jarry, litho published as a poster for the performance in 1896.

24. M. P. Oulianov, *Schluck and Jau* by G. Hauptmann, dir. V. Meyerhold, Moscow, Studio Theater, 1905. Doc. Th. Lib. Moscow.

23

1905 was a critical year for Stanislavsky. Could naturalist techniques help him translate the inner soul or create a sense of beauty that would resemble the pictures of a Vrubel or the plays of a Maeterlinck? Did the theater have to lag behind the other arts? After all, music was moving away from harmonic melodies and the new style of painting renounced traditional realist techniques in favor of a new spatial vision which advocated the free composition of forms and colors. Stanislavsky was full of doubts. How was he going to reveal the ineffable and the surreal? He hoped to find the answers to all these questions in the work of Meyerhold, an actor and director who had been a part of the Moscow Art Theater since its inception and whom Stanislavsky had invited to take charge of the experimental workshop at the Studio Theater.

"The stage is like a work of art. Take a good picture, cut out the nose and replace it with a real nose. That would make the picture seem real, but it would be ruined." This quotation from Chekhov may seem surprising when one thinks of what Chekovian "realism" meant to Stanislavsky, but Meyerhold kept it uppermost in his mind when he was preparing his productions for the Studio Theater in 1905. Like the poet Briussov and the playwright Andreyev, he opted for a stylized theater in which the spectator would be a sort of "fourth creator," after the author, the director and the actor: a theater in which everything was not told or shown to the pub-

27

24

25

25. N.N. Sapunov, *The Death of Tintagiles* by M. Maeterlinck, dir. V. Meyerhold, Moscow, Studio Theater, 1905. Doc. Th. Lib. Moscow. **26.** M.V. Dobujinsky, *Petrushka* by P.P. Potemkin and V.F. Nouvel, dir. V. Meyerhold, Loukomoriye Th. 1908. Bakhrushin Mus. Moscow. Photo. Petitjean.

lic, and in which the setting was created in the spectator's mind as a consequence of the harmonious relationship between the music, rhythm, movements, words, lines and colors.

Along with such painters as Sapunov, Soudeikine, and Oulianov, Meyerhold attempted to strike the death blow to the naturalist theater. He destroyed the realistic scenic universe and replaced it with a series of "impressionist sketches." Abandoning the principle of the model, he even tried to reduce the stage to the two dimensions of a painting and to include all of the characters within that surface area. For Hauptmann's *Schluck and Jau,* assisted by Oulianov, he brought to life the spirit of that age and dramatized the action using stylized elements and suggestive symbols. Staging Maeterlinck's *The Death of Tintagles,* with sets by Sapunov, struck him as a task similar to that of the "icon painter" who depicted hieratic figures on a gold background.

The Studio Theater never actually opened, but the experience was instructive for Meyerhold. As a person who constantly experimented, he discovered that it was difficult to adapt the conventions of painting to

28

26

27

27. A. Golovine, *Masquerade* by M.I. Lermontov and A. Glazunov, dir. V. Meyerhold, Petersburg, Alexandrinsky Th. 1917. Bakhrushin Mus. Moscow. Photo P. Willi. Symbol of luxury at the end of the regime. *Masquerade* took place Feb. 25, 1917, the first day of the Revolution.

the theater because of the principal role played by the actor. The only valid solution was statuary art: that is, the painter's contribution was limited to designing a set that would serve as a conventional background for the action and that would not compete with the actor on the same level, as in Dobujinsky's ingenious scenery for *Petrushka* that Meyerhold produced in 1908.

In this way the painter became one of the chief craftsmen of the stylized theater that Meyerhold then supported. He did not hesitate to push the actor towards the public by having him play on an extended forestage. In 1910 the "aesthete of imperial sets" staged *Don Juan* in St. Petersburg with sumptuous settings by Golovine (the painter of the Ballets Russes) that "threw the light veil of a perfumed and golden Versailles-like kingdom" on Molière's play. It was a magnificent production in which the director tried to restore the same relationship between the actor and audience that bound them together during the seventeenth century. Rather than reconstitution, an extraordinary sense of invention unified Meyerhold's principles. Anything was considered good that closed the gap between the actors and the public. For example, there was no curtain; the scenography provided the transition between the auditorium and the background of the stage where successive backdrops evoked the different places of the action. And lastly, the lights were not dimmed in the auditorium during the performance.

A few years later Meyerhold and Golovine used basically the same methods in

29

staging Lermontov's *Masquerade.* There again the scenography united the stage and the auditorium. As in the warp and woof of a tapestry, each scene, richly decorated, produced a harmony of colors that was perfectly suited to its atmosphere and action. The luxurious symbol of the end of an era, *Masquerade* was performed for the first time on February 25, 1917, the night the Revolution broke out. In later works the stage sets that Meyerhold designed became more bare and austere, with the constructivist "object" replacing the decorative background, certainly an original contribution to the new stylized theater.

In 1907-1908 Stanislavsky staged works about the destiny of man and the unreal world. With the aid of the painter he created a universe that combined philosophical drama and impalpable enchantment.

Egorov and Oulianov designed the sets for Knut Hamsun's *The Drama of Life* (1907). The deliberate distortions of the figured elements corresponded to the chaos of passions unleashed in the drama, while the shock of the colors created a visual balance that underscored its unreal and exaggerated aspects. Another fantasy — the fluid, misty visions suggested by Maeterlinck's *Blue Bird,* which was performed in 1908 at the Moscow Art Theater. The sets by Egorov resembled illustrations from a folk tale leaving the spectator with the impression of having rediscovered the naivete of his childhood.

Without using painted hangings, Egorov also designed the scenery for Leonid Andreyev's *The Life of Man* (1907). Stanislavsky, having discovered the value of black velvet, used it as an abstract background against which the actors could speak about eternity, as he sketched in the different worlds in which Andreyev's schematic characters moved. Egorov's sets were just as schematic. On a black background, symbolically colored lines (white, pink for man's youth, gold for the ball) were drawn to suggest the stylized forms of the windows, door and properties. The actors, who also wore costumes of black velvet outlined in white, were an integral part of the scenery, which seemed to serve as a burlesque counterpoint to the language they spoke.

This production indirectly introduced modern art into the theater, and excited all of the Moscow theatergoers who were enthusiastic about Picasso, Matisse and the Fauves. Stanislavsky, however, had paid his debt to Symbolism and could not help feeling that he had failed. What was the importance of the scenery if nothing had been done to enrich the art of the actor? Critical of this venture which he considered essentially negative, Stanislavsky returned to realism. How could he have guessed that the stage designs for *The Life of Man* and *The Drama of Life* anticipated the productions of the Expressionists as well as those of Pitoeff?

28, 29. A. Golovine, costumes for *Masquerade* by M.I. Lermontov and A. Glazunov, dir. V. Meyerhold, Petersburg, Alexandrinsky Th. 1917. Bakhrushin Mus. Moscow. Photo P. Willi.

28
29

30
31

30. V.E. Egorov, *The Drama of Life* by K. Hamsun, dir. C. Stanislavsky, Moscow Art Theater, 1907. Doc. Th. Lib. Moscow. **31.** V.E. Egorov, *The Blue Bird* by M. Maeterlinck, dir. C. Stanislavsky, Moscow Art Theater, 1908. Doc. Th. Lib. Moscow. In *The Drama of Life* Stanislavsky brings to the stage an allegory of the destiny of man, and in *Blue Bird,* an intangible fantasy in which each person thinks he has rediscovered the innocence of his childhood.

32

32, 33. V.E. Egorov, *The Life of Man* by L. Andreyev, dir. C. Stanislavsky, Moscow Art Th. 1907. Doc. Th. Lib. Moscow. The director discovers the value of black velvet; here is an abstract background against which the players discuss eternity. With just a few lines of color, Egorov schematically designed this stylized decor.

33

Reinhardt: A Transition

As if it were a rule that a prominent director had to sacrifice something to collaborate with the painter, Reinhardt, like Stanislavsky, called on the painter for plays which were not limited to descriptions of the daily relationships between people, but attempted to reveal the very mystery of beings and things. Only the painter seemed capable of feeling and evoking this mystery with the fluid imprecision necessary for its expression.

In 1903 Reinhardt staged *Pelleas and Melisande* at the Neues Theater in Berlin; Impekoven was responsible for having the action occur behind a veil of gauze that blurred its unreal and secret visions. Three years later Edvard Munch, a precursor of the Expressionists who had already worked with Lugne-Poe, crystallized the atmosphere in Ibsen's *Ghosts* by means of a deliberately styl-

ized decor that emphasized the weight of fatality. The room faced a fjord, but through the window could be seen the oppressive presence of a mountain. Without contradicting reality, the elements in the set increased the dramatic tension by the selective way they were used and by the subtle arrangements of lines and colors. Yet Munch's set did not look as if it existed independently or as if it reproduced a preexistent milieu. Rather it seemed to emerge out of the very substance of the play itself, revealing its internal life. In other words, it translated the impressions that the painter felt when he read Ibsen, and materialized a spiritual vision. What mattered were the elements of real expressive value with respect to the psychological drama that enveloped the characters.

Yet the painter had no more than a transitory influence on Reinhardt's work. Reinhardt's eclectic and fundamentally innovative spirit kept him from freezing his creations within the confines of a formula.

34

33

35

36

34. E. Munch, *Ghosts* by H. Ibsen, dir. M. Reinhardt, Berlin, Kammerspiele, 1906. Kunst. Mus. Coll. Basle. Photo. Hinz.
35, 36. Idem. Munch Mus. Coll. Oslo. The intervention of the director, M. Reinhardt, permitted two Scandinavian artists, the writer Ibsen and the painter E. Munch, to meet on the Berlin stage. The sense of harmony that helped to blend their respective sensibilities guaranteed the essential unity of the production.

88271

FERNALD LIBRARY
COLBY-SAWYER COLL.
NEW LONDON, N.H. 0

37

38

37. L. Bakst, *Scheherazade* by N. Rimsky-Korsakov, chor. M. Fokine, Paris Opera, Ballets Russes of Serge de Diaghilev, 1910. Mus. Arts Deco., Paris. "I search for rich, magnificent, spell-binding nuances" (L. Bakst). 38. L. Bakst, *Judith,* an opera by A. Lerov, Paris, Th. du Chatelet, Ballets Russes. 1909. Doc. Gall. del Levante, Milan. 39. L. Bakst, *Le Dieu Bleu,* ballet by J. Cocteau and F. de Madrazo, Mus. R. Hahn, chor. M. Fokine, Paris, Th. du Chatelet, Ballets-Russes, 1912. Doc. Gall. del Levante, Milan.

34

39

The Ballets Russes (first period) or the triumph of exoticism

1909 marked the appearance of the Ballets Russes at the Theatre du Chatelet. "Like a paved stone in mud," the Company unleashed public passion and enthusiasm. Serge Diaghilev, who later asked to be surprised, began by surprising the public.

As his compatriots Mamontov and Volkonsky had done before him, Diaghilev commissioned artists to design the decors and costumes for the ballets that he produced during the first period (1909-1913). Then he turned to those artists who formed part of his review *World of Art,* Benois, Bakst and Golovine, who had reacted against the realism of the "Ambulants." These men found the themes of their inspiration in past centuries, refused imitation and tried to return painting to its function as an art that created form out of the imagination. After awhile, however, their decorative "impressionism" was not enough. As of 1914 Diaghilev called more and more on artists who represented the new artistic movements, first on Russian painters and then on the most well known members of the School of Paris.

What was the reason for the immediate triumph of the Ballets Russes? In an era dominated by technical progress, mechanization, industrialization and social problems, Diaghilev's company provided the spectator with a momentary escape from his civilization. His ballets presented vast, dreamy visions of distant or unknown worlds that were simultaneously primitive and barbaric, refined and voluptuous. With richness and sumptuosity, the Ballets Russes incarnated the poetry, and translated artistically the aspirations of the Belle Epoque.

Here was the fabulous Orient of *Scheherazade, Thamar* and *The Nightingale,* the Egypt of *Cleopatra,* the Greece of *Helen of Sparta, Daphnis and Chloe* and *The Afternoon of a Faun,* the primitive universe evoked in *The Rite of Spring,* the fantastic world of *The Firebird,* the popular imagery of *Petrushka,* and with *Armide's Pavilion,* the splendors of the age of Louis XIV. A dizzy world of one surprise after another!

Diaghilev's collaboration with painters showed his desire to work with people who were more concerned with the pictorial than with techniques and virtuosity. He chose artists who were capable of imagining vast decorative syntheses in which stylization and the arabesque played major roles. Like Alexandre Benois, he saw the ballet as a Gesamtkunstwerk, the manifestation of a total art unifying music, painting and choreography. The painter's contributions were extremely important. He not only became the true artistic consultant within the company and participated in the collective work that went into designing and staging the ballet, but he frequently was responsible for the plot. (Bakst was the author of the story of *Scheherazade, Thamar* and *The Afternoon of a Faun,* Roerich of *The Rite of Spring.*) With regard to staging, Bakst helped Nijinsky in *The Afternoon of a Faun* rediscover the plastic value of the paintings on ancient Greek vases, and more generally, he gave the ballet the visual qualities that raised it to the level of a pictorial work. "The decor," wrote Mauclair, "is conceived of as a picture in which the actors move like shifting color values." And according to Leon Bakst, the decor should be designed "like a picture in which the figures are not yet painted, not as in landscape or architecture."

40

40. L. Bakst, *The Afternoon of a Faun,* mus. Cl. Debussy, chor. V. Nijinsky, Paris. Th. du Chatelet, Ballets-Russes, 1912. Mus. Nat. Art Mod. Paris. Photo. Agraci. "The decor is conceived of as a painting in which the characters move about like shifting color values."

The scenic material was simplified, and the overall effect was one of great stylization that, far from excluding ornamental richness, implied it. Bakst liked sets to be "beautiful, rich and powerful," and Benois thought that they should "flatter" the senses of the spectator. The variety and seductive richness of the colors testify to this.

If the painters who worked with the Ballets Russes revolutionized this art form and held the public spellbound, it was not so much by the choice of their decorative forms which were integrated into a vision that altered reality without making an abstraction of it, even in such a conventional ballet as *Petrushka*. A more important factor was the apparent novelty of their palette, the way in which they associated color with the music and the story of the ballet. "Now this is color!" exclaimed Maurice Denis, and Jean Louis Vaudoyer found the "polychrome orgies" irresistible. "Color must express a visual joy," affirmed Leon Bakst and added: "I seek rich, magnificent, dazzling shades of color."

41. A. Benois, *Petrushka* by I. Stravinsky and A. Benois, chor. M. Fokine, Th. du Chatelet, Paris, Ballets Russes, 1911. The fair. Courtesy Wadsworth Atheneum Hartford. Phot. Blomstrann. 42. A. Benois, *Armide's Pavilion*, ballet by A. Benois and N. Tcherepnin, Th. du Chatelet, chor. M. Fokine, Paris, Ballets Russes, 1909. Courtesy Wadsworth Atheneum Hartford. Phot. Blomstrann. 43. A. Benois, *Petrushka*, pic. 2, variant 1925. Courtesy Wadsworth Atheneum Hartford. 44. A. Benois, *Les Sylphides*, mus. F. Chopin, chor. M. Fokine, Paris, Th. du Chatelet, Ballets-Russes, 1909. Carr Doughty Coll. London. 45. N. Roerich, *Decor and Polovtsian dances from Prince Igor* by A. Borodin, chor. M. Fokine, Paris, Th. du Chatelet, Ballets-Russes, 1909. V. and A. Mus. London.

42

43
44

45

The desire to create "symphonies of color" that would echo and correspond to the "symphonies of sound," the attempt to symbolize the dramatic action and themes in the scenic image so that they would make a powerful impact on the audience, the concern with the optical unity of the production — all explain the way in which the painters chose the color schemes for their sets and harmonized them with the costumes they designed. Freed from the restrictions of naturalism, color, as it intensified, exploded in a burst of dramatic expressiveness. The audience discovered the exaltation of color while the painter saw his "picture" transformed according to the rhythms of the choreography.

Indeed, it was because of such an exuberant use of color that Jean Cocteau discovered "a greenhouse of passion" in *Scheherazade.* The scenery included a heavy green hanging with black and orange-pink motifs of Persian inspiration, a background dominated by greens and blues that were successively bathed by shadow and mysteriously filtered light, and a geranium-red floor that favored the development and eruption of passion. Everything was "green, blue, red, and orange-colored; in other words, instinctive, sensual, vertiginous" (Peladan). There was not the slightest trace of white in this ensemble of colors that appeared, merged, disappeared or were juxtaposed with each other. Was it still a ballet? Andre Levinson could only respond: "It is above all a decor animated by interchangeable elements."

Once the unquestionable contributions of Bakst, Benois, Roerich, and Golovine have been acknowledged, let us place the first period of the Ballets Russes in its artistic context. The Ballets Russes were received with enormous enthusiasm because, despite their decorative novelty, the Company did not shock or offend the customs of the audience. Their profusion of color was only extravagant by comparison with the grayness of everyday life and the faded tones of traditional theatrical decoration. But in relation to the works of the Fauves, a Van Gogh or the French Impressionists, the Ballets Russes lose much of their revolutionary virtue. The scandals surrounding the Company had nothing to do with the painters; it was the choreography of *The Afternoon of a Faun* that was judged pornographic, and Stravinsky's music that caused the uproar for *The Rite of Spring,* not the mild, temperate settings by Roerich. The pictorial and decorative universe of Bakst and Benois was quickly assimilated by the public, who needed to

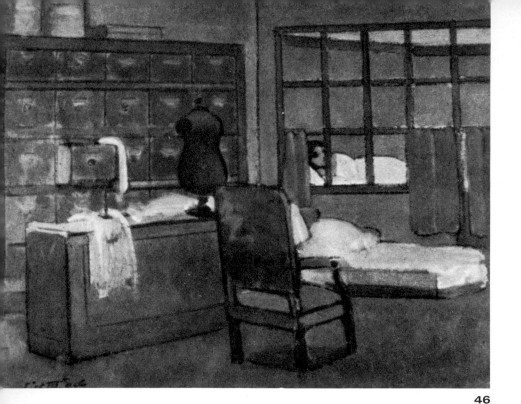

46

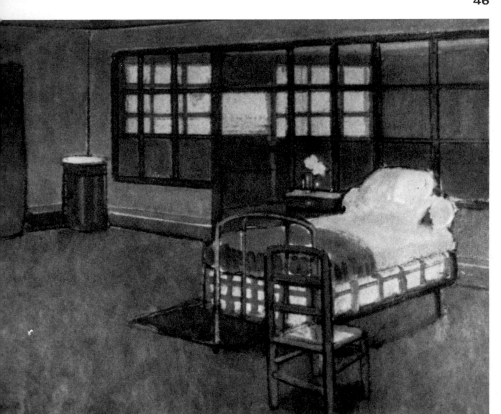

47

be stimulated by fresh surprises. Diaghilev was aware of this and anticipated what the public wanted.

Jacques Rouché and "good taste"

The end of the first period of the Ballets Russes also marked the closing of the Theatre des Arts that Jacques Rouché had opened in Paris in 1910 with a performance of *Carnaval des Enfants* by Saint-Georges de Bouhelier, sets and costumes by Maxime Dethomas.

Rouché's ambition was "to make staging correspond to the artistic visions of contemporary painters, to make it harmonious with the general movement of ideas and sensitivities that paradoxically the scenic art had not until now followed." He regarded staging as only "one aspect and dependent on the other plastic arts," and wanted the performance to possess the homogeneous qualities of a "moving fresco." Not surprisingly, therefore, he too appealed to the painters.

The artists Rouché chose reflected his ideas on the subject of decor. He wanted neither to distort nor "to decorate the play excessively, but only to accentuate its main lines and the particular nature of its beauty." In all of his productions he was concerned with stylization, synthesis and the simplification of the scenic means of expression, as he tried to apply the rules of "good taste" and a sense of proportion. Painters with quiet, unobtrusive talents, such as Maurice Denis, Guerin, Laprade, Piot, Dresa, and Dethomas among others, created the poetic and evocative settings for his works. Reality was portrayed in a simplified way, with allusions to it,

46, 47. M. Dethomas, *Le Carnaval des enfants* by Saint-Georges de Bouhelier, (**46.** the shop, acts I and III. **47.** the rear of the shop, act II), dir. A. Durec, Paris. Th. des Arts, 1910. Bibl. Arts Deco., Paris. A stylized realism that evoked dramatic expression. The painter noted: "The importance attached to color contributed to creating the atmosphere. The effects of the lighting variations were as subtle as intonations in a dialogue. The gray-blue and ochre set, stressing the black and steel colors worn by certain characters, united the wine and blood of the defrocked and the masks." (M. Dethomas.)

48

48. M. Dethomas, *Thesee* by J.B. Lully, Paris. Th. des Arts, 1913. Mus. Arts Deco., Paris.

and the painter too displayed his abilities rather unpretentiously. Decor became "decoration and not painting." Even when the scenic space was logically organized, it remained in the background as a decorative element enhanced by muted or delicate hues against which were contrasted the solid colors of the costumes. "A green and blue harmony," wrote Dethomas about *Salome*," with white uniquely reserved for the costume of the leading character as a way of making her the shining center of the ballet. And as for the work he did for *The Brothers Karamazov*, Dethomas added: ..."Once again at the Theatre des Arts I wanted to keep the audience from feeling as though they were the indiscrete witnesses of a contemporary and overly realistic drama. I wanted to make them feel as if they were the spectators of a human story that was taking place a little bit farther away from the footlights than usual."

During the first phase of collaboration between painter and director, the contributions of the former were far from negligible. With the production now the result of a collective effort, the decor became suggestion, and not mere description or reproduction. Its power did not emanate from its resemblance to reality — all of the apparatus of the naturalist theater had been destroyed — but from the expressive means available, lines and colors, and from the interrelationships that were established between the play and the scenic picture in a theatrical universe which still recognized and even observed convention. The decor functioned either as

49

50

49. R. Piot, *Idomeneo* by W.A. Mozart, Paris, Th. des Arts, 1912. Bibl. Arts Deco. Paris. 50. R. Piot, *Le Chagrin dans le palais de Han* by Laloy and G. Groulez, dir. A. Durec, Paris, Th. des Arts, 1912 Bibl. Arts Deco., Paris.

background or decorative fiction, if not as a pictorial interpretation of the environment; or it perhaps symbolized the fundamental elements of the play. Given these conditions it is easy to understand why the collaboration between painters and the stage has been a continual process in spite of the vicissitudes related to their selection as well as their individual development, and even though we tend to take this link for granted. The influence of the painter is often challenged by those who fear the subordination of the theater to the plastic arts, by those for whom the action and the acting are the most important elements, and those who expect scenography not to illustrate the dramatic text but to organize the scenic space in which it unfolds.

51

51. A. Appia, design of the rock for Wagner's *The Valkyrie,* 1892. D. Oenslager Coll. New York. Phot. P.A. Juley. **52.** A. Appia, design for *Tristan and Isolde* by R. Wagner, 1896. Appia Foundation, Berne. **53.** A. Appia, design for R. Wagner's *The Rhinegold,* 1892. Appia Foundation, Berne. **54.** A. Appia, design of the forest in R. Wagner's *Parsifal,* 1896. Appia Foundation, Berne.

52

door life exalted man's corporal awareness; this preoccupation was reflected artistically. Think of Rodin, Hodler, Loie Fuller, Isadora Duncan, the Dalcrozian rhythmics, etc! What was necessary then was to insure the artistic character of the performer's presence, which would be accomplished by a "lighting that emphasized the actor's plasticity and a plastic scenic arrangement that emphasized his attitudes and movements."

The scenic space had to be rigorously conceived of, and organized to serve the performer. First it had to be a plastic organization of volumes so that the vertical scenery harmonized with the sculptural aspect of the actor, and furnished him with the properties that supported his dramatic expression. Towards this end, Appia envisioned decors that had a functional, geometrical

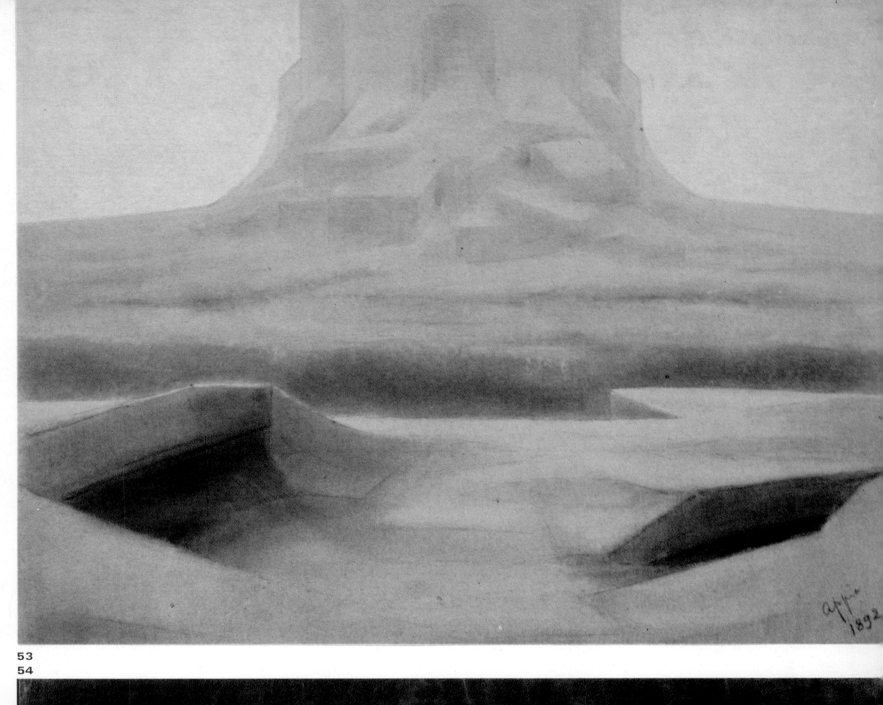

53
54

55. E.G. Craig, *The Vikings at Helgeland* by H. Ibsen, act II. dir.
E.G. Craig, London, Imperial Theater, 1903. Craig Coll. Bibl. Arsenal, Paris. At the dawn of the 20th century, Appia and Craig
were the two strongest proponents of the idealist movement.
Both men tried to regenerate the theater by transforming its
aesthetic foundations.

56. A. Appia, *Echo et Narcisse,* ballet-pantomime by E.J. Dalcroze, Geneva, Jaques-Dalcroze Inst., 1919, Appia Foundation, Berne. **57.** A. Appia, *Rhythmic Spaces: the stairs,* 1909. Th. Mus. Munich. Although Appia seemed to be a prisoner of a "compelling Wagnerian romanticism" in his first designs, his desire for simplification never ceased. He constantly devised new scenic architectures which tended to eliminate the descriptive and anecdotal elements.

style. At first they were figurative and neo-romantic (set designs for the *Ring, Parsifal, Tristan and Isolde*), but Appia soon turned to the architectonic rigor of his "rhythmic spaces" inspired by the experiments of Jaques-Dalcroze (1909-1910). These consisted of arrangements of platforms, ramps, staircases, compositions of landings, columns, and planes in which shadowy areas contrasted with lighted ones. The effect of these compositions was a theatrical architecture that suggested the confrontation between man and the real volumes of the stage space. When he drew models for *Orpheus,* or his late sketches for Wagnerian and Shakespearean dramas, and Greek plays, Appia blended the concept of luminous functionalism with his intense requirements for dramatic expression.

45

56

57

58-60. A. Appia, *Rhythmic Spaces,* 1909. Geometric compositions of planes and volumes, the rhythmic spaces are supposed "to underscore the value of the human body as imposed by the music." **58.** *The clearing.* Appia Foundation, Berne, **59.** *The shadow of the cypress tree.* Th. Mus. Munich. **60.** *Evening circle.* Jaques-Dalcroze Inst. Geneva. Phot. Bibl. Nat. Switz. **61.** A. Appia, design for *Orpheus and Eurydice* by C.W. Gluck, Champs-Elysees, 1926. Appia Foundation, Berne.

61

His architecture required light; not simply a lighting that 'illuminated' but a lighting that 'animated' the action as well. Appia felt the mysterious bond that linked light with music. Light became the visual equivalent of music, blending the elements of the play visually as music orally unifies the musical score. Appia relied on lighting to enhance the actor in space, to fuse the various visual components, to contribute to the decor or to replace it by permitting the lighting to evoke the places and dramatic mood. For example, a neutral background, a few hangings, beams and spots of light on the ground were enough to evoke a clearing; or, the shadow of a cypress tree would constitute the entire decor, present through its very absence. Furthermore, Appia, not content to use light as a creator of spiritual atmospheres, moods and moral distances between characters, invented light projections to complete, modify, animate or even create the decor as early as 1891.

What then was the role of color in this system? There is no doubt that Appia was more sensitive to volume. Yet, although his sketches were in monochrome, Appia attributed a very precise role to color. Just as he had freed the actor from his bondage to the painted set, he allowed color to become alive and exist independently. Color was no longer merely "indicated;" it became a property of the scenic object or a fluid carried by light and capable of metamorphosis. Its newly acquired independence enabled it to play an active role in the drama.

But Appia's work was by no means limited to reforming the decor, or restructuring aesthetic factors, however significant these may have been. He dreamt of a "living art" in which the spectator could totally participate, a vision partially inspired by the Dalcrozian rhythmics. What was at stake was more than just a transformation of the setting and its function, more than an emphasis on the value of the scenic space. The concept of a "living art" implied a new organization of the physical relationship between the public and the play, that is, a new style of theatrical architecture. Appia had foreseen this possibility in *Music and Mise en Scene* before he stated (1918): "Sooner or later we will have what will be called the hall, a cathedral of the future that in a large, free transformable space, will receive the various manifestations of our social and artistic life and will be the place *par excellence* in which dramatic art will flower — *with or without spectators...*"

Appia had not designed any Wagnerian sets before 1914 that corresponded to his desires and ideals. Sievert's sets for *The

62. A. Appia, sketch for the enchanted garden in *Parsifal* by R. Wagner, 1922. Appia Foundation, Berne.

63, 64. *The Rhinegold* by R. Wagner, dir. O. Walterlin according to Appia's ideas, Basle, Th. Municipal, 1924. Doc. Th. Mus. Munich. **65.** A. Appia, *The Valkyrie,* by R. Wagner, dir. O. Walterlin based on Appia's conceptions, Basle, Th. Municipal, 1925. Doc. Th. Mus. Munich. Only much later did Appia influence the theater with his theories of stage design and his ideas on Wagnerian scenography. However, he did not have at his disposal all the technical devices which would have allowed him to more fully carry out his ideas; and he had few occasions to test his theories.

66

66. An exhibition of rhythms in the auditorium of the Jaques-Dalcroze Institute at Hellerau demonstrating Appia's ideas in 1911, Jaques-Dalcroze, Geneva. In 1918, of all his desires, Appia called for "the *auditorium* of the theater to be as a cathedral of the future, a vast, free and transformable space which could dramatize the diverse manifestations of our social and artistic life and which would be the place *par excellence* for dramatic art to flourish *with* or *without an audience.*" The Hellerau auditorium foreshadowed his ideas of a free space.

63

64

65

67

68

67. A. Appia, *Orpheus and Eurydice* by C.W. Gluck (the descent into Hell) Hellerau, Jaques-Dalcroze Institute, 1912-1913. Phot. Boissonnas-Borel, Geneva. **68.** A. von Salzmann, *Tidings Brought to Mary* by P. Claudel, Hellerau, Jaques-Dalcroze Institute, 1913. In K. MacGowan, *The Theatre of Tomorrow,* New York, 1921. Rather than concentrating on the decor, his essential concerns were directed towards organizing space and devising a scenic architecture.

69

Rhinegold, however, presented in Friburg in 1912, seemed to concretize Appia's ideas, although by then, Appia had already gone beyond his earlier vision. The Jaques-Dalcroze Institute that opened in Hellerau that same year helped to make Appia's ideals on theatrical architecture more practical, just as the scene, the descent into hell in Gluck's *Orpheus,* which was presented on a stage Appia had contrived, confirmed the value of his scenic use of light and space.

The hall was about 150 feet long, 51 feet wide and 37 feet high. On one end were fixed rows of steps for an audience of 600; on the other, an empty space in which for each production, there was a new scenic arrangement using standard scenic elements (steps, curtains, slopes, etc.). There was *no proscenium arch* and consequently no break between the action and the audience. Behind the sheets of white canvas that defined the area of the theater and through which the lighting was filtered, thousands of electric bulbs created a luminous environment that was pierced by the beams of the spotlights. When Jaques-Dalcroze staged an uncut version of *Orpheus* here in 1913, Ernest Ansermet proclaimed enthusiastically: "It is no longer a dramatic subject illuminated from the outside by the designer, adorned with gestures and amplified by music. It is the drama itself that radiates and gives meaning to each of the elements in the production ..."

In 1913 Paul Claudel's *Tidings Brought to Mary* was produced at the Hellerau workshop, the settings designed by A. Salzmann. The structure was reminiscent of Appia's architectures but also introduced innovative arrangements consisting of a number of playing areas on various platforms and levels, linked together by slopes, steps, etc. The action unfolded in successive scenes or simultaneously in several places without any break which preserved the unity of the inter-

69. L. Sievert, *The Rhinegold,* by R. Wagner, Freiburg-in-Breisgau, 1912. Inst. Th. Cologne, Sievert's decors for Wagner in 1912 seemed directly inspired by Appia.

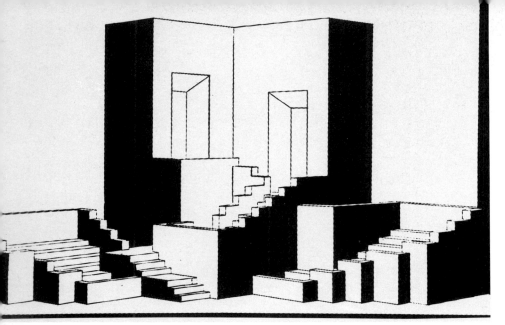

70
71

nal development of the drama. The continuous performance, inspired by the medieval stage, was to considerably enrich the theater of the future.

To measure the scope of Appia's work would require a review of the development of modern theater, pointing out the traces of his influence on the way. Significantly, this influence extends beyond the questions of stage design into every aspect of the theater. There are marks of his thinking in Constructivism, Expressionism, Copeau's work as well as in the ventures of scenographers like Dulberg, Urban, Pillartz and Svoboda, to name only a few. Even today we are constructing the type of theater of which Appia dreamed. It may not be the cathedral, but that hardly counts, as long as it is a structure that gives the drama the free space required.

70. E. Dulberg, *Oedipus Rex* by I. Stravinsky, dir. O. Klemperer, Berlin, Krolloper, 1928. Inst. Th. Cologne. **71.** E. Dulberg, *Fidelio* by L. van Beethoven, dir. O. Klemperer, Berlin, Krolloper, 1927. Inst. Th. Cologne. **72.** T.C. Pillartz, *Oedipus* by Sophocles, dir. E. Keller, Darmstadt, Hessisches Landestheater, 1922. Inst. Th. Cologne. Dulberg and Pillartz share an indisputable resemblance to Appia. Having applied the lessons of their mentor, both regarded the stage as a space for constructing geometric volumes.

72

73. J. Svoboda, *Oedipus Rex* by Sophocles, dir. M. Machacek, Prague, Th. National, 1963. Photo. Jar. Svoboda. It would be difficult not to see this immense staircase as the synthesis and epitome of all the staircases designed by Appia. Aside from their distinctive originality and the fact that half a century has passed, both Appia and Svoboda affirmed the importance of integrating the stage space and the actor, and the unique role of lighting in their productions.

Craig: The Willed Totality

The prophet of the modern theater . . . an idealistic prisoner of chimerical dreams . . . a belated romantic . . . a genius or a charlatan . . ! This is only a sampling of the passionate and contradictory opinions that Craig aroused. His own fondness for paradox and sarcasm helped to confuse many issues. What matters, however, is the work he did, which was both deeply rooted in his time and far ahead of it. Craig liked the Pre-Raphaelites and had a sense for beauty that linked him to Ruskin, but just as Kandinsky tried to find the "independent empire" for painting,

74

Craig searched for the "independent empire" in the theater.

Actor, draftsman, engraver, director, designer, theoretician and art historian, Craig was surely versatile. His crucial work was accomplished between 1900 and 1914. In these fourteen years he overthrew the foundations of the theater of his time and revolutionized the art of decor.

At thirty three, after staging seven productions in which he interpreted the texts, designed the sets and costumes and directed the actors, Craig wrote his first important theoretical work in the form of a dialogue, *The Art of the Theater*. "The art of the theater is neither acting nor the play; not the stage setting, nor the dance. It is composed of all of the elements of which these things

74. E.G. Craig, *The Vikings at Helgeland* by H. Ibsen, act II, dir. E.G. Craig, London, Imperial Th., 1903. Craig Coll., Bibl. Arsenal, Paris. (Cf. color reproduction, fig. 55). **75.** Idem, act IV. Craig. Coll., Bibl. Arsenal, Paris.

75

76

76. E.G. Craig, *The Vikings at Helgeland,* costume by Sigurd. Craig Coll. Bibl. Arsenal, Paris. **77.** E.G. Craig, *The Vikings at Helgeland,* costume design. From *Deutsche Kunst und Dekoration.* **78.** E.G. Craig, costume for *Acis and Galatea* by G.F. Handel, London, Great Queen St. Theater, 1902. Th. Samm. Vienna. Craig coordinated the extreme simplicity of the scenery with the highly stylized costumes, without regard for archeological authenticity.

are composed: the drama, the setting and the dance: of gesture, which is the soul of acting; of words, which are the body of the play; of line and color which are the very heart of the decor; and of rhythm which is the essence of the dance." Craig's well known and enlightening definition bases the theater on the harmonious union of a certain number of absolutely interdependent auditory and visual elements. The director had to assume the powers of the director, designer and lighting engineer while Craig waited for the Master Artist of the Theater of the Future to create masterpieces without the assistance of the playwright. The theater, according to Craig, should break away from literature and purge itself of all the parasitical tyrannies that accompanied it, including that of the painter as well as the actor. Realism, a synonym for degeneracy, was obviously out of the question. The scenic language Craig had in mind was stylized and symbolic.

He rejected photographic exactitude beginning with his first productions (*Dido and Aeneas,* for example). Drawing his inspiration directly from the play which he reduced to its essential components, he created a total vision that at each moment corresponded to the different phases of the dramatic action, and a decor that blended with the visions of the poet. He was less concerned with the places of the action than with the symbolic meaning of the drama that was reflected in them. Therefore he tried to materialize a universe on the stage which evoked the main elements. Simplification, selection and synthesis were the basic precepts that he applied to his art.

In 1899-1900 Craig designed one of his first revolutionary sketches for Scene 4, Act II of *Hamlet,* consisting of bare walls, rectangular surfaces and a lighting which projected zones of mysterious shadows and

77

78

53

79

79. E.G. Craig, *Elektra* by H. von Hofmannsthal, probably conceived around 1905. Th. Samm. Vienna. Craig never staged
Elektra; however, this sketch represents the final state of his
conceptions. At first he imagined a high door as the central element and heart of the tragedy. Later, he decided to leave the
space empty.

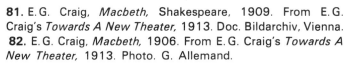

80

81

81. E.G. Craig, *Macbeth,* Shakespeare, 1909. From E.G. Craig's *Towards A New Theater,* 1913. Doc. Bildarchiv, Vienna.
82. E.G. Craig, *Macbeth,* 1906. From E.G. Craig's *Towards A New Theater,* 1913. Photo. G. Allemand.

82

light. The hallmark of what came to be known as the Craigian style resides in the deliberate simplification of the scenic picture, an architecture reduced to elementary geometry. For *Macbeth* and *Hamlet* he envisaged other architectural spaces that featured a series of undated walls, cubic and parallelepipedic volumes, occasionally of gigantic proportions, which dwarfed the characters and gave the drama a more universal significance. In 1908 his designs for *King Lear* called for an almost abstract architecture, an accumulation of cubes that formed a specifically theatrical place. Sometimes he reduced the set to a few hangings that emphasized certain areas of the stage and concealed others, leaving the spectator's imagination wander at leisure. He also organized his decor around a central object that expressed its basic idea: a rock for the first scene of *Macbeth,* a door for *Electra,* a large round table for the second act of *The Vikings at Helgeland* whose circle was echoed by a huge iron crown that dominated the stage, and for the fourth act, a bare domed mound. The background of the set served only as a conventional boundary, unless it was used in

83

83. E.G. Craig, sketch for *Psyche,* 1907. Th. Samm. Vienna. Serge de Diaghilev, director of the Ballets Russes, accustomed to the pictorial conceptions of Bakst and Benois considered Craig's spatial vision here too bold.

84

84. E.G. Craig, *Elektra,* H. von Hofmannsthal, project probably dating around 1905. Th. Samm. Vienna. Cf. Color reproduction, fig. 79.

a more indefinite way to evoke the no man's land out of which the tragic tensions were meant to arise.

In Craig's work the setting participated in the action to the degree that line, color, materials and light were the means of composition and expression. Color was used to reveal the drama and help the spectator receive its impressions. When Craig staged *Hamlet* in Moscow (1912), he wanted to show through his very setting the tragedy of a solitary man lost in a perverted world he could not and must not relate to, and with good reason. Gold, which decorated the background as well as the costumes of the king and queen and their court, was the symbol of the cunning and deceitful world of appearances against which Hamlet, dressed in black, fought alone. The lighting, a creation of beauty, freed the audience from the usual naturalist imitation and interpreted the drama. The enormous shadow of Polyphemus underlined the danger threatening *Acis and Galatea* (1902).

However, Craig's scenographic achievements were not limited to merely simplifying the decor. It is as if his own development encouraged him to abandon successive sets in favor of a single architectural structure. His

85

88

86

85-88. E.G. Craig, *The Steps*, project dating around 1905 published in E.G. Craig's *Towards A New Theater,* London, 1913. This was envisioned as a "silent drama," and in four sketches, he suggested four different times and four moods. The steps are simultaneously the theme, the framework, the character and title of the drama. **85.** First mood. **86.** Second mood. **87.** Third mood. **88.** Fourth mood.

87

experiments led him to conceive of apparently two contradictory solutions (a fixed stage architecture and a mobile one) both of which made the traditional scenographic structure a virtual anachronism.

In 1905 Craig imagined a *drama of silence* with the mysterious title *The Steps* for which he drew four sketches that suggested four different atmospheres and four different times. In fact, the staircase was all at once the theme, the framework and the main actor in this drama. From 1905 Craig expressed his desire for a single stage architecture that would be capable of illustrating the diverse phases of a dramatic action.

When in 1912-1914 he was working on

the staging of *Saint Matthew Passion* (a project that never materialized), instead of a series of settings he created a stable, fixed architecture containing several playing areas — a structure inspired by a humble romanesque church in the Tessin. In the arrangement of the choir, crypt and nave Craig saw a symbol of the Christian world, earth, heaven and hell. His own architecture recreated these structures to some degree, for example in the way he symbolically organized space by introducing separate little stages or mansions that were superimposed on one another. Through each phase the action defined the scenic elements.

Another totally different solution which also permitted Craig to reconcile unity and multiplicity, permanence and change was his idea that a scene could be changed in full view of the public — an idea that should be viewed in the context of his experimental attempts to create an art of movement. Craig traced the origin of the theater back to that concept. From 1906-1907 he began to dream of an art of movement that would transcend the theater, an art that would generate constantly changing forms. He imagined an interplay of parallelepipeds which could rise or fall, mobile screens and a subtle effective lighting to animate the whole design. His copper engravings of 1907 illustrate what this new type of theater might have been like. In any case, the art he envisioned anticipated the innovations of painters who were searching for an expression of movement (particularly Delaunay and the Futurists), and heralded the kinetic arts of today.

Faced with the technical impossibility of realization, Craig, nevertheless, applied some of his ideas to the theater. The screens, the famous "screens" that he designed in 1907 and continued to experiment with until 1923, constitute the fundamental element on the stage for his poetical drama. Instead of a series of independent sets, Craig relied on a single architectural unit made up of mobile panels that moved (turned, advanced, receded, folded, etc.) as the director wished and thus created the successive places where the action unfolded without any interruption. The screens he used in his famous Moscow production of *Hamlet* suggested a stylized staging that "progressed like the drama" (Piot).

Craig's influence on the theater was substantial in terms of both theory and practice, but it was even more important in the domain of scenography. How many crea-

89

90

89. E.G. Craig, sketch for *Saint Matthew Passion* by J.S. Bach, 1913. Craig Coll., Bibl. Arsenal, Paris. For Bach's work Craig envisioned a balanced architecture consisting of multiple playing areas which was inspired by a humble romanesque church in the Tessin (Ticino, Switzerland), San Nicolao de Giornico. 90. E.G. Craig, *Scenes* (Hell), copper engraving, 1907. Bibl. Art et Archeologie, Paris. The series of engravings that Craig created in 1907 entitled *Scenes* reflects his search for an art of movement, generating forms in a perpetual metamorphosis animated by lighting. 91, 92. E.G. Craig, *Hamlet* (Wm. Shakespeare), dir. E.G. Craig, Moscow Art Th., 1912. Doc. Mus. Art. Th., Moscow. 91. The king and queen. 92. The final scene.

91

92

93

93. C. Czeschka, *King Lear* (Wm. Shakespeare), dir. M. Reinhardt, Berlin, Deutsches Theater, 1908. Doc. Inst. Th. Cologne. 94. O. Strnad, sketch for *Hamlet* (Shakespeare), 1923, design not used in the production. Th. Samm. Vienna. 95. J. Svoboda, *Hamlet* (Shakespeare), dir. J. Pleskot, Prague, National Th. 1959. There is no real conceptual break from the time of Craig's *Hamlet* until Svoboda's, including the creations of Czeschka and Strnad. The styles of each designer may vary but the motivation permeating all of their productions was to make the stage space more expressive and simplify the architecture.

94

95

theater" of whom he dreamed. However, outside of his own country Wyspianski's work is known only to a handful of specialists. There are undoubtedly many reasons for his isolation and the general lack of knowledge that surrounds his activity: his oppressed country, the fact that he died young, that his theatrical abilities were not immediately recognized by his contemporaries, and that he was only able to stage one of his works with his own sets, *Boleslas the Bold* (1903).

Like Craig, Wyspianski belonged to both the past and the future. His plays place him with the Symbolists, although they also clearly anticipated Expressionism and Surrealism. He did not reject the notion of the Gesamtkunstwerk. On the contrary, he regarded the theater as the ideal meeting place for a synthesis of all the other arts — poetry, music, acting and painting. To some extent he participated in the pictorial current of theatrical reform, perhaps because painting inspired his activities as a playwright, and

96. S. Wyspianski, *The Legend,* by S. Wyspianski, dir. L. Solski, Lvov, Municipal Th., 1905. Dramatist, poet, painter, draftsman, creator of stained glass windows, director and stage designer, Wyspianski is the founder of modern Polish scenography.

96

tions in our century, and even among the most recent, recall in their stylization the simplified architectures of Craig: from Orlik to Roller and Strnad, from Sievert to Alexandra Exter, from Bel Geddes to Pitoeff, Wieland Wagner and Josef Svoboda! Craig was not the founder of any of the great movements of the modern theater — Expressionism, Constructivism, Epic Theatre, etc. — but there are few artists who are not at least partly indebted to him for their accomplishments. Craig's work was much more than just a style.

The Wyspianski Case

There is something paradoxical about the case of Stanislav Wyspianski. He was at the same time a poet, playwright, painter, draftsman, director, designer and creator of stained glass windows. Craig saw him as his mentor, and as one of those "artists of the

97

97, 98. S. Wyspianski, *Boleslas The Bold* by S. Wyspianski, dir. S. Wyspianski, produced by J. Sosnowski, Crackow, Municipal Th., 1903. Photo. Zaiks. The costumes bear witness to the encounter in Wyspianski's works between the European currents of "great reforms" and Polish national traditions.

62

98

color was one of his favorite means of expression. But his monumental conceptions and the importance he accorded to light make him akin to Appia and Craig. In short, it is difficult to classify him. Wyspianski was the founder of modern Polish scenography; that he belonged to the European movement of theatrical reform does not diminish the national character of his work in which there is a deep feeling for his native soil and traces of folklore. The costumes he designed for *Boleslas the Bold* recall those of the Polish peasantry of his time.

If Wyspianski's work is less well known than Craig's and Appia's, it is probably because his departure from traditional ways was apparently less radical, since he remained subject to the visions of his times and retained a personal fondness for realistic figuration even though he simplified it in his own work. It is necessary, however, to look beyond first impressions and study the scenic indications that he wrote for his plays or his notes on staging *Hamlet.* In these remarks, as Strzelecki pointed out, it is obvious that he attached tremendous importance to his basic ideas and aspirations. An admirer of Giotto, Wyspianski replaced the use of successive settings for *Hamlet* by introducing a stage consisting of multiple playing areas with arches that could be opened or closed with a curtain. His notes for two of his works, *The Judges* and *The Woman from Warsaw* show to what degree he rejected the purely descriptive use of color, the idea of matching the colors of the costumes with the moral qualities of the characters. As for properties, Wyspianski used them with the greatest economy; they were never simply objects. He created some which became real dramatic characters possessing a symbolic role.

There is one work by Wyspianski, the playwright, that says a great deal about his scenographic aspirations, *The Liberation.* In 1903 he thought of having his play performed on a bare stage without a curtain. He wanted the actors to put on their costumes in front of the public, and the stage crew to come and move or remove the few pieces of decor that suggested the places of the action on this conventional stage. But the illusionist stage merely served here as a raised platform. In the same way as Meyerhold and Craig, Wyspianski, working from within a somewhat realistic framework, precipitated the downfall of illusionist realism.

TOWARDS A NEW THEATRICAL ARCHITECTURE

S. Wyspianski: "I envision my theater, it is enormous; I see large spaces, filled with men and shadows. I am there and I enter into their thoughts."

Romain Rolland (1903): "All I need for a popular theater is a large room or auditorium, or a place used for public gatherings like the Huyghens and Salle Wagram, preferably built on an incline so that everyone can see; and in the rear (or in the center if it's a circus), a high, wide bare platform."

E. G. Craig (1905): "I see a large building containing thousands of people. At one end is a gigantic platform on which enormous, heroical figures can move about."

Wyspianski, R. Rolland and Craig dreamed of new spaces to escape from the

WINTERMÄRCHEN · PALAST DES LEONTES· AUFFÜHRUNG · 1905

99. E. Orlik, *A Winter's Tale* (Shakespeare), dir. M. Reinhardt, Berlin, Deutsches Theater. 1905. Inst. Th. Cologne.

suffocating confines of the illusionist theater. They desired a new theatrical architecture, and they were not the only ones.

The illusionist stage was neither infallible nor immortal, the product of a civilization, it corresponded to determined social structures and prescribed ways of thinking and performing. At a time, therefore, when attempts were being made to transform the theater into a ceremony or rite in which everyone could participate, it was obvious that an architecture that separated the action and the audience would be condemned. But, as reformers tried to rediscover the traditional nature of the spectacle, they naturally tended to discard any arrangement which was partial to forgetting conventions. However, while illusionist stage structures were gradually being destroyed, painters were also beginning to question the Albertienne perspective (an inheritance from the Renaissance), in their search for new spatial conceptions.

There were many in the theater who preferred the raised platform, a free, concrete space in which the actor could develop three-dimensionally to an empty box filled with the mirages of the painted canvases. As they looked for new theatrical spaces they naturally returned to the models employed during the great periods of the European and Asian theaters, or to other forms of entertainment such as the circus.

All of the reformers at the beginning of the century were preoccupied with creating a new theatrical space. Craig's ventures as well as Appia's cathedral of the future can be seen in this light. Some artists occasionally discarded the usual theatrical edifices while others used them as a precondition for renewing their art.

Nostalgia for the Elizabethan Stage

In the winter of 1896-1897 Lugne-Poe was in London, where, at the Merchant Taylor's Hall, he saw a performance of Shakespeare's *Two Gentlemen of Verona*. Struck by its unusual structure, the director of the L'Oeuvre returned to Paris and described with much enthusiasm this production of "Shakespeare without decor." What excited him most about William Poel's efforts to stage an authentic Shakespearean play was not the director's fidelity to the original text but the manner in which he had organized the theatrical space. The public surrounded the stage on three sides, and Poel used a conventional architectural background, that, with

100

100. R. Hista (sketch of Flasschoen published in *Le Petit Bleu de Paris,* 1898) *Measure for Measure* (Shakespeare), dir. Lugne-Poe, Paris, Cirque d'Ete, 1898. In searching for a theatrical setting that would approximate Shakespeare's original creation, Lugne-Poe tried the circus arena. It didn't matter that the setting was not exactly Elizabethan, since he respected the general principles of the Elizabethan stage. That is, there was close contact between the actors and spectators, unlike their usual separation on the Italian stage.

two doors and a balcony, recalled the structures of the Elizabethan stage. His techniques were evidently effective since, with a little imagination, the audience was easily able to transform the single setting into successive places.

It was not surprising, therefore, that in 1898 Lugne-Poe tried to do something similar with *Measure for Measure,* when he introduced an Elizabethan stage in the ring of the Cirque d'Ete. Near the entrance to the stables, was the stylized facade of a house with a raised balcony and three doors which opened onto a large platform that stretched out over the ring, surrounded by tiers of seats. The circus only provided the general framework. It hardly matters whether or not Lugne-Poe's arrangement was an exact reproduction of the Elizabethan stage. What counts is that he respected its general principles, and established a close contact between the actor and the spectator, which terminated their mutual isolation.

Nostalgia for the Bare Stage
Jacques Copeau and the Vieux Colombier

"Let the other marvels vanish and, for the new works, leave us with a bare stage!" When he founded the Vieux Colombier in Paris in 1913, Copeau intended to use his theater to combat all theatrical forms of commercialism and exhibitionism. Restoring real majesty and purity to the stage required first of all the reinstatement of the actor and the play itself to their prominent positions in the production. He therefore repudiated all exterior complicity (excessive decoration, extravagant lighting) as pretense, and all cumbersome machinery. The decor was reduced to its absolute essentials and only one or two properties sufficed to create the atmosphere.

The director of the Vieux Colombier explained his nostalgia for the bare stage. "The empty stage, free to create fiction," said Mallarmé. These words stir my heart and evoke for me the whole miracle of the theater. "Le petit treteau nu, four benches in a square with four or six boards above" that Cervantes talked about in one of his prologues, the simplest arrangement of all, symbol of the greatest freedom, and which in the purest way demands the utmost from the poet's imagination. Farce springs up, magic is suggested with a rustle of garland and feathers, mystery does not surrender its majesty, and even the supernatural can be awakened. The world, at our summons, can fill that platform, and its three or four steps are enough to stage, according to their rank, demons, beasts, flowers, man, his passions and his gods."

A far away but omnipresent ideal — to achieve gradually. For Copeau the year 1913 was a starting point. He gave Francis Jourdain the task of restoring the traditional stage at the Athenee Saint Germain. Jourdain endowed it with a vast proscenium that brought the actor closer to the public, a forestage forward of an inner proscenium that made it possible to create two separate playing areas, and mobile hangings that could be colored by the lighting. Subordinate to the action and the actor for whom it served as a background, the decor was reduced to the greatest simplicity and often suppressed completely. In his productions several hangings were borrowed from Craig, and only a few props suggested the mood and environment (screens for Heywood's *A Woman Killed With Kindness,* and blocks that replaced seats for *Twelfth Night*). During this first phase Copeau emptied the stage in order to liberate it, but he had not yet undertaken its reconstruction. The underlying aesthetic principle recalled the Munich Art Theater,

66

101. L. Jouvet, the stage and auditorium of the Vieux-Colombier in 1913 after its restructure undertaken by F. Jourdain; the first step towards the architectural stage that Copeau inaugurated after the first World War. Reproduction dating from 1919. Jouvet Coll. Bibl. Arsenal., Paris.

101

102

founded by Georg Fuchs, but without Fuch's 'relief-stage'. From the year 1913, Copeau proposed a 'poor' theater in which the play was "expressed mainly through the acting."

After the First World War Copeau and Louis Jouvet remodeled the Vieux Colombier by erecting a permanent structure, an architectural innovation for which Copeau partially owes his fame. Prior to its establishment, he experimented with different arrangements, and during the war learned a great deal from his visits with Craig and Appia as well as from his fruitful collaboration with Jouvet. His productions in the United States at New York's Garrick Theater were mounted on a 'dispositif' similar to the future one in Paris. A large projecting apron with two conventional doors on each side and in the center, a stage with a proscenium arch, framed by two stairways leading to a balcony. This structure was adaptable, varying only slightly from one production to another by adding a few elements. The scenography for *Pelleas and Melisande* bore similarities to *The Tidings Brought to Mary* at Hellerau, or

102. F. Jourdain, *A Woman Killed with Kindness,* by T. Heywood, dir. J. Copeau, Paris, Vieux-Colombier, 1913. From *Le Theatre,* 1913. The decor, reduced to the greatest simplicity and even to its suppression, simply accompanies the action and is also subordinate to the actor, serving as a background for him. **103.** L. Jouvet, *Pelleas and Melisande* by M. Maeterlinck, dir. J. Copeau, New York, Garrick, Th., 1919. Copeau Coll. Bibl. Arsenal, Paris. The stage of the Garrick Theater consisted of multiple playing areas and marked another step towards the development of the "dispositif fixe," or permanent stage of the Vieux-Colombier.

103

276

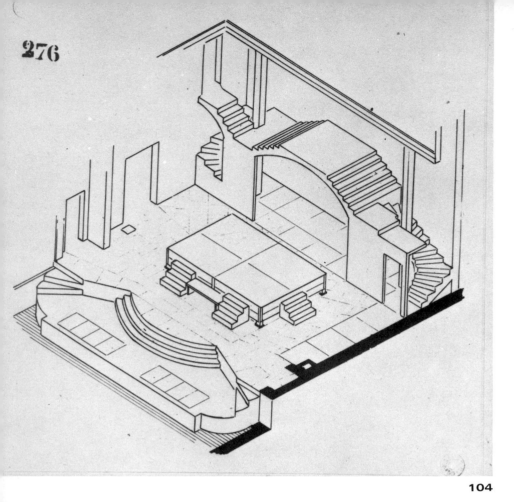

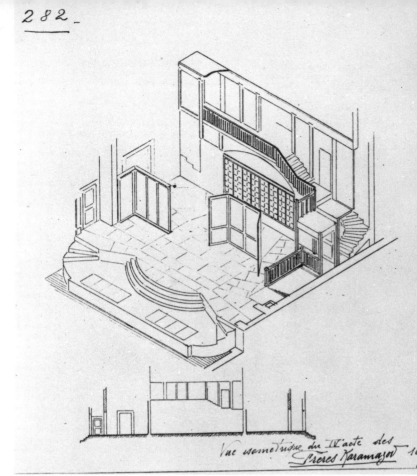

Vue isométrique du IV.e acte des
Frères Karamazov 10

104

106

105

107

74.

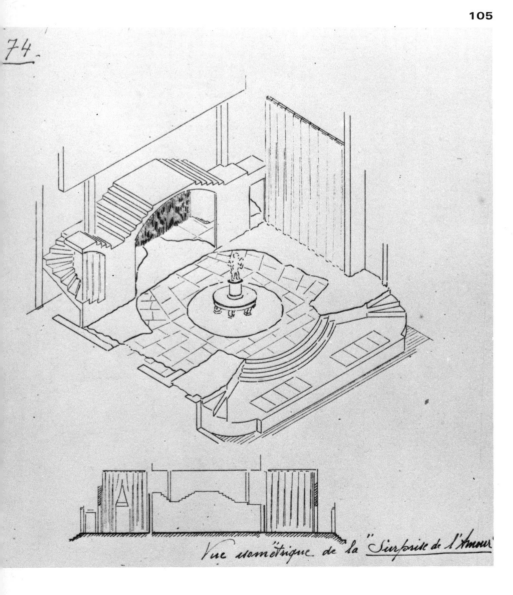

Vue isométrique de la "Surprise de l'Amour"

104. L. Jouvet, stage of the Vieux-Colombier, sketched in 1919. L. Jouvet Coll., Bibl. Arsenal, Paris. Photo. P. Willi. In his plans Jouvet combined two of Copeau's nostalgic inspirations for a permanent stage, fusing the "music-hall" techniques of farce with the main principles applied to the stages of Elizabethan times. **105.** L. Jouvet, *La Surprise de l'Amour* by Marivaux, dir. J. Copeau, Paris. Vieux-Colombier, 1920. L. Jouvet Coll. Bibl. Arsenal, Paris. Photo. P. Willi. **106.** L. Jouvet, *The Brothers Karamazov* by F. Dostoievsky, dir. J. Copeau, Bibl. Arsenal, Paris. Photo. P. Willi. Some rare scenic elements have been added (folding screens and balustrades) to complete the basic stage architecture.

107. L. Jouvet, *La Mort de Sparte* by J. Schlumberger, dir. J. Copeau, Paris, Vieux-Colombier, 1921. J. Copeau Coll., Bibl. Arsenal, Paris. Photo. P. Willi.

to the Molieresque farce, *Le Medecin Malgre Lui.*

In Paris (1920) the Vieux Colombier received its rigorous and definitive scenic architecture. The proscenium arch had been eliminated and a projecting apron joined the stage with the auditorium. In the rear were raised playing areas and an inner stage inspired by the Elizabethans. Hangings, properties and other scenic elements could of course be added to this permanent stage, which paradoxically combined freedom with restraint so that *The Brothers Karamazov, La Surprise de l'Amour* or *La Mort de Sparta* could all be performed on it. Now that the Vieux Colombier resembled the nave of a church, the frontal relationship linking the public to the dramatic action was modified from what it had been in the illusionist theater. The action was not supposed to extend beyond the limits set by the frame. A certain perspective had been achieved by

concentrating on this sculptured stage formation, in which evidently cubism had clearly left some traces.

While the architecture of the Vieux Colombier proved to be too rigid, the idea of a permanent stage *(dispositif fixe)* dominated the scenographer's thinking for many theatrical productions of the twentieth century. It became apparent that each play required its own setting and that predetermined architectures were not always suitable, especially when a new formula for decorating was required. Copeau himself was undoubtedly aware of this when, with Andre Barsacq in Florence, he designed the scenography for *The Mystery of Santa Uliva,* staged in the courtyard of the Santa Croce cloister (1933), and later *Savonarola* on the Piazza della Signoria (1935).

108. A. Barsacq, *Savonarola* by R. Alessi, Piazza de la Signoria, 1935. Doc. Bibl. Nat. Paris. **109.** E. Stern, *A Midsummer's Night Dream* (Wm. Shakespeare), dir. M. Reinhardt, Berlin, Deutsches Theater, 1913. The model belongs to the Th. Samm. in Vienna. In an atmosphere of poetic realism Reinhardt constructed an entire forest on a revolving stage, which moved and turned as it presented new imaginative images.

108   109

Nostalgia for the Arena Theater: From the Circus to the Grosses Schauspielhaus in Berlin

Of all of the innovators during the first decades of our century, Max Reinhardt was undoubtedly the least inclined to theory and the most eclectic. His apparent versatility, however, masked one of his principal concerns, namely, to find for each production a rapport between the public and the dramatic action that would be appropriate for the form and atmosphere of that particular work. For this reason he refused exclusive formulas and instinctively experimented with new theatrical spaces.

Beyond his eclecticism Reinhardt possessed an intuitive sense of drama as well as a strong desire to reach the "soul" of the spectator, to touch him spiritually while awakening his senses. Consequently he used all of the material elements available (color, light, etc.) to compose a total spectacle. At the same time Reinhardt attempted to restore the collective emotions that were part of the theaters of Greek antiquity and the Christian Middle Ages.

We can understand why Reinhardt, once having worked in a theater laboratory for a hundred people, began to dream of a theater that would reach maybe five thousand. Curiously, he was never tempted to draw his inspiration from the Elizabethan stage. Even for his productions of Shakespeare he used the most perfected techniques of the modern

110

110. *Oedipus Rex* by M. von Hofmannsthal, dir. M. Reinhardt, Berlin, Schumann Circus, 1910. A gouache by E. Orlik of the production. Inst. Th. Cologne. The setting was created by A. Roller, the costumes by E. Stern. 111. *Oedipus Rex,* photograph from the production of the crowd scene. Doc. Th. Mus. Munich. Reinhardt thought that the architecture of the circus was the most suitable space for staging classical Greek tragedies and applying their great principles in his own modern revivals.

111

theater, staging *A Midsummer Night's Dream* on a revolving stage that emphasized and exalted movement. But for the Greek tragedies, he decided to return to the principles and architectural forms of the Greek theater, and use a circus arena. When in 1910 he staged *Oedipus Rex* at the Schumann Circus, the empty ring, free of all decorative accessories, was reserved for the chorus. A wide staircase connected the ring to a platform which was surrounded by six massive columns, behind which was an austere-looking wall containing a central door. This served as the facade of Oedipus' palace as well as the architectural background of the *skene* in the Greek theater. The audience sat on rising tiers of steps; there was neither a

112

112. A. Roller, *The Oresteia* by Aeschylus, dir. M. Reinhardt, Berlin, Schumann Circus, 1911. **113.** E. Bertin, *Oedipus, King of Thebes* by Saint-Georges de Bouhelier, dir. F. Gemier, Paris, Cirque d'Hiver, 1919. Gemier did not "copy" Reinhardt. However, if his productions at the Cirque appeared less radical than those of the Berlin director, the conceptions of the two men were still quite similar.

72

curtain nor a proscenium arch, and the action no longer took place "elsewhere." The walls were alive and encompassed the masses of spectators, as the actor's emotions spread out, into concentric waves from the center, reached the tiers and reverberated throughout. Illusionist perspective was completely abandoned because the relationship be-tween the audience and the stage was not purely frontal. The actor could be seen from several sides simultaneously, as he stood out in sharp contrast to the audience, who was also part of the play. This sort of theater anticipated the less radical productions of Gemier, notably his *Oedipus Rex at Thebes* which was staged at the Cirque d'Hiver in

113

1919. While he was a rather unique individual, Reinhardt should nevertheless be considered as a participant in the global artistic movements that were disengaging from traditional spatial conceptions.

When he staged *The Miracle* at the Olympia Hall in London, Reinhardt and his designer Stern played with several conventional devices and scenographic ideas. Lighting was used to enlarge or restrict the playing areas, which consisted of a huge sinking stage in the center of the arena and a framed stage, used alternatively or simultaneously to reveal a universe elaborately constructed in the realistic fashion. A new dimension, however, was added. Stern transformed the entire auditorium of the Olympia Hall into the nave of an immense cathedral which was surrounded by tiers of steps on three sides for the spectators. An overall Gothic motif was maintained in the structure, vaults, ogival arches and stained glass windows. With this permanent decor which was either cast in shadow or brilliantly illuminated, Reinhardt plunged the spectator into the center of the dramatic universe.

114

114. E. Stern, *The Miracle* by K. Vollmoeller and E. Humperdinck, dir. M. Reinhardt, London, Olympia Hall, 1911. Niessen Coll. Inst. Th. Cologne. **115.** Idem., sketch by J. Duncan. Doc. V. and A. Mus. London. In staging *The Miracle* Reinhardt transformed the Olympia Hall in London into a vast cathedral.

115

The productions at the Circus in Berlin and at the Olympia Hall in London constituted various stages in Reinhardt's work. From a figurative church he moved on to a real one. At Salzburg in the choir of the Kollegienkirche (1922) he staged Hofmannsthal's *The Great World Theatre* and also *Jedermann* (based on the medieval *Everyman*) on the square in front of the cathedral (1920). Reinhardt was mostly responsible for the rediscovery of the arena theater in the twentieth century and its transposition into an elaborate theatrical architecture. Plays by Aeschylus, Shakespeare and Romain Rolland were produced at the Grosses Schauspielhaus in Berlin, which was built according to his ideas by Hans Poelzig and inaugurated in 1919. For *Danton* the entire space was transformed into a popular assembly hall with no separation between the actors and the spectators, and the public was again invited to participate directly in the performance.

In 1933 at the Felsenreitschule in Salzburg, Reinhardt created *Faust,* his last attempt to develop a theater of the masses. The staging pointed to a return to figurative realism. An enormous space was used to build Faust's city in its entirety, and yet all of the playing areas could be perceived simultaneously by the public.

Many of Reinhardt's productions made significant advances in the revolt against illusionist perspective. While the illusionist theater was still prevalent, new creations were constantly undermining its structures by showing that they clearly belonged to the past.

116. E. Stern, *Danton* by R. Rolland, dir. M. Reinhardt, Berlin, Grosses Schauspielhaus, 1920. Niessen Coll., Inst. Th. Cologne. The auditorium of the Grosses Schauspielhaus in Berlin was directly inspired by Greek and Elizabethan theaters. The principles of these classical theaters formed a basis for Reinhardt's production of *The Miracle* in London.

116

The Reign of "isms"

Cubism, Expressionism, Constructivism and Futurism are many convenient, although somewhat artificially contrived terms used to classify artistic currents. Reality, however, does not always fit into a category. During the first few decades of our century, movements tended to overlap, boundaries were uncertain, and the personalities of the creators eluded the labels that were pinned on them. Often the labels themselves comprised heterogeneous subjects. Nevertheless, the abundance of "isms" that arose during that time testify to the actual existence of movements, no matter how difficult they were to define. And although they were like many waves breaking on the surface of artistic history, these movements shared similarities and differences with one another as they made their impact. In most cases they encompassed more than one art form. Expressionism, for example, affected painting, poetry, music, theater and the cinema.

THE EXPRESSIONIST PERSPECTIVE

The Scandinavian artist Edvard Munch painted *The Cry* in 1893. In the center of the picture a haggard figure lets out a cry of terror which deforms his whole body while he clasps his emaciated face in his hands. His emotions are echoed by the concentric waves in the surrounding landscape. This work "staged" Expressionism for the first time. The title, the distortions in the 'decor', and the technique which invites the viewer to share the figure's perceptions — all announce the Expressionist theater. Yet, it was not until 1918 that the actor Ernst Deutsch, playing in *The Son* by Hasenclever, expressed feelings and assumed a posture which recalled Munch's figure.

Expressionist painting and theater emerged shortly before World War I. It was during the war, however, and particularly just afterwards that Expressionism became an important form of theatrical expression — as if a global conflagration were needed to transform human anguish into tragic emptiness and encourage the poet to materialize his visions on the stage.

Expressionism, generally speaking, was not a predefined style but a highly personal way of viewing things, and an active description of man's rebelliousness. According to expressionist philosophy, the individual often rejected the real world because it failed to contribute to his security and stability. Or, as an alternative to complete rejec-

117

117. E. Stern, *The Beggar* by R. Sorge, dir. M. Reinhardt, Berlin, Deutsches Theater, 1917. The expressionist designer transmits visually the anguish of his characters through their rigid postures, distorted gestures as well as through the deformation of the scenic elements.

tion, he substituted his own visions with the intention of dominating his environment. It was apparent that the expressionist artist would have to restructure reality from his subjective viewpoint, and that he would have to repudiate established laws, parody conventional rules and destroy the natural and logical relationships that normally existed between people and objects. Consequently, the art form which emerged was symbolic, abstract and replete with fantasy.

These characteristics guided the theatrical Expressionists as well. They also condemned the passivity of the naturalist and impressionist movements, and advocated freedom for the imagination to express the bizarre or extravagant without fear of offending the public. The goal of the Expressionist *metteur en scene* was not to *represent* in the illusionist fashion a coherent situation with all of the changes of fortune in the lives of the characters, their relationships with one another, etc., but rather to reveal the essence of the play, to emphasize the *leimotif* or primitive force motivating the drama. Clearly the stage had to be *denaturalized* and the anecdotal form abandoned.

Whatever did not pertain to the drama's essence was rejected, including visual elements that only reflected everyday appearances without touching the "soul." Accordingly, the expressionist setting was usually symbolic and tended to become more and more abstract with regard to line, color, form and object. Since this designer did not want to depict a *real* world, he did not visualize a *real* place, nor did he try to define a locale outside of the dramatic action. The play suggested certain visions to him, which he wanted to concretize in his setting to create a sort of "sphere of atmosphere" for the drama. Like the actor, the decor could interpret the play, illuminate the inner feelings of the characters, their interrelationships or simply the state of mind of just the principal character. Finally, the decor might underscore some aspect of the plot, or perhaps transform the action as the situation changed.

In reality the expressionist theater established two different tendencies in its decor which were integrated with one another to present the idea of a total theater. The first was inclined to distort reality and the second offered a rhythmical organization of space. The two tendencies, particularly apparent in the German theater of the twenties, also existed in other countries of Central Europe (Czechoslovakia, Poland), although modified by their individual national characteristics, in

118. L. Sievert, *The Son* by W. Hasenclever, dir. R. Weichert, Mannheim, National Th., 1918. Inst. Th. Cologne. **119.** L. Sievert, *Drums in the Night* by B. Brecht, dir. R. Weichert, Frankfurt, Stadtische Buhnen, 1923. Inst. Th. Cologne. An expressionist designer's first intention is never to define a locale which is preexistant to the dramatic action. He never *sees* the place but rather has visions which *suggest* a room, etc., and then attempts to make these visions concrete in his decor, thereby creating a "sphere of atmosphere" for the drama.

118

119

120

Scandinavia, and to a certain degree in the Soviet Union.

Distortion of the dramatic universe! "A bowl smashed to bits," was how Sievert defined his idea of a synthetic decor for *Drums in the Night.* The theatrical space he designed, somewhere between heaven and earth, suggested that this was not merely the designated place, but a duality within the characters themselves. In this strange room without a ceiling the immediate framework of the action and the omnipresent city were merged into a single vision. This was a recurrent theme among the Expressionists and can be found, for example, in Reigbert's sets in which he superimposed the vision of a large city on the immediate and successive places of the action. Fragmented settings, distortions of reality, a composite of images united into several actual scenes which the viewer was not accustomed to perceive simultaneously!

120. L. Sievert, *The Great Highway* by A. Strindberg, dir. F. P. Buch, Frankfurt, Schauspielhaus, 1923. Inst. Th. Cologne. **121.** E. Stern, *From Morn till Midnight* by G. Kaiser, dir. F. Hollaender, Berlin, Deutsches Theater, 1919. Th. Samm. Vienna.

121

KAISER: VON MORGENS BIS MITTERNACHT   CESAR KLEIN

122

122. C. Klein, *From Morn till Midnight* by G. Kaiser, dir. V.
Barnowsky, Berlin, Lessing Theater, 1921. Inst. Th. Cologne.
123. R. Neppach, *Transfiguration* by E. Toller, dir. K. H. Martin,
Berlin, Tribune, 1919. Doc. Th. Mus. Munich.

123

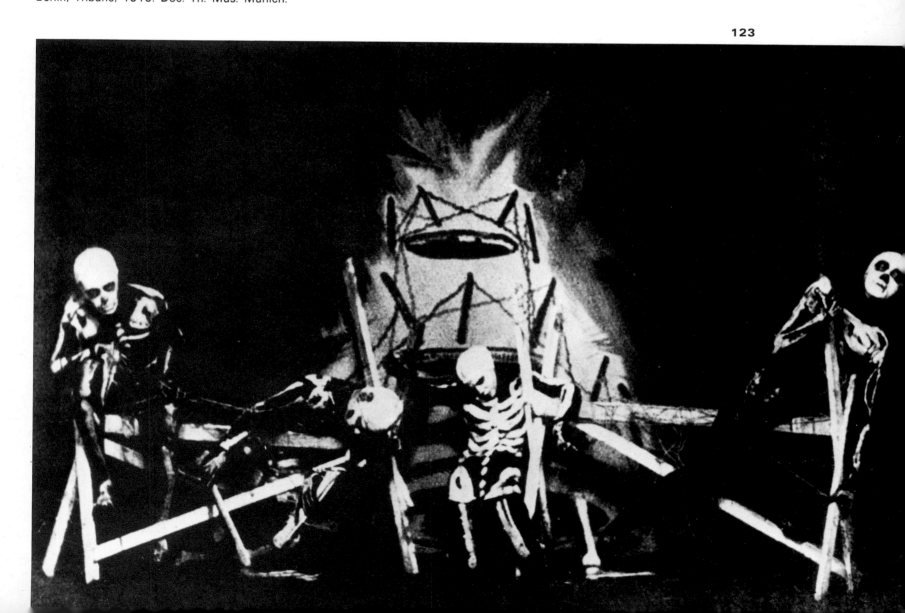

124-127. O. Reigbert, *Drums in the Night* by B. Brecht, dir. O. Falckenberg, Munich, Kammerspiele, 1922. Th. Mus. Munich. **124.** Original sketch, act IV. **125.** Same scene in the production. **126.** Original sketch. Street scene. **127.** Another scene from the production. It is worthwhile to compare Reigbert's sets for Brecht's play with those designed by Sievert (cf. fig. 119).

In connection with distortion, which made the sets for the film *The Cabinet of Dr. Caligari* famous, Worringer's idea of *Abstrakionsdrang* should be mentioned. Worringer believed that if an object were uprooted from the logical world, then the artist could give it some absolute value or independent life. It should not be forgotten that the atmosphere created by the designer formed a "second self" for the actor, that is to say that the decor was frequently perceived through the tormented soul of the main character, and thus played an active role in the action.

Distortion was also a source of motivation. The best way to extricate an object from the real world, give it its own "soul" or spiritual essence and shape it into the plastic expression of the artist's emotions was to systematically deform it. For example, vertical walls were often tilted, as if to defy the laws of gravity, windows became triangular or trapezoidal holes, apertures that looked out onto an anguished and mysterious world. The scenic elements seemed to be animated by some chaotic inner emotion, like the doors Troster designed for *The Inspector General* (or *Le Revizor*) which gave the impression that a "dance" was carrying them off and trying to destroy them.

Another tendency is found by extending the ideas of Craig and Appia. Recall that the essential ingredient for them was the dynamic organization of the stage space which sup-

124

125

126

127

128. V. Hofman, *The Hydra* by J. Maranek, dir. K. Dostal, Prague, Municipal Th., 1921. From M. Rutte and F. Bartos, *The Modern Czech Stage,* Prague, 1938. A favorite theme among expressionist dramatists and scenographers alike was to present an anxious and uneasy city by the systematic visual distortions of the setting.

128

129

ported the play and was integrated with all of its elements. To paraphrase the director, Jessner: external impressionism has been replaced through the presentation of an 'actual lived experience' which should be represented in a "real" fashion by using concise scenic suggestions. These mere indications of place are similar to the central symbols or characteristic elements that Craig had in mind, and include such examples as the schematic-looking tree erected by Brunner in 1914 for Kleist's *Penthesilea*, the vague outlines of windows by Stern for *The Beggar* (Sorge), and the grilled window Sievert placed against the black velvet background of his set for *The Son,* the only opening onto the panorama of a threatening city. Still other examples of these "scenic abbreviations" are the panels designed by Neppach which stand out in his shadowy setting to summarily suggest the various "stations" in Toller's play *Transfiguration;* or Desdemona's bed, placed alone on the stage by the designer Pirchan for Jessner's *Othello;* or finally the mill of Isaac Grunewald in the third act of *Samson*

129. E. Pirchan, *Othello* (Shakespeare), dir. L. Jessner, Berlin, Staatschauspielhaus, 1921. Inst. Th. Cologne. Color is not merely a descriptive element here but has become an agent of dramatic expression. 130. E. Pirchan, *Wilhelm Tell* by F. Schiller, dir. L. Jessner, Berlin, Staatliches Schauspielhaus, 919. The empty road. Th. Samm. Vienna. The "Stufenbuhne" (an imaginative use of levels and steps) contributed to an abstract staging of mythical events. 131. E. Pirchan, *Othello,* same production. Desdemona's bed. Doc. Theatermuseum, Munich.

130

131

and Delilah. The scenic place became the focal point of dramatic tensions that permeated the entire stage space.

Nostalgic for a certain vitality, the Expressionists attempted to animate the space indirectly by modifying it into what might be called an "expressive trampoline" for the actor. To follow the progression of the action, an architectural arrangement was constructed in which it was possible to adapt a decor that was simultaneously figurative, functional and symbolic (as in Sievert's decor for *Penthesilea*), or one which might be more abstract, (note the spatial organizations of the Polish designer Pronaszko and the Czech Hofman). Even better examples perhaps are the productions in Berlin by Jessner and his designer Pirchan, their creations of "an abstract stage for mythical events." For *Wilhelm Tell* the principal element was an enormous staircase which suggested the underlying motif of the play. In *Richard III* there wasn't the slightest historical indication of place; only a platform raised below a grayish-green wall that represented the menace

132

132, 133. C. Klein, *Napoleon* by C.D. Grabbe, dir. L. Jessner, Berlin State Theater, 1922. Doc. Th. Mus. Munich. **134, 137.** E. Pirchan, *The Marquis of Keith* by F. Wedekind, dir. L. Jessner, Berlin, Staatliches Schauspielhaus, 1920. The sketch (Th. Samm. Vienna), and the production (From Bab, *Das Theatre der Gegenwart,* 1928). **135, 136.** E. Pirchan, *Richard III* (Shakespeare), dir. L. Jessner, Berlin State Theater, 1920. (**135.** Doc. Th. Mus. Munich. **136.** Design of the staircase, a plastic and metaphorical interpretation of the rise and fall of King Richard. Inst. Th. Cologne).

133

134

135

136

137

138. H. Heckroth, *The Green Table,* chor. K. Joos, Essen, Stadt, Buhnen, 1932. Niessen Coll. Inst. Th. Cologne. **139.** The realization. This most famous of expressionist ballets is still performed by modern repertory companies.

threatening everyone, the ever-present Tower of London, symbol of the reign of terror in England. Periodically, a monumental staircase leading to the platform was incorporated into the action. This red staircase, red for the royal mantle and the blood of many victims, presented a spatial description of the rise and fall of Richard. Jessner and Pirchan, like other Expressionists, recognized the expressive value of color and took advantage of its dramatic and symbolic power to evoke emotion.

The two tendencies described above, although clearly defined, were not completely isolated from one another. On the one hand, the scenic space was sometimes subjected to extreme distortions that undermined its stability and gave it a sort of baroque twist (the designer Drabik). On the other, the requirements of spatial organization did not

140

140. L. Sievert, *Cain* by Byron, dir. J. Tralow, Frankfurt, 1923. Theaterabt, St. U. Frankfurt Lib. 141. I. Grunewald, *Samson et Delila* by C. Saint-Saens, Stockholm. Royal Opera, 1921. Drottningsholms Theatermuseum.

141

necessarily exclude the interplay of pictorial surfaces (cf. Handel's *Herakles* staged at Munster in 1927 with sets by Heckroth).

However, the expressionist picture would have been incomplete, spiritless and most likely ineffective if not for the developments in lighting which animated and emphasized its dramatic expressiveness. A sort of auspicious semi-darkness could achieve Rembrandt-like effects or beams of light might streak across the stage. In both time and space the expressionist director depended heavily on the use of contrasting light. Moreover, instead of general illumination, he preferred selective lighting in zones, spots and flashes which enabled him to catch the actor's expression with a strong beam of light, and in an "ecstatic moment," isolated him from his environs. Furthermore, the intensive interplay of shadow and light accentuated the actor's presence and tended to enlarge and exaggerate his image. (cf. sketch by Cesar Klein for *Holle, Weg, Erde*). As a reinforcement and integral part of design, lighting was also independently important. It created speedy shifts of scenes, underscored relationships between characters, and of

142

142. C. Klein, *Holle, Weg, Erde* by G. Kaiser, dir. V. Barnowsky, Berlin, Lessing Theater, 1920, Inst. Th. Cologne.

143. H. Heckroth, *Theodora* by G. Handel, dir. H. Niedecken-Gebhard, Munster State Th., 1927. Doc. Th. Mus. Munich.

143

144
145

88

144. W. Drabik, *As You Like It* by Shakespeare, dir. L. Schiller, Warsaw, Boguskawski Th., 1925. **145.** V. Hofman, *Herakles* by O. Fischer, dir. K.H. Hilar, Prague, Municipal Th., 1920. Sect. Th. Mus. Nat. Prague, Photo. O, Hilmerova.

146. V. Hofman, costume for Shakespeare's *Richard III*, dir. J. Bor., Municipal Th. Prague, 1934. **147.** V. Hofman, costumes for *King Lear* by Shakespeare, dir. K.H. Hilar, Prague, National Th., 1929. From *The Modern Czech Stage*, op. cit.

146

147

course, engulfed the audience with its magical fluctuations.

The emotional impact of Expressionism produced by the use of shock and other effects which acted directly on the spectator's nerves cast a spell that suspended his critical faculties. Obviously, those who advocated a more lucid form of theater refused such dramatic effects and the spiritual isolation it created for the individual. Expressionism was also condemned by those who wanted to portray man's role in History in order to achieve certain political goals. A new objectivity called Constructivism was developed by artists who did not accept the fatality of tragic tensions and insisted on another perspective of the world.

CONSTRUCTIVISM AND POLITICAL THEATER

Just as the expressionist movement was centered in Germany, the heart of Constructivism was in the Soviet Union. Any analysis of it must take into account historical events and situate the artists in the context of the Russian Revolution. It is also clear that the influence of this movement extended beyond the Soviet Union, especially into Cen-

148

148-150. Y. Annenkov, *The Storming of the Winter Palace*, collective work, dir. N. Evreinov, Petrograd, Place Uritski, 1920. **148.** Design by Y. Annenkov. Bakhrushin Mus. Moscow. **149.** From the production: The red stage. Doc. Th. Mus. Leningrad. **150.** The white stage. Doc. Th. Mus. Leningrad.

151. C. Malevich, *Victory over the Sun* by A. Kruchenykh and → M. Matyushin, dir. C. Malevich, Saint-Petersburg, Luna Park, 1913. Th. Mus. Leningrad, (From *Projekt*, Warsaw, 5, 1967).

149

tral Europe, where, however, it gave rise to all sorts of variations and perhaps lost some of its original purity. Nevertheless, Constructivism established new theatrical forms which were combined with new means of expression.

90

The Soviet Union of the Twenties

November 7, 1920. The enormous Uritski Square in Petrograd, the site of the original event, saw 150,000 people relive one of the most crucial times in their history: *The Storming of the Winter Palace.*

At one end of the square was the Palace itself with its sixty-two huge windows all lit up; the final struggle could be seen through these windows in the form of profiles created by shadow-boxing. At the other end were two vast circular platforms that rested against the semi-circular buildings. On one side was the "red stage" consisting of scaffolded levels, high brick walls and imitation factory chimneys. The revolutionary spirit erupted from this spot. On the other side was the "white stage," the domain of the Kerensky and provisional government. Between the two was the arch of a bridge which was the meeting point of the conflict. These three scenic areas encircled the square and the spectators. In the first part of the play the action wandered from one stage to another; in the second part it reached the Palace. Armored trucks and soldiers of the Red Army advanced through the crowd of spectators for the assault. Machine guns fired and cannons thundered until the lights in the windows

150

were extinguished and fireworks announced victory for the people.

This was the most famous of the mass festivals that took place in revolutionary Russia; grandiose spectacles reminiscent of those during the French Revolution or the desires of a Romain Rolland, encouraging the spectators to abandon their passivity and participate in, relive and exalt their victory! Moreover, theater was supposed to complete the political education of the masses and open the doors of artistic knowledge to them. Annenkov, the scenographer of this mystical, revolutionary stage design on the public square, instinctively returned to the scenic principles of the medieval mystery plays and the concept of differentiated zones for his inspiration. The stage, which was divided into various playing areas permitting the action to flow easily from one to the other, also eliminated the traditional barriers between actors and spectators.

Many other mass festivals took place in the Soviet Union, but the year 1920 marked their apotheosis. Their popularity further indicated the tendency during revolutionary times to theatricalize life. People had extraordinary confidence in the powers of the theater so that these mass productions had a strong impact on the leading creators of the Soviet Theater. Mayakovsky dreamed of destroying the walls of traditional theater, while Meyerhold hoped to build an edifice that would restore the atmosphere and conditions of a public square. Einstein staged some of the scenes for *Gas Masks* in a factory. In the thirties Okhlopkov and his designers Knoblock and Shtoffer were influenced by the mass festivals for the staging of their productions at the Realistic Theatre in Moscow, where they established new spatial relationships between actors and spectators.

In 1913 Mayakovsky declared: "The great social upheavals that we have undertaken in all realms of beauty in the name of the art of the future, the art of the Futurists, will not come to a halt and will not be confined to the theater alone." In December of the same year the first Futurist Theatre in the world produced Vladimir Mayakovsky's *A Tragedy* on the stage at Luna Park in Petersburg with backdrops by the painters Filonov and Skolnick, and *Victory over the Sun*, a Futurist opera using the idea of "alogical" language. For the latter, Malevich designed the sets and staged the work himself. His costumes looked like geometrical forms, brightly colored to fit the stage space and

were not based on a precise style. The actors wore masks over their faces which denaturalized their characters. Oskar Schlemmer designed his costumes in a similar fashion for his *Triadic Ballet*. Malevich's cubistic style backdrops marked a transition from Cubo-Futurism to the Suprematist movement. Some of his backgrounds depicted a chaotic universe in which objects such as houses, chimneys, sun dials, staircases, musical notes and abstract signs were combined with one another. Others were reduced to purely geometric forms; one had a square in its center intersected by a diagonal that formed two triangles, one black and the other white. (Painters at this time were putting a black square on a white background). The unique pictorial style of Malevich's costumes and backdrops were not his only achievements. Thanks to his original use of stage lighting, the characters, who were by now reduced to merely decomposable motifs, were integrated into the action.

This significant, although isolated experience introduced into the development of modern theater an alliance between the artist's need to experiment and his search for a plastic, three-dimensional setting. During the first years of the Soviet Revolution an extraordinary flurry of creative activity spread among the artistic avant garde, who for the most part identified with the new regime. Perhaps not all of the artists were as committed as Meyerhold. Their enthusiasm was strengthened, however, by the hope that the new government would promote the absolute freedom of artistic expression. At first their aspirations seemed to be fulfilled. Then Stalin imposed the ideas of Zhdanov on the Soviet artists, and a fascinating period of theatrical creativity was terminated.

In the years immediately following the Revolution, Alexander Tairov upheld a purely aesthetic ideal at the Kamerny Theater in Moscow. He believed that the theater should be completely autonomous, of life, political ideologies, etc. and also that it not simply illustrate a literary work. Theater was to be a "living synthesis" of language, sound, stage design, costumes, lighting and the actor, the latter being the fundamental source of theattrical emotion. Alexandra Exter's concern for plasticity was apparent in her setting for *Famira Kifared (Famira the Harpist)*, in 1916. She fashioned a playing area composed of raised platforms and levels that emphasized the physical movements of the actor, and organized the volumes of the three-dimensional space rhythmically to blend with the work and delineate the various elements of

152-154. C. Malevich, *Victory over the Sun,* dir. C. Malevich, Saint-Petersburg, Luna Park, 1913. In the backgrounds Malevich inaugurated his suprematist concepts. In this monumental although isolated experiment, the play tended to become rather abstract and decomposed into motifs; the characters were integrated into the action by the clever use of lighting — which was not explicitly called for in the script.

152

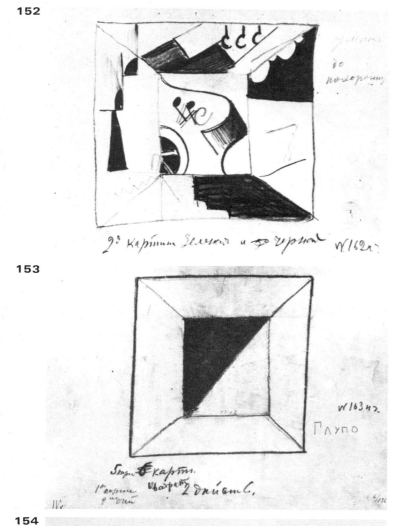

153

154

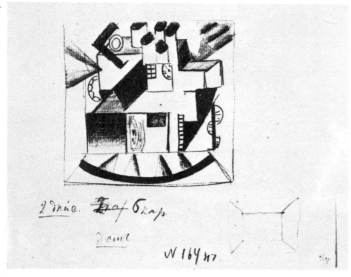

the decor. Tairov's strikingly original style at this time combined the ideas of Appia with ''pictorial cubism.''

Three different productions will illustrate this style. For *Salome* Alexandra Exter constructed a masterful architecture consisting of steps leading to various raised levels surrounded by massive columns. There was a kind of symmetry in this assymetrical arrangement. The rhythm of the volumes was echoed in the composition of brightly colored fabrics, a red here, brown there or a golden streak cutting across the blue of an abstractly-drawn sky. Draperies or curtains were raised and lowered to indicate changes of time and place, and at the same time, modified the color balance. This ''dynamic'' decor, as a parallel to the dramatic action, reflected the emotional and aesthetic values of the play and made the spectator sensitive to its special attributes.

The world of *Phaedra* as, conceived by the architect A. Vesnin, could be characterized as untamed and unstable. In the absence of clear horizontal and vertical lines the geometry of the stage space was chaotic. A sloping stage made the ground appear to rise towards the background as if some geological movement were lifting it. A stone rested against a concavely-shaped wall, while in another corner a cylindrical object struggled with a flatly-shaped form. Colorful triangular flaps hung above the stage and cut into the space. Tension was created in this mixture of objects and empty space from the outpouring of tragic emotion that emanated from the statuesque, cyclopean forms. This universe was perhaps not the one Ràcine intended, but it was a powerful production because it captured the essence of the original myth. The ''sculptured, living'' creatures wore masks, which together with their costumes removed them entirely from modern life; *Cothurnoi* emphasized their height and added a hieratic quality, and the production achieved a total plastic unity.

There was no barbarism in *Princess Brambilla.* Jacoulov designed sets for this kaleidoscopic fantasy that featured a fairyland under cubist influence. Curved forms seemed to join right angles and flat surfaces, sharp edges were blunted by arabesques and draperies created a balance to the volumes. The spiral staircase was twisted and broken. Cubism was overpowered by a baroque elegance, and it was obvious that attempts to expel painting from the theater had not been completely successful.

This type of expressive construction in which the representational vision was re-

155

155. A. Exter, *Salome* by O. Wilde, dir. A. Tairov, Moscow, Kamerny Th., 1917. The constructed model. Th. Samm. Vienna. A colorful arrangement in which one can see the orderly imposition of the artist's will. **156.** A. Vesnin, *Phaedra* by J. Racine, dir. A. Tairov, Moscow, Kamerny Th., 1922. Constructed design. Th. Samm. Vienna. The emptiness of these cyclopean forms provides the tension.

156

157. A. Vesnin, *Phaedra* by J. Racine, costume design, Inst. Th. Cologne. **158.** S.M. Eisenstein, *Macbeth* by Shakespeare, dir. V. Tikhonovich, Moscow, Polenov Th., 1921.

159. I. Gamrekeli, *Anzor* based on V. Ivanov's *The Armored Train 14-69,* Tibilsi, 1928. Doc. Bakhrushin Mus. Moscow. In the work of this Georgian designer, the style is essentially representational, although the perspective is somewhat deformed.

160

160-162. I. Nivinsky, *The Princess Turandot* by C. Gozzi, dir. E. Vakhtangov, Moscow, Vakhtangov Th. 1922. Bakhrushin Mus., Moscow. Vakhtangov and Nivinsky proposed nothing less for this comedy than a Chinese setting with a commedia dell'arte script — all of which unfolds like a piece of modern art.

161

162

tained although somewhat distorted can be found in the works of the Georgian designer Gamrekeli, in the creations of Eisenstein for *Macbeth* and in those of Nivinsky for *The Princess Turandot*. Staged by Vakhtangov in 1922, the spirit of *Princess Turandot* was different. While the action was supposedly taking place in China, the characters emerged from the Italian *commedia* and Nivinsky's setting seemed like a prism of modern art machinations. Behind the chaotic appearance of this highly-charged atmosphere filled with gaiety, there was the dynamism and warmth of the actors' continual improvisations. The sloping stage had a wall in the background penetrated by angular or curved openings and a balcony. A series of hangings and mobile curtains were hung in full view of the public, who by now were receptive to all sorts of suggestions. And a suspended disc, symbol of the play, was raised or lowered to represent either the sun or the moon. Anything could happen in this puzzle of forms and objects. The atmosphere, like a fairground, reminded the audience in case they had forgotten that the theater was purely an art form.

In the year Malevich worked on *Victory over the Sun*, Tatlin designed the sets and costumes for *Ivan Sussanin*. Only a soothsayer could discover in these sketches any signs of Tatlin's future artistic inclinations. They contained no revolutionary elements, considering the works by other painters in the theater. But Tatlin's unique style was evident even at this time in the extraordinary

163

164

165

163, 164. V. Tatlin, costume designs for *Ivan Sussanin* or *The Life For The Tsar,* by M. Glinka, 1913. Bakhrushin Mus. Moscow. **165.** V. Tatlin, sketch of the decor for *Ivan Sussanin* or *The Life For The Tsar* by M. Glinka, 1913. Tretyakov Gall. Moscow. Photo Petitjean. Who could imagine from these sketches what the artistic future of Tatlin would be like! The counter-reliefs he would create the following year.

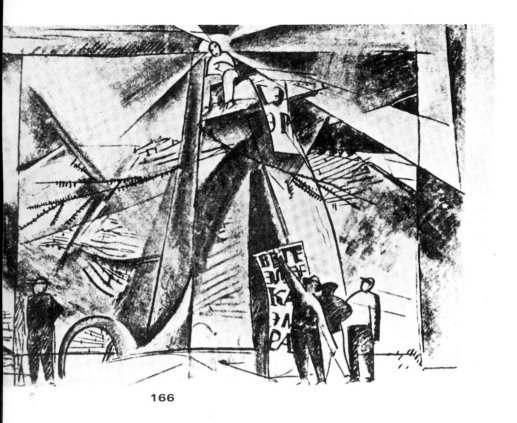

166

166, 167. V. Tatlin, *Zanguezi,* by Khlebnikov. Petrograd, 1923.
166. The design.   **167**. The constructed model. Th. Samm.
Vienna.

rhythm and emphasis on simplification of composition. Yet, who knows if this theatrical experience contributed to the artist's transition into the field of sculpture? The following year Tatlin created counter-reliefs in which real materials (glass, wire, metal) sculptured empty space. This was an important step in the complex development of Constructivism and Tatlin was one of the main, if not the principal promoter.

The spirit of counter-reliefs can be found in Khlebnikov's *Zanguezi.* Tatlin devised a concrete structure for these dialogues in "trans-sense" (*zaumny* in Russian) language by combining surfaces made of different materials and treating them in various ways.

167

168, 169. V. Dimitriev, *The Dawns* by E. Verhaeren, dir. V. Meyerhold and V. Bebutov, Moscow, R.S.F.S.R. Th. No. I, 1921. Leningrad Th. Mus. **168.** Sketch. **169.** A scene. Dimitriev's stage presents a composite of cubo-futuristic ideas and Tatlin's counter-reliefs. The production seems to be a prologue for scenic constructivism.

168

Mobile spotlights animated and emphasized their particular characteristics.

Zanguezi was an isolated production among Tatlin's post revolutionary works, and curiously it was staged when Constructivism had already made inroads into the theater, thanks to the convergence of the ideals of such plasticians as Popova, Stepanova, and Meyerhold. In 1920 Dmitriev's scenery for *The Dawns* represented a prologue to scenic constructivism. Non-descriptive elements that were not directly related to the action played an aesthetic role and suggested a world gripped by revolution (practicables, grayish-silver cubes, a red circle, suspended objects like a yellow triangle, an iron pipe,

169

170

170. N.I. Altman, *Mystery-Bouffe* by V. Mayakovsky, dir. A.M. Granovsky, Moscow Circus, 1921. Th. Mus. Leningrad. The particular style of performing in the circus as well as the special rapport the circus enjoyed with a large audience, captured the imagination of many Russian directors and scenographers during the first few years of the new Soviet regime. The circus here in this play furnished a theatrical space which of course did not conform to the rigors of the Italian stage.

crossed ropes). In this composite image Cubo-Futurism was blended with Tatlin's style of counter-reliefs. The performance provided Meyerhold with a pretext for announcing his own scenic ideal: "Joyfully abandoning their brushes, our artists will arm themselves with axes, hammers and picks to cut out scenic ornaments from the materials offered by nature!"

In the autumn of 1921 Meyerhold was a frequent visitor at the first constructivist Exhibition in Moscow entitled "5 x 5 = 25." How could he not have been charmed by the "constructivist models" of such artists as Popova, Rodchenko, Exter, Stepanova and Vesnin! The Constructivists denied beauty was the supreme goal of art. Rejecting figurative tendencies and any decorative ornamentation, they advocated an art that would be as useful as work or science. For example, such an art would produce objects that were not imitative of another real form but would have an autonomous existence. And this could be achieved through the artistic structuring of raw materials like wood, metal, glass, etc. Geometrical creations during this period reflected the general enthusiasm for technology and industrial machinery among a people busily engaged in the rebuilding of their society. Like others before and after him, the revolutionary director Meyerhold wanted a theater that would serve the people. Violently against illusionism, he absorbed the ideas of his fellow artists, particularly with regard to plasticity in design.

There was yet another factor which contributed to the close relationship between the stage and the artistic currents of that time; namely, the attraction of many men in the theater to the circus. Granovsky used the circus to stage Mayakovsky's *Mystery-Bouffe* not simply because it was an unusual theatrical place, but because the circus had a unique spirit and a powerful appeal to the popular audience. Here was an art based on theatricality, on a fresh and direct image that was not emasculated by psychological analysis, an art that required perfect mastery by its performers. While the "eccentric" actor was assimilating the techniques of clowns, stuntmen, and trapeze artists, the constructivist stage designer was enchanted with the scenic elements and properties of the circus. From such inspirations came the scene in hell Annenkov designed for *The First Distiller* (1919), which featured suspended and mobile platforms, flying trapezes and poles that facilitated the performance of the actor-acrobat; Eisenstein's (1923) adaptation of Ostrovsky's *Enough Stupidity in Every Wise*

171

172

171. Y. Annenkov, *The First Distiller* by L. Tolstoy, dir. Y. Annenkov, Petrograd, Hermitage Experimental Th. 1919. Bibl. Arsenal, Paris. **172.** S.M. Eisenstein, *A Wise Man* based on *Enough Stupidity in Every Wise Man* by A. Ostrovsky, dir. S.M. Eisenstein, Moscow, Proletkult, 1923.

173

173-175. L. Popova, *The Magnificent Cuckhold* by F. Crommelynck, dir. V. Meyerhold, Moscow, Actor's Theatre, Group of students from Meyerhold's Theatrical Workshop, 1922. **173.** Basic outline. **174.** The model. Bakhrushin Mus. Moscow. **175.** The production. Doc. Kunstgew Mus. Zurich. A bare stage except for Popova's "machine for acting," divided into levels and linked by steps. The platform no longer evoked a fictitious world; it was rather the true place of the action and completely functional.

174

175

Man staged in a theater transformed into a circus arena; and the production of *The Magnificent Cuckold* by Meyerhold.

For *The Magnificent Cuckhold,* the stage was bare, stripped completely of its traditional decorative properties — curtains, hangings, footlights, etc. — denuded of everything but the brick wall which served as the background. The dramatic action alone animated the empty space. The stage, which did not represent another world or evoke faraway images was the actual place of the action, presenting "that which is" and entirely functional.

On this unencumbered stage, rising directly from the ground and without any attachment to the wings, was an open-work construction like the tower Tatlin dedicated to the Third International. Illuminated by visible spotlights none of the objects in this skeletal assemblage were hidden from view. The construction was linear and consisted of scaffoldings, slides, platforms, steps, a sled, revolving doors and revolving elements such as windmill sails which indicated the shifting settings — bedroom, balcony, etc. Among the revolving discs which turned according to the rhythm of the emotions expressed by the actors, there was one, which like a graph of Lissitzky, traced the name of the playwright,

176. G.B. Jacoulov, *Princess Brambilla* by E.T.A. Hoffmann, dir. A. Tairov, Moscow, Kamerny Th., 1920. Inst. Th. Cologne. "To intimately unify all of the elements on an unencumbered stage, to capture the fantasy and engulf the audience in a swirl of theatrical phantasmagoria — that was my objective in *Princess Brambilla*." (A. Tairov).

177

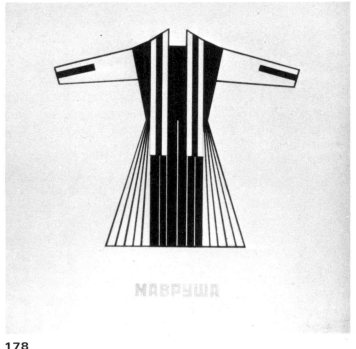

МАВРУША

178

ПОЛУТАТАРИНОВ

179

Crommelynck. Such was the "machine for acting" out *The Magnificent Cuckold.* The actors, dressed in the overalls of a stage-crew, were free to develop their "bio-mechanical" movements in the three dimensional space of the stage.

In *The Death of Tarelkin* Stepanova's original set consisted of a series of non-figurative elements that were all slatted and contrasted with the background of the stage.

Were these sets really "abstract"? or were they rather an assortment of working instruments for the actors, who manipulated and assigned various functions to them while the action unfolded. As the eccentricities increased during the course of the performance, the functional and ludicrous roles of these objects were underlined.

To modify this radical type of Constructivism, both *Earth in Turmoil* and *The Forest* introduced objects from everyday life or realistic elements that were isolated from their usual context. The aesthetic principle of

177-179. V. Stepanova, *Death of Tarelkin* by A. Sukhovo-Kobylin, dir. V. Meyerhold, Moscow, G.I.T.I.S. Theater, 1922. **177.** The model. Doc. Th. Mus. Leningrad. **178, 179.** Costumes. Bakhrushin Mus. Moscow.

180, 181. V. Fedorov, *The Forest* by A. Ostrovsky, dir. V. Meyerhold, Moscow. T.I.M. Th., 1924. **180.** The model. **181.** A scene from the production. Doc. Th. Mus. Leningrad. In this production the radical constructivist style was tempered by the introduction of real objects or realistic elements which were not related in their usual way.

180

181

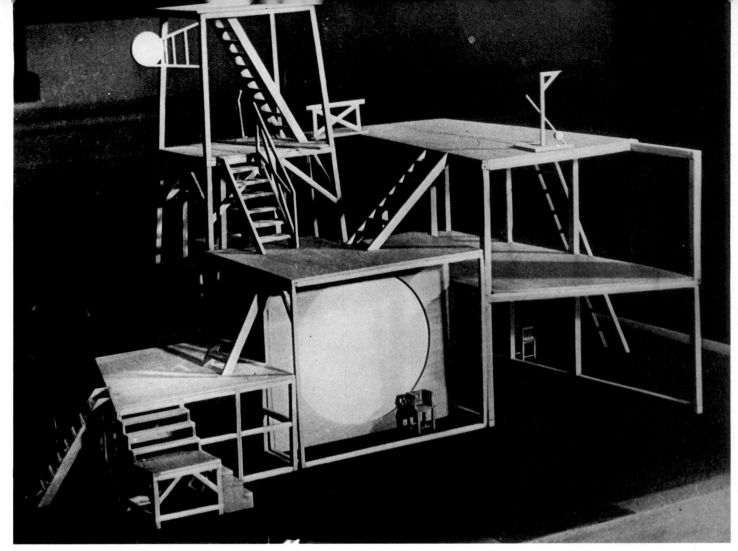

182

182. V.A. Shestakov, *Lac Lyul* by A. Faiko, dir. V. Meyerhold, Moscow, Theater of the Revolution, 1923. Doc. France and Soviet Union. **183.** V.A. Shestakov, *Man and the Masses* by E. Toller, Moscow, Theater of the Revolution, 1923. Doc. France and Soviet Union.

184. S.M. Eisenstein, *Heartbreak House* by G.B. Shaw, unrealized project, dir. V. Meyerhold, Moscow, Zon. Th., 1922. **185-187.** El Lissitzky, *Victory over the Sun* by M. Matyushin and A. Kruchenykh. Conceived of in 1923 as an electro-mechanical project. Unrealized production. Published as lithographs, Mun. Mus. Amsterdam. Cf. Color reproduction, fig. 227.

183

184

collage is evident as the tension grew out of the confrontations between the different aspects of reality. In *Earth in Turmoil,* a motorcycle, automobile, field kitchen, and tractor symbolized the important tasks of the moment (transportation, electrification, etc.) while appropriate captions and commentaries were projected on screens. In *The Forest,* a long ramp, symbolizing a path, curved downward onto the stage and a few descriptive elements (fences, gate to the property, etc.) specified the place and its surroundings. Shestakov designed a set for *Lake Lyul* (as he did for *Man and the Masses*) that was based on an extremely dynamic architecture, including platforms, steps, bridges, elevators, illuminated titles and advertisements, cinematographic projections — all of which were intended to construct a synthetic image of the modern city. Without copying reality, Constructivism in this play proposed an alternate version of it. The productions of *Earth in Turmoil, The Forest,* and to a certain degree, *Lake Lyul* explain what Meyerhold meant by his contention that: "The stage cannot sustain either absolute abstraction or absolute naturalism. The true substance of the contemporary theater and probably of theater in general lies in the fusion of these two elements."

Constructivist ideas remained present for a long time in Meyerhold's works even though it seemed that his personal artistic development would have driven him towards other scenographic experiences. Some of his projects that were never staged are worth mentioning: *Heartbreak House,* for which Eisenstein conceived the scenography, at the same time brings to mind the sets of Popova, Stepanova, and Tatlin. There was also the joint effort with El Lissitzky, *I Want A Child* by Tretyakov, that took several years to stage (1926-1930) because of difficulties with the censors.

If a Constructivist pursued his convictions to their logical conclusions, would it have been possible for him to permit the presence of a person on the stage? Either he had to agree to place his art at the disposition of the theater, or else, if he wanted to create a "pure" Constructivist production, he had to be the director as well as the controller of the objects he had invented. Then, together with his plastic decor, it would be possible for him to conceive of a purely mechanical work. Lissitzky chose the second alternative, as did the future members of the Bauhaus. One of his efforts which remained just a project was described in a portfolio of

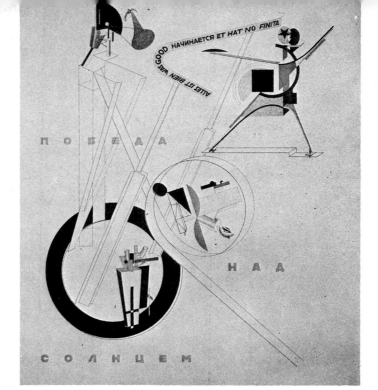

185

186

187

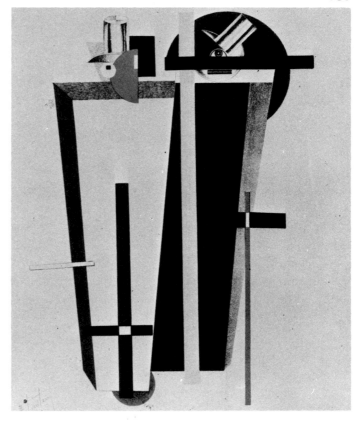

107

188. El Lissitzky, *I Want a Child* by S. Tretyakov, dir. V. Meyerhold, Moscow, 1926-1930. Unrealized production. Reconstructed model. Bakhrushin Mus. Moscow. The organization of the theatrical space as proposed by this model is close to what Vakhtangov and Barkhin had created for Meyerhold when the construction was interrupted.

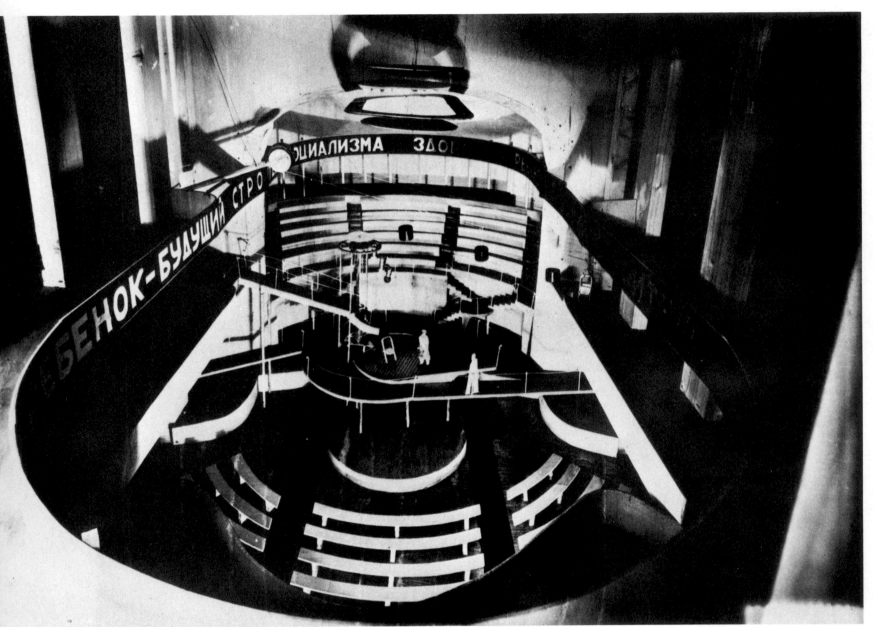

188

189

189. Y. Annenkov, *Gas* by G. Kaiser, dir. Khokov, Petrograd, Great Dramatic Theater, 1922. Th. Mus. Leningrad. This production was staged the same year as Meyerhold's *Magnificent Cuckhold.*

190

191

190. N. Akimov, *Mister Magridge Junior* by Triger, dir. N. Petrov, Leningrad, Volnaia Comedia, 1924. 191. N. Akimov, *Tartuffe* by Moliere, dir. N. Petrov and V. Soloviev, Leningrad. Gosdrama Th., 1929.

colored lithographs that was published in Hanover in 1923. Like Malevich ten years earlier, he worked on *Victory over the Sun* but his conceptions of this work were very different from the other artist. Lissitzky proposed a stationary "machine setting" consisting of all moving parts, and accessible from all sides. A series of "acting bodies" could traverse this machine in all directions. Both the "machine" and the "acting bodies" would be directed by a single artist located in the center of the apparatus, who with the help of electro-mechanical devices would coordinate the movements, sounds and lighting. The light would be transmitted through prisms and through their reflections on varied surfaces. Only the text itself of this Futurist opera by Kruchenykh forced the designer to give the "figures" something of a human anatomy.

In their endeavors to create an art of movement and of lighting that went beyond the theater, this important project should be inserted between the engravings of Gordon Craig for *Scenes* and some of the productions of Nicolas Schoffer.

One can only imagine what the production of *I Want A Child* would have been like with Lissitzky's scenography and Meyerhold's intention to stage it in the form of a debate that the spectators could have interrupted. This production would have undoubtedly advanced scenic constructivism beyond the accomplishments of Popova and Shestakov. A model of the reconstruction has survived showing a stage with two superimposed levels and several catwalks which would have been built in the theater that Vakhtangov and Barkhin designed for Meyerhold; its actual construction, however, was abruptly halted while Stalin was in power.

The majority of significant constructivist productions were unquestionably put on by Meyerhold, but the influence Constructivism had in other theaters in the Soviet Union should not be forgotten. Many stage designers worked in that general style either out of conviction or perhaps simply out of a desire to be in vogue. In any case they succeeded in designing certain scenes that seemed only possible in a realistic or traditionally academic style. Indeed, Constructivism continued long after Meyerhold had begun searching for new forms of expression.

The year Meyerhold produced *The Magnificent Cuckold,* Annenkov in Petrograd designed the set for *Gas.* A sort of "integral rationalism" pervaded his decor which combined an elaborate stage and a complex architecture of more or less figurative ele-

ments. Akimov, too, was part of these artistic trends. Notice his designs for *Mister Magridge Junior* and his sets for Molierè's *Tartuffe,* which were inspired by the circus.

Constructivism at the Kamerny Theatre was less ascetic and more colorful. The gay production of the operetta *Girofle-Girofla* captured the rhythm of the music hall and reflected the extent to which Tairov was seduced by popular entertainment. Jacoulov's scenery blended the atmospheres of the cabaret and circus to achieve rapid and continual shifting scenes that contributed to the light, spirited movement of the action. The scenic structure provided the actor at every moment with the accessories and "acting instruments" he needed. Some kind of screen opening here and there through a system of trap doors, a few staircases, mirrors and ladders that appeared and disappeared — nothing more was required for Tairov's acrobat-actors to perform.

If it is difficult to recognize the stage de-

signer of *Princess Brambilla* in the scenic architecture of *Girofle-Girofla,* who would believe the same Vesnin created the sets for both *Phaedra* and *The Man Who Was Thursday?* One features a massive cubist structure, the other a complex scaffolding. This apparent versatility is an indication of the scenographer's need to adapt to different works and also of Vesnin's fondness for experimenting. Furthermore, it shows how quickly scenic forms evolved during this period of intense questioning, and the facility with which a personal artistic style could be transformed into a means of expression. Constructivist ideas were applied to Vesnin's setting for *The Man Who Was Thursday.* His use of platforms, steps, skeletal structures, kinetic elements as well as the suggestive powers of the whole production invite a comparison with Shestakov's *Lake Lyul.* Constructivism in these works did not seem to be a consequence of our technological and industrial civilization, but a means to describe it. The actor's participation was vital here and the properties he used were more "realistic" than those in the machine of the *Magnificent Cuckold.*

Tairov's work evolved into a new form of Constructivism that employed symbolic elements and at the same time maintained a certain aestheticism. From 1924-1931 his collaboration with the Sternberg brothers illustrated his ideas. *The Hairy Ape* displayed a cross-section of a ship. Representing both a place to live and a pontoon bridge, the Ark in *The Thunderstorm* was symbolic of the passing from one end of life to another and symbolic too of the drama's main character, the omnipresent Volga. The rigorous architecture and symmetrical beauty of *Saint Joan* inspired many imitations and showed that Constructivism could be applied for decorative purposes. Rabinovich's ingenious setting for *Lysistrata* at the Musical Studio of the Art Theater included the usual construc-

195. V.A. Stenberg and K. Medunetsky, *The Thunderstorm* by A. Ostrovsky, dir. A. Tairov, Moscow, Kamerny Th., 1924. Model. Th. Samm. Vienna.

192. G.B. Jacoulov, *Girofle-Girofla* by Ch. Lecocq, dir. A. Tairov, Moscow, Kamerny Th., 1922. Inst. Th. Cologne. Tairov could not refuse the seducing operetta, *Girofle-Girofla,* which captured the modern music hall spirit. A mixture of the rhythms of the music hall, circus, etc. Jacoulov's colorful and adaptable setting contributed to a spirited production.

193. A. Vesnin, *The Man Who Was Thursday* by G.K. Chesterton, dir. A. Tairov, Moscow, Kamerny Th., 1923. Doc. Th. Mus. Munich. **194.** V.A. and G.A. Stenberg, *The Hairy Ape* by E. O'Neill, dir. A. Tairov, Moscow, Kamerny Th., 1926. Doc. Th. Mus. Munich.

195

196. V.A. and G.A. Stenberg, *Saint Joan* by G.B. Shaw, dir. A. Tairov, Moscow, Kamerny Th., 1924. Th. Samm. Vienna. Doc. Fratelli Fabbri Editori.

196

193
194

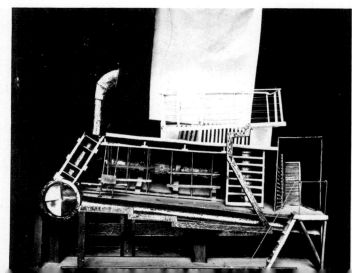

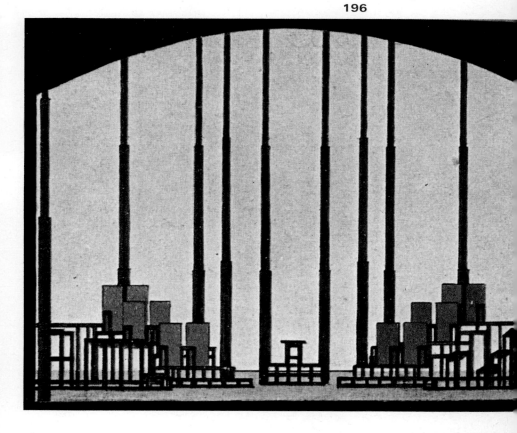

197

197. I. Rabinovich, *Lysistrata* by Aristophanes, dir. Nemirovich-Danchenko, Moscow, Musical Studio of the Moscow Art Theater, 1923. From *Art et decoration,* 1925. With this mobile arrangement, constructivism had lost its purity, ensnared by the charms of Neo-Grecian elements.

198. A. Exter, design of a constructivist decor. 1924. V. and A. Mus. London.

198

tivist components, staircases, raised levels, and a revolving stage that made it possible to view the scenery from different angles and modified its rapport with the actors. The designer, however, added various realistic elements; through his skillful use of neo-Greek columns, he removed some of the modernity from the scenery. It was perhaps more like the Museum of Modern Art in Paris.

Mayakovsky mocked the "sweet Futurism for ladies" that he thought was practiced at the Kamerny Theater, his sarcasm probably directed at Alexandra Exter. In 1930 she published her theatrical designs which were elegant, like so many embroideries of clever variations on the constructivist theme, because most of them were designed with no specific work in mind. It seemed as though Constructivism possessed a new virtuosity and was entering the realm of the decorative arts.

Many of Alexandra Exter's later sketches seem intended for the dance. Curiously, Constructivism exerted a relatively minor influence on the ballet compared with its

199

199. A. Exter, *Maquette de theatre,* Paris. 1930. She contributed to this book which was published in Paris in 1930; A. Tairov wrote the Preface. E. Neumann Coll. Frankfurt.

200. A. Pevsner and N. Gabo, *La Chatte* by H. Sauguet, chor. G. Balanchine, Monte-Carlo, Ballets Russes, 1927. Doc. Part. Coll. Paris. Photo. P. Willi. In a space designed to receive reflections and images, the scenographer presented a strange, mysterious world out of shiny or transparent plastic materials.

200

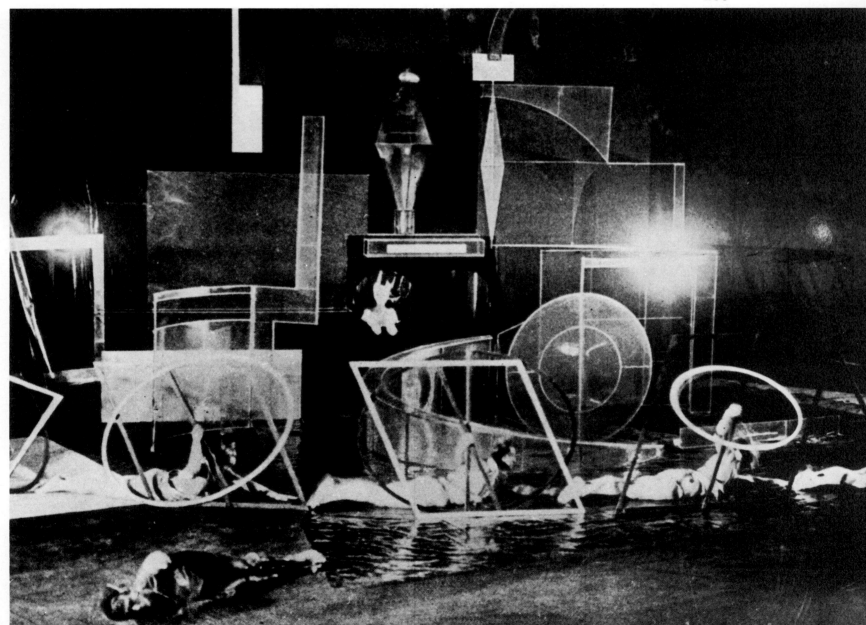

effects on the dramatic theater. While the movement should have inspired choreographers and broadened their scenographic experiences, even Diaghilev who was always eager to integrate new artistic trends into his ballets, called on the Constructivists only twice, and then, not before 1927. A complex architecture was designed for *La Chatte* by Gabo and Pevsner. The stage was covered with a waxed, black piece of cloth which was stretched to create the backdrop. Into this mysterious black universe that absorbed all reflections of light, Gabo inserted plastic, translucent forms, some curved, some rectangular. The new effects created by this transparency were unique and quite important for the development of choreography.

The spirit and theme of *Pas d'Acier* differed from *La Chatte*. To those outside of the Soviet Union the ballet was chiefly a picture of the "new Russia in the process of reconstruction." The scenery was somewhat similar to *The Magnificent Cuckold* and *Lake Lyul* in that it served as a trampoline for the dancer and presented a picture of a society striving for industrial growth. The set was an elaborate composition of staircases, a rope ladder and various objects used in transport and factories, (pulleys attached to driving belts, overhead cranes, semaphores, and in the distance, an image of a locomotive).

While these two ballets were performed one after another in France, Meyerhold in the Soviet Union had already moved away from Constructivism. Perhaps he understood more quickly than others the dangers of this aesthetic principle and realized the constructivist style would not be suited to a theater whose function was to educate man in the spirit of socialism. His passion for the movies soon led him to incorporate certain aspects of cinematography into the theater. For instance, he suggested screen projections during the performance, adapting dramatic works into episodes with sequences successively ordered as in silent films, and the systematic use of expressive or rhythmical movements of the scenic structures.

Give Us Europe! (1924) and *The Warrant* (1925) reflected this new direction. Although Meyerhold's art remained opposed to illusionism, the period of scaffoldings was over. Panels were now in fashion. In *Give Us Europe!* cherry-lacquered walls moved, rolled on wheels and turned according to the rhythm of the action, successively representing different places — a street, square, or interior. . . For certain scenes the walls intervened directly in the action, such as one in which they began to converge and then slip-

114

201

201. G.B. Jacoulov, *Pas d'acier* by S. Prokofiev, chor. L. Massine, Paris, Sarah-Bernhardt Th., Ballets Russes, 1927. Photo. part. Coll. Paris. The setting for this ballet depicted contemporary Russia. **202.** I. Shlepyanov, *Give us Europe!* by M. Podgaetsky, dir. V. Meyerhold, T.I.M. Th. of Moscow on tour in Leningrad, 1924. Doc. Th. Mus. Munich. *Give us Europe!* suggests a new orientation for Meyerhold's artistic endeavors. After scaffolding had gone out of style, panels became important.

203

203, 204. I. Shlepyanov and K. Soste, *The Warrant* by N. Erd-mann, dir. V. Meyerhold, Moscow, T.I.M. Th. 1925. **203.** The model. Kunstgew. Mus. Zurich. **204.** The production. In *Pour l'amour de l'art*, 1925. In harmony with the actors' perform-ance, the double revolving platform and mobile panels rein-forced the social satire.

204

205

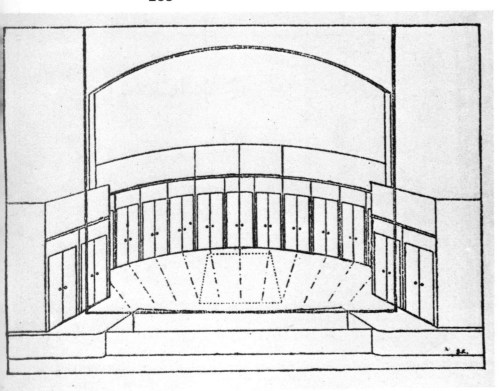

206

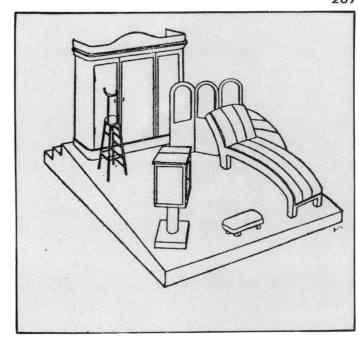

207

ped passed each other, or the one in which the motion of the walls suggested a chase. The actor here was able to conceal himself and finally exit behind a panel. In *The Warrant* the panels were combined with a double revolving stage and an impressive number of objects belonging to the middle class while a vaudeville type of gag routine reinforced the social attire. Turning in different directions, two panels kept the lovers from meeting each other at every moment they thought they were at last going to succeed.

For *The Inspector General,* the summit of his career, Meyerhold abandoned moving panels and replaced them with fifteen doors set in a mahogany wall to form an abstract and symbolic background. The action was often concentrated on a small, steeply sloping platform filled with objects that looked real but were actually subtly exaggerated. The platform moved towards the center of the stage. Never before had a director succeeded in creating this degree of tension and in blending total abstraction with absolute naturalism. He thus prepared the way for a new realism that had nothing to do with the formalism later known as socialist realism.

Meyerhold's development is sufficient to show that it would be arbitrary to label the Soviet theater of the 1920's as strictly Constructivist, although it is often tempting to put very different experiences into a convenient, single category.

More attention should be paid to the role of the scenic arts at the Kamerny Jewish Theater in Moscow and the Habima Theater during the 1920's in the Soviet Union. There were of course traces here and there of the prevailing constructivist mode, but the productions at these theaters expressed a special poetry that was created from the

205-207. V. Kisselev, based on Meyerhold's sketches for Gogol's *Inspector General,* dir. V. Meyerhold, Moscow, G.O.S.T.I.M. Th., 1926. 205. Photograph of a scene. Th. Mus. Leningrad. 206. Outline of the entire stage space. 207. Outline of the small stage with all of its scenic elements.

208. M. Chagall, sketch for *Playboy of the Western World* by J.M. Synge, 1920-21. Never realized. Property of the artist. Photo. P. Willi.

208

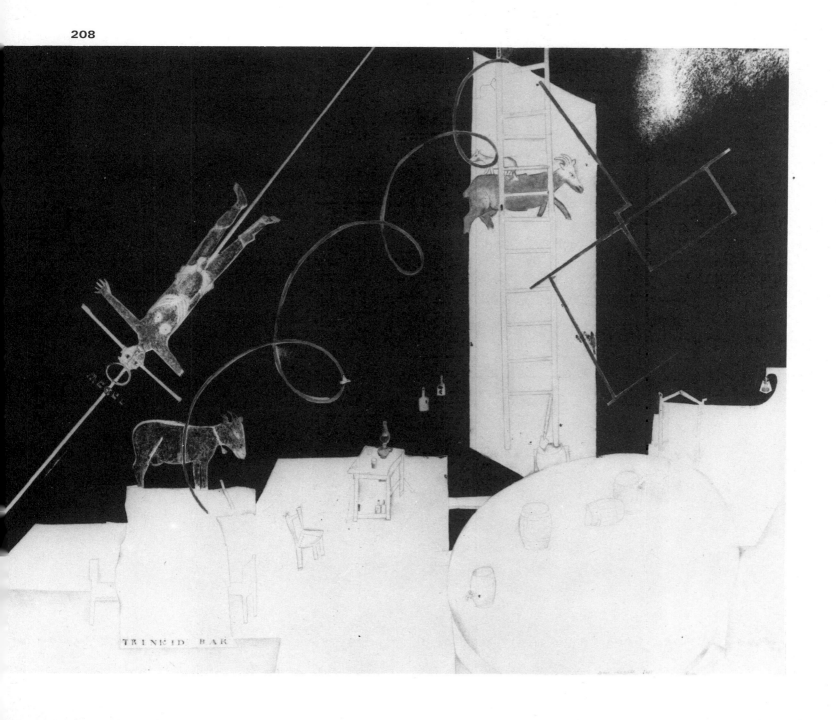

209

209. M. Chagall, *The Agents* by S. Aleichem, dir. A. Granovsky, Moscow, State Jewish Theater, 1921, sketch from 1919. Property of the artist. Photo. P. Willi.

210

combination of expressionist techniques and tradition.

Marc Chagall had designed some settings that were rejected for several projects. Among them were his sketches for *The Gambler* and *Marriage,* intended for the Experimental Theater of the Hermitage, and those in 1920 for *The Inspector General.* The Art Theater was equally unreceptive to his designs for *Playboy of the Western World.* These sketches presented juxtaposed playing areas, a world of many constructivist objects (ladders, ropes, etc.), embedded, however, in the intangible space of the poetic imagination. A man slipping on a wire, the double-faced Chagallian goat that was like two sides of a mysterious, spiritual universe, impregnated with obsessions and dreams. And always, the element of surprise was present for those who could not penetrate Chagall's world of the surreal and "alogical".

Verisimilitude can be more easily grasped in Chagall's sketches for Sholem Aleichem's "miniatures", especially *Mazel*

210, 211. M. Chagall, *Mazel Tov* by S. Aleichem, dir. A. Granovsky, Moscow, State Jewish Theater, 1921. **210.** Sketch from 1919. Property of the artist. Photo. P. Willi. **211.** From the production.

211

120

212

213

214

212, 213. I. Rabinovich, *The Sorceress,* based on Goldfaden's play, Moscow, State Jewish Theater, 1922. 214, 215. R. Falk, *A Night in the Old Market* by Peretz, Moscow, State Jewish Theater, 1924. From *Das Moskauer Judische Akademische Theater,* 1928.

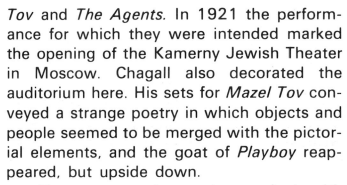

216. *David's Crown,* by Calderon de la Barca, Habima Theater, 1929. Doc. Th. Mus. Munich. 217. N. I. Altman, *The Dybbuk* by S. Ansky, dir. E. Vakhtangov, Moscow, Habima Th., 1922. Doc. Inst. Th. Cologne.

215

216

217

Tov and *The Agents.* In 1921 the performance for which they were intended marked the opening of the Kamerny Jewish Theater in Moscow. Chagall also decorated the auditorium here. His sets for *Mazel Tov* conveyed a strange poetry in which objects and people seemed to be merged with the pictorial elements, and the goat of *Playboy* reappeared, but upside down.

The scenographers who worked with Granovsky, the director of the Kamerny Jewish Theater, deserve an independent study. For *The Sorceress,* Rabinovich contrived an adaptable scaffolding that recalled the superimposed levels of the Constructivists, with ladders and staircases to facilitate the movements of the acrobatic actors. The tumultuous universe was shaped by an extremely expressive dynamism in which humor and anguish were merged in a picturesque Jewish village, that was but faintly suggested. As for the actual place of the carnival in *The Night in the Old Market,* Falk created a terrifying decor composed of leprous-looking walls and a gigantic hand suspended above the stage.

"The poor, bare synagogue, the broken lines of the cupboard where the Torah was kept, a table strangely-reduced in size on top of which stood the marvellous rabbi, all in white. Suddenly this gentle rabbi took on the dimensions of a thaumaturge as he cast an anathema on the dybbuk. The whole atmosphere was bathed in non-distinct chiaroscuro effects . . . dazzling contrasts, the bride's shining white long gown against the greenish rags worn by the poor, the bright white tablecloth on the tzadik's table, and in the corners, the menacing darkness containing the obscure forces of the cabala." This was the description by Nina Gourfinkel of the famous production of *The Dybbuk*, staged by Vakhtangov at the Habima Theater. For this mixture of social caricature, grotesque and supernatural elements, Altman designed a set that was constantly subjected to expressive distortions, similar to those by German Expressionists but very different by virtue of his choice of subject matter, his conceptions and manner of execution.

The 1920s represented a brilliant period whose importance is still far from exhausted. How many contemporary creations imitate the spirit of the past without being able to recapture that sense of adventure! The 1930s were less fruitful years in the Soviet Union due to the change in governmental policies which led to the gradual impoverishment of the theater. However, this was not the only reason. It seems that after every period of intense questioning and invention there comes a time when revolutionary practices lose their ability to shock. Bold innovations become assimilated as experimentation yields to syntheses.

Tairov moved in the direction of ''concrete realism,'' best exemplified by Ryndin's

219. A.G. Tishler, *Richard III* by Shakespeare, dir. K. Tverskoi, Leningrad, Great Dramatic Theater, 1935. Th. Mus. Leningrad.
220. V. Favorsky, *Twelfth Night* by Shakespeare, dir. V. Gotovtzev and S. Zhiatzintova, Moscow, 1934. Bakhrushin Mus. Moscow.

218. V.F. Ryndin, *The Optimistic Tragedy* by V. Vishnevsky, dir. A. Tairov, Moscow, Kamerny Th., 1933. Bakhrushin Mus. Moscow. ''When we say that 'simplicity is indispensable,' in all of our works and in this one in particular, we are thinking of a kind of simplicity that is the result of enormous effort, of a simplicity that is precise, crystal clear and directly reaches the spectator...'' (A. Tairov).

218

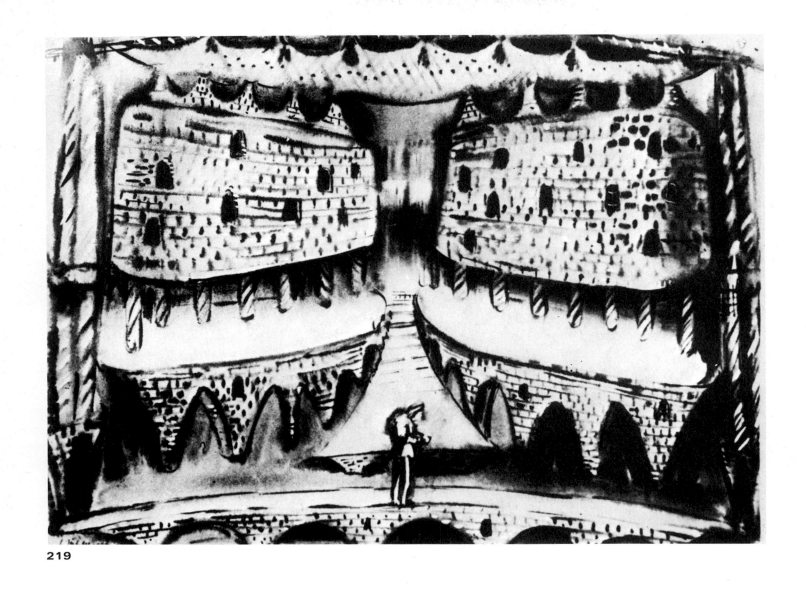

219

220

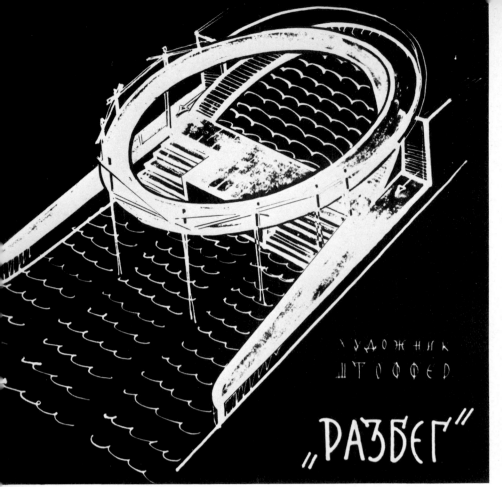

 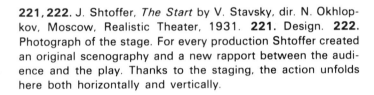

221

223

221, 222. J. Shtoffer, *The Start* by V. Stavsky, dir. N. Okhlopkov, Moscow, Realistic Theater, 1931. 221. Design. 222. Photograph of the stage. For every production Shtoffer created an original scenography and a new rapport between the audience and the play. Thanks to the staging, the action unfolds here both horizontally and vertically.

124

222

224

223, 224. J. Shtoffer, *The Mother,* by M. Gorky, dir. N. Okhlopkov, Moscow, Realistic Th., 1932. **223.** A design. **224.** A scene photographed during rehearsal. Doc. Kunstgew. Mus. Zurich.

remarkable stage architecture for *The Optimistic Tragedy.* For *Richard III* Tishler infused his setting with romantic and at times symbolic elements. Favorsky's cleverly designed revolving stage for *Twelfth Night* combined the decorative, such as painted canvases, with a realistic construction which again clearly demonstrated the conventional aspects of this production.

The most important theatrical experiences of those years, however, were carried out by one of Meyerhold's students, Okhlopkov, who renewed the scenography of the mass spectacles and attempted some of the abortive plans of Meyerhold and Lissitzky. Okhlopkov's scenographic revolution extended beyond the redefinition of the fixed stage space and its various furnishings. Together with his designers Shtoffer and Knoblock, he relocated the seating and all of the playing areas in the auditorium, the precise arrangement of which varied with each work. Moreover, he dramatically transformed the physical and psychic relationships between objects and the public; overall, the modes of perceiving the spectacle were so altered to permit a real participation of the audience in

the theatrical event.

Certain similarities are apparent between the scenography of *The Start* and Lissitzky's model for *I Want A Child.* Both employed a double stage with two superimposed levels, raised circular ramps, and similar seating arrangements for the public on either side of a composite playing area. The realities may have been different, but the underlying principles of the two plays were identical.

Okhlopkov designed a composite stage with theater in the round seating for *The Mother.* There was a central, circular platform surrounded on all sides by a series of steps which extended outward into a concentric wave formation. Three strips connected the platform to the gangways of the auditorium where there was another circular playing area.

For Pogodin's *Aristocrats* he installed two stages that were shaped to form a diagonal as they touched each other at one of their angles. The audience sat in the empty spaces between this double platform.

These are just a few of the original solutions that Okhlopkov conceived of to promote greater contact between actor and

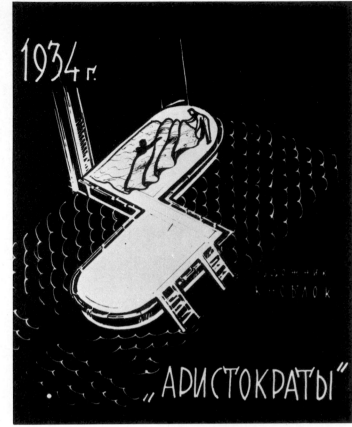

225

226

225, 226. B. Knoblock, *The Aristocrats* by N. Pogodin, dir. N. Okhlopkov, Moscow, Realistic Th., 1934.

spectator. Whether or not the stage design was an integral imitation of reality is inconsequential. Okhlopkov used objects from everyday life which gave an undeniable authenticity to his highly stylized productions, even when the objects were brought in and removed from the stage in full view of the public. Inspired by techniques in the Chinese theater, his metaphorical manner of expressing reality sometimes led him to give his actors blue uniforms. What we see in Okhlopkov's theater is the tension Meyerhold tried to establish between abstraction and naturalism, a tension which was considerably more potent here due to the greater intimacy Okhlopkov initiated between the audience and the dramatic action.

Adolphe Appia had dreamed of this close contact, but Okhlopkov actually achieved it, although in a different way and for different purposes. The inspiration he gave his designers brought about such striking and original scenographies that he became one of the most important directors of the 30s. As paradoxical as it may seem, his productions anticcipated both Grotowski's *Akropolis* and *1789* by the Theatre du Soleil.

Anti-Expressionism in Germany

While Expressionism was prevalent in the twenties, it was also rejected by many artists. Indeed art history is full of examples of the dialectical adventure in which oppos-

227. El Lissitzky, *Victory over the Sun* by A. Kruchenykh and M. Matyushin, project for an electro-mechanical spectacle, conceived of in 1923 but not realized. Published as lithographs. Mun. Mus. Amsterdam. Cf. Reproductions of the characters' activities. fig. 186-187.

227

ing currents borrow one another's formulas and techniques until eventually new artistic forms emerge. Affirmations and condemnations revealing man's perspective of reality!

Everyone did not react in the same way to the war and its accompanying social-political upheavals. In Germany, the Expressionists responded to troubled times by adopting a sentimental, romantic attitude as they dreamed of a world in which all men would be brothers. The Dadaists, on the other hand, advocated the end of art, which they declared was simply a bourgeois notion; in short, ''art is just a lot of crap.'' But there were those who refused the sentimental individualism of the Expressionists, condemned the principle of aestheticism, and yet refused to deny the value of art. They felt it was important to overcome negativism and put art at the service of man, to depict his role in History. The director Edwin Piscator was one of them.

The Piscatorian Theater of Action

In the aftermath of the First World War Germany was shaken by economic crises and bloody confrontations. Men began to direct their artistic struggles toward political ends, and agitprops in the form of slogans, captions, newsreels, etc. made striking inroads into the dramatic action. Piscator was committed to a theater that would bear witness to the struggles of the proletariat; theater was to become a profession of faith to help the working class find political awareness. The artist no longer depicted man as an isolated victim of his own moral and psychological conflicts but as a political being, the instrument of his historical development. What counted was not the destiny of one man but of all mankind. Of course the stage had to be enlarged to accommodate the new ''expansion of materials into space and time.''

These ideas required a new dramaturgy along with an appropriate theatrical space. Piscator conceived of such an architecture, and together with his friend Gropius completed designs for the *Total Theater*. Rejecting the illusionist box stage, he envisaged an adaptable unit containing the most modern technical advances that would give the director a number of ways in which he could alter the relationship between the auditorium and the stage. Everything imaginable to jolt the spectator out of his usual passive role! While this theater was unfortunately never built for want of funding, it has been a source of inspiration for some of the boldest projects in theatrical architecture.

228

229

228, 229. T. Otto, propaganda plays at Kassel, 1926. Doc. Th. Mus. Munich. His means of expression were as striking as they were simple.

230. L. Moholy-Nagy, project for a cover for E. Piscator's book *Das Politische Theater,* photomontage. Kunstgew. Mus. Zurich. A picture showing theatrical technique serving the masses.

230

231

231. Traugott Muller, *Storm over Gothland* by E. Welk, dir. E. Piscator, Berlin, Volksbuhne, 1927. Doc. Th. Inst. West Berlin.

Piscator introduced new means of expression into the more classical stages he was obliged to accept. He did not experiment, however, to gratify his ego. Recent theatrical innovations were assimilated by him for the purpose of making his art serve revolutionary ends. But because of his fondness for new techniques he was called the "theatrical engineer," though to be sure there was nothing scientific about his methods. Piscator thought technology would be a liberating force and saw the inevitable connection between technological and social revolutions, both of which he felt would enrich art with new techniques. All of this technical progress was used to "raise the drama to a historical level" by having the action unfold in an "epic" manner.

In 1920 he staged *The Hour of Russia (Russlands Tag)* at the Proletarian Theater in Berlin. The settings created by John Heartfield illustrated Piscator's ideas. "...a map," wrote Piscator, "showed the geographical location and described the obvious political meaning of the scenes. It was not only an element of the 'decor' but a social, economic, historical and geographical diagram as well. The map was an integral part of the performance ... intervening at times as the action occurred. It in fact became a dramatic element." No embellishments; the 'decor' was not intended to please but to clarify what was happening. Thus it was addressed to the intelligence of the spectator who was called upon "to read" its meanings.

Three of Piscator's productions are most

233-237. Traugott Muller, *Hurrah, We Live!* by E. Toller, dir. E. Piscator, Berlin, Piscator Theater, 1927. **233.** A bare stage; on the screens the shadow box profile of Piscator. Doc. Th. Mus. Munich. The metallic scaffolding, 36 ft. wide and 38 ft. high, is both functional and symbolic. **234, 237.** Sketches by Traugott Muller. Th. Inst. West Berlin. They form a photomontage. In the production the photos are replaced by the film projections. **235, 236.** Photographs of the stage. Doc. Th. Inst. West Berlin. The utilization of the scenic space varies during the course of the action.

233

232

232. E. Suhr, *Tidal Wave (Sturmflut)* by A. Paquet, dir. E. Piscator, Berlin, Volksbuhne, 1926. From J. Bab, *Das Theater der Gegenwart,* 1928. The film serves as the catalyst for the dramatic action, which is divided between the live action on stage and the motion picture projections — a kind of complimentary act.

234

235

236

237

238

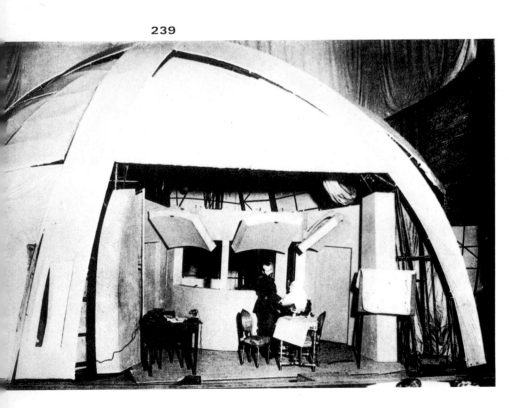

239

238, 239. Traugott Muller, *Rasputin* by A. Tolstoy and P. Shtchegolev, dir. E. Piscator, Berlin, Piscator Theater, 1928. **238.** Photomontage used to advertise the play. Doc. Th. Inst. West Berlin. **239.** The main quarters of the Tsar. Doc. Th. Mus. Munich.

famous: *Hurrah, We Live* and *Rasputin* (1927) and *The Good Soldier Schweik* (1928). Aspects of Russian Constructivism were apparent in Traugott Muller's architecture for *Hurrah, We Live*. A metallic scaffolding 36 feet wide and 27 ft. high was divided into three dimensional 'cells' which permitted various events to occur simultaneously on the stage. The structure was functional, but also symbolic because it presented a cross section of the society that Toller depicted. Screen projections, used to comment on the live action on stage, were made against the backgrounds of these various cells, which were like so many pieces of a vast collage.

A similar combination of functionalism and symbolism reappeared in the scenery for *Rasputin*. Through this memorable character Piscator was able to give European dimensions to the origins of the Russian Revolution. On a revolving stage there was a globe, obviously representing an image of our world. The machinery opened to reveal different locations, and portions of scenes in which different events were unfolding, sometimes on the stage level, sometimes above the stage, and at times on both simultaneously.

"What we wanted to do in *Schweik*," said Piscator, "was to focus the projectors on the satire of war itself without neglecting to bring out the tremendous power of humor in this work." This explains the caricatural and clownish aspects of the production which was based on the idea of Schweik's journey through an uninterrupted swirl of events that unfold over a rather long period of time. Two treadmills which moved in opposite directions transporting the character and containing a minimum of scenic elements animated the action, while in the background Grosz's cartoons were projected onto a canvas that served as a screen.

The use here of multiple projections was one of the principal means of expression in Piscator's scenography. He was certainly not the first to make use of moving pictures, but he employed them so systematically and gave them so many functions that it was clear that these films had nothing to do with any naturalist extension of the drama.

In *Hurrah, We Live* the images were projected through the technique of photomontage which made the scenic place even more dramatic. "At the back of the stage," said George Grosz, "Piscator set up a huge drawing board covered with white paper on which he drew large hieroglyphs as a commentary on the live action. In this way he created new possibilities for modern graphics." Then, in

240

240. Traugott Muller, *Rasputin*. Doc. Th. Inst. West Berlin. The staging of *Rasputin* combines functionalism with symbolism. On a revolving stage, a globe-like structure, symbolizing our world. The machinery can open up into different sections to reveal small portions of scenes; the action unfolded sometimes on the stage itself, sometimes on a higher level, and sometimes, like here, simultaneously.

241. G. Grosz, *The Good Soldier Schweik* by J. Hacek, dir. E. Piscator, Berlin, Piscator Theater, 1928. Doc. Th. Mus. Munich.

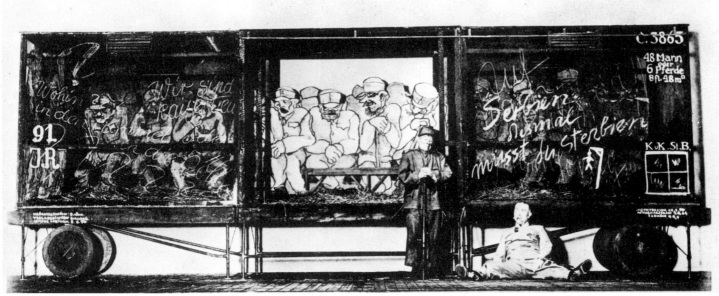

241

242. E. Suhr (scenic architecture) and G. Grosz (projections), *The Drunken Ship* by P. Zech, dir. E. Piscator, Berlin, Volksbuhne, 1926. Doc. Ak. d. Kunste, West Berlin.

242

243

243. W. Baumeister, *Liberty* by H. Kranz, dir. F. Skuhra, Stuttgart, Deutsches Theater, 1920. Margaret Baumeister Coll. Stuttgart. **244, 245.** W. Baumeister, *Transfiguration* by E. Toller, dir. F. Skuhra, Stuttgart, Deutsches Th., 1920. Margaret Baumeister Coll. Stuttgart.

244

245

Das Trunkene Schiff (The Drunken Ship), 1926, the three scréens forming the backdrop allowed Grosz to project three unrelated settings, consisting of highly enlarged, caricatural figures in outline form. In *Schweik* the backdrop is the drawing board itself onto which these cartoon figures are projected. Some of these figures are characters or objects Schweik encounters on his trip. There were also motion pictures of real places projected onto that background to situate the action.

Films thus played a basic role in some of Piscator's most important productions. Of course, the time had come for movies and cinematic experiments. In 1925 Abel Gance filmed *Napoleon* which was meant to be shown on a triple screen. In 1927 the first talking pictures were made, and Paul Claudel wrote *Christophe Colombe* in which an important place was accorded to films. Piscator's use of film, however, was not intended as a simple formula for *total theater,* but as a means of encouraging the spectator to reflect upon what he was seeing. Motion pictures appeared as early as 1924 in Piscator's production of *The Flags,* and two years later in *Tidal Wave.* In the latter, the film is the principal bearer of the dramatic action which was divided between live action and projections. In *Rasputin* (1928) the films served diverse functions: According to Piscator the *didactic film* "presents objective facts..., develops the subject in time and space...., whereas the *dramatic film* intervenes in the unfolding of the action and replaces the spoken scene..... The *film* that acts as a *commentary* accompanies the action like a chorus." There was a genuine counterpoint as the sequence of events alternated between the live action and the films, and within the stage space, between the different surfaces which received the projections — on the exterior surface of the globe erected in the center of the stage, on a screen located on the upper stage, and on a gauze screen placed at the side of the stage.

Some critics have accused Piscator of injecting impurities into the theater. In fact his contributions enriched theatrical language and made the spectacle a scientific collage. Furthermore, he paved the way for the collaboration between theater and motion pictures that is continuing today — for example, in the works of Josef Svoboda; and, Piscator's work represents a decisive stage in the development of "realism" in the twentieth century. Like Meyerhold's productions, those of Piscator prepared the groundwork for the flowering of epic realism.

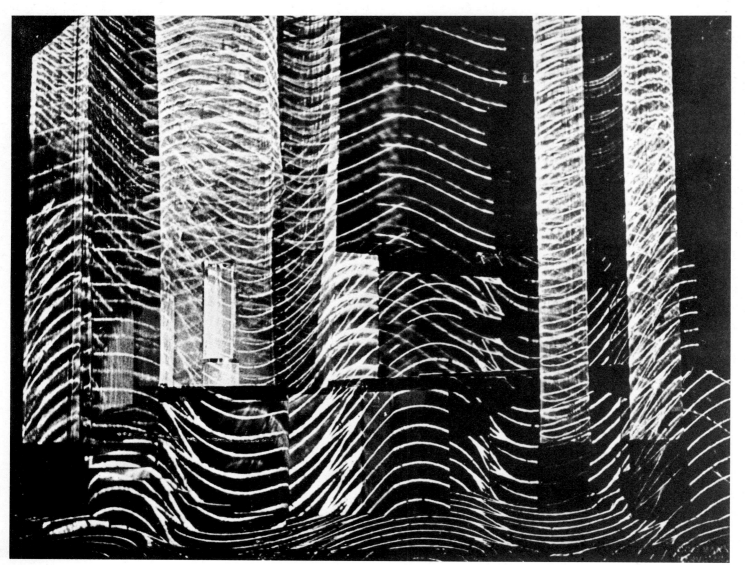

246

Anti-Romantic Variations

In the Germany of the twenties the tendency toward Constructivism was not confined to Piscator's political theater. In diverse forms Constructivism represented the general desire of all artists to free the stage from romanticism, and to arrange space somewhat geometrically. Emotion, however, was rigorously controlled, although not excluded, so that the "truth" of the dramatic works could emerge

It is interesting to compare the expressionist sets that Neppach designed for Toller's *Transfiguration* with those for the same work by Willi Baumeister. In both productions a black background served as a contrast for the "scenic abbreviations," but in Neppach's set the figurations were subjected to distortion; whereas in Baumeister's everything appeared more normal — familiar rectangular or trapezoidal panels and objects in their usual forms. The geometrical rigor that was displayed in the surfaces also occurred in the volumes for Baumeister's *Macbeth* and again in his architectural designs for Handel's *Ariodante* that consisted of

246. L. Schenk von Trapp, *Schwanda, the Piper* by J. Weinberger, dir. R. Mordo, Darmstadt, Hessisches Landestheater, 1930. Inst. Th. Cologne. **247.** L. Schenk von Trapp, *Tannhauser* by R. Wagner, dir. R. Mordo, Darmstadt, Hessisches Landestheater, 1929-30. Doc. Th. Mus. Munich.

247

248

just a few steps and abstract columns. "The painter of scenes no longer exists," wrote Baumeister in 1926. "What counts now is the relationship of architectonic forces to surfaces painted with simple but precise doses of colors. The extraordinary potential of stage lighting will do the rest." This citation suggests that the painter had been more or less converted to the ideals of Adolphe Appia.

Because of their functional value and expressive power, Appia's architectural structures and rhythmic spaces attracted the attention of many directors and designers. Jessner and Pirchan exploited Appia's designs for their expressionist virtues, while others profitted from their rigor and absence of ornamentation. Similar rigorous struc-

248. L. Schenk von Trapp, *Woyzeck* by A. Berg, dir. R. Mordo, Darmstadt, Landestheater, 1930-31. Doc. Th. Mus. Munich.
249. H. Heckroth, *Radamisto* by G.F. Handel, dir. Niedecken Gebhard, Gottingen, Handel Festival, 1927. Doc. Th. Mus. Munich.

249

250

251

tures appeared in Ewald Dulberg's *Fidelio* and *Oedipus Rex,* or in Lothar Schenk von Trapp's more decorative, academic style in *Tannhauser, Lohengrin,* or in Hein Heckroth's *Theodora* and *Ezio* by Handel. The ease with which Lothar Schenk von Trapp or Heckroth varied their styles showed their capacity to adapt to the particular work, and also the degree to which the style itself often became the substantive part of the work. (Recall the development of Russian Constructivism.) Heckroth's scenography for Kurt Weill's *Royal Palace* incorporated photo montage and films. Lothar Schenk von Trapp, for Strauss' *Intermezzo,* created a universe that was a collage of unrelated objects and real people; in addition, the flats and hang-

250. L. Schenk von Trapp, *Intermezzo* by R. Strauss, dir. R. Mordo, Darmstadt, Landestheater, 1929-30. Doc. Th. Mus. Munich. **251.** W. Reinking, *News of the Day (Neues vom Tage)* by P. Hindemith, dir. A.M. Rabenalt, Darmstadt, Landestheater, 1929-30. Doc. Th. Mus. Munich.

252

252. H. Heckroth, *Royal Palace* by K. Weill, dir. E. Engel, Essen, Opernhaus, 1929. Doc. Th. Mus. Munich.

ing panels were covered with inscriptions and pictures that were not logically related, such as the titles of musical works and enlarged playing cards, etc.

Piscator had already experimented with combining style and content. Like Meyerhold, he communicated with the audience in diverse ways — by means of the action, the plastic elements of the scenography and by written texts which he projected through a proscenium arch. This undoubtedly brings to mind cubist techniques, but Piscator really aimed at the spectator's intelligence, at forcing his detachment from the scenic event so that he could get a better perspective of its dimensions and mechanisms.

During the twenties in Germany, the most important scenic experiments in Con-

253

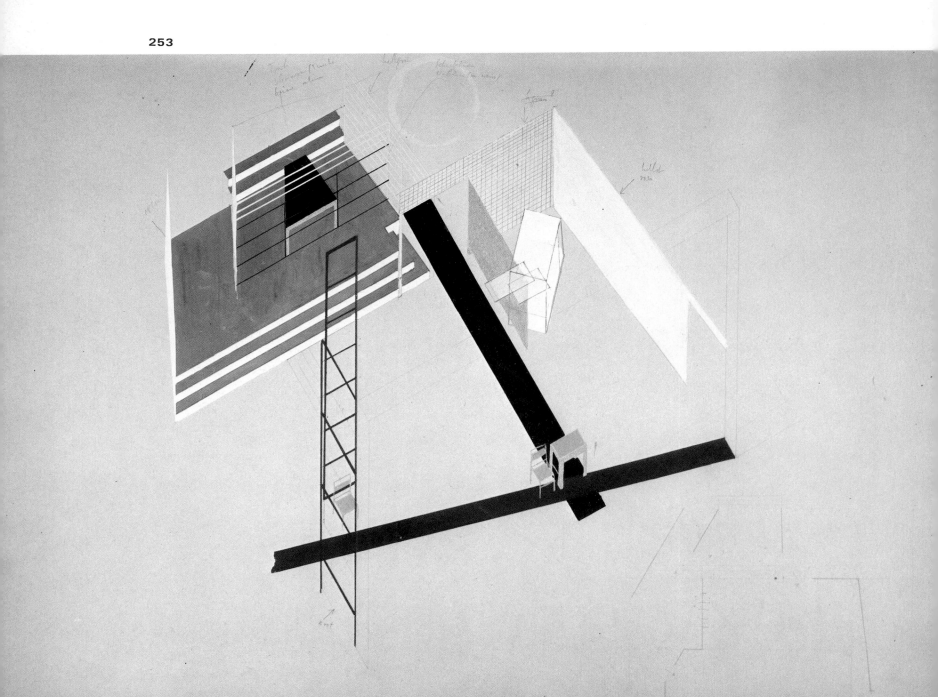

structivism were undertaken by Moholy-Nagy at the Krolloper theater. He and other directors tried to create modern musicals and revive musical staging with its means of visual expression. In 1920 Moholy-Nagy collaborated with Piscator on Upton Sinclair's *Prince Hagen,* and later in 1929 on *The Merchant of Berlin,* but the actual productions did not live up to the qualities set forth in the original projects. That same year, however, his scenography for *The Tales of Hoffmann* was an extraordinary success, as described by Hans Curjel. The historical vision along with all traces of middle class romanticism had been eliminated. The spectator discovered a scenic universe that was both modern and fantastic in which the use of mechanical devices did not exclude emo-

tions. Moholy-Nagy designed a transformable laboratory made up of aerial scaffoldings, and rectilinear objects and surfaces whose transparencies played with the brilliancy of the lighting; (metallic pieces of furniture by Marcel Breuer were shown on the stage for the first time). The various components of this architecture were like so many objects to trap the light, which then reflected everything on the backdrop in double images to give multiple perspectives. At the same time the dramatic action was intensified by the double image of the live actors and the film. "An extremely rich spatial articulation," wrote Moholy-Nagy, "and yet perfectly intelligible." His fairy land world worked so well because it was supported by the principles of precision and clarity.

253, 254. L. Moholy-Nagy, *The Tales of Hoffmann* by J. Offenbach, dir. E. Legal, Berlin, Krolloper, 1929. **253.** Design. Inst. Th. Cologne. **254.** Design. Klihm Gall. Coll. Munich. "An extremely rich articulation of space which is, however, perfectly capable of being understood." (Moholy-Nagy).

254

255

256

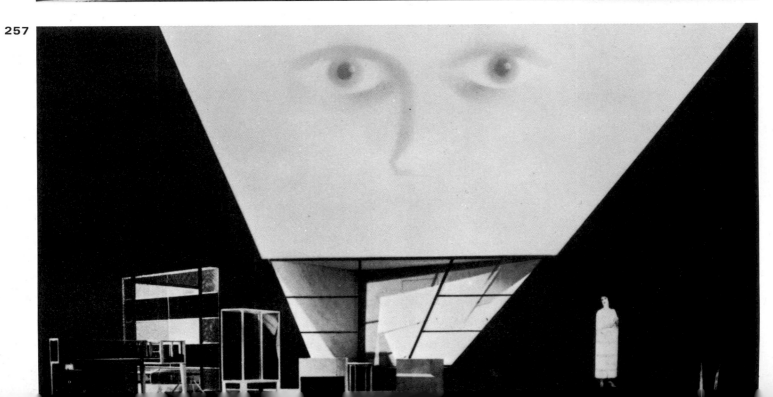

257

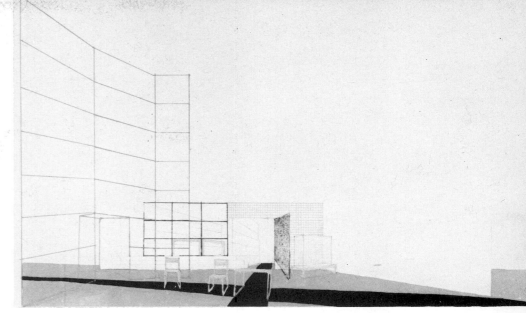

258

259

255-259. L. Moholy-Nagy, *The Tales of Hoffmann* by J. Offenbach. **255.** Phot. Lucia Moholy-Nagy, Zurich. **256.** Doc. Sibyl. Moholy-Nagy, New York. **257-259.** Inst. Th. Cologne. A universe filled with modern extravagances. A transformable laboratory made up of aerial scaffolding, of objects and rectangular surfaces in which transparencies play with the effects of brilliancy. A delicate ensemble whose elements are like traps that capture the light, which in turn, reflects the images against the backdrop giving the viewer multiple perspectives. Sometimes the action is reinforced by the joint intervention of the actor and the film.

260

260. L. Moholy-Nagy, *Madame Butterfly* by G. Puccini, dir. H. Curjel, Berlin, Krolloper, 1933. Doc. L. Moholy-Nagy Coll. New York.

Moholy-Nagy's decor for *Madame Butterfly* (1931) was just as remarkable although less revolutionary. Having eliminated the saccharin tone along with the meaningless exoticism of former productions, his scenography recreated a Japan that looked like a modern art tableau. The architecture combined wood, screens and transparent elements. Using a black and white print the designer evoked the image of a port in the background, and on the center stage, the suggestion of a house which could be moved in its entirety or in part. Thanks to kinetics and cinematographic devices, Moholy-Nagy and the director Curjel could project the action close-up or make certain parts of the scenery seem remote. The interplay of light and shadow turned this very 'real' structure into a surrealist one, and when necessary the action appeared like a vision or dream sequence, so that the constructivist elements of this production were infused with an impalpable poetry.

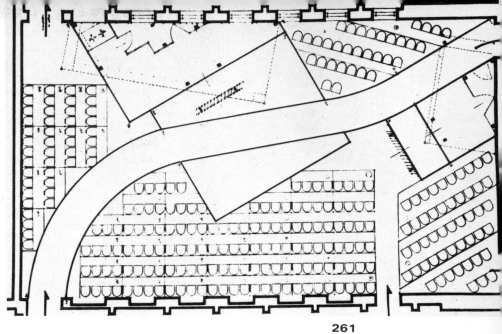

In the Heart of Europe

There are movements that do not affect certain countries. Constructivism, for example, hardly influenced stage design in Poland. The productions of Szymon Syrkus, especially his *Sacco and Vanzetti Case* (1933), showed an affinity with Okhlopkov's creations only by virtue of the similarities in their rapport between the audience and the dramatic action. None of the great Polish designers between the two world wars, however, (Frycz, Drabik, Pronaszko, or Daszewski) could be called strict Constructivists. Pronaszko's boldly articulated settings that juxtaposed planes and geometrical volumes were clearly more sympathetic to cubist principles. All of the designers mentioned made

143

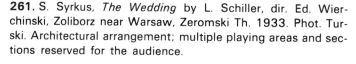

261. S. Syrkus, *The Wedding* by L. Schiller, dir. Ed. Wierchinski, Zoliborz near Warsaw, Zeromski Th. 1933. Phot. Turski. Architectural arrangement; multiple playing areas and sections reserved for the audience.

262. S. Syrkus, *Boston,* by B. Blume, dir. E. Weichert, Zoliborz, Warsaw. Zeromski Th. 1933. Photo. Turski.

262

263

263. W. Drabik, *The Undivine Comedy* by Z. Krasinski, dir. L. Schiller, Warsaw. Boguslawski Th., 1926. **264.** K. Frycz, *Julius Caesar* by Shakespeare, dir. L. Schiller, Warsaw, Polski Th. 1928. Phot. Turski.

264

265

265. A. Pronaszko, *Forefather's Eve* by A. Mickiéwicz, dir. L. Schiller, Warsaw, Polski Th., 1934. Phot. Turski. 266. A. and Z. Pronaszko, *Achilleis* by S. Wyspianski, dir. L. Schiller, Warsaw, Boguslawski Th., 1925.

266

sure that the universe they created did not extend in the illusionist way beyond the stage frame. The settings by Daszewski for *War For War* (1927) might have qualified as constructivist if it were not for their humoristic and satirical vein that made fun of Russian Constructivism. In the spirit of 'persiflage' that characterized much of modern Polish scenography, the decors were "lightly mocking interpretations of the conventions of previous theatrical epochs," according to the scenographer and scenographic historian Z. Strzelecki. Daszewski became an expert in this tendency, but at the same time moved in the direction of a neo-realism that united principles of cubist composition with his own greater concern for reality.

The situation in other central European countries was different. During the interwar years Czechoslovakia emerged as one of the most lively centers for the theatrical arts, and became a kind of crossroads at which vari-

267. A Pronaszko, *The Undivine Comedy* by Z. Krasinski, Lvov, Wielki Th, 1935. **268, 269.** W. Daszewski, *War for War* by A. Nowaczynski, dir. L. Schiller, Warsaw, Polski Th., 1927. Sketch (268), Warsaw Th. Mus. Phot. Turski.

akt 1 i 2.

268

269

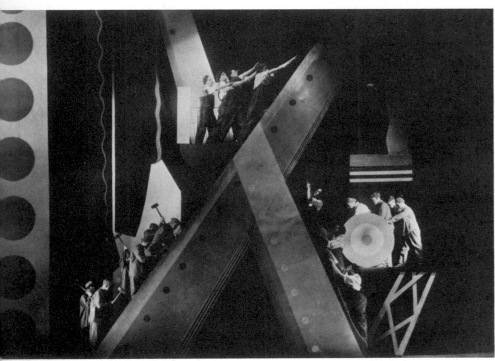

270

271

ous aesthetic currents and styles confronted each other, Dadaism with Expressionism, Surrealism with Constructivism. From B. Feuerstein and J. Capek to F. Troster, there was a large group of excellent stage designers to attest to the vitality of Czechoslovakian scenography. Because of his creative talents and amazing ability to assimilate different styles, V. Hofman was undoubtedly the most outstanding among them. *The Hussites,* staged in 1919, showed this designer to be quite adept at pictorial expressionism, but his *Antigone* of 1925 could easily have been conceived of by either Appia or Dulberg. In 1926 his production of *Hamlet* recalled the ideas of Craig, while the following year, *The Man Who Was Thursday* proved that he was equally capable of incorporating constructivist elements. For *R.U.R.* (1929), he made use of the techniques of collage, and then in 1932 with *Oedipus Rex,* the remarkable spirit of synthesis in his architecture made Hofman *the* brilliant explorer of all possible scenic styles at that time.

During this same period, however, even more radical ventures took place which were either resolutely constructivist or extended and enriched former Soviet stage experiments. In *Thesmophoriazusae* (1920) as in *Cirkus Dandin* (the title based on Molière's comedy staged by J. Frejka at the Liberated Theater in Prague), Antonin Heythum easily recaptured the more ludicrous aspects of Constructivism. The scanty scaffoldings to which he added a few ladders were truly "acting instruments" in the real sense of the word. In this decor the stage was reduced to representing the concrete reality of its ob-

270,271. T. Gronovsky, *The Tower of Babel* by A. Slonimski, dir. L. Schiller, Warsaw, Polski Th, 1927. Phot. Turski.

272, 273. B. Feuerstein, *Edward II* by Ch. Marlowe, dir, K.H. Hilar, Prague, National Th. 1922. Nat. Th. Mus. Prague. Phot. O. Hilmerova.

272

273

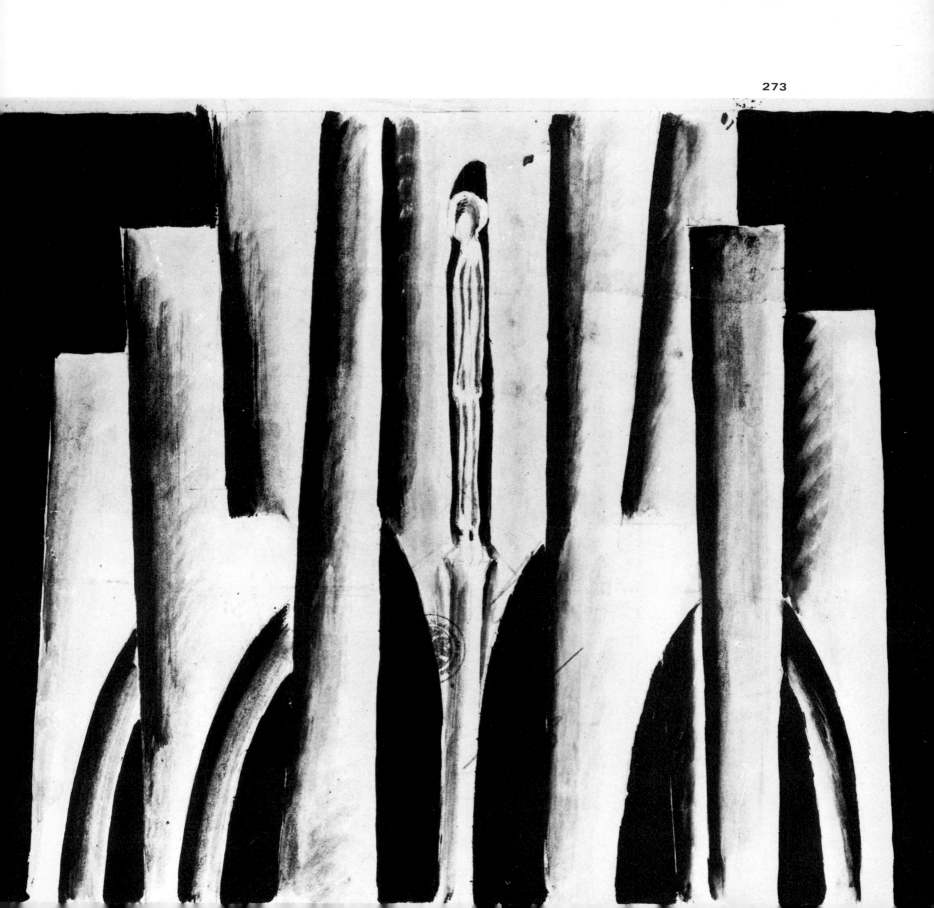

274

275

274. F. Troster, *Svatopluk* by I. Stodola, dir. V. Sulc, Bratislava, National Th., 1934. In *The Modern Czech Stage,* 1937. **275.** F. Troster, *Fidelio* by L. van Beethoven, dir. V. Sulc, Bratislava, National Th. 1936. In *The Modern Czech Stage,* 1937. **276.** V. Hofman, *A Man Named Thursday* by G.K. Chesterton, dir. K. Dostal, Prague, National Th. 1927. Sect. Nat. Th. Mus. Prague. Phot. O. Hilmerova. **277.** V. Hofman, *R.U.R.* by K. Capek, dir. J. Hodicek, Prague, National Th., 1929. Sect. Nat. Th. Mus. Prague. Phot. O. Hilmerova. A functional and expressive architecture that lends itself to photomontage.

276

CHESTERTON: KAMARÁD ČTVRTEK. 1.J.   Arch. Vlastislav Hofman 1927

277

278

279

278. A. Heythum, *Thesmophoriazusae* by Aristophanes, dir. J. Frejka, Prague, Osvobozene Divadlo, 1926. In *The Modern Czech Stage*, 1937. **279.** A. Heythum, *Cirkus Dandin* based on Moliere, dir. J. Frejka, Prague, Osvobozene Divadlo, 1925. In *The Modern Czech Stage*, 1937. Heythum discovers here the ludicrous virtues of constructivism. The steps and ladders are really "the players' instruments" in the full sense of the word.

jects that were endowed with meaning by the dramatic action. The wooden structure he built for *Desire under the Elms* was both functional and descriptive.

In the thirties the collaboration of the director Burian with his scenographic team (Kouril, Novotny, Raban) fostered the creation of a scenic polyphony on the small stage of his theater. This was not a *Gesamtkunstwerk* in which each art form fulfilled the unique function assigned to it, but a dynamic ensemble in which the roles of the actor, plastic elements and music were interchangeable, and all of them were capable of conveying the dramatic action.

In Burian's work the stage was generally reduced to a few elements such as a panel or narrow screen, a gallery, step-ladder, and some sort of emblem or symbol. With the exception of the properties, the scenic elements were created through the lighting and the projections of slides and shadows. Burian and Kouril, who soon became his official scenographer, perfected a true *theater of light*. In *Spring's Awakening* (1936), *Eugene Onegin* (1937) or *The Sorrows of Young Werther* (1938) they combined the acting with the use of slides and films in such a way that the meaning of the work was equally divided between the text, the dramatic action and the projected images. Indeed, the meaning sprang from the confrontation and tensions between these different media. In addition, the films were projected on transparent surfaces so that at certain moments in *Spring's Awakening,* it looked as though the actors were part of the projections. Many of the slides and films exhibited enlarged or selected details that conferred an unusual

280. A. Heythum, *The Silent Canary* by G. Ribemont-Dessaignes, dir. J. Honzl, Prague, Osvobozene Divadlo, 1926. In *The Modern Czech Stage,* 1937.

281, 282. A. Heythum, *Desire under the Elms* by E. O'Neill, dir. K. Dostal, Prague, National Th, 1925. Sect. Nat. Th. Mus. Prague. Phot. O. Hilmerova. Aside from the basic latticed structure, there was a number of possible combinations.

281

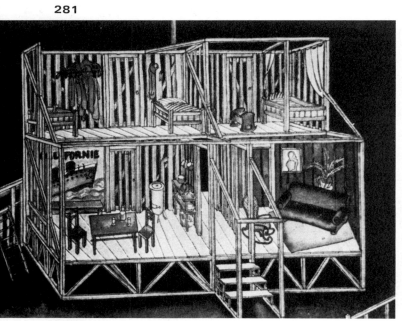

282

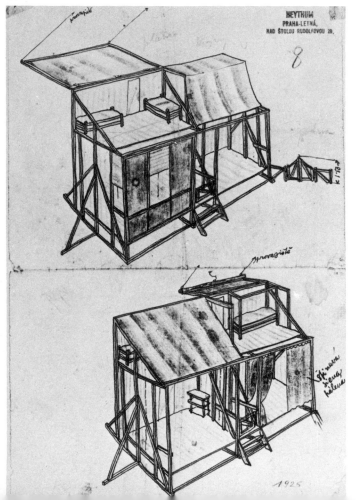

283

283. M. Kouril, *The Barber of Seville* by Beaumarchais, dir. E. F. Burian, Prague, D. 37 Th. 1936. A Burian Arch. Strahov.

284. M. Kouril, Novotny and Raban, *John B. Conquers the World* by F. Wolf, dir. E. F. Burian, Prague, D. 35 Th. 1934. Doc. M. Kouril Arch.

285. M. Kouril, *Spring's Awakening* by F. Wedekind, dir. E. F. Burian, D. 36 Th. 1936. Doc. Th. Inst. Prague.

154

power on some part of the drama. "The scenography for *Spring's Awakening,*" wrote Jan Grossman, "was not a realistic description of the places where the action occurred but a representation so to speak of the symbolic and expressive awakening of the different sequences of the drama. The scenic architecture which was sensitive to all of the components was thus able to 'follow' and accentuate the changing rhythms and tones of the play..."

The pursuits of Burian and Kouril, together with those of Piscator and Traugott Muller opened the door for new forms of theater whose scenographic means were the architectonic structure, lighting and projected images instead of the canvas and the artist's paints. The birth of today's audio-visual civilization!

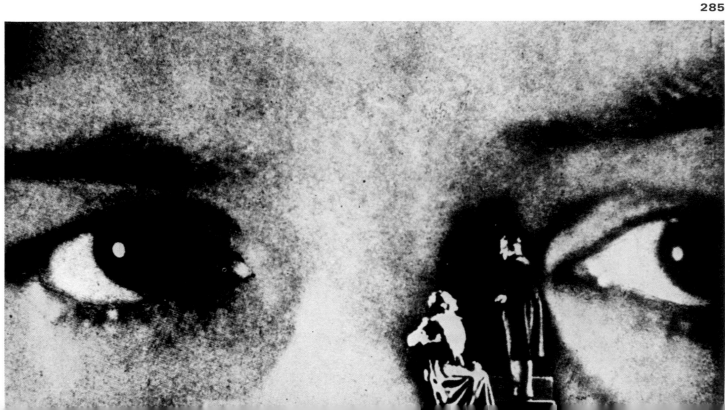

Aesthetic Quests and Pictorial Adventures

1917. While World War I was raging and Russia was undergoing its own revolution, *Parade* burst forth with a provocative freshness. More than anything else the play showed the vitality of a theater that offered escapist entertainment, and proved that the collaboration between the painter and the scenery was very much alive. Indeed the pictorial 'avant-garde' was represented here by none other than Pablo Picasso. It was obviously a pleasure for the painter to leave the narrow framework of the canvas for the task of animating a three-dimensional space. Furthermore, it was an opportunity for him to test the validity of his own pictorial pursuits, and enlarge his field of artistic creation, especially since he could now initiate theatrical experiments and not merely collaborate with others (Cf. Oskar Schlemmer at the Bauhaus).

During the effervescent years of the twenties the painter played a substantial role. Above and beyond the 'isms', discounting eclecticism, various productions with their diverse pictorial visions and contradictory styles confronted one another. The painter essentially affected choreography and was connected to official companies like the Ballets Russes or the Ballets Suedois, but his search for new forms of theatrical expression led him to experimental adventures in the laboratory as well.

THE SCHOOL OF PARIS AND THE BALLET

"Give painters their freedom; they know what they want. It's they who will pave the way even for musicians." Diaghilev's statement is indicative of the confidence he had in the painter. "Surprise me," he asked of Jean Cocteau. But because of this desire the creations of Bakst and Benois were not inspiring enough and made him turn to the most modern forms of plastic expression. He asked the greatest painters of the School of Paris to work with him along with Rolf de Mare of the Ballets Suedois and the company of the Ballets Russes of Monte Carlo. The artists who were called upon belonged to the major artistic currents of his time, namely, Futurism and Constructivism.

But before he requested Picasso, Braque, Rouault or Miro to assist him, or before he engaged in a pictorial cosmopolitanism that reflected the diverse themes of his ballets and an astonishing variety of composers ranging from Stravinsky to Satie, Diaghilev first drew his inspirations from vital artistic sources in his own country which gave him the means

for the visual renewal of his productions. The early works of Gontcharova and Larionov who remained with Diaghilev during the entire existence of his company marked a transitional period in his ballets. While with their assistance Diaghilev remained faithful to ideas from his native country, he also chose other modern painters and the best representatives from the Rayonist movement. The two Russian designers were situated at the crossroads of contemporary artistic trends and certain arts of the past, as they succeeded in blending fauvist and cubist influences with their nostalgia for icons and peasant or folk imagery.

Gontcharova abandoned the imitation of reality in a more radical manner than did Bakst, and accorded a really significant role to imagery. The reds and golds of her sumptuous palette for *Le Coq d'Or* (1914) danced across the entire setting. The luxuriant colors were then offset by the unusual proportions of the arabesques that were used as decorative motifs. In what was an innovation for those times, she integrated choral groups with the decor and placed them on both sides of the stage. Then in the working models that she made for *La Liturgie* (a ballet which was never realized) she merged decorative cubism with the art of icon painting. For *Les Noces,* however, the decorative elements were suppressed and there was a return to a more conventional staging. Two pianos were placed on the stage by Stravinsky and scenic allusions were most discrete. Simply one or two small windows and a hut against two neutral backdrops were enough to evoke the setting for the ceremony.

The sets that Larionov designed for *Midnight Sun* and *Contes Russes* caused Leon Bakst to exclaim, "Old Russia appeared flamboyant and comical in a vision in which the byzantine was strangely wedded to the frenetic dances of Russian workers." He went on to admire the "luminous decors and glittering costumes." *Chout* staged in 1921 was even more audacious. In the decor as in the costumes made of paper, waxed canvas and cardboard, the brightly colored surfaces of this cubo-futurist composition echoed one another, while in *Le Renard,* constructivist elements arose in the center of more figurative objects.

Sometimes the decor served only as a background or enlarged picture that through its harmonious forms and colors merged with the general atmosphere of the ballet even though it did not have a direct and logical rapport with the action. This was the kind of relationship preserved by Rouault in *The*

286

286, 287. N. Goncharova, *Le Coq d'or* by N. Rimsky-Korsakov, chor. M. Fokine, Opera de Paris, 1914. 286. The curtain. V. and A. Mus. London 287. Set for the great square. The Mus. Mod. Art, N.Y.

287

288

288-290. N. Goncharova, *Le Coq d'or* by N. Rimsky-Korsakov, chor. M. Fokine, Opera de Paris, 1914. Costume designs. V. and A. Mus. London.

289

290

291. M. Larionov, *Histoires Naturelles* by M. Ravel, project dating back to 1916. Never realized. Mme. Larionov Coll., Paris.
292. M. Larionov, *Chout* by S. Prokofiev, chor. M. Larionov and T. Slavinsky, Paris, Gaiete-Lyrique, Ballets Russes, 1921. Set for the 5th act. Mme. Larionov Coll. Paris.

291

292

Prodigal Son in which the settings displayed the stained-glass style that is present in many of the painter's works. However, this was not the case for either Sonia Delaunay's working models for *The Four Seasons* or Ernst and Miro's canvases for *Romeo and Juliet.* The decor was independent here of the ballet or rather expressed in a parallel way other elements of the composition. Apart from the pictorial style this conception was not so far removed from the decorative principles applied at Paul Fort's Theatre d'Art.

The decor was not necessarily limited to functioning as a backdrop. In spite of the extreme simplification of the scenic elements the settings also offered a synthetic pictorial vision which suggested the places where the

294

293

293. M. Larionov, *Midnight Sun* by N. Rimsky Korsakov, chor. L. Massine, Geneva, Grand Theatre, Ballets Russes, 1915. Costume design. Courtesy Wadsworth Atheneum Hartford. Phot. Blomstrann. **294, 296, 297.** M. Larionov, *Chout* by Prokofiev, chor. Larionov and T. Slavinsky, costumes. Mme. Larionov Coll., Paris. **295.** M. Larionov, *Renard,* ballet by I. Stravinsky, chor. B. Nijinska, Opera de Paris, Ballets Russes, 1922. Mme. Larionov Coll. Paris. This sketch is a variant of 1927.

295

296

298

297

299

298, 299. G. Rouault, *The Prodigal Son* by S. Prokofiev, chor.
G. Balanchine, Sarah-Bernhardt Th., Ballets Russes, 1929.
Courtesy Wadsworth Atheneum Hartford.

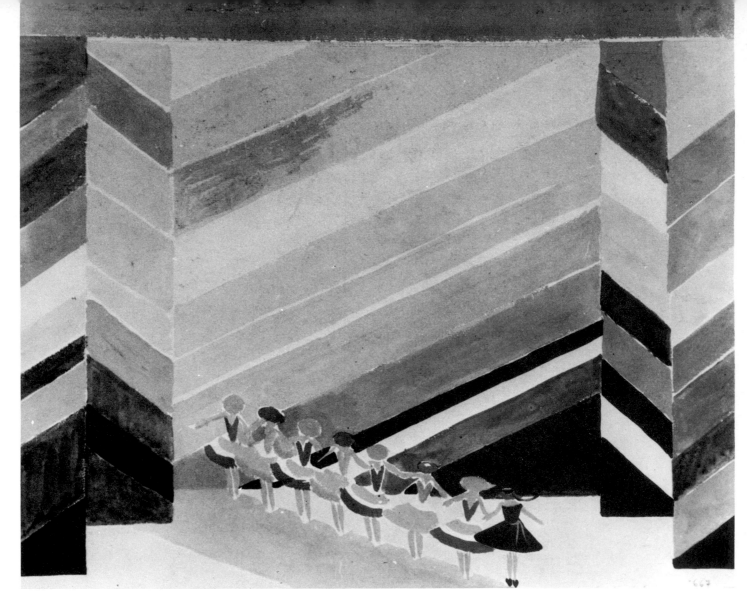

300

300, 301. S. Delaunay, *The Four Seasons*, ballet, project of 1928-29. Sonia Delaunay, Paris.

301

action occurred and became integrated with the theme of the ballet, as they expressed its spirit and provided a visual equivalent for the music.

This latter tendency was illustrated in Picasso's sets for *Le Tricorne*, known as *The Three-Cornered Hat,* and *Pulcinella.* In *The Three-Cornered Hat* a few canvases with soft colors, appearing bleached by the sun, and a lightly outlined drawing created a synthetic image of Spain that owed nothing to folklore: a large arch, a small humpbacked bridge in the distance, and the mere sketch of a village. The whole atmosphere was created

302. M. Ernst, *Romeo and Juliet* by C. Lambert, chor. B. Nijinska, Monte-Carlo, Ballets Russes, 1926. Courtesy Wadsworth Atheneum Hartford. Phot. Blomstrann. Ernst's composition seems to be independent of the ballet, or rather, it is a parallel expression of other elements of the work.

302

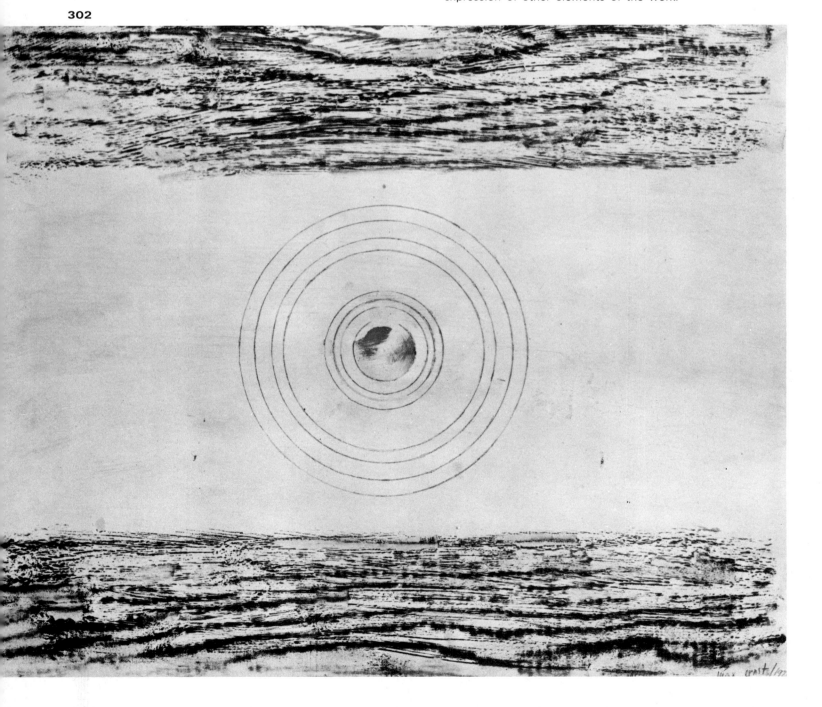

303

303. J. Miro, *Romeo and Juliet* by C. Lambert, chor. B. Nijin-ska, Monte-Carlo, Ballets Russes, 1926. Courtesy Wadsworth Atheneum Hartford. Phot. Blomstrann. **304.** J. Miro, Signed by Miro in 1925. Courtesy Wadsworth Atheneum Hartford. Phot. Blomstrann.

304

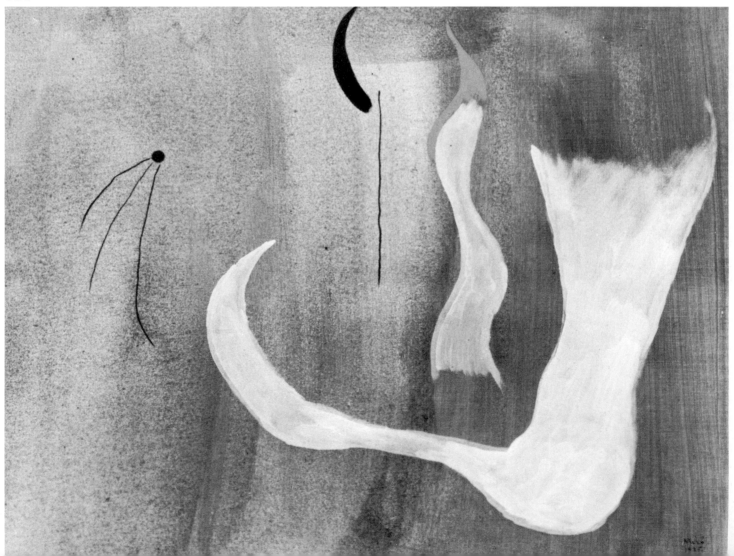

305

305. J. Miro, *Jeux d'enfants* by G. Bizet, chor. L. Massine, Monte-Carlo, Opera, Ballets Russes of Monte Carlo, 1932. G. Cramer, Mies Coll. Switz. Phot. Grivel. "Miro makes the world of toys surrealistic, constructivist and abstract with a naivete, truculence in the use of colors and freedom in design that are indicative of the artist." (R. Cogniat).

306

from the bursting colors of the costumes — yellows, scarlets, blues, pinks and greens blended against a subdued background. The settings for *Pulcinella* consisted of a backdrop, friezes, an entirely white stage floor, and a large three-paneled screen on which motifs of houses and a boat were painted to suggest Naples. Once again the bright costumes were contrasted against a harmonious decor in black, gray, white and blue, as Picasso managed to combine the spirit of popular theater with contemporary modes of plastic expression.

Braque's decors for *Les Facheux* (1924) featured an ocher colored architecture and dark green foliage that looked as though it had been cut out of paper with an artist's scissors; those by Chirico for *La Jarre* and *Le Bal* employed the artist's well known metaphysical style to create a mysterious, frozen world of ruins in which the costumes of the dancers, decorated with symbolic and cabalistic symbols, blended with the architectural elements. Although Juan Gris' decors for *Les Tentations de la Bergere* were more traditional, all of these settings shared a common aesthetic ideal. Whatever their graphic and plastic beauty, and however innovative their pictorial style may have been, the spirit of these decors was not basically different from the one in the early period of the Ballets Russes. While the scenography blended with the rest of the ballet it did not participate directly in the action. The decor

166

306. P. Picasso, *The Three-Cornered Hat* by M. de Falla, chor. L. Massine, London. Alhambra Th. Ballets Russes, 1919. Doc. Ed. Cercle d'Art, Paris. **307.** a,b,c,d. P. Picasso, costumes for the *Three-Cornered Hat*. Doc. Ed. Cercle, d'Art, Paris. Here is the synthetic picture of a Spain which is not due to folklore. The whole atmosphere is created from the animated interplay of the costumes of the colors against the soft, muted backdrop.

307 a

307 b

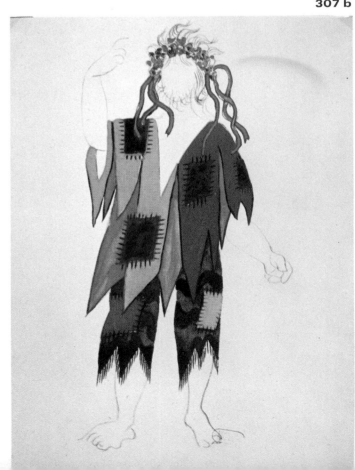

308

308. P. Picasso, *Pulcinella* by I. Stravinsky, chor. L. Massine, Opera de Paris, Ballets Russes, 1920. Part. Coll. Paris. Doc. Ed. Cercle d'Art, Paris. In spite of its tremendous originality, this project was never realized; Picasso wanted to extend the auditorium onto the stage.

307 c

307 d

309

309. P. Picasso, *Pulcinella* by I. Stravinsky, chor. L. Massine, Opera de Paris, Ballets Russes, 1920. Doc. Fratelli Fabbri Editori. The brilliant colors of the costumes stand out against the harmonious gray, blue, black and white setting; a synthetic vision combining the spirit of popular theater and contemporary styles of plastic expression. **310.** G. Braque, *Les Facheux* by G. Auric, chor. B. Nijinska, Monte Carlo, Ballets Russes, 1924. V. and A. Mùs. London. **311, 312.** G. de Chirico, *Le Bal de V. Rietti,* chor. G. Balanchine, Monte Carlo, Ballets Russes, 1929. Courtesy Wadsworth Atheneum Hartford. Phot. Blomstrann.

310

311

312

continued to preserve its illustrative functions and complementary role, forming the contrast against which the performers stood out.

This is tantamount to saying of course that these productions were not terribly revolutionary. Picasso's *Parade* or Fernand Leger's *La Creation du monde,* however, were certainly quite audacious. According to Jean Cocteau, the decor did not simply 'attend' the ballet, it enacted it. The scenography became an integral part of the performance and another means of its expression like the music and choreography. And the costumes were no longer simply clothing but together with the dancer formed a single expressive totality. The ballet went beyond the movements of the dancers to become a single entity whose expressive power grew out of the way the various elements counterbalanced each other in time and space without giving up their independence.

Parade. Abandoning sentimentality and all traces of Impressionism and Wagnerianism, Picasso created the delightful world of the circus, fair and *cafe-concert* (coffee houses where artists performed in the evening)! "Picasso gives us," wrote Leon Bakst, "his personal vision of a fair where Chinese acrobats and fair barkers move about in a kaleidoscope both fantastic and real. A large 'deliberately old-fashioned' curtain separated these flowers of the 20th century and the fascinated spectator." The spectacle, based on contrasts, reversal of values and the tension that existed between opposing elements, had a decidely cubist character which stemmed not from external forms but from its very composition. The decor seemed like an exploding collage. There was the suggestion of ruins behind a romantically designed curtain with such figures as the Harlequin appearing on the draperies. The area beyond the proscenium arch was left empty, and the travelling show performed between two railings above which were walls and windows. Of course everything was deliberately distorted. The managers wore cubist-styled Picassian costumes that made them look 10 feet tall, like "moving human-decor portraits," while the inspiration for the acrobat and young American girl came directly from the world of the circus. In the final confrontation, however, these unreal figures reduced the live dancers to mere puppets, which led Apollinaire to speak here of "surrealism" and Cocteau to describe Picasso's method as "truer than truth."

Picasso further integrated the decor with the production in *Mercure.* Without a story or plot this ballet was conceived of as a series of

313-316. P. Picasso, *Parade* by E. Satie, chor. L. Massine, Paris, Th. du Chatelet, Ballets Russes, 1917. Doc. Ed. Cercle d'Art, Paris. **313**. The set. **314**. A Manager. **315**. Another Manager. **316**. The Horse.

314

313

315

316

"plastic poses" combining dancers wearing classical costumes with mobile forms wearing outlines of clothing. It wasn't clear whether they were decorated dancers or animated decors. The frontier between performer and decor had vanished. In Miro's world of *Jeux d'Enfants* the dancers were transformed into toys. The costumes and schematic forms dotting the background were treated like colored paper that a child might have cut out and glued together. "With Miro," wrote R. Cogniat, "the world of toys became surrealist, constructivist and abstract. And it did so with that naivete, that truculence of colors and freedom in drawing unique to Miro."

Fernand Leger dreamed of a mechanical choreography and mobile decor that would oblige the audience to be interested in the entire stage and not in the dancers alone. He wanted to make "objects act" and treated the performer as part of the materiel available for the creator's disposal, like the lighting or cinematographic projections. *Skating*

317. P. Picasso, *Parade* by E. Satie, chor. L. Massine, Paris. Th. du Chatelet, Ballets Russes, 1917. The Curtain. Mus. Nat. Art Mod. Paris.

317

318

318-320. P. Picasso, *Mercure* by E. Satie, chor. L. Massine, Paris. Th. de la Cigale: "The Count of Beaumont's evening soirees in Paris, 1924, Doc, Ed. Cercle d'Art, Paris. 318. The curtain. Mus. Nat. Art Mod. Paris. 319,320. Pictures of the stage: the abduction of Proserpine; The Three Graces with Cerberus.

319

320

321

321. F. Leger, *Skating Rink* by A. Honegger, chor. J. Borlin,
Paris. Th. des Champs-Elysees, Ballets Suedois of R. de Mare,
1922. Doc. Museum of Dance, Stockholm. "I tried to achieve
the greatest scenic intensity by applying pure, flat colors." (F.
Leger).

Rink (1922) did not fulfill his dream: "I tried," he wrote, "to achieve the greatest scenic intensity using the technique of applying pure, flat colors." But already in this evocation of the big city the lighting and dancing seemed to animate the immobile geometric forms that dominated the stage. With *La Creation du Monde* (1923) Leger took a step forward. Inspired by the black statues and dances of Africa, Blaise Cendrars, Darius Milhaud and he created a ballet in which the audience witnessed "the birth of men, plants and animals under the aegis of three African gods about 26 feet tall." These mobile forms, or performers, who were hidden behind costumes that transformed them into objects, made *La Creation du Monde* a landmark in the development of the kinetic arts. A continually evolving plastic totality was created out of the white, black, ocher and blue harmonies. That same year Leger launched his film *Le Ballet Mecanique (The Mechanical Ballet)* which represented the logical outcome of his pursuits. Other painters, too, like Jean Hugo *(Romeo and Juliet),* wanted to bring about a decorative fusion of the settings and costumes.

One year after *La Creation du Monde* the spontaneous ballet *Relache,* called *No Performance,* introduced the Dadaist spirit into the domain of choreography. Dadaism had already made inroads into the dance with Sonia Delaunay's *Gas Heart. Relache* was undoubtedly intended as a "piece of anti-art," an "anti-ballet", but it was above all a hymn to modern life freed of all conventions. The scenarist and author, Francis Picabia, said his ballet showed "the happiness of unreflecting moments," and he added triumphantly: "Automobile headlights, pearl necklaces, delicate and curvaceous forms of women, advertising, music, an automobile, a few men dressed in black, movement, noise, play, clear transparent water, the pleasures of laughter, that is Relache. *Relache* was the ballet of a painter who had replaced painting with lighting and cinema. The background consisted of dozens of electric lightbulbs in the center of their reflectors. During the interval between the acts there was a film, *L'Entr'acte,* by Rene Clair, that was a kind of "visual stammering" in which the projected image, "diverted from its function of conveying meaning," led "to its concrete existence."

The Ballets Suedois unified cinema and scenography during the years that Piscator was working towards the same ends. A few years later in *Ode,* in a scenic space that was filled with metallic ropes, Tchelitchew employed real dancers and puppets that resembled them. He also made use of cinema and the magic lantern, neon lights and dipped the costumes in phosphorus. The ballet seemed to assimilate new techniques and means of expression. The painters' adventures in the theater were not limited to the use of forms and colors at a time when there was an overall tendency to deprive man of his importance as a hero and turn him into a scenic object.

TOWARD AN ABSTRACT THEATER

When Gordon Craig created his art of movement, he in fact invented a sort of abstract theater. When Malevich used spotlights to give the performers in *Victory over the Sun* a fragmentary appearance, he also tended towards an abstract theater in which man was no longer the supreme center but existed as one factor of expression among many others. Although apparently isolated, these two manifestations belonged to a theatrical current that went beyond figurative representation. The risk was that the performer might be excluded from the stage or that his presence there might be limited or distorted since the performer always remained the sign of man and could not be treated like other theatrical materials (sound, color, form, etc.).

Wagner had not been successful in his attempts to promote the *Gesamtkunstwerk.* However, the very idea of a "total theater" remained more alive than ever and inspired avant-garde painters and musicians. It was not by chance that Scriabin composed his symphonic poem *Prometheus* for voice, orchestra and clavier/color organ (invented by Rimington) in an attempt to fulfill his old dream of synthesis of the arts. At about the same time, between 1909 and 1913, Arnold Schonberg's score for *Die Gluckliche Hand (The Lucky Hand)* provided for colored lighting to interpret the drama and to act as a counterpoint to the music. Schonberg was also a painter and friend of Kandinsky's.

Kandinsky and Mondrian

No sooner had Schonberg's composition been completed than in 1912 Kandinsky published two important texts in the almanac of *Der Blaue Reiter* ("The Blue Rider") that he had written three years earlier. The texts, "On Scenic Composition" and "The Yellow Sound" elucidate one another and should not be considered separately.

322

323

324

322-326. F. Leger, *La Creation du monde* by D. Milhaud, chor. J. Borlin, Paris. Th. des Champs-Elysees, Ballets Suedois, 1923. **322, 323, 324.** Costume designs. Museum of Dance, Stockholm. **325.** Design of the stage. Part. Coll. Basle. **326.** Photograph of the set. Doc. Museum of Dance, Stockholm.

325

326

327

328

327. S. Delaunay, *The Gas Heart* by T. Tzara, dir. M. Sidersky,
Paris. Th. Michel, 1923. Delaunay designed only the costumes. Doc. S. Delaunay, Paris. **328.** F. Picabia, *Relache (No
Performance)* by E. Satie, chor. J. Borlin, Ballets Suedois, 1924.
Doc. Museum of Dance, Stockholm. "Automobile headlights,
pearl necklaces, round, fine womanly forms, advertisements,
music, an automobile, some men dressed in black, movement,
noise, transparent and clear water, and the joy of laughter, that
is *Relache*" (F. Picabia).

329

329. P. Tchelitchew, *Ode* by N. Nabokov, chor. L. Massine,
Paris. Th. Sarah-Bernhardt, Ballets Russes, 1928. Courtesy
Wadsworth Atheneum Hartford. For *Ode,* Tchelitchew used
neons, movies and the magic lantern. The ballet seems to assimilate new techniques.

In the first, Kandinsky explained his theoretical ideas about "stage composition," and in the second he furnished a concrete example of what he intended. Violently attacking the theatrical art of the nineteenth century and its three narrow branches — drama, opera and ballet — he accused the Wagnerian utopia of *Gesamtkunstwerk* of only uniting external means in a purely external fashion so that they came together without creating any unity. Kandinsky believed that the total work of art depended on an *inner* necessity and on the *inner* unity of its diverse elements (music, painting, movement, etc.). "The Yellow Sound" is a scenario based on the belief in the fundamental sameness of the arts and in a correspondence which would make their interrelation possible. "The Yellow Sound" was a "composition" in both the artistic and chemical sense of the word.

"The composition consisted of three elements which served as the external methods to transmit the *inner values:*

1. The musical sound and its movement;

2. The psychic-physical sound and its movement expressed through beings and objects;

3. The chromatic tone and its movement (a specific possibility for the stage).

Thus the drama finally consists here of the complex inner experiences (spiritual vibrations) felt by the spectator himself."

The fusion occurred at the level of the 'sound' and the 'movement'. The various elements — more or less vaguely defined characters, music, visible or backstage voices, mobile colored forms and lights — were taken apart and then recomposed, acting sometimes simultaneously and sometimes separately. A form such as a hill, flower, or rock appeared, developed and blossomed, while the colors were transformed under a constantly changing light. The color and lighting did not illustrate the music any more than the music commented on the drama. In fact the "drama" resided precisely in the joint action of the multiple voices that composed Kandinsky's scenic polyphony.

Kandinsky never realized this scenario in spite of Hugo Ball's efforts in 1914 nor did he stage other similar works that he wrote during this same period: *The Green Sound* and *Black and White* (1909) and *The Violet Sound* (1913). We can, therefore, only conjecture about these works. One thing is certain, however, and that is, that although *The Yellow Sound* anticipated abstract theater, it did not exclude all figuration. Perhaps Kandinsky's paintings after 1909 may help us to imagine what the plastic reality of his scenarios might have been like.

In 1923 Kandinsky clarified his ideas more precisely in an essay entitled "On a synthesis of abstract scenic composition." Five years later at the Friedrich Theater in Dessau he was given a chance to design and stage Mussorgsky's *Pictures at an Exhibition.* The work was composed of sixteen scenes, but it was only during two of them that two dancers resembling marionettes appeared. The abstract ensemble reflected the pictoral development of the painter. The scenic universe was animated by the musical forms and the mobile ones played with colors and lighting as each scene was composed and decomposed in absolute harmony with the musical movements.

Kandinsky's example is sufficient to show that the painter played a determinant role and took the initiative in the evolution towards an abstract theater. The same is partially true for the Futurists, but certainly the case for those that experimented at the Bauhaus. With Mondrian it is really a question of a meeting between a play *The Ephemeral is Eternal,* written by Michel Seuphor, who was both a painter and theoretician of modern art, and another painter, Piet Mondrian, who discovered in this work a form of literary neoplasticism that corresponded to his own pictorial researches. According to Seuphor, his play was meant to depict the end of "traditional, psychological theater", while also showing that it was a means of composing a new "authentic theatrical spectacle" — in the way that he used sound, rhythm, verbal music, color and direct contact between the stage and the audience. Mondrian grasped his intentions and in 1926 designed three sets in the familiar geometrical style of his paintings that animated the spatial counterpoint of the colors. There was no movement except for the successive settings. As for the actors, Mondrian preferred them not to be seen and only heard. With this unstaged project Mondrian joined a cohort of other artists who wanted to drive the human presence from the stage.

The Futurist Explosion

While Kandinsky and Mondrian each approached the theater in an original way, the works of Prampolini, Depero, and Balla were part of a general artistic movement that affected painting, music and poetry as well as the theater. Futurism was nothing more than a violent revolt against the entire heritage of the past, especially that of the nineteenth century. It was the rebellion of sons against fathers. Futurist manifestoes were like challenges to a fight, vibrant proclamations combining provocation with the affirmation of new ideals. Led by the poet Marinetti, the Futurists praised motion, speed, dynamism and simultaneity as expressions of modern civilization. They worshipped energy and aggression, going so far as to advocate war as the culmination of all they admired. The Futurists proclaimed a new cult of beauty: the automobile was more beautiful than the *Victory of Samothrace.*

In manifestoes published in 1915, *The Futurist Synthetic Theater,* and in 1922, *The Theater of Surprise,* the Futurists defined some of their theatrical ideals: to abolish theatrical techniques from the moribund past, to give dramatic expression to all of the recent discoveries concerning the subconscious and the imagination, and to provoke and reawaken the sensibilities of a passive audience. Old forms such as tragedy, comedy, vaudeville and farce were to be replaced by Futurist *sintesi* which were short 'synthetic' dramas, or animated poems that used improvisation, alogical language, simultaneity, objects rather than actors, and presented the rapid succession of disparate sensations. This anti-psychological, anti-naturalistic theater was not a representation but a presentation based on the interplay of the unreal, chance and surprise, which explains why the Futurists were fond of the circus and music hall.

330

331

330-332. V. Kandinsky, *Pictures at an Exhibition* by M. Moussorgsky, dir. B. Kandinsky, Dessau, Friedrich-Theater, 1928. Inst. Th. Cologne. The work consists of 16 scenes. Th abstract ensemble reflects the pictorial development of the painter; while the music evoked in his imagination the shapes and configurations that animated his scenic universe, mobile forms play with colors and light; and each scene is composed and decomposed in absolute harmony with the musical movements.

332

333

333-335. P. Mondrian, *The Ephemeral is Eternal* by M. Seuphor, project in 1926, photographs of the original maquette. Doc. Neumann, Frankfurt. M. Seuphor thought that *The Ephemeral is Eternal* could be an ''authentic theatrical spectacle: with sound, rhythm, music, language, color and direct contact between the stage and the public.'' Mondrian understood Seuphor's wishes, and in 1926, designed three sets for a stage without much depth in which the painter's own style animated the spatial counterpoint of the colors.

334

335

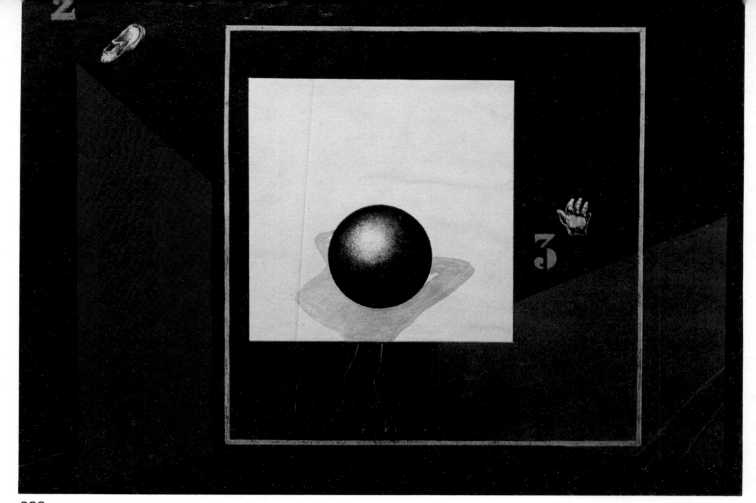

336

337

During this period of manifestoes on drama, the painter Enrico Prampolini attempted to describe the new stage in his "Manifesto on Futurist Scenography" (1915), and "Futurist Scenic Atmosphere" (1924). Rejecting any kind of realism, he called for a total synthesis of the material expressions of the stage, and insisted that: "Colors and stage design should incite emotional responses different from anything suggested by the poet's words or the actor's gestures." Instead of painted scenery, he imagined a "colorless electro-mechanical architecture, powerfully vitalized by chromatic variations streaming out of a luminous source," a dynamic stage which tended toward abstraction, an illuminating stage that would radiate with the range of colors required by the dramatic action. The

338

336. E. Prampolini, *The Merchant of Hearts,* chor. plot by E. Prampolini and F. Casavola, chor. E. Prampolini, Paris, Th. de la Madeleine, Cie du Th. de la Pantomime Futuriste, 1927. Private Coll. Rome. **337.** Idem. Phot. Perotti, Milan. **338.** E. Prampolini, *Parallelepiped* by P. Buzzi, Prague, Svandovo Th., Cie. du Th. Synthetique Futuriste, 1921. Private Coll. Rome. Phot. Perotti.

theater should not focus on the actor since Prampolini envisaged his abolition in favor of vibrations, luminous forms that would wriggle and writhe energetically, authentic 'actor-gases'. The stage of the future will rest on a synthesis, on plasticity and will therefore be a dynamic stage in which the mood within this polydimensional space will echo a multi-expressive dramatic action.

Although Prampolini was indebted for much of his program to Gordon Craig, the novelty and originality of his ideas were apparent in spite of an often unreliable phraseology. While some of the ideals of the Futurists may seem visionary and difficult to carry out, Prampolini and others tried to translate their convictions into theatrical productions and plans.

Prampolini's most daring works were rather abstract. He regarded the stage as a character in a play and animated it with a moving decor. For example, in *Parallelpiped* the screens were organized to form an ab-

339. E. Prampolini, *The Fire Drum* by F.T. Marinetti, Prague, National Th., 1923. Private Coll. Rome. Phot. Perotti.

stract architecture consisting of light and shadowy areas, and in *The Fire Drum,* the entire stage was devoted to the dazzling interplay of brilliant colors. In *Parallelpiped* and *The Merchant of Hearts* he constructed a space that seemed both spiritual and material out of flats, frames and screens on which shadows were projected like symbolic signs filling emptiness. Such a stage was suited to the confrontation between live actors and figure-like marionettes, who became little more than costumes that appeared and disappeared into the black background.

In 1924, the same year that Leger filmed his *Mechanical Ballet,* Prampolini designed a model for a "magnetic theater" which he presented at the International Exhibition of Decorative Arts held in 1925. With this undertaking he came close to translating his ideas into reality. The stage itself expressed the dramatic action; the decor and actors were replaced by a constructivist ensemble, "a polydimensional, electrodynamic architecture of luminous plastic elements in the center of the theatrical space." The action unfolded through the interplay of human voices, lighting and the "actor-space."

Gordon Craig's theory of the "ubermarionette" had given rise to a number of interpretations which sometimes contradicted one another. Indeed as the Futurist experience indicates, there are several stages on the way to marionettization. Or, perhaps the marionette aspect might dictate the acting technique or voluntarily limit the actor's physical means of expression (his bodily movements) from the beginning, that is, because of the text itself. Such was the case for Marinetti's *Feet* (1915) in which the curtain was raised to show only the actors' feet and legs while the rest of the body remained hidden). Similarly the action in the play *Hands* consisted simply of hands gesturing above a curtain which was stretched across the stage. One could also do what Picasso had done for the Managers in *Parade* (1917), that is, dress the actors in costumes which completely deformed their shapes and inhibited their movements. Ivo Pannaggi used this technique for his *Mechanical Ballets* as did Depero in *Machine of 3000* (1924) which was another 'mechanical' ballet set to the music of Casavola.

In the final stages of marionettization the actor disappeared completely and was replaced by a new kind of real marionette that was assembled according to cubist principles. Prampolini used such marionettes, in different sizes, to stage his *Matum and Tevibar* (1919) at the Piccoli Theatre; however,

340

340. E. Prampolini, *The Psychology of Machines* by S. Mix, Milan, Odeon Th., 1924. Doc. Kunstgew. Mus. Zurich. 341. E. Prampolini, *The Merchant of Hearts,* chor. E. Prampolini, Paris, Th. de la Madeleine, 1927. Cf. Reproductions of the designs, fig. 336, 337. 342. E. Prampolini, *Cocktail* by F. T. Marinetti and S. Mix, Th. de la Madeleine, Cie. du Theatre de la Pantomime Futuriste, 1927.

341

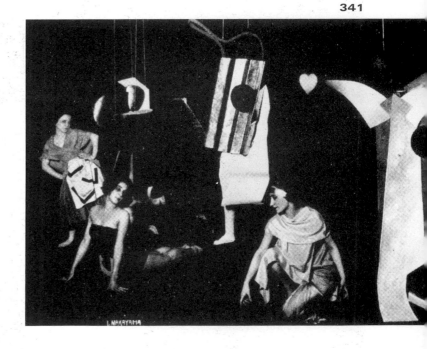

342

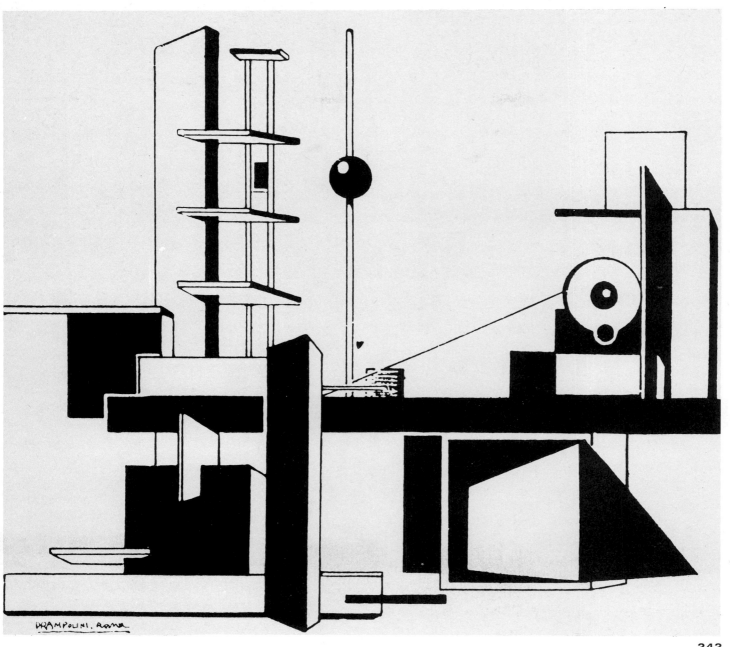

189

343

344

343. E. Prampolini, project for a magnetic theater, 1925. Without doubt this project brought Prampolini closer to his ideal for an art of movement. He created a "poly-dimensional electro-dynamic architecture composed of luminous plastic elements in the center of the theatrical space cavity." The action is expressed through the sound of human voices, the lighting, and the performance of the "actor-space." **344.** V. Marchi, project for a ballet, *Balla del 2,000,* 1922. Marchi Coll. Rome.

345

346

347

345-348. F. Depero, *The Song of the Nightingale* by I. Stravinsky, chor. L. Massine; S. de Diaghilev refused this project in 1917 but later asked the painter H. Matisse to do the decor. G. Mattioli Coll. Milan. **345.** The model. Phot. Perotti. **346.** Mandarin Costume. Phot. G. Sinigaglia. **347.** Lady of the Chinese court. Phot. Perotti. **348.** Lady of the Court. Phot. Perotti.

those created by Fortunato Depero were by far the most famous.

Depero is the author of a 'synthetic' abstract play entitled *Colors,* a drama growing out of four abstract shapes, each colored differently: gray, red, black and white. In 1916 at the request of Diaghilev, he designed the decor and costumes for Stravinsky's *Song of the Nightingale,* but his plans were never realized. The settings called for a fantastic floral imagery in which various geometrical volumes created a world of strange vegetation while the angular costumes pointed out his tendency to treat the dancers as marionettes. However, Depero's fame in theatrical history stems from the robot-like marionettes he made for his *Plastic Ballets* (1918). After attending some of the rehearsals, the Italian poet Settimelli voiced his enthusiasm for the work:

"Depero's marionettes transport us into a deformed and rigid world of new harmonies which elicit our most childlike and unsophisticated responses and immerse us in an intensely naive sensation of joy. The effects are difficult to understand and analyze because life today has become so feverishly complicated. . . . .

"Finally these ballets are one of the most futuristic expressions of our modern spirit. Paintings become dances, and colors and volumes are like musical compositions."

348

What was marionettization but a tendency to replace the actor with the object-actor. In this light Marinetti's 'synthetic' piece called *Vengono (They are coming)* brought no surprises. A "drama of objects," it consisted of eight chairs and a sofa that moved about the stage while the various lights accentuated their live presence. During this period it is apparent that art attempted to eliminate the disparities between man and object.

It was possible to go still further and do away with the problem of turning the actor into a marionette. By excluding any human presence (or a substitute for it) from the stage, the active element in the drama would become the stage itself. Prampolini favored this solution when he devised his Magnetic Theater (1924). But, in 1917 Balla approached this idea in his ballet *Fireworks,* based on Stravinsky's music. Earlier, in 1914, Balla had designed a ballet entitled *Macchina Tipografica (The Typewriter)* in which the ten letters of the word *tipografia* were reproduced dissymmetrically on a backdrop and side flats; the performers were supposed to move about making mechanical gestures and noises that imitated the sound of a typewriter. *Fireworks* was much more

191

349

349. F. Depero, "I miei balli plastici," 1918. Painting. G. Mattioli Coll. A view of the ensemble of the ballets produced by Depero at the Teatro dei Piccoli in Rome in 1918 with the help of the musicians Tyrwhitt, Shemenov, Casella and Malipiero. "In a word these ballets are the most futuristic expression of our modern spirit. There are scenes which become dances, colors and volumes that seem to become like music." (E. Settimelli).

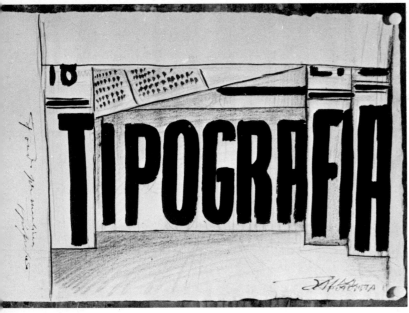

350

350. G. Balla, decor for *Machina Tipografica (The Typewriter)* Onomatopea Rumorista, project of 1914. L. Balla Coll. Rome.
351. *Fireworks* by I. Stravinsky, decor and lighting by G. Balla, produced by S. de Diaghilev, Rome. Costanzi Th. Ballets Russes, 1917. L. Balla Coll.

351

daring; actors and dancers were replaced by lights and decor. The setting resembled Balla's paintings at that time: volumes and shapes with hard or curved edges defined by wide surfaces of bright colors (greens, red, or violets). Other volumes were superimposed, striped with lines in lighter colors, and made transparent so that they could be illuminated from the inside. The whole spectacle consisted of a combination of music with luminous plastic forms. During the few minutes that the ballet lasted, forty-nine different lighting effects altered the appearance of the plastic stage: illumination from the front, from within the transparencies, on the black backdrop and through the play of shadows.

Balla created the "illuminating" stage that Prampolini had desired. Discarding the dead scenery of the past he breathed a vital, dynamic spirit into his settings. Diaghilev certainly never produced anything more audacious than *Fireworks,* which not only anticipated contemporary light-shows but emphasized the importance of Futurism in the development of the modern theater.

The Era of the Bauhaus

While the futurist adventure unfolded amidst the confusion of manifestoes and provocative gestures, the German experimental theater was nourished in the atmosphere of research and teaching at the Bauhaus, which was founded in 1919 by Walter Gropius. The general spirit and goals of the Bauhaus school are well known and have much in common with William Morris' thinking: to reunite the fine and applied arts, to link architecture, craft work and industry for the common good. The leaders, from Gropius to Klee, and Schlemmer to Kandinsky, each imposed his particular point of view; however, their individual affirmations harmed neither the ideals nor the productions of the group.

From the very beginning the Bauhaus had a theatrical workshop, led at first by the writer-painter Lothar Schreyer. Prior to the Bauhaus, Schreyer had directed the Sturm-Buhne group, and from 1919-1921, the Hamburg Kampfbuhne where he had free rein to create in his own abstract expressionist style. In Hamburg he staged a number of different plays, including some of his own, notably *Kreuzigung* which was interpreted by masked, marionette figures (1920). The work resulted in a real scenic composition of seventy-seven water colored engravings. Schreyer undoubtedly had a sharp sense of satire and parody which linked his

works with the Dadaists. However, it was his mystical, expressionist spirit that did not coincide with the rationalism practiced at the Bauhaus school. When Schreyer left the Bauhaus in 1923, Oskar Schlemmer took charge of the theatrical activities.

Painter, sculptor, maker of bas reliefs, stage designer — Schlemmer's tastes were a natural result of his fondness for using a variety of materials. Recall his creations for Stravinsky's *Song of the Nightingale* (1929), Schoenberg's *The Lucky Hand* (1930) or his famous setting for Hindemith's *Murder, Hope of Women (Morder Hoffnung der Frauen).* But as far as the theater is concerned, Schlemmer's real originality was not so much in his stage designs as in the conceptions behind his ballets and the experiments in plastic forms connected with them. A new approach was apparent when the sculptor decided to overcome the immobility of his reliefs by animating them using theatrical means.

Schlemmer's most frequently mentioned work is without doubt his *Triadic Ballet* with its fantastic characters straight out of the modern art movement. His ideas for this ballet date back probably to around 1912, when, after hearing Schoenberg's music, he thought of basing his ballet on the perfect union of musical and colored fluid substances; the *Triadic Ballet* was staged in Stuttgart in 1922. "An apotheosis of the trinity," the dance consisted of variations on the number three: trilogies of form, color and space, of height, depth and width, of dance, costumes and music. Performed by two males and one female dancer, the ballet was divided into three parts: the first, a comical burlesque piece set against lemon-yellow curtains; the second, a solemn and festive section played against a rose setting; and the third, a mystical fantasy danced against a black background. The spatial-plastic costumes, both symmetrical and assymetrical, were the most striking and original elements of the ballet. With their surprising forms based on the circle, semi-circle, cylinder, cone, spiral and ellipse — all of which inhibited bodily movement — the costumes, often made of padded cotton fabrics, were coated with metallic paint or brightly lacquered. "The interplay of colors and forms tends to dematerialize or gives more physical movement to the actors whose movements were not "mechanized, but organized ... to a high degree of exactitude and precision, corresponding to the mathematical essence of the costumes." (O. Schlemmer).

After this ballet Schlemmer's approach

352-354. *Fireworks* by I. Stravinsky, decor and lighting by G. Balla, prod. and dir. by S. de Diaghilev, Rome, Costanzi Th. Ballets Russes, 1917. Reconstructed model with the different lighting effects. Obelisco Gal. Rome.

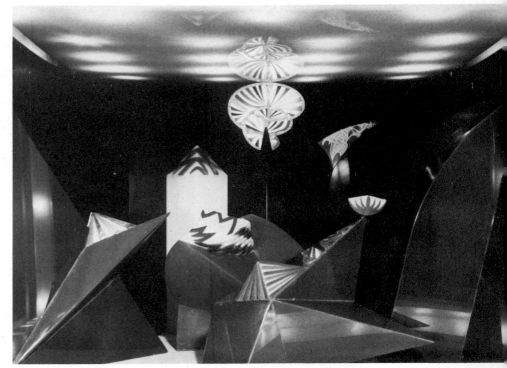

352

353

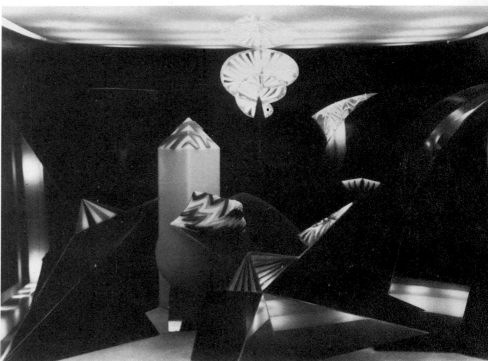

354

355

355. O. Schlemmer, *The Nightingale* by I. Stravinsky, Breslau, Stadttheater, 1929. Tut Schlemmer Coll. Stuttgart. 356. O. Schlemmer, *The Triadic Ballet,* chor. O. Schlemmer, Stuttgart, Landestheater, 1922. Dress rehearsal for the dancers, 1920. Busch-Reisinger Mus. Harvard Univ.

356

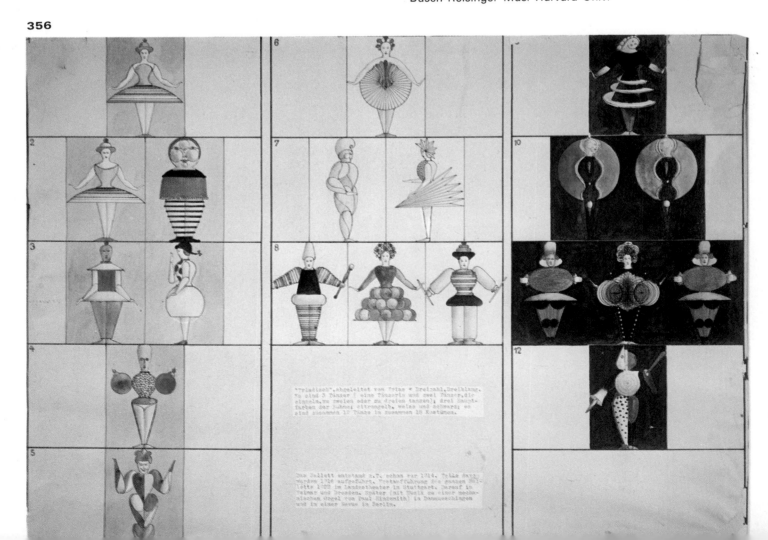

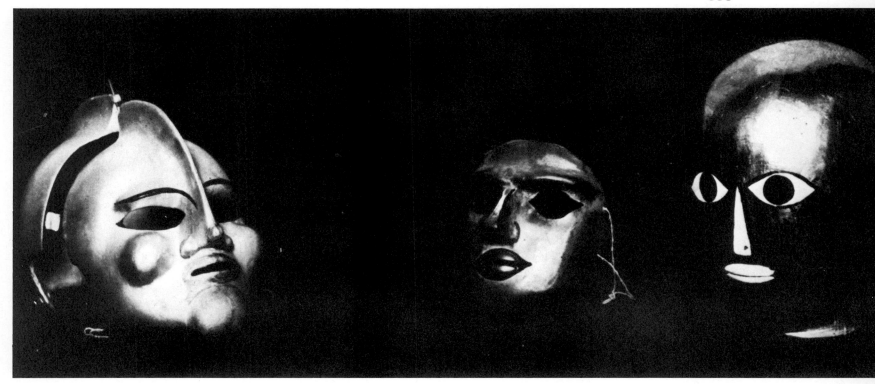

357-359. O. Schlemmer, *The Triadic Ballet.* **357.** Figures reconstructed for the Berlin Exhibition, 1963. Doc. T. Schlemmer. **358.** Masks. Doc. T. Schlemmer. Phot. W. Lucking. **359.** Golden ball. Doc. T. Schlemmer.

359

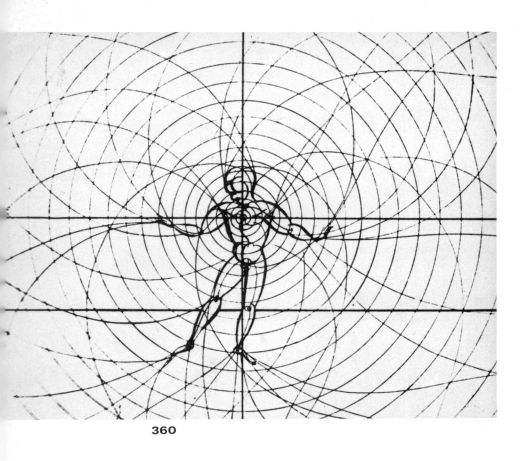

360

to experimentation in the theater was clear. In a period of artistic stagnation, official conformity and commercial art, it was important to start all over, beginning with a practical analysis of each of the elements of the stage in order to find a scenic grammar that would result in their renewed expression and new arrangements. Schlemmer realized that mechanization and abstraction were central principles of his own time, and he worked to create the Gesamtkunstwerk or total art; an art of the personal and superpersonal, of the universal and individual; an art form in which abstraction would be the ultimate means of simplification, the reduction to the essential and primary, opposing unity to multiplicity.

Once the Bauhaus was transferred to Dessau and had an experimental stage, Schlemmer was free to try a series of experiments which managed to combine a deep,

198

360. O. Schlemmer, *Egocentric Delineation of Space,* 1924. Doc. T. Schlemmer. 361. O. Schlemmer, *Figure and Delineation of Space,* 1924. T. Schlemmer Coll.

361

serious approach with the festive spirit of burlesque. If the Futurists had soirees, so did the members of the Bauhaus. Schlemmer noted in his diary of May, 1929: "The formula for the Bauhaus theater is very simple: as few prejudices as possible; regard the world as if it had just been created; don't think things to death, let them develop gradually, freely in their own way; be simple, but not poor ('simplicity is a very great word'); too simple is better than elaborate or pompous; be witty rather than sentimental. Which is to say everything, and say nothing! Begin with elementary things. What does that mean? Start with the point, line and simple surface; start with the construction of simple surfaces, with the body and simple colors like red, blue and yellow, black, white and gray. Begin with materials; feel the different textures of glass, metal, wood, etc.

and then assimilate them. Begin with space, its laws and mysteries and let yourself be 'bewitched' by them. Again, everything has been said, and yet, nothing has been said until these words and ideas have been lived and charged with meaning. Begin with the positions of the body, from its simple presence to the positions of standing, walking and finally leaping and dancing. To take a step, raise a hand or even wiggle a finger is an adventure." Schlemmer might have added: "use the simplest accessories, opaque or transparent screens, blocks and balls, and play with either transparent or projected lighting." The well defined ideas of Schlemmer inspired the titles of his creations such as "Space Drama," "Form Dance," "Gesture Dance," "Dance of Sticks," "Dance of Metals," "Hoop Dance," all of which date back to the years 1926 to 1929.

362. O. Schlemmer, *Figure in Space,* Bauhaus, 1924. T. Schlemmer Coll. "Start with the elementary . . . start with the point, the line, . . . the body." (O. Schlemmer).

362

363

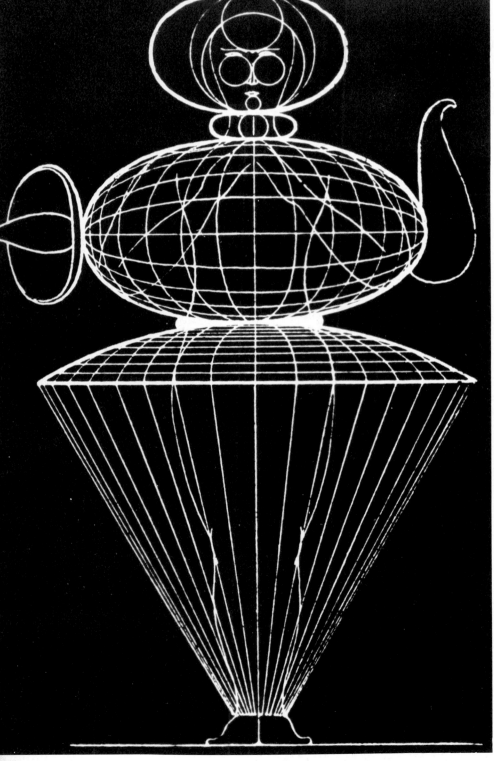

364
365

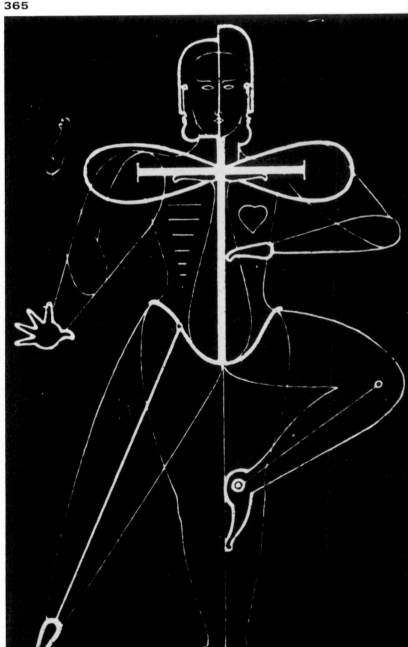

363-366. O. Schlemmer, Course in theatrical theory, Bauhaus Stage. Doc. T. Schlemmer. **363.** *Technical Organism,* the laws of motion governing the human body in space. A Negative. **364.** *Ambulant architecture,* laws of the surrounding cubical space. **365.** *Dematerialization,* The metaphysical forms of expression. **366.** *A jointed puppet,* The functional laws of the human body in their relationship to space. A negative.

366

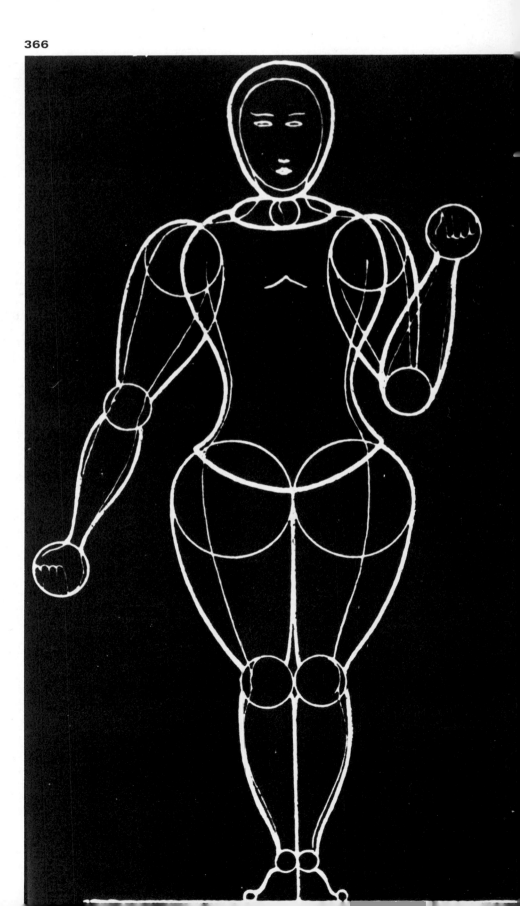

367

368

369

367. O. Schlemmer, *Gesture Dance,* Dessau, Bauhaus, 1926. Doc. T. Schlemmer. **368.** O. Schlemmer, *Dance of Sticks,* Dessau, Bauhaus, 1927. Doc. T. Schlemmer. **369.** O. Schlemmer, *Dance in Metal,* Dessau, Bauhaus, 1929. Doc. T. Schlemmer.

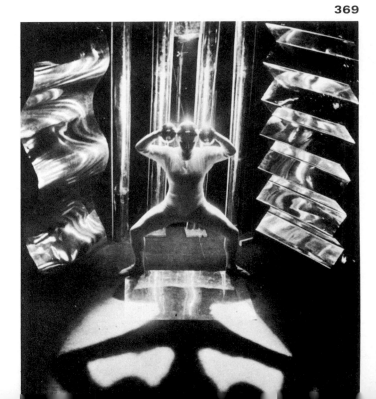

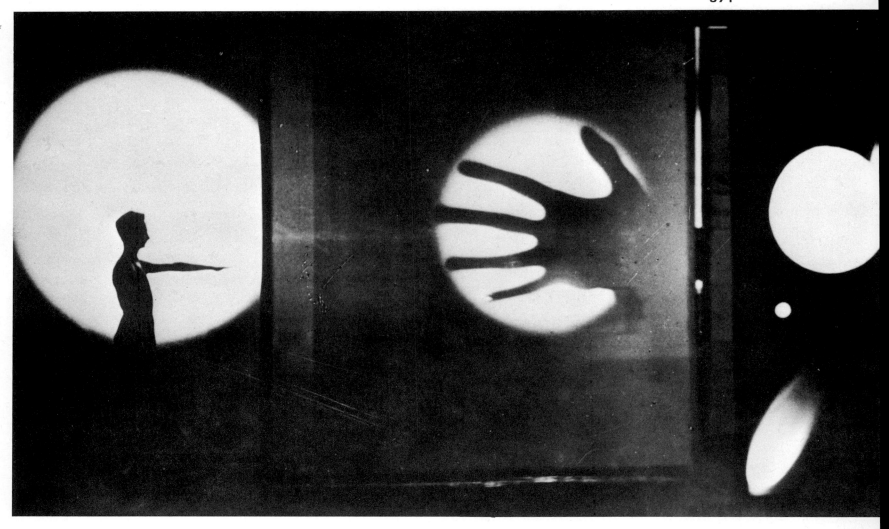

370. O. Schlemmer, *Dance of Hoops,* Dessau, Bauhaus, 1927. Doc. T. Schlemmer. **371.** O. Schlemmer, *Light Play, with Projections and Translucent Effects,* Dessau, Bauhaus. 1926-27. Doc. T. Schlemmer. **372.** O. Schlemmer, *Curtain Play,* Dessau, Bauhaus, Doc. T. Schlemmer.

370

371

372

373

373. O. Schlemmer, *Equilibristics,* Bauhaus, Doc. T. Schlemmer. **374.** O. Schlemmer, *Meta or the pantomime of places,* Bauhaus, 1929. Doc. T. Schlemmer. **375.** O. Schlemmer, *Farce on the staircase, sketch of a musical clown,* Dessau, Bauhaus, 1925. Doc. T. Schlemmer.

374

375

Schlemmer did not reject the human presence even when the costume and mask deprived the actor of his individuality. He admired this being of flesh and blood, intelligence and conscience whom he considered the most perfectly constructed mechanism. For this reason he had certain reservations about the mechanical stage. Although he conceived of "a theater in which the action consisted essentially of the movements of forms, colors and light," he also imagined a stage in which the human figure would confront two enormous marionettes. In spite of its appearances his "Figural Cabinet," presented in several different versions between 1922 and 1926, was not a mechanical ballet. "Half shooting gallery, half metaphysicum abstractum," it was composed of twenty grotesque, brightly colored figures, whose simple movements — according to the spatial axes — were controlled by people hidden beneath their costumes.

This was also true for the "Mechanical Ballet" by K. Schmidt, G. Teltscher and F. W. Bogler, which was presented at Jena in 1923 during "Bauhaus week." Abstract painted forms moved about in space, but were animated by dancers who remained invisible in their black costumes. In the same spirit, George Adams-Teltscher presented another "Mechanical Ballet" where again human presence, as the manipulator, was not excluded from the stage.

The only truly mechanical ballets were those devised by Andreas Weininger, Heinz Loew and, outside of the Bauhaus, Kiesler. Weininger designed a mechanical stage for a musical revue which involved moving vertical and horizontal bands of different colors. Loew's maquette proposed various geometric forms, among them two discs, which moved along three rails that were parallel to the proscenium arch.

376

Kiesler's experiments were the most systematic. For the Vienna Festival of 1924 he conceived of a *railway-theater*. During this forty-five minute show he projected objects made of wood, velvet, gauze and canvas onto a mechanical stage. At the beginning there was a kind of rectangular funnel, after which various shapes were separated and recombined in different ways. These new images were further developed before the initial composition was again projected. Earlier, in 1922, Kiesler had designed an 'electro-mechanical' setting for Capek's *R.U.R.* It was very much like an animated sculptural relief composed of different sections, one of which served as a movie screen while the entire design was subject to the impact of moving colored lights.

All of these experiments indicate how important the idea of a mechanical stage with an animated setting was to the artists of the theatrical avant garde, from Lissitzky to Loew, and from Prampolini to Kiesler. Generally speaking, historians of the kinetic arts have ignored most of their ventures although they admit that the artists of the experimental theater made significant contributions to the development of films. But should their works really be considered theatrical? When Craig conceived of the tools and means of expression for an art of movement, wasn't he right perhaps to claim that he had discovered an art form which transcended the theater?

These attempts, however, to create abstract theater soon stopped until after the Second World War when they reappeared as possible techniques to be applied in some play. The Nazis condemned the Bauhaus members into exile and Schlemmer was put on the black list of "degenerate artists" — thus bringing to a brutal close one of the richest theatrical adventures in our century.

376. O. Schlemmer, *The Figural Cabinet I,* chor. O. Schlemmer, Weimar, Bauhaus (Bauhaus Festival), 1922. Doc. T. Schlemmer. Despite its appearances, *The Figural Cabinet* with its many different versions that were staged between 1922 and 1926, is not a mechanical ballet. "Half shooting gallery — half metaphysicum abstractum," the ballet consists of twenty flat figures, all grotesque and brightly colored, whose simple movements were controlled by people hidden beneath their costumes.

377

377. A. Schawinsky, *Spektro-drama,* scenic elements, Dessau, Bauhaus, 1926. 378. A. Schawinsky, Spektro-drama, montage, Bauhaus, 1926-36. In *O. Schlemmer und die abstrakte Buhne,* 1961.

378

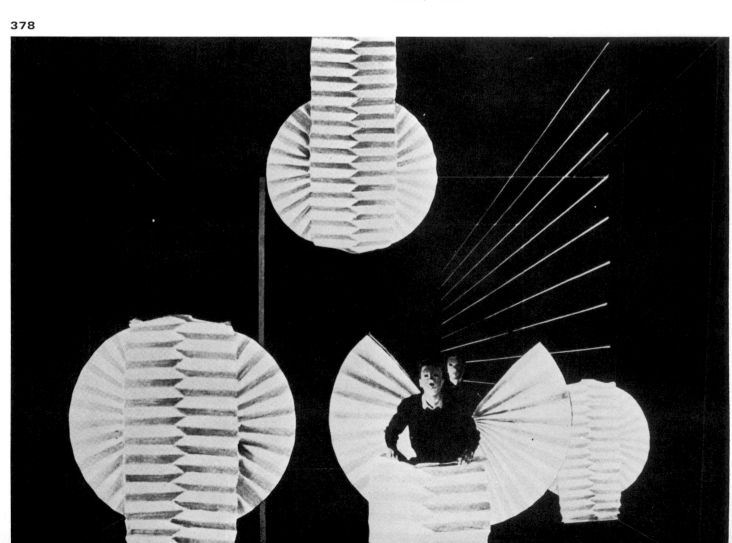

379

379. K. Schmidt, project for a *mechanical ballet,* Jena, Bauhaus, 1923. Doc. Kunstgew. Mus. Zurich. **380.** A. Weininger, *Revue, Mechanical Stage,* Dessau, Bauhaus, 1926. Inst. Th. Cologne.

380

REVUE | mechanische bühne

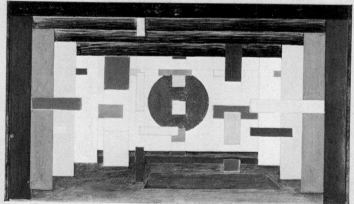

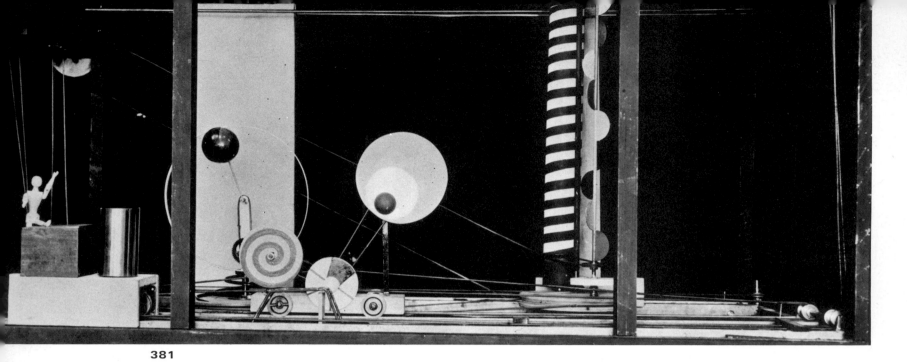

381

382

383

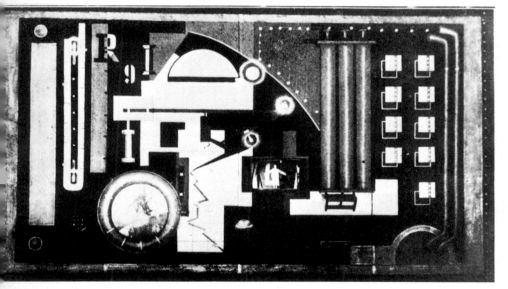

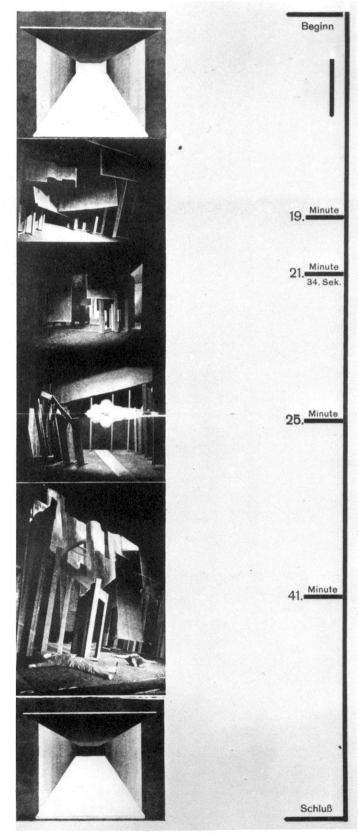

381. H. Loew, Maquette of the *mechanical stage,* Dessau, Bauhaus, 1926-27. Doc. Kunstgew. Mus. Zurich. **382.** F. Kiesler, *R.U.R.* by K. Capek, Berlin, Kurfurstendamm Th. 1922. Doc. Inst. Th. Cologne. **383.** F. Kiesler, *Six continuous actions of a spatial mechanical set,* Berlin, 1923. Doc. Th. Mus. Munich. In the beginning there is a rectangular funnel, after which the various shapes are separated and recombined in different ways. These new images are further developed before the initial composition is again projected. Such was F. Kiesler's mechanical spectacle.

Experiment and Synthesis

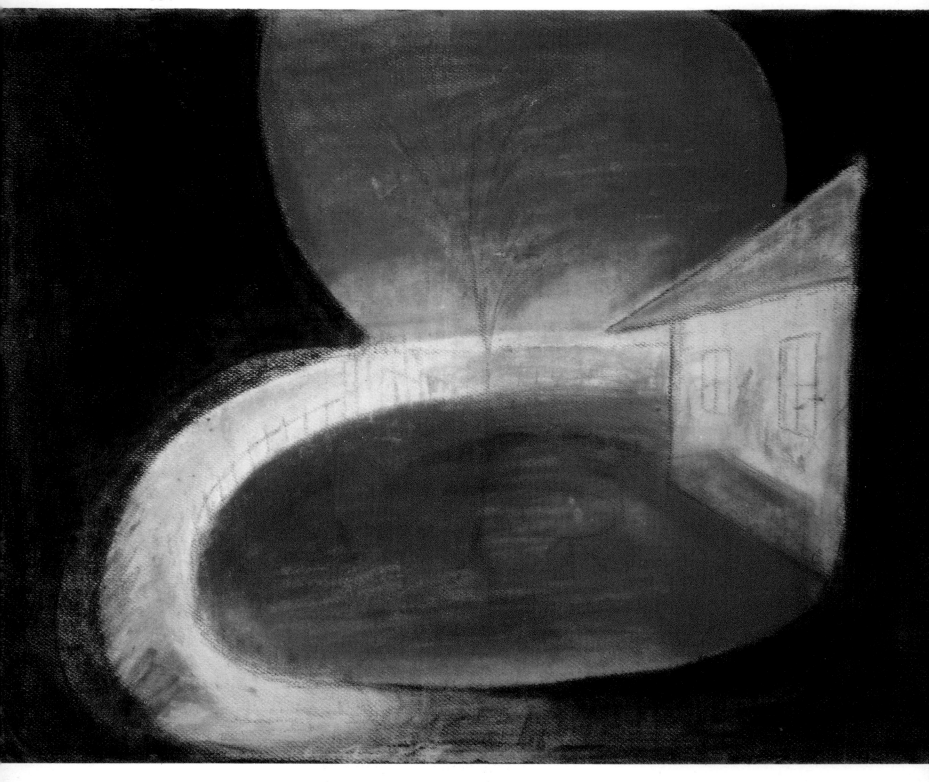

384. G. Pitoeff, *Liliom* by F. Molnar, dir. G. Pitoeff, Paris, Comedie des Champs-Elysees, 1923. Pitoeff Coll. Bibl. Arsenal, Paris.
Phot. P. Willi.

The nature of an 'ism' is that it is born in a specific place and then extends its influence in concentric waves which weaken as they spread out from the center. Some countries may never be touched by a particular movement. In France, for example, between the two wars, practically nothing was known about the Constructivist movement and very little about Expressionism. Indeed Giraudoux was worlds away from either Hasenclever or Toller.

Currents develop simultaneously, sometimes overlapping or becoming confused with one another. While in one artistic milieu a movement may reach extremes, in another that very same tendency may be diluted or assimilated. In this way a radical idea may end up seemingly harmless, its extreme aspects forgotten and only a few of its basic principles retained. Contributing to this development, too, are the individual national, social and artistic characteristics which interfere and complicate any rational analysis of a subject which by nature escapes systematic reasoning.

The development of the theater demonstrates over and over this kind of dialectical process in which syntheses transcend theses and antitheses without necessarily maintaining either their original attributes or impact on each other. What is revolutionary in one period is often assimilated by the next. There were times when it seemed that the destructive phase of a revolutionary movement had terminated and that a more constructive period was about to begin. To a certain extent this was the situation in both France and the United States during the interval between the two world wars, and should explain rather than minimize either the doctrines or aesthetic importance of the productions of that period.

FRANCE DURING THE CARTEL

Even though the above may not entirely apply to the following movement, it is important to mention the experimental ventures of a rather unknown but significant group of people and their theatrical works. The group, known as *Art and Action* was founded by the architect Edouard Autant and his actress wife Louise Lara. Between 1911 and 1951 they gave 402 performances, usually using amateur actors, of 112 plays written by 82 different writers. Their most productive and meaningful period, from 1921-1933, started when the Autant-Lara couple transformed the attic of their house in Montmartre into a simple theater.

What were the goals and methods of this group? To paraphrase the director's explanation:

It was a matter of establishing general rules for the director so that all of the elements of the drama would be coordinated — text, setting, dialogue, lighting, and actors' interpretations.

The principle of scenic dominance should be perfectly justified and remain simple. However, it should come about as the final result of a tested and laborious synthesis undertaken by the entire group in search of an individualized production.

That is why there must be total collaboration of all of the active elements on the stage.

Unlike the members of the Bauhaus they had no intention of starting from scratch by reevaluating each of the dramatic elements. Their interests lay in experimenting with improvisational dialogue, dramatic effects, all kinds of staging possibilities and scenography, as they produced plays that were seldom, if ever, performed, new plays, montages or works that were not originally destined for the stage.

The scenography of the *Art and Action* group concerned both decor and theatrical architecture. Given their limited monetary resources which hampered their search for new devices, the group showed great artistic imagination and concentrated on formulating principles. With their rejection of complicated techniques, old machinery and all traces of naturalism, the directors showed a clear inclination for a more or less abstract symbolism in which the decor became the "emblematic suggestion of the play." Decors were symbolic, allegorical, or even epigraphic *(The Thief* by Apollinaire), and conceived according to very different scenographic ideas. There were single, successive, kinetic and finally simultaneous settings, such as in Claudel's *The Golden Head* (1924). Generally the settings combined a number of simple elements; transparencies were significant in *Les Saintes Heures de Jeanne d'Arc* while for Claudel's *Break of Noon,* screens followed by projections were used. In *Theodicee* simple black and white volumes were piled up like building blocks against a white backdrop; and in *Ecce Homo* the lighting together with a single panel that moved into different positions was all that was needed to create the diverse scenic envi-

385
386

388

387

385. *The Thief* by G. Apollinaire, Paris, Art and Action, 1922. The heads of four players appear on a distant screen. Art and Action Coll. Bibl. Arsenal, Paris. **386.** E. Autant, *The Temptation of Saint Anthony* by G. Flaubert, dir. L. Lara, Paris, Laboratory Art and Action, 1931. Art and Action Coll. Bibl. Arsenal, Paris. **387.** Akakia-Viala, *The Wedding* by S. Wyspianski, Paris, Art and Action, 1923. Paper Marionettes. Art and Action Coll. Bibl. Arsenal, Paris. Phot. P. Willi. **388.** *La Fanfare d'un jour de printemps* by G. Garine, Paris, Art and Action, 1930. Art and Action Coll. Bibl. Arsenal, Paris.

389. F. Masereel, animated shadows for *Liluli* by R. Rolland, dir. L. Lara, Paris, Art and Action, 1922. Art and Action Coll., Bibl. Arsenal, Paris. Phot. P. Willi. For Romain Rolland's play, the crowd is largely depicted through these shadow-boxed figures that were projected onto a screen.

Les OUVRIERS.

La FOULE.

Les MAIGRES.

Les GROS.

LILULI de ROMAIN ROLLAND

Ombres Articulées de Franz Masereel

390

214

ronments. For *La Fanfare d'un Jour de Printemps,* an animated decor was seen through a pattern of grill-work. All ingenious solutions! Still one more example is the setting for Romain Rolland's *Liluli* in which the crowd of characters was represented by the shadows of Franz Masereel's marionettes projected onto a screen.

Most of these settings were designed by Autant himself along with his son Claude Autant-Lara and his niece Akakia Viala. Two painters also made important contributions: Fauconnet, who created the symbolic, comical costumes for *Le Dit des Jeux du Monde,* and Joseph Sima, whose surrealistic spirit was perfectly in tune with his friend Ribemont-Dessaignes' play, *The Executioner of Peru.*

In the domain of theatrical architecture the directors of *Art and Action* designed different structures to correspond to their dramatic productions. Their main project, however, was a Theater of Space which was supposed to stage enormous spectacles *(The Metals, The Fabrics,* etc.) for the International Exhibition of 1937. Unfortunately the project was abandoned at the last minute because of administrative difficulties.

The Autant-Laras were extremely knowledgeable about all aspects of the theater. For example, they had been to see I. Solska's Theater of Space at Zolibor near Warsaw which had been built by the architect Szymon Syrkus. In Syrkus' Theater plays were staged in many areas with simultaneous settings that were spread among the spectators. Edouard Autant used similar structures for his own Theater of Space and added other ideas. In the center he placed a vast rectangular parvis which contained the audience as well as several playing areas with diverse kinds of settings. And all around, on three sides was another rectangular structure for still other settings and large chorale groups. Therefore the audience was both inside and in front of the spectacle at the same time. It was an important project, because like the productions of Okhlopkov, this theater anticipated a number of the scenographic structures that have been designed during the last ten years.

Certainly the accomplishments of the Art and Action group should be judged with a critical eye. Although they contributed to the development of the modern theater, not all of their ideas were new. Often the directors dressed up their experiments in abstract theories and confusing verbiage. But beyond the negative aspects of their work, it is clear that no other group in the twentieth century

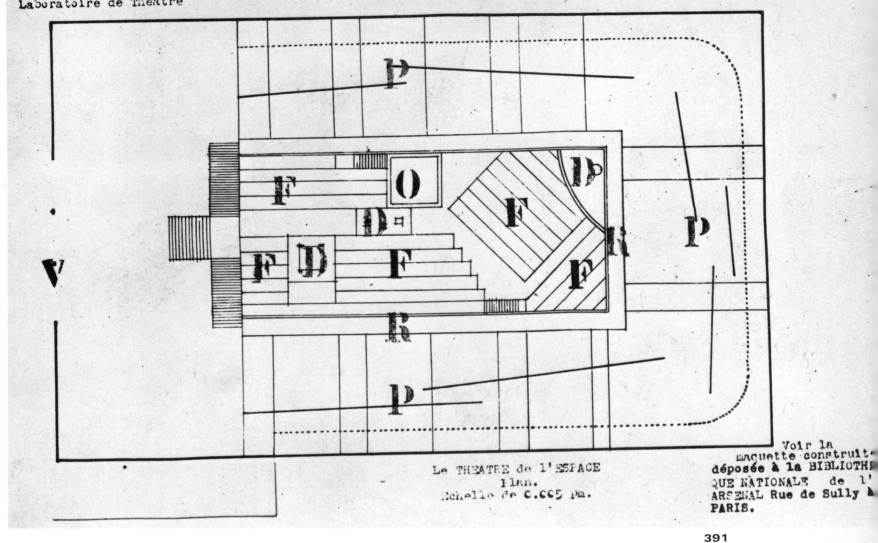

ART et ACTION
Laboratoire de Théatre

Le THEATRE de l'ESPACE
Plan.
Echelle de C.CC5 pm.

Voir la
maquette construit
déposée à la BIBLIOTHE
QUE NATIONALE de l'
ARSENAL Rue de Sully à
PARIS.

391

215

390. J. Sima, *The Executioner of Peru* by G. Ribemont-Des-saignes, dir. L. and E. Autant-Lara, Paris, Art and Action, 1927. Art and Action Coll. Bibl. Arsenal, Paris. **391.** Ed. Autant, plan for the *Theatre of Space*, 1937. Art and Action Coll. Bibl. Arsenal, Paris. The audience is seated in the midst of, as well as in front of, the spectacle. This novel project for the theatrical space anticipated many of the scenographic structures that have been constructed during the past ten years.

had made such an original effort to clear new ground for the theater.

At that time the productions of the Cartel directors were much better known even though they also worked under precarious conditions. Formed in 1927 by four men, this group opposed naturalism, commercialism and demanded more serious theatrical critics. Their backgrounds were as dissimilar as their aesthetic approaches and actual productions.

Dullin and Jouvet had collaborated with Copeau and retained their mentor's influence long after both men left the company. Baty was familiar with the Kunstlertheater's activities in Munich, Reinhardt's work, and had also collaborated with Gemier, particularly for the Cirque d'Hiver's production of *Oedipus Rex at Thebes.* And Pitoeff brought to France his pre-World War I experiences from his native Russia, where his theatrical group had opposed Stanislavskian realism. He had also worked at Hellerau where he was influenced by Jaques-Dalcroze and indirectly by Appia, and where he discovered the importance of rhythm.

Dullin was above all an actor and a teacher of acting. His repertory varied in quality and the plastic settings of which he was fond were quite eclectic. Nevertheless, a

392

216

392, 393. Cl. Autant-Lara, *The Metals,* unrealized project for the Theatre of Space shown in the International Exhibition of 1937, Art and Action, 1937. Art and Action Coll. Bibl. Arsenal, Paris. 392. Acrobats climbing. 393. The Corporate house.

393

few basic principles motivated his work. He was wary of those who gave the main role to the decorator, and in his opinion, if the theater pursued that path, "it courted disaster." Dullin did not believe in progress through the use of new machinery because he felt that brought no "real understanding of the art. Compared to the creation of illusion, such progress was minimal, and absolutely to be despised when compared with the imagination." Moreover, he strongly opposed the prestidigitation of Robert Houdin. The only new medium that seduced him was lighting, which he believed should be used

394

394. A. Artaud, *Life is a dream* by Calderon, dir. Ch. Dullin, Paris, Vieux-Colombier, 1922.

like music to touch all of the senses. In his words: "Light is a living element, part of the flow of the imagination, but decor is dead." And so he declared: "The most beautiful theater in the world is a masterpiece presented on just four bare boards!" He had not forgotten Copeau's "treteau nu."

The stage, however, preserved an air of mystery for Dullin; it was "a world outside of the real world," and not a place for vulgar imitation. In his productions he tried to achieve a coordination of "color, sound and plastic expression." There is an apparent contradiction in his remarks. Although his ideal

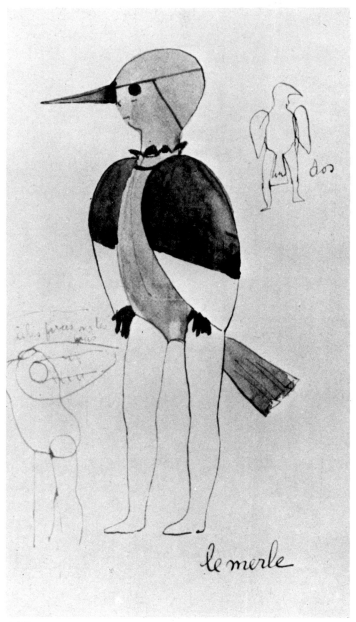

395

was simplicity, Dullin wanted to retain the maximal power of theatrical expression. And while he criticized the role of the painter, it did not stop him from asking artists, sculptors or architects whenever he felt there was a special affinity between the play and that particular artist's own temperament.

In some of his first productions Dullin used curtains and a bare platform; later for *Tsar Lenin* he opted for a sloping stage and formal decor. For *Life is a Dream*, Antonin Artaud presented Dullin with a rigorous structure that was reminiscent of Appia (but an Appia slightly altered by expressionist distortions). Lucien Coutaud's decor for *The Birds* (Aristophanes) consisted of simple but disparate elements that suggested the atmosphere of the circus. There were fewer settings for *Volpone* which permitted Dullin to focus "on the text, the performance and silhouette of the actor, and the precise expression of emotions, in short, upon the essential." His first step was to 'purify' the work, although each of Andre Barsacq's settings was highly decorative in spite of its rigorous construction. The production was certainly a long way from the bare platform stage; still more complex were Touchagues' creations for Balzac's *Le Faiseur*. Indeed, Dullin's eclecticism is readily explained. He detested rigid theories, but he also realized

396

397

398

395-397. L. Coutaud, *The Birds* by Aristophanes, dir. Ch. Dullin, Paris, Th. de l'Atelier, 1928. Doc. Ed. Cercle d'Art, Paris. **398.** A Barsacq, *Volpone* based on B. Jonson's play, dir. Ch Dullin, Paris, Th. de l'Atelier, 1929. Barsacq Coll.

that a significant alteration of the settings would only be possible if the Italian stage were replaced.

Louis Jouvet also attempted to transcend the limitations of the picture frame stage during the period of his collaboration with Copeau and in the first few years with his own group. But, gradually he returned to the Italian stage and used his imagination to create some charming effects. As he was familiar with all aspects of a theatrical production including staging, Jouvet at first designed his own settings. For such plays as *Knock, Malborough s'en va t'en Guerre* and *Siegfried* he composed simple decors based on unusual geometric forms that produced a cold, distant feeling. He liked to play with different materials (wood, moleskin, satiny materials, etc.) and preferred to use subtle lighting but without shadows in order to give the stage complete clarity. He refused, however, to subscribe to any particular theory of stage design: "There is no theory or system of stage design, no aesthetic principles which

399

399. H. G. Adam, *The Flies* by J. P. Sartre, dir. Ch. Dullin, Paris, Th. de la Cite, 1943, Mme. Adam Coll. Phot. Cauvin.

400

401

402

400-402. H.G. Adam, *The Flies* by J.P. Sartre, dir. Ch. Dullin, Paris, Th. de la Cite, 1943. Masks. Mme. Adam Coll. Phot. Cauvin.

403

222

404

"Knock" 2ème acte
Le cabinet du Docteur Knock.
14 5bre 1923
louis jouvet

403. L. Jouvet, *Malborough s'en va-t-en guerre* by M. Achard, dir. L. Jouvet, Comedie des Champs-Elysees, 1925. In *Art et Decoration,* 1925. **404.** L. Jouvet, *Knock* by J. Romains, dir. J. Jouvet, Comedie des Champs-Elysees, 1924. In *Art et Decoration,* 1925. **405.** O. Tchelitchew, *Ondine* by J. Giraudoux, dir. L. Jouvet, Paris. Th. de l'Athenee, 1939. Lipnitzki Arch. Paris.

405

406

407

408

409

can teach you how to create a setting or a theatrical place. Only the emotions emanating from the play itself can help to create the decor or to imagine the type of place for the action. A decor is not deduced from reasoning, but from sensitivity to feelings."

Jouvet soon turned to other stage designers for help. From time to time he worked with Guillaume Monin and Pavel Tchelitchew, who did the sets for *Ondine* (1939). With Berard he began a more permanent type of collaboration; the two men worked as a team, mutually respecting and understanding one another. During Berard's association with Jouvet, the painter suppressed his pictorial inclinations, and elegant gouache style which was in vogue, as well as the marvelous couturier fashions he used in his ballet designs. A number of productions showed the influence of Jouvet's geometric style, in the balancing of decorative colors and stylized forms *(L'Ecole des Femmes, Don Juan, Les Fourberies de Scapin,* and *La Folle de Chaillot).*

Here is what Berard wrote about the setting for the first act of *The Madwoman of Chaillot:* "The most beautiful settings were created by Meyerhold in Russia. They were beautiful because they seemed to consist of almost nothing. It was an art of "allusion." In Ostrovsky's *The Forest* everything was suggested by a board and three steps: how marvelous! The decor for Stanislavsky's production of *Anna Karenina* was absolutely perfect, and made of a mere nothing. But this *nothing* was everything . . . everything that had been stripped away.

225

406-409. Chr. Berard, *The School for Wives* by Moliere, dir. L. Jouvet, Paris. Th. de l'Athenee, 1936. **406,408.** *The enclosed garden,* realization (Phot. Bernand, 1947) and sketch (Mme. Faurer Coll. Paris, Phot. P. Willi). **407,409.** *The open garden,* realization (on stage L. Jouvet and D. Blanchar. Phot. Bernand, 1947) and sketch (Mme. Faurer Coll., Paris. Phot. P. Willi).

410

411

412

410, 411. Chr. Berard, *Don Juan* by Moliere, dir. L. Jouvet, Paris, Theatre de l'Athenee, 1947. **410.** The forest. Lipnitzki Arch. **411.** Don Juan's house. Phot. Bernand. **412.** G. Braque, *Tartuffe* by Moliere, dir. L. Jouvet, Paris, Th. de l'Athenee, 1950. Doc. Kunstgew. Mus. Zurich.

"In order to have nothing as a result, you do not, however, begin with nothing. You begin by putting in everything, and then taking things away, one by one. Thus . . . for *The Madwoman of Chaillot* (the setting for Act One, on the terrasse chez Francis), I began by imagining a very complete setting, with the chestnut trees, the front of the cafe and the building above. Then I removed things and left only the essential. I took away the trees but kept the bench because the bench was necessary to the action. I added a little touch of gray to suggest the Avenue Montaigne, but the facade of the building seemed too heavy, so I took out the walls leaving the windows hanging in space; and they were quite enough to suggest the building."

Berard's death was a great blow to Jouvet. He wondered whether Georges Braque, who designed the sets for his *Tartuffe,* could become Berard's successor. However, shortly after this production Jouvet's death put an end to their collaboration.

Baty's position was quite different: "As I understand it my task is not to arrange words but to coordinate color, gesture and sound in order to create, alongside the real world, the illusion of another world which would be still more beautiful. I am a descendant of chorus

413

leaders and masters of ceremonies and not of philosophers." This declaration explains Baty's violent diatribes against *'Sire le mot'* (Our Lord the Word) and every conception of theater based on the predominance of the text. He was not a theatrical Jansenist; his conception of the universe was Thomistic so that he tended to view the decor as a "living polyphony" which was capable of transcending the verbal and evoke the mystery of beings and things, of everything alive.

With this statement in mind, Baty also refused to enlarge the role of the decor. He declared that "the settings exist only as a function of the text and of the actor's interpretation." He opposed all a priori theories about design (such as a realistic work demands a realistic setting), all excess, but he did want to make use of a wide variety of elements — "colored, luminous and plastic means of expression, acting, mime rhythm, noises, music, etc."

"Thanks to them, we can escape from old constraints, explore new frontiers, and

413. G. Baty, *Maya* by S. Gantillon, dir. G. Baty, Paris, Studio des Champs-Elysees, 1924. Lipnitzki Arch. 414. G. Baty, *Tetes de rechange* by J.V. Pellerin, dir. G. Baty, Paris, Studio des Champs-Elysees, 1926. Doc. Bibl. Arsenal, Paris. 415. G. Baty, *The Dybbuk* by S. Ansky, dir. G. Baty, Paris, Studio des Champs-Elysees, 1928. Lipnitzki Arch.

414

415

416

416. G. Baty, *Cri des coeurs* by J.V. Pellerin, dir. G. Baty, Paris, Th. Montparnasse, 1928. Lipnitzki Arch. 417. E. Bertin, *Phaedra* by J. Racine, dir. G. Baty, Paris, Th. Montparnasse, 1940. Lipnitzki Arch.

417

translate our integral vision of the world into an integrable drama."

This point of view somewhat explains why Baty was not concerned with finding a unique style for his settings, all the more so since his repertory included very different kinds of plays and authors, ranging from Gantillon and Ansky to Shakespeare, Brecht and Racine. There was, nevertheless, throughout all of his realizations (whether he had created the settings himself or had inspired other designers such as Emile Bertin) a unified vision, a kind of realistic romanticism transfigured by lighting, that created more of a sense of atmosphere than of space. His sensitive use of light made him a virtuoso in this respect. Carefully placed effects of light, shadow or darkness lent a mysterious aura to most of his productions.

To the list of those whom he considered "artists of the theater," there was one whom Gordon Craig made sure not to omit: Georges Pitoeff. Simultaneously an actor, director and set designer, he was very close to Craig as far as certain aspects of his theatrical ideals were concerned. Pitoeff, whose works were the most unified, was also the director in the Cartel Group most concerned with creating a plastic scenography.

418, 419. *Liliom* by F. Molnar, dir. G. Pitoeff, Paris, Comedie des Champs-Elysees, 1923. **418.** A sketch. Pitoeff Coll. Bibl. Arsenal, Paris. Phot. P. Willi. **419.** Picture of the stage. Doc. Pitoeff Coll. Bibl. Arsenal, Paris. Phot. Treatt.

Pitoeff did not consider the theatrical arts as a synthesis of other art forms. "While the theater uses the other arts as its basic materials, it also recreates and transposes them. The art of the theater is as undefinable as life itself. For if in the other arts man is the creative source, in the art of the stage, he is both the creator and the instrument." Because scenic art is completely independent from the other arts, the director must remain absolute master and not bound by principles and methods. Nor should he try to be original at all costs. Rather he should enter into communion with each work, discover its "secret truth", and then inspire the designer to express the deep motif of the play in his settings.

Pitoeff's work has sometimes been de-

418

419

420

421

scribed as an "art of rags and tatters." It is true that he often had to make poverty a virtue, but sometimes his plastic compositions reflected a cubistic inclination or the pictorial avant garde of the Russian twenties.

Sometimes plain strips of material against a sky-colored background, or against velvet, were enough to suggest the atmosphere and places in the play, as in Lenormand's *The Eater of Dreams*; or else he might use hangings stretched diagonally across the stage to evoke a Scandinavian landscape *(Brand).* On other occasions, there appeared one startling object as the central motif of the set which was supposed to determine the way the viewer should perceive the play: for example, the elevator which brought the six characters in search of an author on stage, or the oval medallion which precisely dated *The Lady of the Camellias.* After denuding the space of all superfluous objects, Pitoeff reconstructed the stage and divided it into compartments for *The Failures* or into simultaneous settings for Bruckner's *Criminals.* The setting for *Liliom,* however, was truly poetic. Like the vision of the sky, a number of poetic elements were combined on stage to compose so many pieces of a dream that had become reality.

420. G. Pitoeff, *Brand* by H. Ibsen, dir. G. Pitoeff, Paris. Th. des Mathurins, 1928. Pitoeff Coll. Bibl. Arsenal, Paris. Phot. P. Willi. **421.** G. Pitoeff, the "medallion" in *The Lady of the Camellias,* by A. Dumas, dir. G. Pitoeff, Geneva, Plainpalais auditorium, 1921. Doc. Bibl. Arsenal, Paris. **422.** G. Pitoeff, *The Hairy Ape* by E. O'Neill, dir. G. Pitoeff, Paris. Th. des Arts, 1929. Doc. Bibl. Arsenal, Paris. Phot. P. Willi.

233

422

423

No doubt Pitoeff's greatest achievements as a designer were in the stage apparatus that he contrived for his Shakesperean productions of *Hamlet, Macbeth* and *Romeo and Juliet;* he himself understood their importance. The changes he made in the set designs for *Hamlet* show a desire for simplicity and purification. In the beginning he used movable screens, reminiscent of Craig's in Moscow, but in the end, he decided upon a single, fixed structure. The plastic arrangement also emphasized a symbolic usage of color; Hamlet, dressed in black, struggled for purity, and in the final scene, Fortinbras and his soldiers, all in white, arrived to close the tragedy.

The architecture for *Macbeth* was quite different; composed of vaults, depressed ogival arches, and stairs that lead to some undefined place, the crossroads of the tragedy perhaps. "The setting for *Macbeth*," wrote Pitoeff, "did not represent or evoke any place at all; it was neither an interior nor an outdoor scene; nor was it a place that imitated another milieu; nor was it a place known to men or nature. It was purely imaginary from the very top to the very bottom of the stage. Now today, when I try to recapture the meaning of this setting, it seems to me a place that brought together or separated the realities and unrealities of life, that is to say, this *decor is the plastic translation of the world in which the whole play takes place.*" There is also his description of the setting for *Romeo and Juliet:* "The single decor for *Romeo,* which was visually inspired by early Italian artists, has nothing in common with the set for *Macbeth,* except that it is a single setting. It shows houses, the sky, the cell, the public square, that is, known, public places, but these different elements are connected by lines which do not represent anything, the same spirit as the setting for *Macbeth.* The lines are there to separate or connect different places, *and mark those moments in the play in which Shakespeare's characters seem to leave the earth and fly off into the unknown.*"

A few slight changes, or the addition of temporary secondary elements completed the composition. Lighting was used to bring out the playing areas, and at the same time suggested the atmosphere. In his work, the idea of decor was already approaching the modern conception of the scenic arrangement.

423. G. Pitoeff, *Hamlet* by Shakespeare, dir. G. Pitoeff, Geneva, Plainpalais Auditorium, 1920. Doc. Pitoeff, Coll., Bibl. Arsenal, Paris. Phot. Treatt.

424

424,425. G. Pitoeff, *Macbeth* by W. Shakespeare, dir. G. Pitoeff, Geneva, Plainpalais Auditorium, 1921. Pitoeff Coll. Bibl. Arsenal, Paris. ''...a place which does not imitate any other place, a place unknown in nature and unclassified by man, a purely imaginary place.'' (G. Pitoeff). 424. A scene. Phot. Treatt. 425. A sketch. Phot. P. Willi.

425

426

427

426, 427. G. Pitoeff, *Romeo and Juliet* by Shakespeare, dir. G. Pitoeff, Paris, Th. des Mathurins, Sketch in 1922. Realization in 1937. Pitoeff Coll. Bibl. Arsenal, Paris. **426.** Detail. Notice that the stage is divided into multiple, simultaneous playing areas. **427.** The entire sketch.

did not envisage radical departures from traditional ways. Even when they condemned the tyranny of language, these men still considered themselves interpreters and not creators. In short, they were faithful to European theatrical traditions.

The prophet of the future was Antonin Artaud, whose ideas did not constitute an orderly system but rather a combination of poetic visions, philosophical reflections, the observations of a man of the theater who had been deeply moved by Oriental Dramas, and the aspirations of a man whose life was marked by tragedy. After reading his lecture on the subject of "Staging and Metaphysics," given on December 10, 1931, or his "First Manifesto of the Theater of Cruelty," which he published on October 1, 1932, it is clear that he did not want to make the theater more theatrical (retheatraliser le theatre) but to bring it to life again by banishing everything having to do with psychology or daily events. Artaud was against any theatrical form that was first addressed to the audience's comprehension because he felt that was restrictive and tended to make the theater assume a passive role.

"I maintain," wrote Artaud, "that the stage is a concrete, physical place that must be filled up and made to speak in its own special language." He wanted a theater that would engage the actors and audience simultaneously, a magical, ritualistic theater of ceremonies, impregnated with a "mythical and touching reality" in which the spectator would find himself confronted by his passions and greatest desires; he leaned toward the ideal of the 'total theater' in which violent physical scenes would stir up or hypnotize the spectator's senses, making him a captive of the play and caught in a whirlwind of higher forces.

Only then would the text lose its supremacy. Gestures, sounds, movements, colors, lights and space were the many elements of this concrete theatrical language, capable of acting upon the senses, the intellect and nerves of the audience — all at the same time.

Such a theater required much more than a change in architecture. It demanded a new kind of place which Artaud described in his visionary manner. There would be a single area with no separation between the audience and the stage. Imagine a barn or a garage. Place the audience in the center so that the action unfolds simultaneously or successively in four different corners, assaulting the viewer from all sides. In order to increase and diversify the different possible kinds of action

Whatever had been its importance, the work of the Cartel was not the starting point for a new movement but a climax. And if their aesthetic ideals survived in France, they became part of an eclectic approach to the theater — as some of the directors had already exhibited. In a short time, however, the temptation to 'decorate' triumphed over the rigorous integrity each of them had advocated in his own way.

The members of the Cartel did not really demand a new kind of theater. They were not in the habit of preaching like Craig or Appia. Their experiences in the theater made them 'practical craftsmen' possessing the nobility and limitations inherent in this definition.

Although for the most part they felt the need to create new relationships between the theatrical event and the audience, they

and movement at both height and depth, Artaud imagined galleries or catwalks running all the way around the room, and added that the action could if necessary, revert to the center and take place in the middle of the room. Thus, no fixed or tangible barrier existed between the actor and the audience, but instead, a network of actions and reactions were pushed sometimes to a state of paroxysm.

This was a frontal attack upon the Italian style theater, occurring at the time Okhlopkov was staging his productions, which is proof that Artaud's desires were shared by others. As part of a powerful subcurrent whose effects would be felt later on, Artaud was ahead of his time. But the theater was not ready for the translation of his conceptions into reality.

THE UNITED STATES
IN SEARCH OF AN IDENTITY

The European pioneers of naturalism were Antoine, Stanislavsky and Brahm, while in the United States, David Belasco became master of the art of photographic illusion. The settings in the early American theater were also traditional, with misty, faded colors and an excessive number of historical-geographical motifs. At the beginning of the 20th century, the artistic notion of a 'set designer' did not exist.

As it had in Europe, the American Theater went through a period of great reforms, when the "new stagecraft," as it was called, began to oppose old traditions and the vulgar imitation of reality. The movement, however, adapted to local conditions. Although it is an oversimplification, it may be said that the art of stage design was imported, or perhaps, that European innovations had to be assimilated before being adapted to the American situation. No doubt this explains why new ideas lost some of their radical qualities, and why there were no traces in the American theater of the twenties and thirties of pure Constructivism, Futurism, or any tendencies towards abstract theater. Moreover, the theater occupied a special place in American society; often a production depended on an individual undertaking which made it difficult for continual collaboration between a director and a designer; also, the repertory was quite varied, including plays, operas and musical comedies, all produced with more or less realistic settings.

Starting around the time of the First World War, there were, nevertheless, some 'great' American stage designers (such as Robert Edward Jones) who emerged out of the confrontation between European artistic ideals and their own aspirations. Both Jones in *The Iceman Cometh* and Lee Simonson in *Liliom* went beyond the limitations of naturalism and created settings which evoked a world that transcended our immediate reality.

"Imported" into the United States took many forms. First of all there were foreign designers who came to live in America. This was the case of the Austrian, Joseph Urban, who was asked in 1912 to collaborate at the Boston Opera on musical comedies and revues. Later he designed the settings at the Metropolitan Opera in New York for *Faust, Tristan and Isolde, Parsifal* and *Electra.* With his curious eclecticism Urban moved easily from one style to another although he especially tried to create a synthesis from several influences — the colorful palette of the Ballets Russes and the architectural concepts of Craig and Appia whose ideas were known in a vulgarized form in the U.S.A. through Urban's manipulation of volumes, surfaces and lighting. Another example is the Russian Boris Aronson who had studied under Alexandra Exter. In his designs in the U.S. for the Yiddish Art Theater or the Schildkraut theater, there are reminders of Altman's constructivist style. His work, however, became a crossroads of various currents which reflect the diversity of the works he tried to serve. Mordecai Gorelik, who became the chief set designer in Harold Clurman's Group Theater, also came from Russia. The American theater undoubtedly benefited from the melting pot of many nationalities.

There was another type of 'import': the

428. R.E. Jones, Project for staging *The Cenci* by P.B. Shelley, 1913. J. Mielziner Coll. N.Y. Phot. Juley.

428

influence of foreign theater group productions. Max Reinhardt's *Sumurun,* produced in the U.S. in 1913, was an example of 'total theater', liberated from naturalism and based on the enriching union of music, dance and color. In 1917 Jacques Copeau presented a lesson in asceticism, the purified architecture of a few simple lines stripped of all ornament.

Another factor was that many American artists had gained first-hand knowledge of the European theater. Jones' work would undoubtedly not have developed as it did, if this admirer of Craig had not gone to Florence before the war, or had not attended the performances of *The Tidings Brought to Mary* at Hellerau, or had not actually collaborated in Berlin with Max Reinhardt. Each of these experiences which deeply impressed Jones, were explained to his fellow Americans in his critical works. Two books among others played a significant role in disseminating European ideas: Kenneth Mac Gowan's *The Theatre of Tomorrow* (1921), and Mac Gowan's and R.E. Jones' *Continental Stagecraft* (1922). In these books each reader discovered for himself the art of Craig and Appia, Copeau, Reinhardt and the German Expressionists.

The best American stage designers showed their originality in the way they assimilated European ideas, adapted them to the American situation — notably to a theatrical literature dominated by the forceful personality of Eugene O'Neill — and succeeded in imposing their own personal styles. While they were not revolutionary artists, they were indeed artisans·of a new type of stagecraft in the U.S.A.

Two currents seemed to exist: the most eminent representatives in the first group were R.E. Jones, L. Simonson and Norman Bel Geddes. Whatever their backgrounds may have been, these men were more like architects than painters in their approach to stage design.

Simonson wrote the following about his friend Jones: he was as much an artist as he was a unique combination of craftsman, romantic spirit, mystic and Puritan. Jones himself defined his ideal:

"A good stage design must not be a picture but an image ... everything real must undergo a strange metamorphosis before it can have a theatrical reality.

"This presents a curious mystery.

"You recall the quote from *Hamlet*:

" — My father! — methinks I see my father!

" — Oh, where my Lord?

" — In my mind's eye, Horatio."

"The setting must be created for the mind's eye. There is the outer eye which observes and an inner eye which sees.....

"The designer must be careful not to be too explicit. A good setting, I repeat, is not a picture. It is something seen, but it is also something suggested: an emotion, an evocation. Plato said somewhere: It is beauty I seek, not beautiful things. That is what I mean. A setting is not only a beautiful thing, or a collection of beautiful things, it is a presence, a state of mind, the symphonic accompaniment to the play, a powerful wind which must embrace the drama. It emphasizes, animates, sends back an echo. It is an expectation, a foreboding, a tension. It says nothing but gives everything."

429

430

431. R.E. Jones, *Macbeth* by Shakespeare, dir. A. Hopkins, New York, Apollo Th., 1921. In *Drawings for the Theatre*. Ogival arches reduced to abstraction in this set suggest the world as seen through the tormented minds of the protagonists.

No one was more capable of adapting his designs to the spirit of the play than Jones. For some he constructed a monumental architecture or a stylized realistic one that was full of mystery; sometimes his settings were expressionistic, or decorative and ornamental, or full of modern imagery. But behind these diverse styles his work expressed a unity that was due to his training and the nature of his artistic sensibilities.

His sets for *The Man Who Married a Dumb Wife*, produced by Granville Barker in 1915, made him famous. The brightly colored costumes stood out against the black and silver background of this highly stylized production. With a complete break from the naturalist tradition, Jones introduced symbolism into the American theater. It would be interesting to study the diverse facets of this talented man, however, his Shakespearean settings may give us some idea of his accomplishments.

For *Richard III* he designed a courtyard with massive walls so high that the sky was invisible; in the center, for each scene he added a symbolic element: curtains, a prison cell, and for the last scene, the dark silhouette of a net against a blood red sky — the only conceivable sky for this tragedy.

For *Hamlet,* Jones imagined a large impersonal hall with a platform that sloped upward towards a central doorway — the whole design suggesting a distant echo of Craig's arrangement for *Saint Matthew Passion.* The lighting accomplished everything else.

In *Macbeth* his setting concretized the evil spirits of the play in the form of three gigantic masks that dominated the stage. The scenic world was visualized through the minds of the tormented protagonists. For the sleep-walking scene Jones devised a series of arched window frames on the stage through which and against Lady Macbeth made her appearances.

However, this same Jones also designed a typical American farm for *Desire Under the Elms*. By the year 1913 he had already planned his most original and revolutionary production, *The Cenci*, which was intended to be performed in an arena type theater, as if Jones had foreseen the important role that the theater-in-the-round was to have in America.

One of the founders of the Theater Guild and for a long time, its usual stage designer, and one of the most important American writers on the history of the theater was Lee Simonson. Although he was formally trained as a painter, he thought like an architect, and

432. R.E. Jones, *Macbeth* by Shakespeare, from the same production. In *Drawings for the Theatre*. The three witches. Three enormous masks represent the materialization of the evil spirits which inspired them.

believed that "the decor should be a plan of action," an idea which he owed to Meininger and Appia. His immediate concern was to resolve the technical problems presented by each play. After that, he knew how to construct a setting, make bold use of colors, even create grotesque tones. He also liked to base his setting on a single fixed structure that could be modified or completed by adding other elements, as in *The Tidings Brought to Mary*. The armored ship he fashioned for *Roar China* was impressively realistic. However, the sails of the sampan that came to hide the large vessel introduced a poetic touch. For Toller's plays he designed expressionist settings. When looking at his scenography for Wagner, it is clear that this man who detested Craig, was a spiritual son and passionate admirer of Appia. But Appia was not an eclectic, and would never have combined the subtle mixture of realism and expressionism as Simonson did for *Liliom.*

Of the three men, Norman Bel Geddes had the strongest architectural sense. He declared that "most important of all, is *to orchestrate the entire production by using all of the means available,* harmonizing the setting, rhythmic associations, costumes, movements of the actors or dancers, speech . . . and the lighting, a magical element but which is not, however, more important than the actor's performance." His most popular play was unquestionably *The Miracle,* presented by Max Reinhardt in New York (1923) in a traditional Italian style theater that Bel Geddes converted into the apse of a cathedral. But despite its originality and daring, this gothic structure was much less radical than the arrangements he later conceived of for either *Hamlet* or *Jehanne d'Arc* (by de Acosta). For these plays his architecture was abstract, grouping different volumes and connecting them by steps on which the action took place. Often his settings were planned along a diagonal, where dissymetry played within symmetry, and the lighting delineated the playing areas.

Bel Geddes was both a designer and a director. It was not by chance that he devoted his energies to staging. His talent here was apparent from the sketches and models he made for projects that were never realized: his primitive and barbaric proposals for *King Lear,* or his dramatic version of *The Divine Comedy* (Bel Geddes himself cut the scenes from Dante's poem). In the latter, he envisioned a great crater rising in circular levels and changing its appearance. The lighting either revealed, hid, or gave the crater a moving vitality.

244

433. R.E. Jones, project for *Pelleas and Melisande* by C. Debussy, 1921. Never produced. Yale Univ. Wickes Coll. An intangible evocation combining abstraction and symbolism.

434

435

434. L. Simonson, *The Valkyrie* by R. Wagner, 1948. 435. L. Simonson, *Roar China!* By S. Tretyakov, 1930. Phot. Vandamm. 436, 437. L. Simonson, *Dynamo* by E. O'Neill, dir. Moeller, New York. Th. Guild, 1928. Phot. Usis.

436

437

438

439

440

438. N. Bel Geddes, *Saint Joan* by M. de Acosta, dir. N. Bel Geddes, Paris, Th. de la Porte Saint-Martin, 1925. Design of the trial. Hoblitzelle Coll. Th. Arts Lib. The Univ. of Texas at Austin. **439.** N. Bel Geddes, *The Eternal Road* by F. Werfel, dir. M. Reinhardt, New York, Manhattan Opera House, 1937. Doc. Hoblitzelle Th. Arts Lib.

440-442. N. Bel Geddes, *The Divine Comedy,* based on Dante, 1921. Model of the project. Not produced. Hoblitzelle Coll. Th. Arts Lib. The Univ. of Texas at Austin. N. Bel Géddes, is a designer-director. For this project N. Bel Geddes himself cut the scenes from Dante's work for the stage. He envisioned as the playing area an enormous crater which changed its appearance through the clever use of lighting. The lighting either revealed, or hid, or gave the crater a moving vitality.

441

The second group of designers was more eclectic than the first. They had already assimilated the discoveries of the theatrical reformation so that various styles became the means of expression from which they could choose the one that was suitable for each play. This is especially true for Oenslager. Although he was at first influenced by Jones and the Expressionists, (cf. *Brand* or *The Emperor Jones*), he gradually became the unwavering and faithful interpreter of the text. He thought that the designer must be a combination of painter, sculptor, engineer and graphic arts specialist. Oenslager worked on all kinds of productions (dramas, ballets, musical comedies and operas) for which he designed realistic, surrealist, impressionist or expressionist settings depending on the work in question. One year he worked on *Mac-*

443

444

445

443. D. Oenslager, *Brand* by H. Ibsen, dir. G. Pierce, Yale Th.,
1928. Phot. Juley. **444, 445.** D. Oenslager, *Emperor Jones* by
E. O'Neill, dir. G. Pierce, Yale Th., 1931. Phot. Juley.

446

447

beth with a particular view in mind, but ten years later, with another, he chose a completely new approach.

Gorelik's conception of the designer's role was different. His works, which show the influence of Jones, Simonson, Bel Geddes and Soudeikine, are also, at times, infused with an epic vision. Gorelik seriously admired the political theatrical ventures of Piscator and Brecht, the latter still unknown in America. Using a variety of styles, he did not simply try to recapture the ambiance of a play in his sets, but wanted to find a metaphorical image that would express the different levels and significance of the work. Yet, even when he became associated with a theatrical undertaking, he never was a partisan of a particular school of thought.

The eclectic tastes of Jo Mielziner were apparent. "Every new play," he said, "requires a new approach, different methods and a fresh vision. I cannot speak of preconceived ideas that govern the way I go to work on each play." When the curtain first went up, he preferred not to have his set in the limelight. Rather he wanted his decor to enhance the key scenes and underscore the climactic moments. Often he seemed to be inspired by Craig, whom he admired (as, for example, in *Panic, Journey to Jerusalem,* and *Winterset*), but he could also create a Renaissance type of setting as in *Romeo and Juliet.* Most of his sketches were enveloped in a light, translucent mist, an impalpable poetic veil that captured the mystery of beings, things and their interrelationships. Mielziner became the designer for Tennessee Williams.

A number of comparisons can easily be made between the development of stage design in France and the United States. In both countries scenographers gradually abandoned preconceived ideas because of their impracticality for general application, and adapted styles according to their suitability, and the special view of reality of each work. But one might ask if the stage designer is capable of expressing multiple visions of the world, and indeed, should he? Can he play with reality without becoming a chameleon? Is eclecticism the sign of a fertile imagination or of decadence? As history has alternated between periods of strict, radical doctrines and compromises, no answer has as yet been provided, although it seems that compromises have inevitably elicited violent reactions. The last thirty years is full of confrontations between those who have advocated a fashionable eclecticism and those who have looked for new approaches that would introduce new relations between the spectacle and the audience and between a certain vision of man and reality.

446. M. Gorelik, project for *They shall not die* by J. Wexley, 1934. 447. M. Gorelik, *Thunder Rock* by R. Ardrey, dir. E. Kazan, New York, Mansfield Th., 1939. 448. H. Hermanson, *Triple A-plowed under,* by the Living Newspaper, dir. J. Losey, New York, Biltmore Th., Federal Theatre, 1936. Shadow boxing is employed in this social and political form of theater which tried to achieve in the theater something similar to the printed newspaper.

448

449

450

451

449. J. Mielziner, *Panic* by A. MacLeish, dir. J. Light, New York City, Imperial Th., 1934. Phot. Juley, **450.** J. Mielziner, *Winterset* by M. Anderson, dir. G. MacClintic, New York, Martin Beck Th., 1935. Phot. Juley. **451.** J. Mielziner, *Yellow Jack* by S. Howard and P. de Kruif, dir. J. Harris, 1934 project. Phot. Juley. **452.** J. Mielziner, *The Glass Menagerie* by T. Williams, dir. E. Dowling and M. Jones, New York, The Playhouse Th., 1945.

452

Thirty Years of Scenography

453

454

453. T. Otto, *Faust* by J.W. Goethe, dir. G. Grundgens, Hamburg, Deutsches Schauspielhaus, 1958. Inst. Th. Cologne.
454. M. Bignens, *Tales of Hoffmann* by J. Offenbach, dir. Pscherrer, Munich. Th. am Gartnerplatz, 1966. Inst. Th. Cologne.

The last thirty years have witnessed the emergence of a new generation of designers, while three of the greatest scenographers of our time — Christian Berard, Frantz Merz and Caspar Neher — and two directors, who more than anyone else transformed the aesthetics of the production — E.G. Craig and E. Piscator — have died.

During this period there have been thousands of theatrical productions throughout the world and hundreds of stage designers participating in the development of a constantly changing art. It would be extremely presumptuous for us to try and analyze these fertile, passionate times within the framework of the last chapter. Clearly, as we approach the present, the various currents are more difficult to separate. Moreover, since we ourselves are taking part in a living, evolving reality, we experience all sorts of impressions which, for the lack of an historical perspective, remain hopelessly unclarified. I will therefore not attempt to reconstruct our present, multi-faceted theatrical era, but will limit myself to a few general remarks which I hope will be explained by illustrated examples and observations.

UNDER THE SIGN OF DIVERSITY

First observation: Anyone examining the contemporary theater must be struck by the extraordinary diversity of styles. Leafing through recent reviews of stage design, the photos indicate many conflicting tendencies. In some pictures the stage is encumbered by pompous motifs that have especially appealed to a Wakhevitch, a Cecil Beaton, or a Eugene Berman — the designer who wants to seduce his audience using any means, academic or otherwise. In others, poverty is the goal, a bare stage ready to accept language and gesture. Side by side one discovers an overwhelming constructivist style with traces of functional elements, a selective kind of realism combined with an illustrative surrealism, abstract symbolism and so on. Whether they are labels, styles, means of expression or merely formulas depends entirely on the integrity of the designer and the nature of his commitment. A period of confrontation, or perhaps open defiance!

The causes of this diversity are numerous. First of all, they are the inevitable consequence of the variety of dramatic, musical and choreographic works. Let us look for a moment at the French repertory of the Fifties. There were the mediocre "Boulevard"

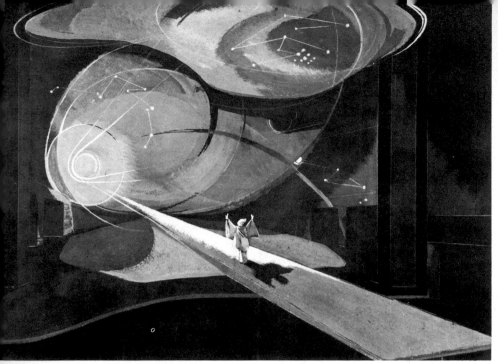

455

plays, which were usually set in some tastefully decorated bourgeois living room; the great classics; works from the theater of the absurd (in these the stage was often emptied so that the character remained alone to face his anguish or desperate wait; Cf. Beckett's *Waiting for Godot,* where the lonely silhouette of a jagged tree serves as man's companion;) plays from the theater of derision, such as the one in which mushrooms, symbolic of social and spiritual decay, invade the stage (Cf. Ionesco's *Amedee* or *How to Get Rid of it):* or Ionesco's farce in which the *chairs,* a metaphorical expression of human reality, become characters; lavishly-produced operettas; Brecht's epic dramas; ventures into political theater or purely escapist types of entertainment; harmless farces and Claudel's tragedies.

More generally speaking, our contemporary theater lives off a past which it recreates in its own image (the classics from Aeschylus to the Romantics), and a multifaceted present consisting of traditionally written works, and those that experiment with new means of expression, improvisation and group creativity. Moreover, theater today serves many different purposes. From the "dissemination of culture" to political agi-

455. P. Haferung, *Moses and Aaron* by A. Schoenberg, dir. K. H. Krahl, Zurich, Stadttheater, 1957. Inst. Th. Cologne. **456.** B. Aronson, *J. B.* by A. MacLeish, dir. E. Kazan, New York, Anta Th., 1959. Phot. Galbraith. **457.** A. Giacometti, *Waiting for Godot* by S. Beckett, dir. R. Blin, Paris, Odeon Th., France, 1961. Phot. Pic. The silhouette of a jagged tree is man's only companion. **458.** J. Noel, *The Chairs* by E. Ionesco, dir. J. Mauclair, Paris, Studio des Champs-Elysees, 1956. Phot. Bernand. The chairs? They are the title of the play, the characters, and the expression of a reality full of anguish and derision.

456

457

458

tation and propaganda, from entertainment to ritual, from evasion to commitment or . . . self indulgence, artists of our times exploit known and tried formulas and venture either spontaneously or deliberately into unchartered paths.

Every dramatic work existing in a purely literary form awaits a second birth, namely its life on stage. Each play has its own internal structure, its unique universe to reveal. The last twenty years point to an abundance of new structures and original creations that have overturned conventional notions of time and space (Armand Gatti, Peter Weiss, etc.). Although a few designers prefer a particular kind of repertory, most of them create for many completely different playwrights and adapt their settings to the requirements of each play. Teo Otto, who has designed sets for plays by Goethe, Shakespeare, Giraudoux, Brecht, Durrenmatt and Stravinsky wrote: "When I create a set, I forget everything I did previously. Every author demands a specific means of expression. If a designer has a too clearly defined style, he is likely to become a mannerist. One should not become associated with theories."

The variety of decors during the past thirty years is also due to the number of different methods and styles of directing. Is there any connection between the staging approaches of Vilar and Felsenstein, Wieland Wagner and Engel, Elia Kazan and Peter Brook, Grotowski and Planchon, Visconti and Krejca, or Garcia and Ariane Mnouchkine? Every director in suggesting a specific way of looking at the world either depicts reality or has the spectator discover it for himself, as he imposes his method for making the scenic universe live on stage. Like other creative artists, most directors go through various stages of development, or "periods" that characterize their styles at a particular time.

459, 460. F. Themerson, *Ubu-Roi* by A. Jarry, dir. M. Meschke, Stockholm, Marionetteatern, 1964. Since the last war puppets have become popular. Meschke's work in Sweden points out the expressive possibilities offered by the combination actor-puppet. **461.** W. Znamenacek, *The Marriage of Mr. Mississippi* by F. Durrenmatt, dir. H. Schweikart, Munich, Kammerspiele, 1952. Inst. Th. Cologne. **462.** L. Vychodil, *The Wolves* by R. Rolland, dir. M. Hynst, Brno Th. d'Etat, 1963.

459

460

463

463. M. Scandella, *The Love for Three Oranges* by S. Prokofiev, dir. G. Poli, Spoleto, Festival des deux mondes, 1962.
464, 466. F. Wotruba, *Oedipus Rex* by Sophocles, dir. G.R.
Sellner, Vienna, Burgtheater, 1960. (464: sketch of the costumes; 466: picture of the set (arrangement). **465, 467.** F.
Wotruba, *Oedipus Rex* and *Oedipus at Colonna* by Sophocles,
dir. G.R. Sellner, Salzburg, Felsenreitschule, 1965. (465:
sketch of the set; 467: model in plaster by the sculptor.) The
monumental world of the sculptor meets the world of tragic
antiquity.

464

465

466

467

The Stage and the Plastic Arts

Additional reasons for the diversity of styles in stage design are apparent from examining developments in other arts. Scenography has some of the characteristics of architecture and sculpture, in the way, for example, scenic volumes are plastically arranged, and of painting, in so far as the set proposes a graphic, colored figuration of the world and gives the spectator a rigorously composed (although it should appear to be accidentally) ensemble of shapes, lines and tonalities which do not necessarily have an immediate or direct meaning. Whether the sculptor or the designer is called upon to create the set, it is expected that the special universe of the play, with its required modes of representation, will be recognizable in the artist's designs. The 'transplant' phenomenon has some dangers. However, it seems reasonable to have a connection between the artist's plastic concerns and his theatrical creations. Indeed this association is often precisely what is desired.

Since the last war fewer plasticians (painters, sculptors) have worked in the theater than at the time of the Ballets Russes. Nevertheless, these artists still contribute occasionally, or engage in longer lasting group efforts in which no 'school' of art is *a priori* excluded.

Look at the works of the sculptor Wotruba whose gigantic blocks on stage have fashioned the worlds of classical tragedy and Wagnerian mythology, worlds in which light and darkness lock in continuous combat. Then there are the realizations by Calder, especially his *Nuclea* at the T.N.P. for which he designed a constructivist arrangement composed of tubular elements and dominated by disturbing mobiles that suggested the atomic age. In *Don Giovanni,* Henry Moore's sculptures were simply transplanted as they were onto the stage, and Nicolas Schoffer created moving sculptures to serve as partners for Maurice Bejart's dancers in the rhythmical studies known as *Cisp I.* Later, Schoffer collaborated with the musician Pierre Henry and choreographer Alwin Nikolais on *Kyldex I,* which was a 'total' theater spectacle combining cybernetics and luminodynamics.

Let us not forget the sets by Picasso for *Oedipus,* Chagall's *Daphnis and Chloe* and *The Magic Flute,* Baumeister's *Judith,* Kantor's *Rhinoceros* and *Antigone,* and Dali's *Mad Tristan* or *Scipion en Espagne;* also noteworthy is Miro's project for *L'Oeil-oiseau.* For the decor of the ballet *Phedre,* the poet Jean Cocteau worked as a painter.

263

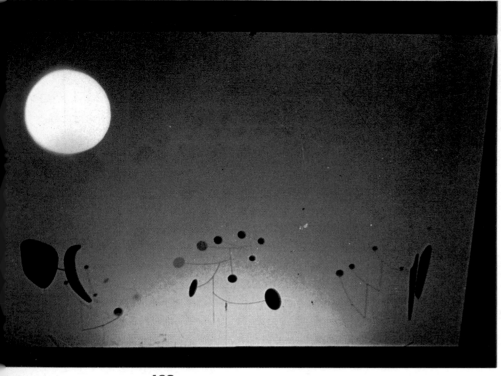

468

469

468. A. Calder, *Work in Progress,* theatrical images coordinated by G. Caradente and presented by F. Crivelli, the electronic music of N. Castiglioni, A. Clementi, B. Maderna, Rome, Teatro dell'Opera, 1968. Doc. Fratelli Fabbri Ed. **469.** A. Calder, *Nuclea* by H. Pichette, dir. J. Vilar, Paris, T.N.P., 1952. Phot. A. Varda. **470.** A. Calder, *The Provocation* by S. Halet, dir. G. Monnet, Comedie de Bourges, 1963. Doc. Kunstgew. Zurich. Mus.

470

Among the many other artists who have been attracted to the theater are: Niki de Saint Phalle, Andy Warhol, Rauschenberg and Dubuffet. Perhaps the stage fascinates certain painters and sculptors because the theater permits them to reach a much larger audience than do the art galleries.

What the sculptor or painter contributes is his vision, his sensitivities, and the materialization of an imaginative world. But, his collaboration invites a certain risk. The plastic artist may impose a universe that does not harmonize with the artistic reality of the play. Sometimes the painter's participation is sought because he is fashionable, in which case the enterprise, relying on snobism, be-

comes more promotional than genuinely artistic.

In the realm of dance there have been two cases of continuous collaboration between the plastic artist and the director. In France, just after the war, Antoni Clave met Roland Petit, and their association brought a period of tremendous success for the Ballets des Champs-Elysees. In recent years, the Ballet Theatre Contemporain has frequently called upon contemporary artists whose styles vary from abstract to kinetic; Karel Appel, Cesar, Jean Dewasne, Sonia Delaunay, Etienne Hajdu, Mario Prassinos, Singier and Soto have all contributed to their productions.

471

471. N. Schoffer, *Cisp I* (Rhythmical Study), chor. M. Bejart,
Marseille, Le Corbusier Festival, 1960. Phot. Descharnes.
Schoffer's moving sculptures become partners of the dancers.

472 a

472. a,b,c,d. N. Schoffer, *Kyldex I,* show by N. Schoffer, P. Henry and A. Nikolais, Hamburg, Staatsoper, 1973. Phot. N. Schoffer. In this 'total' theater, music and dance are joined with cybernetics and luminodynamics; the public also participates.

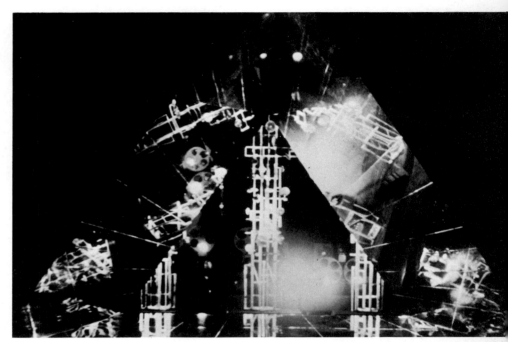

472 b

472 c
472 d

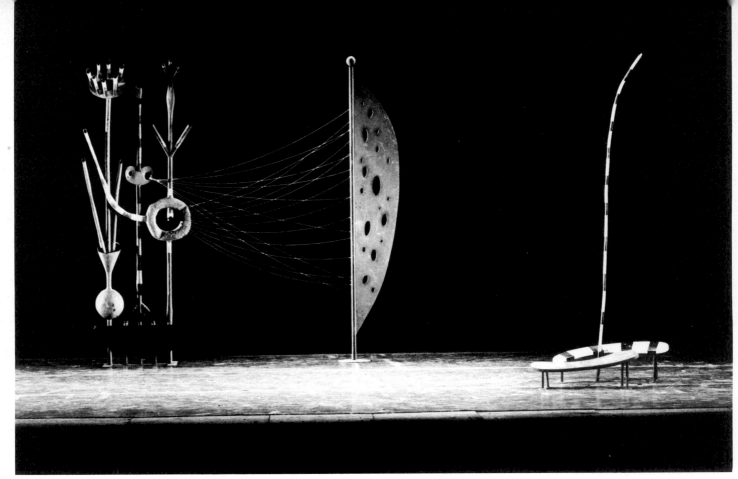

473

474

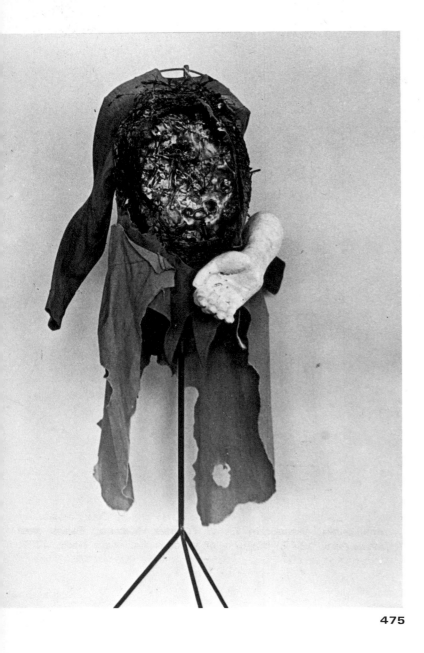

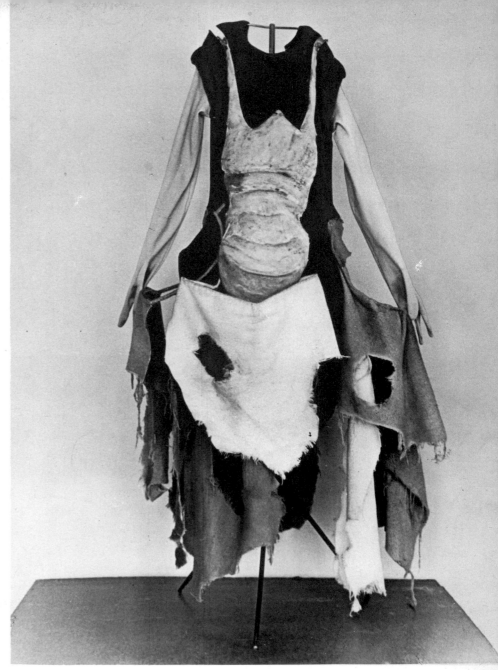

475

476

477

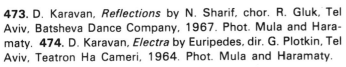

473. D. Karavan, *Reflections* by N. Sharif, chor. R. Gluk, Tel Aviv, Batsheva Dance Company, 1967. Phot. Mula and Haramaty. **474.** D. Karavan, *Electra* by Euripedes, dir. G. Plotkin, Tel Aviv, Teatron Ha Cameri, 1964. Phot. Mula and Haramaty.

475-477. T. Kantor, *Rhinoceros* by E. Ionesco, dir. P. Pawlowski, Cracow, Stary Teatr, 1961. **475,476.** Costumes. Phot. Nowak. **477.** Photo of the stage. Phot. Plewinski.

478

478, 481. M. Chagall, *The Firebird* by I. Stravinsky, chor. A. Bolm, Metropolitan Opera, New York, 1945. Property of the artist. Phot. colors Delageniere, Paris. **478.** Watercolor of the curtain for the first act. **481.** Watercolor of the curtain used in the opening scene.

479, 480. M. Chagall, *Aleko,* ballet by L. Massine, music by Tchaikovsky, American Ballet Theater, Mexico, Palais des Beaux-Arts, 1942. Museum of Modern Art, New York. **479.** Watercolor of the curtain used in the third act. **480.** Watercolor of the fourth curtain.

270

479

480

481

482

483

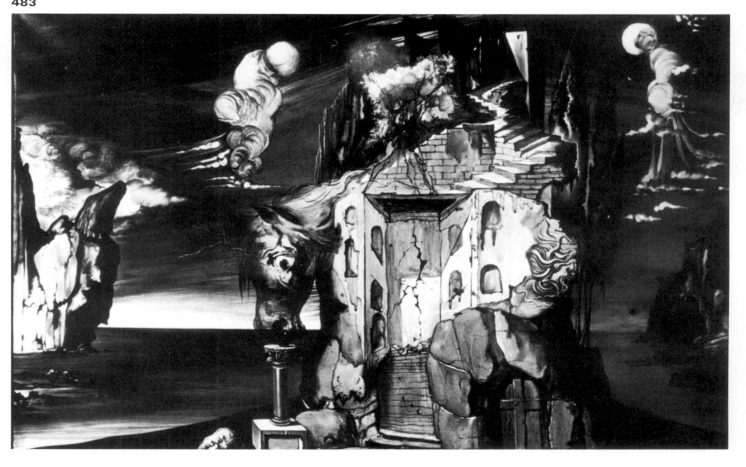

484

485

482. J. Szajna, *Faust* by Ch. Gounod, dir. K. Kad and J. Szajna, Cracow Opera, 1967. Phot. Plewinski. **483, 484.** S. Dali, *Mad Tristan,* ballet by S. Dali based on Wagner's music, chor. L. Massine, New York, International Ballet, 1944. Phot. Descharnes. **485.** A. Warhol (and R. Nelson for lighting), *Rainforest* by D. Tudor, chor. M. Cunningham, Paris, Odeon Th., France, 1970. Phot. Pic. **486.** J. Johns, based on M. Duchamp, *Walk-around Time* by D. Bherman, chor. M. Cunningham, Paris, Odeon Th., France, 1970. Phot. Pic. **487.** N. de Saint Phalle, *Lysistrata* by Aristophanes, produced by N. de Saint Phalle and R. L. Diez, Kassel, Staatstheater, 1966. Phot. Lengemann. The most diverse currents in the plastic arts assault the stage: surrealism, dadaism, neo-expressionism, etc.

486

487

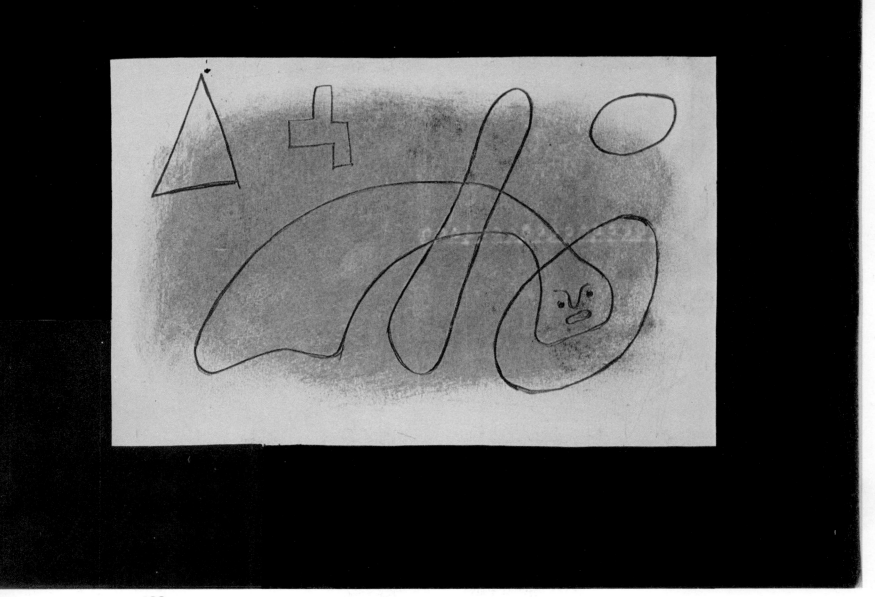

488

488. J. Miro, *L'Oeil-oiseau*, project for the ballet, plot by J. Dupin. Sketch of the curtain, property of the artist. Phot. J. Hyde. Although the ballet was never produced, this project shows that even after *Jeux d'enfants*, Miro continued to think of the ballet.

489. a,b,c,d,e. J. Miro, *L'Oeil-oiseau*. Sketches of the costumes, property of the artist. Phot. J. Hyde. J. Dupin depended on the ideas and sketches created by Miro over a period of several years. The ballet was "a choreographic, musical and poetic spectacle on themes of J. Miro, and an attempt to transpose the artist's plastic and pictorial universe onto the stage." The scenes for this ballet, which had been conceived for presentation at the Maeght Foundation in Saint Paul de Vence, unfolded successively in different places.

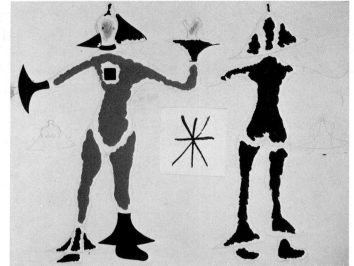

489 b

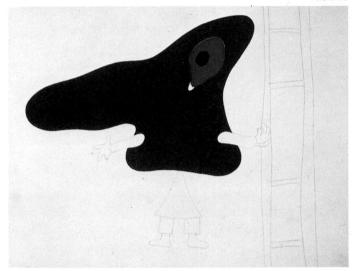

489 c

489 a

489 d

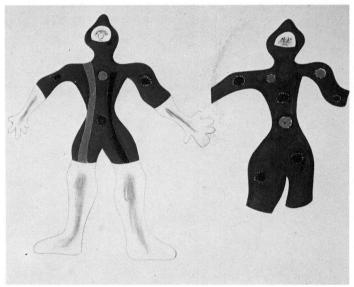

489 e

490

491

490. G. Pellaert (costumes), *Hopop on pop music,* chor. D. Sanders, scen. by Cesar, Amiens, Maison de la Culture, Ballet Theatre Contemporain, 1969. Phot. D. Keryzaouen-Atac. **491.** E. Hajdu, *Cantate profane,* chor. M. Sparemblek, Amiens, Maison de la Culture, Ballet Theatre Contemporain. Phot. S. Lido. **492.** J. R. Soto, *Violostries* by B. Parmegiani and D. Erlih, chor. M. Descombey, Amiens, Maison de la Culture, Ballet Theatre Contemporain, 1969. Phot. S. Lido.

493. A. Clave, *Carmen* by G. Bizet, ballet, chor. R. Petit, Paris. Th. Marigny, Ballet de Paris-Roland Petit, 1949. Sketch of Carmen's room. **494.** J. D. Malcles, *The Lark* by J. Anouilh, Th. Montparnasse, 1953.

492

493

494

Dramatic theater provides us with fewer examples of such systematic collaboration. For example, look at the work of Jean Louis Barrault, who tried to create a 'total theater' in his stagings, which were very much inspired by Claudel. Because not many directors have chosen a more eclectic repertory, his selection of stage designers has also been quite varied, including well known 'decorators-illustrators' such as Malcles, Wakhevitch and Jacques Noel, and painters with very different temperaments, some like Labisse and Masson have worked with Barrault from the beginning.

More typical is the work of Jean Vilar, director of the T.N.P. and Avignon Festival. A number of painters have, of course, worked with him, notably Singier, Prassinos and Pignon; but, if the artist/director association achieved importance, it was largely because of the fortunate encounter between two men who understood each other perfectly, Vilar and Leon Gischia. Vilar broke away from the commercial and mundane Parisian theater, and established a theater for the masses in Avignon which was called a 'theater-festival,' an appellation much misused since then. Convinced that the time had come for more fruitful joint efforts between the director and modern artist, Gischia intended to find out whether his pictorial pursuits were valid in the theater. In one of the first festivals in Avignon he explained how he regarded his role: "The essential role of the painter in the theater, as in front of his easel, is to combine forms and colors according to their internal logical development, a dialectic which is valid in itself and not just in relation to the play being presented. In short, it is a question of combining plastic and dramatic values to form a harmonious synthesis, one which has not previously existed." However, the aesthetics of the T.N.P. — what some have called its 'rhetoric' — has an importance beyond the special problems of the artist-director collaboration, an issue which I shall refer to later.

The relationship between painting, sculpture and architecture on the one hand, and stage design on the other, is indirect perhaps but quite rich and very complex. Within the context of the general evolution of a particular civilization and its sensibilities, the arts furnish an example of the constant exchange among their means of expression, materials and technical processes. While the art galleries offer a whole range of styles and artistic ventures (musical and geometrical abstractions, pop art, etc.), a number of stage designers, whether consciously or not, have

495. F. Labisse, *The Trial* based on F. Kafka's novel, dir. J.L. Barrault, Paris. Th. Marigny, 1947. Phot. Bernand. 496. F. Labisse, *Nights of Wrath* by A. Salacrou, Dir. J.L. Barrault, Paris, Th. Marigny, 1946. Lipnitzki Arch. "A designer should not be chosen for his own style, but for his ability to serve the text. The problem of theatrical decor is not one of either decoration or documentation; it is a problem of culture." (F. Labisse).

495

496

497

498

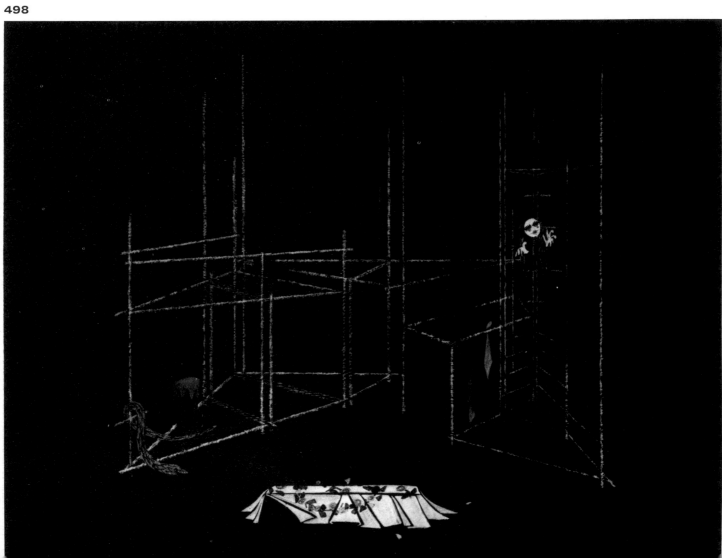

499

497. A. Masson, *The Golden Head* by P. Claudel, dir. J. L. Barrault, Paris, Odeon Th., France, 1960. Doc. Kunstgew. Mus. Zurich. **498, 499.** A. Acquart, *The Blacks* by J. Genet, dir. R. Blin, Paris, Th. de Lutece, 1959. **498.** Sketch of the arrangement; linear and transparent architecture. Bibl. Arsenal, Paris. Phot. P. Willi. **499.** Mask for the white woman. Phot. A. Acquart.

transplanted various elements from these styles into their stage experiences, using them as so many terms for a stage language to address today's audience. Teo Otto has stated that "the artist must be open to all kinds of suggestions, from impressions of nature to the purest abstractions. Even naturalism, which has its limitations as a general approach, can be very useful. In the same way, abstraction can be an excellent means of expression, but can destroy art if it is permitted to become a rigorous theory." At a time when the sculptor's range of materials is constantly being enriched by metals, plastics, plexiglass, etc. so that he can shape empty space with linear structures, it is not by chance that Andre Acquart's setting for *The Blacks* (by Jean Genet) seems to us like an iron-wire piece of sculpture on stage. Contemporary architecture presents us with almost intangible spaces that our eyes can peruse at leisure, transparent constructions in which the interior and exterior are visible simultaneously. How many settings during the last twenty years have played with the

500

501

500. H.U. Schmuckle, *Robespierre* by R. Rolland, dir. E. Pisca-
tor, Berlin, Freie Volksbuhne, 1963. Phot. I. Buhs. 501. A.
Cardile, *Dirty Hands* by J.P. Sartre, dir. F. Piccoli, Bolzano and
Trento, 1963. Doc. Kunstgew. Mus. Zurich. 502. J. Kosinski,
The Dossier by T. Rosewicz, dir. W. Laskowska, Warsaw,
Dramatyczny Th. 1960. Phot. Zaiks. Three decors in different
styles; real collages.

possibility of revealing a number of different spaces all at once to the spectator? For example, a hotel room and the background of the city in which it is located. Walls have become skeletal outlines or simply transparent; limits have been shattered. The audience may discover a composite place in which "here" and "elsewhere" are skillfully combined in a dialectical relationship that is intended to bring out and enrich the meaning of the play. Finally, at a time when the art of collage is imposing its laws, some settings, like those of Schmuckle for Piscator and Cardile for Sartre's *Dirty Hands* look like real collages, as they merge, join and juxtapose images belonging to different worlds.

WHERE POLITICS INTERVENE

In evaluating the developments and tendencies in stage design over the last thirty years, political and economic considerations should be taken into account. Obviously, theatrical history has not been closely related to past political events. Yet, while wars have not necessarily brought artistic endeavors to a halt, they certainly have influenced the life of the arts. Moreover, stage design in

283

502

503

particular, has never been entirely independent from ideologies and political regimes; quite the contrary. During the Nazi era, for example, the official style in Germany was monumentalism, the triumph of an academicism that despised the "degenerate arts." When the shock of the second world war wore off, it is understandable why a number of German designers returned to the expressionist style of the Twenties, even though in many respects that style seemed old-fashioned to them. Elsewhere, between 1948 and 1955, a costly and somewhat pompous version of naturalism was prevalent in the theaters of most Eastern European socialist states including the Soviet Union, where Zhdanovian 'socialist realism' was imposed on all artistic works, and may be regarded as another protuberance of Stalinism. But, very soon thereafter, this style was contested and replaced, especially in countries like Czechoslovakia and Poland, which are today in the vanguard of experimental scenography. Even in the Soviet Union stage design has been evolving, as prominent designers there rediscover the experiments of Meyerhold, Tairov and Vakhtangov. At times their return to the past has brought confusion, but it has also been the source of some remarkable accomplishments, notably those of the Na

Taganke Theater of Moscow and the works of Sumbatashvili.

Economics also play an important part. The enormous variety of contemporary productions is clearly related to the way money is allocated. While one theater, subsidized by the government, may spend large sums on sets, another designer has to make poverty a virtue. It often happens that wealth becomes a poor advisor, and that indeed poverty is the mother of invention, as in the case of a group like the Bread and Puppet Theater. The successes of the Berliner Ensemble and the Piccolo Teatro of Milan, however, should also be a reminder that in enterprises on a large scale, heavy financial backing can sometimes make more serious theatrical experimentation possible. Money traps only those who permit themselves to become ensnared.

Against Geography

Geographic differences account for very little of the great diversity of scenographic approaches. Some countries, of course, are especially active as far as experimenting goes. Others have strong, local traditions and exhibit special characteristics, so that there,

504

505

506

503. J. Sumbatasvili, *The Death of Ivan the Terrible* by A. Tolstoy, dir. L. Kheifits, Moscow, Th. C.T.S.A., 1966. Phot. Sochurek Vilem. **504.** A. Stopka, *The Story of the Glorious Resurrection of Our Lord,* dir. K. Dejmek, Warsaw, National Th., 1962. Phot. Zaiks. **505.** Z. Strzelecki, *Agamemnon* by Aeschylus, dir. K. Dejmek, Warsaw, National Th., 1963. Phot. Zaiks. **506.** Z. Strzelecki, *The Frogs* by Aristophanes, dir. K. Dejmek, Warsaw, National Th., 1963. Phot. Zaiks.

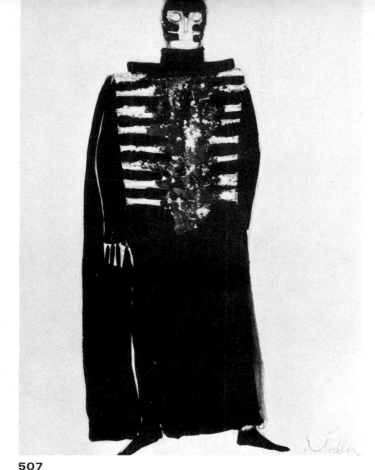

507

507, 508. Z. Wierchowicz, sketches of costumes for *Richard III* by W. Shakespeare, dir. J. Maciejowski, Szczecin, Wspolczesny, Th., 1967. Phot. Turski.

508

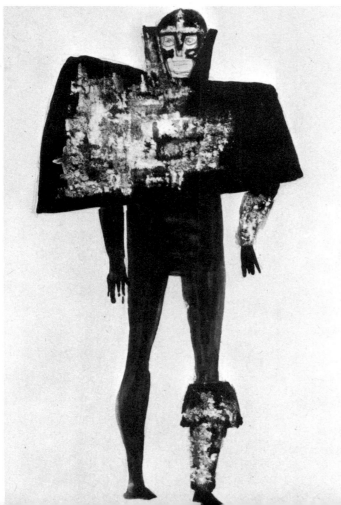

it is almost possible to speak of a national school of theatrical design. Think of the Polish pictorial style which shows a distinct predilection for folklore and inspiration from the common people. Strzelecki, an historian of Polish stage design and himself a designer calls this "persiflage," that is, the self-conscious, slightly ironic use of formulas from the past (such as the simultaneous 'mansions' of the medieval theater, stylized painted backdrops, etc.). Selective realism also comes to mind, as more or less practiced by the Berliner Ensemble of East Germany. Nevertheless, the last thirty years testify to a kind of internationalization, if not uniformity of approaches, an increasingly wider diffusion of new forms in scenography, all of which has led to a number of similarities among designers from countries geographically far apart.

The first two Quadrennials of Scenography in Prague (1967 and 1971) demonstrate this rapprochement. It can no longer be maintained that the most interesting experiments in stage design occur in just a few European countries, and that others subsequently follow that innovation. One of the most interesting designers whose work was shown in 1967 was a young Brazilian, Flavio Imperio, who used the open stage and arena theater in an entirely original way. The 1971 Quadrennial presented the works of another young Brazilian, Eichbauer. He had assimilated the lessons of the Czech designer Svoboda, yet his style was unique, based on an architectural rigor and formal purity. What is apparent is that currents exist and different experiments are taking place, neither of which has anything to do with the political boundaries of nations.

From the Past to the Present

Contemporary theater often contests and challenges some of the forms, but does not completely break away from the past. In fact, in some cases old approaches are extended or repeated. But, thanks to progress in technology, today's theater attempts to realize what might have been formerly only a visionary idea or utopian dream.

Over and over in modern productions one finds the influence, or simply the implicit presence, of those principles that were cherished by reformers around the turn of the century. Since 1951 at the "New Bayreuth," the grandsons of Richard Wagner have tried to translate the elder Wagner's works into a modern idiom, using new techniques and

509. J. Kosinski, *Oedipus-Rex* by I. Stravinsky, dir. K. Swinarski, Warsaw Opera, 1962. Phot. Myszkowski.

510

510. H.U. Schmuckle, *The Officers* by H.H. Kirst and E. Piscator, dir. E. Piscator, Berlin, Freie Volksbuhne, 1966. Inst. Th. Cologne. Phot. Furtinger. The Piscator of the Sixties did not renounce the Piscator of the Twenties. Schmuckle's arrangement for *The Officers* resembles the one Traugott Muller devised for *Rasputin.*

511

511, 512. H. Monloup, *Public chant before two electric chairs* by A. Gatti, dir. A. Gatti, Paris, T.N.P., 1961. The playwright devised an arrangement that exploded the scenic space.

512

scenic means that reflect contemporary art. While Wieland and Wolfgang Wagner realized many of Appia's conceptions, in some sense they went beyond the symbolic "illusion" in which Appia, in spite of everything he did, was caught. Their precursors were evidently various directors and designers from the German theater of the Twenties.

Jessner, Meyerhold and Piscator all strongly marked the development of modern theater. It should be noted that the Piscator of the Sixties did not disown the Piscator of the Twenties. On the contrary, the scenic design of *The Officers,* due to Schmuckle, closely resembled the global stage arrangement for *Rasputin.* The scenographic themes that reoccurred in these later stagings point

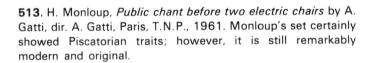

513. H. Monloup, *Public chant before two electric chairs* by A. Gatti, dir. A. Gatti, Paris, T.N.P., 1961. Monloup's set certainly showed Piscatorian traits; however, it is still remarkably modern and original.

out Piscator's permanent and underlying struggles.

Piscator's ideals and methods, however, go beyond the personality of their promoter. (Cf. Hubert Monloup's remarkable decor for *The Public Chant Before Two Electric Chairs*). Looking at the works of one of the masters of contemporary stage design, the Czech Josef Svoboda, inevitably brings to mind Craig or Appia, sometimes Piscator and the Russian Constructivists, or even some of Burian's productions. In no way does this diminish the originality of Svoboda's contributions. It simply proves that innovations do not mask the continuity of history; further, it suggests that our epoch is one of research, exploitation, assimilation, and why not admit it — of vul-

garization of the past. The result is the existing confusion and difficulty when we try to understand contemporary stage design.

The case is the same with regard to certain theatrical desires. Many theoreticians and directors continue to dream of a "total" theater. While some ventures are thoroughly original, the conceptions of these artists indicate that they are really the heirs of Wagner. Consciously or not, they reinvent the notion of the Gesamtkunstwerk, and the visions of Craig, or perhaps of Antonin Artaud. The productions of the last thirty years demonstrate that the best directors seek more than ever to give their works a perfect unity, to fuse language, acting, music, decor and lighting into an intimate union.

514

515

514, 515. L. Ciulei, *Viteazul* by P. Anghel, Teatrul de Nord, 1970. Two different arrangements of the kinetic elements.
516. F. Mertz, *Oedipus Rex* by Sophocles, dir. G. R. Sellner, Darmstadt, Landestheater, 1952. Doc. Kunstgew. Mus. Zurich. The presence of the tragic space: the chorus, shadow and light.

516

same ideals. The decorator is certainly not the "supplier" he was at the end of the nineteenth century. In our present vital theater, he is, along with the author and director, one of the co-producers of the play. Often it is impossible to distinguish between what is due to the director and what has been contributed by the scenographer. But, in the final analysis, the designer is responsible for what Josef Svoboda called with some justification, "the plastic staging of the drama," for it is he who determines the visual style; for instance, for many years Giorgio Strehler's approach was closely identified with some of Luciano Damiani's best creations.

THE BATTLE WITH SPACE

The tendency has been to make scenography part of a total audio-visual picture that exerts an impact on the spectator. Since the beginning of the twentieth century its very function has undergone a singular evolution which has been even more accentuated over the last twenty years. Using the French word 'decor' is convenient because language habits are deeply ingrained, but it is an outdated term, with whose pronouncement we associate display, pomp and ornamentation. Today, primarily in the field of drama, but also in that of ballet and opera, decor has lost its strictly decorative function. The decorator's task is no longer to adorn, embellish or create the setting for the play. Beyond stylistic differences, contemporary decor has become an interpreter of the drama, an actor communicating a message to the spectator, as it simultaneously acts directly or indirectly on his sensibilities. Of course, the set may still pinpoint or evoke the place of the action, or participate in the creation of that "feast for the eyes," required by some genres. But above all the decor embodies, enacts, emphasizes and reveals the dramatic significance of the work.

Creating the scenic space satisfies the first requisite for dramatic action. Designers like Mertz, Neher, Gischia, Svoboda, Koltai, John Bury, Sean Kenny and Acquart, in agreement with their respective directors, conceive of a place where the drama can breathe, an organized space that is adapted to the needs of the play, the staging, the actors and the public. They fashion a platform, mark off playing areas, create scaffolded levels, trace the axes and organize walkways. In short, they erect a scenic architecture in which every element is not only in-

FROM THE DEMIURGE TO THE COLLECTIVE WORK

The first decades of our century offer examples of men capable of both directing and designing their productions: Craig, Appia and Pitoeff among them. Such examples increased after the second world war: Wieland Wagner, Peter Brook, Visconti, Swinarski, Szajna, Zeffirelli, Ciulei to cite only the most famous, keeping in mind, however, that the phenomena still remains relatively rare.

There is yet another way to achieve perfect unity, namely, collective effort. During the interval between the two wars, repertories were formed around a designer and director who worked in close collaboration: Pirchan-Jessner, Berard-Jouvet, Pronaszko-Schiller, and Neher-Brecht are but a few. After 1945 this practice became much more widespread. Vilar-Gischia, Planchon-Allio, Felsenstein-Heinrich, Sellner-Mertz, Kazan-Mielziner, Krejca-Svoboda, Strehler-Damiani are some of the director-designer pairs who have profoundly influenced the theatrical activities of the last few years. In effect, there have been no major productions that have not been the consequence of the concerted efforts of a group animated by the

dispensable but emphasizes the meaning of the player's slightest gesture. Indeed they are the creators of space!

Consequently, many designers prefer the term "scenographer," which is used throughout Central Europe. Forbidding as the word seems, it is well defined etymologically: "The one who designs the scene." It is also clear why some German designers object to the word "Buhnenbild," the German equivalent of decor, but whose exact translation would be "scenic picture." They prefer to think of themselves as creators of "Buhnenraum," of "stage space," which explains the title of this chapter: "Thirty Years of Scenography."

The stage space is therefore constructed, organized, and more or less charged with realistic or abstract, descriptive, symbolic or parodic elements. Of course, there are sets that still rather ponderously 'reproduce' a real or imaginary universe, but the general tendency is to allude to and indicate by means of carefully selected signs. Whether a scenographer tries to touch the public's sensibilities or reach his intelligence, the viewer's imagination must be taken into account. The spectator almost unconsciously reconstructs the complete world of the dramatic action out of a combination of disjointed elements (furniture, decorative flats, slide projections, etc.). In the majority of cases, the art of modern decor tends to be

292

517

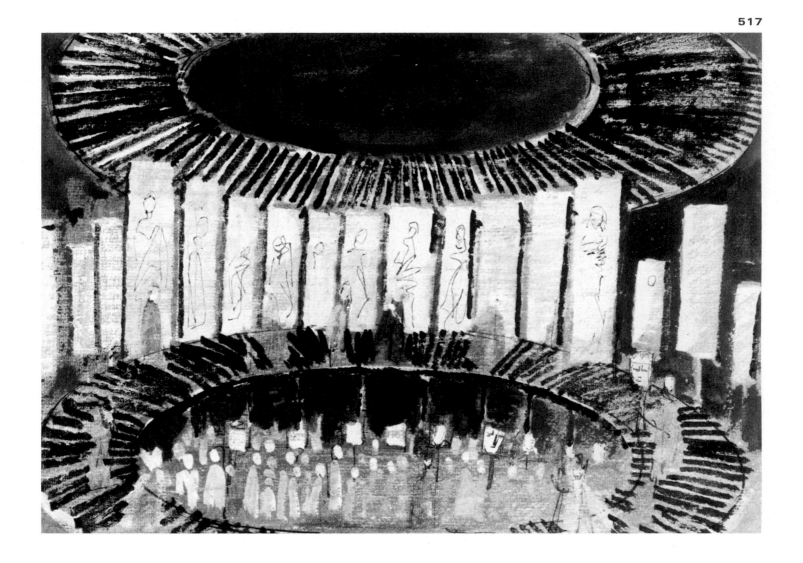

293

518

519

517. C. Neher, *Oedipus Rex* by I. Stravinsky, dir. O. F. Schuh, Vienna Opera, 1958, Inst. Th. Cologne. 518. R. Koltai, *Back to Methuselah* by G.B. Shaw, dir. C. Williams, London, National Th., 1969. The tree of knowledge. Phot. Imperial Chemical Industries. 519. R. Koltai, *As You Like It* by W. Shakespeare, dir. C. Williams, London, National Th., 1969. Phot. Dominic.

discontinuous, the spectator having the same relationship to the performance as he would have to a Cubist painting.

This conception explains the vogue for complex "scenic arrangements." A single structure to which temporary elements are added permits the different phases of the dramatic action to be played while the temporal progression and underlying unity of the play are respected.

In France, the true promoters of intricate "scenic arrangements" were the Festival of Avignon and the T.N.P., two enterprises which exerted an enormous impact on the artistic and sociological life of the French theater. Their influence extended into other countries as well, and cannot be emphasized too strongly.

520

520. J. Bury, *Hamlet,* by W. Shakespeare, dir. P. Hall, Stratford-on-Avon, Royal Shakespeare Theatre, 1965. Phot. Holte. 521. In the Cour d'Honneur of the Palace of the Popes, the first stage of the Festival of Avignon; grill work for the *Cid.* Photographed in 1949 by A. Varda. 522. *The Cid* in an enclosed auditorium, scenic elements by L. Gischia, 1951. Phot. A. Varda. "We offer a bare stage — no trifles, no aesthetic tricks." (J. Vilar).

In 1951 Jean Vilar took over the direction of the T.N.P. "In these anxious, divided times," he wrote, "it is not only important to bring men and women of all political and religious beliefs together . . . there is also our permanent concern to do good, and to do so for a public deprived of joys. For our spectator, wherever he may be, we offer a bare stage — without trifles, aesthetic tricks or decor. Love and the honor of man will uniquely adorn this pine wood platform where tomorrow will gush forth the raptures, the swearing of a pimp or the emotions of the rapacious personality." Like a distant echo some forty years later, these words recall Jacques Copeau's manifesto. Vilar's statement confirmed, with great brio and force, the principles enunciated at the first Festival of Avignon in 1947. His ambition was to direct and not simply stage. He refused the tricks of the cubist decorator, his effects and machinery. Likewise, he rejected the Italian stage because he thought it was imperative to establish direct, efficacious and live contact between the public and the play.

521

295

522

523

524

523, 524. Costumes for *Murder in the Cathedral* by T.S. Eliot, dir. J. Vilar, Paris. Th. du Vieux-Colombier, 1945. J. Vilar Coll. Phot. P. Willi. 525, 526. L. Gischia, costumes for *The Cid,* dir. J. Vilar, J. Vilar Coll. Phot. P. Willi. 525. Costume created in 1951 for a new production of *The Cid* at the T.N.P. with G. Philipe cast in the role of Rodrigue. 526. Costume created in 1949 for the first production at the Festival of Avignon.

525

526

527-530. L. Gischia, costumes for *The Prince of Homburg,* by H. von Kleist, dir. J. Vilar, Avignon, 1951. J. Vilar Coll. Phot. P. Willi.

527

528

529

530

The first festival, in the Cour d'Honneur of the Palace of the Popes, presented a rudimentary, bare geometric stage, consisting of a rectangular platform, backed by a rear wall and preceded by a sloping bridge. As the stage was further adapted to the individual play, the geometry was made even more precise, with patterns of curved and straight lines on the floor, structures out of superimposed surfaces or inclined planes, and strictly delineated playing areas where the lighting was intensified or reduced at will. Leon Gischia described this kind of stage as a "ring" rising up out of the night. During the performance, although the back wall was lost in shadow, its presence could be felt. Once, for *Mary Tudor,* Vilar permitted the effects of projected light and shadow, but Vilar was known not to illuminate historic monuments. Gischia knew that the spatial conception of the stage, in relation to the action, had to be organized in a way that altered traditional spatial perspectives. After they moved to Chaillot, both the director and painter practiced the principles developed in Avignon. An exact reproduction of their Avignon 'dispositif' was impossible, but a good approximation of it was not out of reach. The curtain and footlights were discarded, and a large proscenium about fifty nine feet wide was installed. The proscenium arch, however, was eliminated, leaving the platform in full view of the public. In the background there were often black hangings, which made the colors of the costumes stand out and formed an impalpable space, a no man's land out of which the actors rose up and entered the spotlighted zone of action. The actor appeared on a set that was designed to clarify his gestures, relationships, tensions and liaisons with the other players.

It was not a matter of decor, but as the posters stated, of "scenic elements," parcimoniously chosen and combined for their suggestive value. The most minor prop spoke to the public. "Its importance is, in effect, very great," declared Leon Gischia. "A coat of a specific color thrown on a chair can evoke many things, both plastically and psychologically at the same time. At that point decoration and staging meet. A flag in the *Prince of Homburg* is as important as a costume, suggesting plastically what the text inspired in me. The *oriflammes* of *Lorenzaccio* give the play a special atmosphere. Above all, it is a question of restoring the ceremonial aspect to theater, thereby creating a state of grace, which in my opinion, relates to its very function. And that is more important than the questions of real-

531. C. Demangeat, arrangement for *Don Juan* by Moliere, dir. J. Vilar, costumes by L. Gischia, Festival of Avignon, 1953. Phot. A. Varda. For Moliere, Shakespeare or Kleist, the stage is like "a ring" . . . (L. Gischia). 532. L. Gischia, *Marie Tudor* by V. Hugo, dir. J. Vilar, Festival of Avignon, 1955. Phot. A. Varda.

531
532

ism or non-realism, which are, it must be said, no more than the means... The shed of a cloth merchant suggests the whole fair; a chair should not be an object but the sign of an object; a throne on the stage ought not to be a real throne, but the suggestion of the concept of a throne. These elements function in relation to the actor. Once again, nothing should be gratuitous."

When there was apparently a decor, as in *Ruy Blas,* it was merely a background reduced to its elementary geometry, which required the public to participate actively, to penetrate "behind the curtain" and imagine all of the facets of the scenic universe at the same time. In short, starting with some elements that served as signs, the spectator was meant to recreate the dramatic space in his own mind. This was the aesthetic principle behind the greatest successes of Jean Vilar's T.N.P.: *Richard II, The Cid, Don Juan, Lorenzaccio, The Prince of Homburg* and *The Alcade of Zalamea,* among many others.

But that aesthetic would not have been effective without the imaginative use of two fundamental means of expression — color and light. In spite of the enormous distances that sometimes separated the actor from the spectator, color made him visible. Color was also adapted to suit the psychological make-up of the character and was integrated with the many different tonalities that expressed the drama. As for lighting, it created both the space (a single beam of light without any wall to mark a boundary was enough to evoke Richard's prison), and the atmospheres and places (a few patches of light on the floor suggested the forest for *Don Juan).* At the same time it compelled the spectator to focus his attention on the dramatic action, tensions and rhythms of the play.

A 'scenic arrangement' was therefore built on the stage standing out against a neutral or evocative background. It was an independent spatial structure that might have one or several related playing areas that were temporarily qualified by furniture, secondary elements, accessories or the action itself: settings by Andre Acquart for *A Faceless Banker, The Devil and the Good Lord, The Resistible Rise of Arturo Ui,* by Frank Schultes for *William Tell,* Heinrich Kilger and Thomas Richter-Forgach for *King Lear,* Ming Chow Lee for *Richard III, Peer Gynt* and *Electra.* Or the "arrangement" could be a single structure divided into multiple compartments, as in Ryndin's *Hamlet,* Raffaelli's *America,* or the Living Theater's *Frankenstein.* Another "arrangement" could be a structure capable of being taken apart or re-

300

533, 534. M. Prassinos, *Macbeth* by W. Shakespeare, dir. J. Vilar, Festival of Avignon, 1954. Phot. A. Varda. **533.** Sketch of a costume for Macbeth. **534.** Jean Vilar as Macbeth.

533

534

535. L. Gischia, *Thomas More, A Man for all Seasons,* by R. Bolt, sketch of the arrangement, dir. J. Vilar, T.N.P. 1963. J. Vilar Coll. Phot. P. Willi. Last production staged by Vilar at the T.N.P. His conception of space is similar to one in his first works; a geometry designed to clarify the movements and rapports between the characters, tensions and liaisons which are the heartbeat of the play.

536

536. L. Gischia, *Le Triomphe de l'amour* by Marivaux, dir. J. Vilar, T.N.P., 1955. Phot. A. Varda.

537

537. A. Acquart, *Troilus and Cressida* by W. Shakespeare, dir. R. Planchon, Paris, Odeon Th., France, Repertory of Th. de la Cite in Villeurbanne, 1964. Phot. A. Acquart. 538. A. Acquart, *The Screens* by J. Genet, dir. R. Blin, Paris, Odeon Th., France, 1966. Phot. A. Acquart.

538

539. A. Acquart, *Troilus and Cressida* by W. Shakespeare, dir. R. Planchon, Paris, Odeon Th., France, Repertory of the Th. de la Cite in Villeurbanne, 1964. The set basically consists of moving panels which come apart and are brought together in a rhythmical pattern, as one scene follows another. The panel arrangement creates the places; and by its movement, participates directly in the expression of the drama.

539

540

541

constructed according to the requirements of the action and its more or less symbolist representation; recall the architectural arrangement by Wolfgang Wagner, which contained abstract projections on a cycloramic background for *The Tetralogy,* or Andre Acquart's set for *The Screens* by Jean Genet. The arrangement could also be mobile, involving simple movement, like the revolving stage Busslaev erected for Vishnevsky's *Optimistic Tragedy* in which the spectators could see the successive scenes corresponding to different phases of the dramatic action. More complex movements occurred in the sets of Josef Svoboda, who was a fervent artisan of an essentially kinetic stage, where movement contributed to dramatic expressiveness. In his architectures for *Hamlet, Romeo and Juliet* or *Il Trovatore,* the same elements that were decomposed and recombined before the audience created the successive places of the action, and, by their mobility, accompanied the dramatic progression in a rhythm that acted on the spectator's sensibilities like a musical fluid. Each scene called forth the next in keeping with an apparent variation of the structure.

Finally another kind of "arrangement" was one which involved a container-like structure, as Neher's copper walls for *The Life of Galileo,* or Allio's geographic maps for *Henry IV,* or Karl von Appen's circus tent for *The Resistible Rise of Arturo Ui.* In Appen's set, elements that were lightly colored made the places of the action more precise and at the same time brought out their socio-historical meaning.

542

543

540. A. Acquart, *The Resistible Rise of Arturo Ui* by B. Brecht, dir. G. Wilson, Paris, T.N.P., 1969. Phot. A. Acquart. **541.** Th. Richter-Forgach, *King Lear* by Shakespeare, dir. Kai Brook, Kassel, Staatstheater, 1966. Inst. Th. Cologne. **542.** Ming Cho Lee, *Electra* by Sophocles, dir. G. Freedman, New York Shakespeare Festival, 1964. Phot. N. Rabin. **543.** Ming Cho Lee, *Peer Gynt* by H. Ibsen, dir. G. Freedman, New York Shakespeare Festival, 1969. Phot. N. Rabin.

544

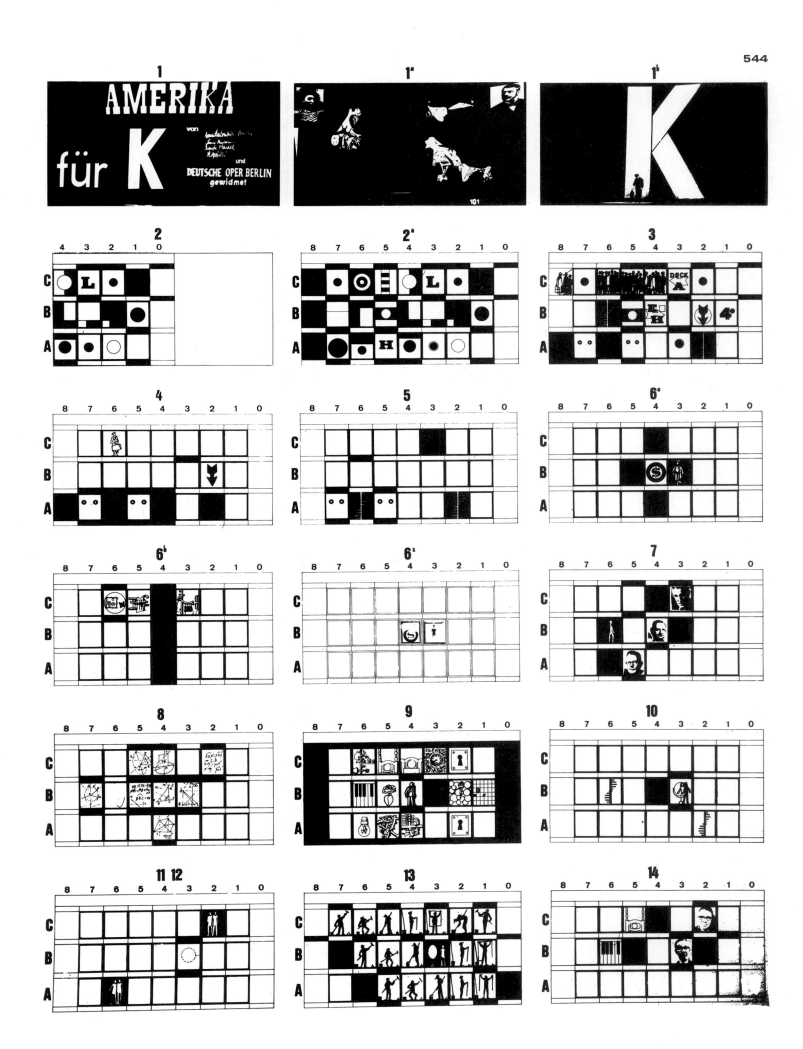

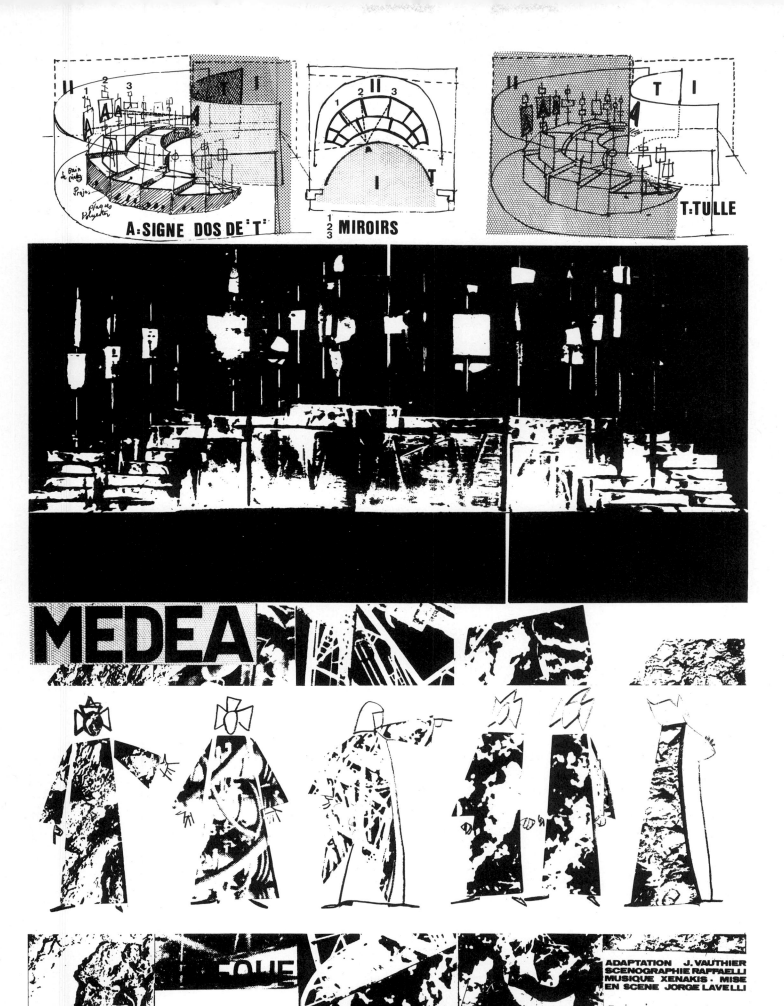

A:SIGNE DOS DE "T"

MIROIRS

T:TULLE

MEDEA

ADAPTATION J. VAUTHIER
SCENOGRAPHIE RAFFAELLI
MUSIQUE XENAKIS · MISE
EN SCENE JORGE LAVELLI

FESTIVAL INTERNATIONAL D'ART
CONTEMPORAIN ROYAN_1967

545

545. M. Raffaelli, *Medea* by Seneca, dir. J. Lavelli, Royan Festival, 1967. For *Medea's* costumes, "I used photomechanical techniques and the silk screen process to create the impressions." (M. Raffaelli).

546 a

546 b

546 c

546. a,b,c. J. Svoboda, *Hamlet* by Shakespeare, dir. O. Krejca, Brussels, Th. National de Belgique, 1965. A trap arrangement in which the moving elements shift more or less towards the spectators and are reflected in a large mirror which dominates the stage at a 45° angle. Interplay of the mirror and double images.

FACING REALITIES

The role of the designer was defined by Rene Allio as follows: "To invent a sort of visual language for each play, that within a chosen expressive style, underscores its various meanings, extending and echoing them, sometimes in a precise and almost critical way, sometimes more diffusely and subtly in the manner of a poetic image where fortuitous meanings are no less important than those that are sought." Cast the world in a certain perspective, transmit a particular vision using definite artistic means that have been adapted to the theatrical work as well as to the designer's conception of it — this too is his task. The diversity of visions, perspectives and means explains the variety of styles.

Mention has already been made of the number of conflicting styles offered on today's stage. Two distinct currents, however, each with many variations, can be discerned: on the one hand, a tendency towards abstraction; on the other, a multi-faceted realism. Their opposition recalls the unending confrontations between symbolism and

547

547. Wieland Wagner, *Tannhauser* by R. Wagner, dir. Wieland Wagner, Festspielhaus Bayreuth, 1965. Doc. Festspiele Bayreuth. Phot. W. Rauh.

naturalism that took place in the Nineties.

Abstraction, as a theatrical style, can be an interplay of forms, materials and colors. Or it may also express a distinct conception of man and his destiny — metaphysical or contemplative man, or the mythical hero; and the set might be an abstract universe where forms, colors and lights are like many symbolic signs and metaphorical elements addressing our sensibilities. In 1972, when Wieland Wagner died, the Bayreuth theater received crossfire from many critics. In the Fifties and Sixties, with the efforts of Wolfgang and even more of Wieland Wagner, the elder Wagner's works were subjected to a true renovation. One day Lothar Schreyer wrote: "The scenic art, like any other, is symbolic, that is, the work of art in its material form expresses a spiritual reality. This is possible because of the expressive value of the means of representation in each work, each of these means taken independently in its turn, as an expressive value ... Light is the creator of colored images. It brings out color. It is *the* means to change physical reality into

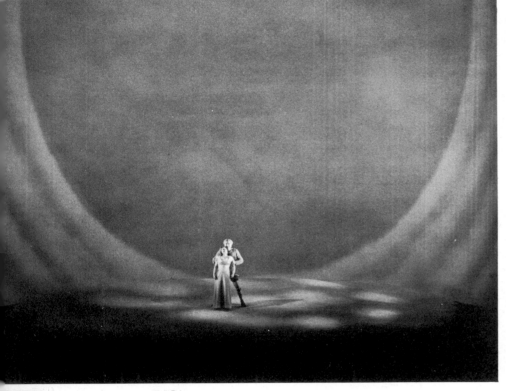

548
549

548. Wieland Wagner, *Siegfried* by R. Wagner, dir. Wieland Wagner, Festspielhaus Bayreuth, 1951. **549.** Wieland Wagner, *The Valkyrie* by R. Wagner, dir. Wieland Wagner, Festspielhaus Bayreuth, 1951. **550.** Wieland Wagner, *Parsifal* by R. Wagner, dir. Wieland Wagner, Festspielhaus Bayreuth, 1959. 548-550. Doc. Festspiele Bayreuth. Phot. Lauterwasser.

550

a moral ideal." Schreyer's text could serve as a commentary to many of the productions of Wagner's grandsons.

The theater at Bayreuth is not an area shaped out of a space that extends beyond the stage. Nor is it a space logically organized by scenery which is disposed of according to naturalist conventions. It is a limited playing area, often disc-shaped, surrounded by an abstract no-man's land, a precisely defined place that stands out against a somewhat vague, almost immaterial, and at times, evocative background. It is a space created and given value by light, which at each dramatic moment, confers tonality and "Stimmung" on it. While Wieland Wagner's production of the romantic tragedy, *The Flying Dutchman* can be considered in the realistic vein tinged with expressionistic elements, *Parsifal* reaffirmed the designer's taste for abstraction, which was also his style for the *Tetralogy, Tristan and Isolde* and *Tannhauser*. Two worlds confronted one another in *Tannhauser:* Venusberg, abstract symbol of physical love, and the Christian world. The first was suggested by an immense, dark and indefinite space, half-animal, half-vegetable, a spongy form that descended from the flies and dominated the stage. For the second, Wieland Wagner arranged an entirely gilded space, that with variations in lighting and a few special props, evoked the places in the drama. That space was none other than the symbol of medieval Christianity, the gold background of primitive painters.

551

551. Wolfgang Wagner, *The Valkyrie* by R. Wagner, dir. Wolfgang Wagner, Festspielhaus Bayreuth, 1960. Doc. Festspiele Bayreuth. Phot. Rauh. **552.** Wieland Wagner, *Tristan and Isolde* by R. Wagner, dir. Wieland Wagner, Festspielhaus Bayreuth, 1962. Doc. Festspiele Bayreuth. Phot. Lauterwasser.

552

553. J. Szajna, *They (Oni)* by S.I. Witkiewicz, dir. J. Szajna, Cracow, Teatr Kameralny, 1968. Phot. Plewinski. **554**. C. Neher, *In the Jungle of Cities* by B. Brecht, dir. E. Engel, Munich, Residenztheater, 1923. Inst. Th. Cologne. **555**. J. Szajna, *The Inspector General* by N. Gogol, Cracow, Nowa Huta Th., 1966. Sketch made in 1963. Doc. Kunstgew. Mus. Zurich. **556**. J. Szajna, *Regarding November* by E. Bryll, dir. J. Szajna, Katowice, Wyspianski Th., 1969. Phot. Z. Lagocki.

555

556

The abstract style can also transmit the anguish man feels in a dangerous world over which he has no control. Such an example is the surrealist universe created by the Pole Szajna, which consisted of highly original forms and numerous objects that the designer had invade the stage. Didn't this staging imply our civilization is becoming more and more artificial, as objects assume an increasingly oppressive reality?

What has been his portrayal of man? As either crushed by historical events or completely outside of any historical framework. At another extreme, man is shown as part of history, the stage representation of which requires a realistic vision of the world.

Photographic verism has virtually disappeared except from boulevard or Broadway type of theaters, and even there it is often only an anecdotal sort of realism. Variations of a more or less stylized realism have replaced older forms. Neo-Realism, as it is sometimes called, has been properly described by Strzelecki as "super-naturalism," for it is essentially psychological, creating an atmosphere for the dramatic action out of an intentionally incomplete picture of reality (cf. Jo Mielziner's sets for *Death of a Salesman*). Seeking unusual and strange forms of expression, this style is particularly suited to such contemporary dramatists as Mrozek. Reality is evoked in certain characteristic ways. Elements, taken from the

real world confer a critical or satirical aspect on the play, sometimes because of the way the elements are strangely related to one another, and sometimes through the passionate and violent nature of the means and materials employed.

One form of realism has significantly marked the theater of the last twenty years, that is the selective realism of epic theater with its modes of expression progressively developed by Bertolt Brecht and his designers, Caspar Neher, Teo Otto and Karl von Appen. Although he worked on a vast repertory, over five hundred productions, Caspar Neher was the first to collaborate with Brecht and elaborate the principal scenographic methods of the Brechtian style. Teo Otto's contributions were decisive at the time of the creation of *Mother Courage,* while Karl von Appen was the pillar of the Berliner Ensemble in all scenographic matters.

Brecht intended in his works to make people conscious of the world and of the possibilities they have to change it. It is a theater that, first of all, addresses itself to our intelligence, because its purpose is to convince and not cast a spell. It is a theater that uses all necessary scenic means of expression, but refuses the Wagnerian concept of the "total work of art."

In 1930 Brecht wrote: "So long as the "total work of art" is seen as a homogeneous mixture of diverse elements, as long as

557

558

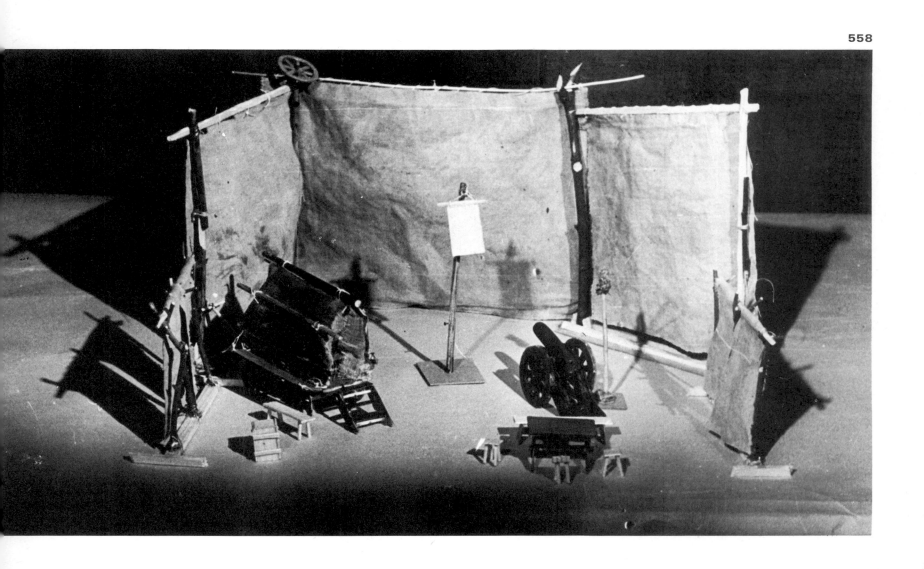

the arts are supposed to be united, the various elements will all be equally shaded, and each will only echo the others and convey the same impressions. Furthermore, the process of fusion extends to the spectator, who gets 'integrated' into the melting pot and becomes a passive (suffering) part of the total work of art. Magic of this sort should be destroyed, as well as whatever produces hypnotic effects, sordid intoxication and foggy minds.''

In 1947 Brecht further clarified his ideas: "The main task of the theater is the exposition of the story, to be communicated by using the appropriate means of 'distancing' (alienation) the spectator from the play. And although nothing may be done without the actor, not everything depends on him. The 'story' is presented, developed and exposed by the entire theater — the actors, stage designers, make-up artists, costumers, composers and choreographers — each one contributing his talents to the joint undertaking without giving up his independence.''

All characteristics of Brechtian theater, especially its settings, stem from these convictions. Partisan of a theater of social reve-

557. J. Mielziner, *Death of a Salesman* by A. Miller, dir. E. Kazan, New York, Morosco Th., 1949. Psychological realism and poetic stylization. **558, 559.** T. Otto, Maquette for *Mother Courage* by B. Brecht, dir. L. Lindtberg, Zurich, Schauspielhaus, 1941. Berliner Ens. Arch., Phot. Paukschta (558, scene 3; 559, scene 11). The model of the set was part of the 1949 production at the Deutsches Theater of Berlin, dir. Brecht/Engel.

559

560

561

lation, Brecht denounced the traditional 'kitchen' type, together with the theaters of evasion and illusion. He believed, however, that theater ought not to hide the fact that it is theater; thus the invention of the Brechtian curtain, the half-curtain that appeared for the first time in the production of *A Man is a Man* at Darmstadt in 1926. The curtain concealed only the lower part of the stage, making it possible to see what was happening between scene changes and during the songs. The background, never illusionist, was neutral gray or almost white. This was not significant in itself, but Brecht used its abstract quality to limit the stage space and prevent the spectator's imagination from escaping; hence too, the compelling discontinuity among the scenic elements which never aimed at presenting an imitation of a real place but simply alluded to it.

Brecht's denial of illusion also engendered a condemnation of naturalism and the search for 'atmosphere', anything which might arouse spectator identification with the characters. The function of lighting is also clear. "We attach," wrote Karl von Appen, "great value to the possibility of control.

Everything on stage should be clearly recognizable to the public and under his control. He must be able to follow the story without impediments. Therefore, there is no need for darkness, chiaroscuro effects to create atmosphere, or partly illuminated actors. For us light is neither a means of creating moods, nor of *coloring* atmospheres. It is for us an objective means of clarification. A cold, even and clear lighting is our goal." There was nothing miraculous about this lighting; Brecht and his scenographers permitted its sources to be clearly visible.

Brecht rejected aesthetics as well, the notion of beauty for its own sake. He also opposed any spatial organization for the numerous practicables of the Stilbuhne, and the decorative or intense, symbolic use of color. If the designer had to suggest, his point of departure was to be neither painting nor construction, but "people," or as Brecht told Neher, their situations and their actions. Depicting the social behavior of people was the prime concern of the Brechtian designer in the sketches (arrangements) he composed, "the anatomy of the action stripped to the bone." When this first phase was completed, the designer could think of his sets or

562

563

318

562, 563. C. Neher, *The Life of Galileo* by B. Brecht, dir. E. Engel, Berlin, Berliner Ensemble, 1957. **562.** Sketch. Th. Samm. Vienna. **563.** Picture of the stage. Berliner Ens. Arch., Phot. Paukschta. A tiled floor and three red copper walls mark the playing space for all of the scenes.

564
565

564, 565. C. Neher, *The Life of Galileo* by B. Brecht, from the same production. 564. Sketch. Th. Samm. Vienna. 565. Picture of the stage. Berliner Ens. Arch., Phot. Paukschta. A few hanging elements, and some on the floor are enough to give the locale and surroundings, while the ''arrangement'' ''created by the scenographer'' reveals the anatomy of the action.''

566

567

568

569

566, 567, 569. K. von Appen, *Drums and Trumpets* based on a
play by G. Farquhar; Berliner Ensemble version, dir. B. Besson,
Berlin, Berliner Ensemble, 1955. 566, 567. Phot. Paukschta.

570

568, 570. K. von Appen, *The Caucasian Chalk Circle* by B.
Brecht, dir. B. Brecht, Berlin, Berliner Ensemble, 1954. A cyclo-
rama in pale or neutral tones exposed on a revolving stage. An
appropriate background for each scene along with scenic elements. The stylized realism of the materials and objects is a
fundamental means of expression of Appen's scenography.

571

572

571, 572. R. Allio, *Henry IV* by W. Shakespeare, dir. R. Planchon. Th. de la Cite, Villeurbanne, 1957. Bibl. Arsenal, Paris. Phot. P. Willi. **573.** R. Allio, *Dead Souls* based on N. Gogol, dir. R. Planchon, Paris. Th. de l'Odeon, Repertory of the Th. de la Cite in Villeurbanne, 1960. Phot. Pic. **574.** R. Allio, *Tartuffe* by Moliere, dir. R. Planchon, Th. de la Cite, Villeurbanne, 1962. Phot. Pic.

573

574

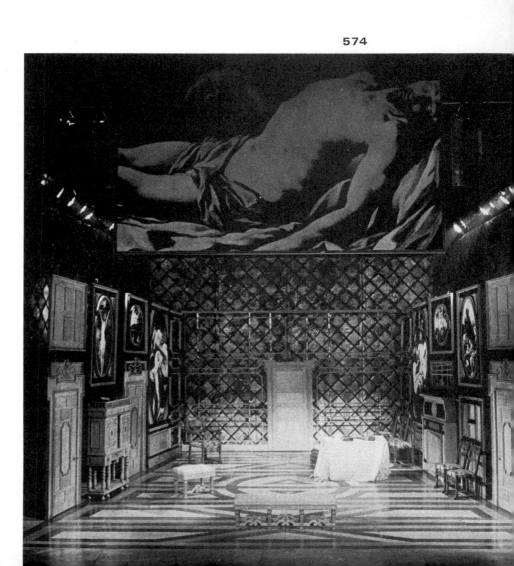

his scenographic style, as he carefully began to select the necessary scenic elements that would bring out the meaning of the play and the characters. At the same time he had to accentuate their realistic qualities; the revolving stage suggested the incessant wanderings of *Mother Courage* or Grusha's flight in *The Caucasian Chalk Circle*, the circus tent, where *Arturo Ui*'s parade was held, and the copper walls that inscribed the *Life of Galileo* within the limits of a world undergoing economic changes.

The designer did not begin with color, but with materials that were chosen and treated to point out their socio-historical context. Leather suggested an army, worn and faded cloth spoke of misery and war, Mother Courage's cart broke down very gradually until its canvas was nothing but tatters, as Mother Courage set out by herself on the highways. Materials illustrated a changing world.

During the twenties Brecht and Neher

575

employed another means: projections. Projections of titles and texts were combined with other scenic elements, while projections of drawings "were placed in front of the events unfolding on stage; overall, they expanded the frame and scope of the action, constituting at the same time an autonomous reality that carried the same value as the text or the music. Lastly, the projections served as an obstacle to the spectator's passivity, preventing him from totally identifying with the characters in the play.

A number of scenographers of the younger generation who have been influenced by the principles of critical realism are, Rene

576

Allio, Luciano Damiani, Horst Sagert, Gunilla Palmstierna-Weiss, Raffaelli and Minks. Each, however, has assimilated the concepts within his artistic and sociological environment and in accordance with his own temperament. Pure, simple imitation and rhetoric have been excluded. In Allio's works (*Dead Souls,* for example), along with traces of Brecht's influence, is the designer's personal search for plastic forms and multiple, plastic spatial perspectives. The robust qualities of a Karl von Appen, in Damiani's work, have given way to the extremely refined usage of materials, tonalities and lighting within the framework of an intelligently-utilized Italian style stage.

Gunilla Palmstierna-Weiss has been in-

575, 576. E. Luzzati, *The Golem* by A. Fersen, dir. A. Fersen,
Florence, La Pergola Th., 1969. **575.** Sketch. Phot. Publifoto.
576. The set. Phot. Marchiori. **577.** H. Balthes, *The Deputy* by
R. Hochhuth, dir. H. Uzerath, Dusseldorf, Kammerspiele, 1964.
Inst. Th. Cologne.

577

580

578-581. L. Damiani, *The Life of Galileo* by B. Brecht, dir. G. Strehler, Milan, Piccolo Teatro, 1963. Studio Phot. Piccolo Teatro. A few properties (furniture and objects in the selective realistic style; pictures of buildings in which the staircase has been turned upside down, etc.) complete the basic arrangement for the various scenes.

581

582

583

584

582. W. Minks, *Schweyk im zweiten Weltkrieg (Schweik in World War II)* by B. Brecht (a continuation of Hacek's military satire), dir. P. Palitzsch, Recklinghausen, Ruhrfestspiele, 1967. Inst. Th. Cologne. 583. W. Minks, *The Robbers* by F. Schiller, dir. P. Zadek, Bremen, Th. am Goetheplatz, 1966. Phot. G. Vierow. 584. W. Minks, *Hamlet* by W. Shakespeare, dir. K. Hubner, Bremen, Th. am Goetheplatz, 1965. Phot. G. Pagerstecher.

clined towards an architecturally and sculpturally unified stage with functional elements and colors. Minks more or less combines pure forms in proportions that have a sort of mathematical poetry, influenced directly or indirectly by Pop Art. As for Horst Sagert, his contemporaries regard him as the poet *par excellence,* the creator of fairy worlds, the inventor of universes.

The opposition abstraction/realism, which exists at the very heart of theatrical history, has not formed an unbridgeable chasm, since between the two are networks of intermediary approaches, compromises, adaptations to special situations, borrowing from various styles and intelligent applications of the right elements. While parody is the dominant feature of one set, the baroque might be recalled in another. Above all, one should remember that every situation, every method has its nuances and depends on the different creators and productions.

585

585, 587. H. Sagert, *The Dragon* by E. Schwarz, dir. B. Besson, Berlin, Deutsches Theater, 1965. Costume. Set. **586, 588.** H. Sagert, *Turandot* or *The Congress of Washerwomen* by B. Brecht, dir. B. Bresson, Zurich, Schauspielhaus, 1969. A costume (Phot. Zubler); a set. Among his contemporaries who practiced critical realism, H. Sagert seems like the poet *par excellence*, the inventor of an original universe.

586

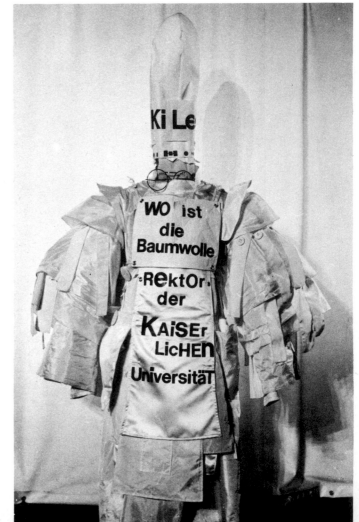

587

588

589. G. Palmstierna-Weiss, *The Song of the Lusitanian Bogey,*
by P. Weiss, collective setting, Stockholm. Scala Th., 1967.
590. G. Palmstierna-Weiss, *Vietnam Discourse* by P. Weiss, dir.
H. Buckwitz, Frankfort, Stadtische Buhnen, 1968. **591.** G.
Palmstierna-Weiss, sketches of costumes for *Marat-Sade* by P.
Weiss. dir. K. Swinarski (Berlin, 1964). P. Brook (London,
1964, New York, 1965), F. Sundstrom (Stockholm, 1965).

589

590
591

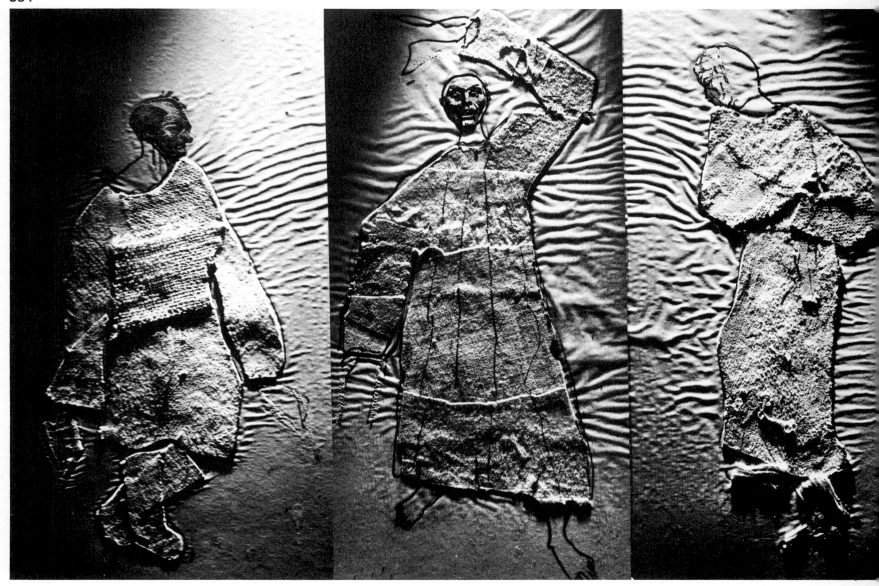

592

593

594. J. Bury, *Moses and Aaron* by A. Schoenberg, dir. P. Hall
and G. Woolfenden, London, Covent Garden, 1965. Phot. H.
Rogers.

594

592. G. Palmstierna-Weiss, *Marat-Sade* by P. Weiss, dir. F. Sundstrom, Stockholm, Royal Th., 1965. Phot. B. Bergstrom.
593. G. Palmstierna-Weiss, *Saint Joan of the Stockyards* by B. Brecht, collective setting, Stockholm, Municipal Th., 1969. The aluminum walls of the set extend to the sides of the theater, which receive the film projections and slides.

PRIVILEGED MEANS OF EXPRESSION

The scenography of each period is characterized by which techniques and means of expression are applied. Our objective here is not to analyze the evolution of scenographic methods during the past thirty years but to stress specific evident phenomena.

Heavy, stereotyped machinery has become outdated and rarely used, except in musical staging. At times it has been built into the structure of some new theaters. The most inventive scenographers prefer to conceive of arrangements especially adapted for each work, using combinations of both traditional and more modern elements. Some, like Allio, consciously or unconsciously borrow from Meyerhold, making sure for example, that the technical equipment is visible. Others, like Svoboda, prefer the technique remain invisible, or exposed only when required by special dramatic effects. Still other scenographers want the actor to be supreme, so they free the stage from sets, machinery and complicated electrical apparatus. Ac-

cording to Grotowski, these elements are all dispensable, because the actor is the principal condition for the theater's existence. Pushing that idea to the limit, Grotowski has made himself the champion of a poor theater. Again, the essence of our times is confrontation, and it seems that no part of the contemporary theater is heading in a single direction.

However, there are two means of expression that play a capital role in today's theater: light and materials.

I have already insisted on the function of lighting in various sections. Undoubtedly progress in the use of electricity in the theater (improvement of organ playing, xenon lamps, low tension devices, even laser

595. H. Palitzsch, *A Modern Dream* by E. Eder and G. Schroer, Linz, Landestheater, 1968. Doc. Kunstgew. Mus. Zurich. **596.** *Messe pour le temps present* by P. Henry, chor. M. Bejart, Avignon, Palace of the Popes, Twentieth Century Ballet Co., 1967. Phot. Kayaert. The lighting reveals and defines the space which it animates or shatters.

597

beams) has increased and diversified its application on the stage. Today lighting is one of the fundamental components of the production. It gives the sconic architecture its true relief and underlines the presence of the actor; it creates the instant space of the dramatic action by making a certain area of the set rise up out of the shadows. Lighting either attracts the spectator's attention to the four corners of the stage, or compels him to concentrate on the actor's expressive face. Whether it evokes atmosphere or serves as a catalyst to emotions, the lighting can tint the scenic space with psychological nuances by creating a certain climate, or it can cast the space in a brilliant light, which would indicate that the director wished the production stripped of any mystery and underline its conventional nature. For naturalist, expressionist, and epic sets, light can be applied in a naturalist, expressionist or epic manner. That is how flexible it is! At the frontiers of the theater experience, in a space deprived of the actor's living presence, the lighting can be an even more determinant factor, as fundamental as any other element. Xenakis' *Polytope* is an example of the type of spectacle based only on the use of synchronized light and music. Spreading out over the space, electronic flashes and laser beams either frighten the public with their aggression or charm them with aesthetic games.

The use of light is indissolubly bound to the use of projections. In this area, experimentation has yielded extremely fruitful re-

597. *The Rites of Spring* by I. Stravinsky, chor. M. Bejart, Th. Royal de la Monnaie, Brussels, 1959. Phot. Kayaert. **598.** J. Svoboda, *The Owners of the Keys* by M. Kundera, dir. O. Krejca, Prague, National Theater, 1963. Phot. Jar. Svoboda. The beams which are projected onto a mirror (the black square) are reflected in the foreground of the stage.

337

598

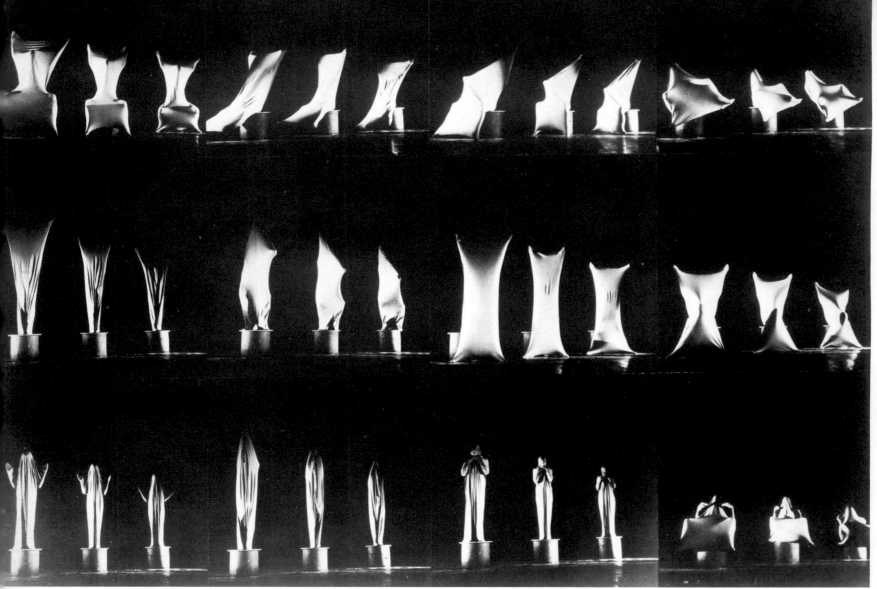

599

599. A. Nikolais, *Masks, Props and Mobiles,* chor. A. Nikolais, Henry Street Playhouse, 1953. Phot. David Berlin. The materials encasing the dancers give their movements an abstract shape. 600. I. Xenakis, *Polytope de Cluny,* Musee de Cluny, Paris, 1972. A sound, music and light show that included laser beams. Doc. Ed. Balland.

600

601

601. J. Svoboda, *Pelleas et Melisande* by Cl. Debussy, dir. V. Kaslik, London, Covent Garden, 1969. Phot. H. Rogers. As they move, the projections harmonize with the musical development. 602. J. Svoboda, *Tannhauser* by R. Wagner, dir. V. Kaslik, London, Covent Garden, 1973.

602

sults during the last thirty years. But, the need for the projected set as a substitute for the painted canvas diminishes to the extent that it is contained within the illusionist perspective. However, the role of projections increases when they serve as critical commentary (epic techniques) or as symbolic abstract commentary. With its Chagallian blues, the lighting created the enchanted garden of *Parsifal*, staged by Wieland Wagner at Bayreuth, and formed the evocative background of many other productions at that theater. The visual interpreter of *Pelleas and Melisande*, Svoboda wedded lighting to the musical world; by subjecting the light to sound, he suggested a fluid, mobile universe that abstractly evoked Monet's water lilies and Klimt's decorative world. Once again, the intimate blending of light and music helped Svoboda suggest the erotic world of Venusberg in *Tannhauser*. Alwin Nikolais, in his ballets, assigned lighting a partnership with his

603

604

603, 604. J. Svoboda, *The Soldiers* by B.A. Zimmermann, dir. V. Kaslik, Munich Opera, 1969. Phot. R. Betz. For this work which blended past, present and future, traditional music, noise and electronic sounds, Svoboda exploded the scenic space and created a collage of projections with his multiple screens.

605

606

605. A. Nikolais, *Echo,* mus. and chor. by A. Nikolais, New York City Center Th., 1969. Phot. S. Schiff-Faludi. The dancer's body serves as a screen projection and becomes integrated with it.
606. A. Nikolais, *Tent,* mus. and chor. A. Nikolais, Tampa U. of South Florida, 1968. Phot. B. Manley.

607. J. Svoboda, *Their Day* by J. Topol, dir. O. Krejca, Prague, National Th., 1959. Phot. Jar. Svoboda. Film and slide projections on multiple screens. **608.** J. Svoboda, *Prometheus* by C. Orff, dir. A. Everding. Munich Opera, 1968. Prometheus' head is contrasted with a highly enlarged televised image. Phot. R. Betz.

342

608

dancers; lighting hid their bodies under the costumes and transformed the dancers into mobile, ever-changing forms — all of which sprung from the imagination of a man who did not forget the lessons of the Bauhaus.

The role of film projections, as introduced into the theater by Piscator, has also been diversified. In creating the *Laterna Magika* (1958), Svoboda made film the indispensable partner of the actor and dancer, as well as of the stereophonic sound; this new form of production was based on the perpetual counterpoint between the image and the live, physical reality. Svoboda soon applied these possibilities to the theater *(Their Day, Atomdeath, The Last Ones,* etc.). Recently, televisual projections have found a theatrical application, thanks to the Eidophor system, which permitted projections on a large screen. Svoboda employed them in Luigi Nono's *Intolleranza,* staged in Boston, and in Virginio Puecher's production of *The Investigation,* which was presented at the Piccolo Teatro of Milan, in exhibition halls and in sports arenas all over Italy. Lately, televisual projections have been effective in theater for the masses, enhancing the gestures, words and general scope of the characters.

The growing role of non-traditional materials on the stage (tin foil, thread, artificial mirrors, foam rubber, polyesters, fiberglass, etc.) should be viewed within the overall evolution of the arts and techniques of our times, notably within architecture and sculpture, which utilize a more expanded range of

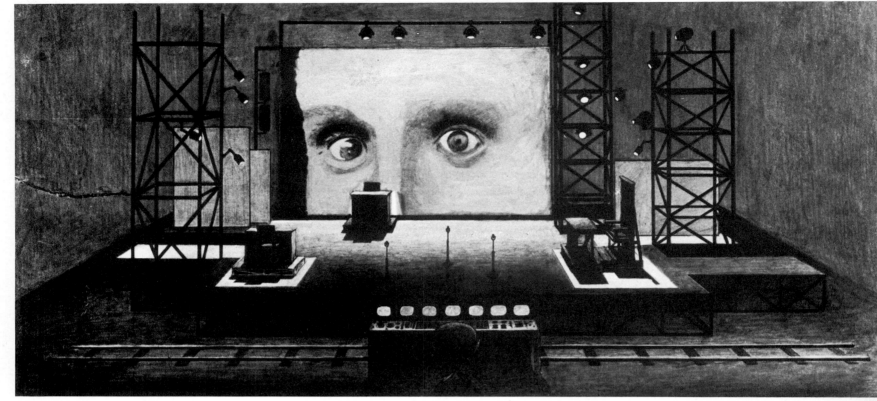

609

609, 610. V. Puecher, *The Investigation* by P. Weiss, dir. V. Puecher, Pavia, Exhibition Palace, Piccolo Teatro Milano, 1967. Phot. Piccolo Teatro. **609.** Design. In the center is a screen that projects slides and moving pictures (films, television projection using the eidophor). **610.** The televised image of the character on the right (a witness) appears over the fixed projections of the portraits of the accused.

610

natural and synthetic materials. The set designer does not depend on these materials for their lightness, solidity, flexibility or acoustical virtues merely so that he can use them in his constructions, for he recognizes these materials are "privileged means of expression." Not only does their appearance suggest a poetic ambiance, dramatic universe or social climate (precious woods, visibly rich metals, tattered cloth, etc.), but, their presence gives a density to the set that creates more of a feeling of reality than do the traditional, painted canvases. Materials create vital relations between the dramatic character and the scenic object or element, and by their resonance evoke the atmosphere, and sometimes the situation of a character or a group. Every performance must be an experience. In these complicated times in which old methods are disappearing and unknown formulas suddenly emerge, the designer has an excellent opportunity to experiment with, and explore the use of new materials.

THE DISINTEGRATION OF SPACE

What will the future historian write when he passes judgment on our heated times? He will have discovered the birth of new theatrical forms, light-shows and mixed media, created by the wizards who learned to ingeniously combine all of the means of expression provided by new techniques. But, perhaps he will decide that the theater is inseparable from the other arts, as he would have had he met them in the Sixties and Seventies at the crossroads of "happenings" and "environments." How then can we read the future? How can we predict the critical judgments of tomorrow?

It is clear that developments in scenography are not isolated from other considerations. Indeed, both the traditional and most modern forms of theater have been shaken up and dealt violent blows. And not only aesthetic forms, but the traditional relations between the spectator and the performance have been overthrown as well.

In 1952 at Black Mountain College, an audience was seated in a large auditorium in four triangular areas that pointed towards a central section where most of the action unfolded. But what kind of action are we talking about? Of an extraordinary mixture of voices and dancing, music and films! John Cage, the animator, gave a lecture; poems were read, a pianist improvised, the Merce Cunningham dancers performed their arabesques. Projections appeared on a ceiling which also suspended Bob Rauschenberg's paintings. The performance assaulted the spectator from every angle, recalling Artaud — an Artaud who would have found during this era of "environments" the confirmation of his prophecies.

In fact, this spectacle was the ancestor of the "happening," although these did not appear until 1959 when the painter Allan Kaprow presented his *18 Happenings in 6 Parts* at the Reuben Gallery in New York. "The line between art and life must remain as flexible as possible," declared Kaprow; and Rauschenberg wrote: "Painting is bound to art and life. Neither can be manufactured. (I try to create in the gap that separates them)." The happenings, therefore, penetrated this gap, creating a spectacle in which art identified with life, and life mingled with the arts. In the unique event of the happening, the distinction between the actor and the spectator terminated, as the latter was invited to a total participation of his mind and emotions. The events of the happenings unfolded in a completely 'alogical' way, the better part given to chance, which triggered a new kind of theatrical *shock*. The artist was looking for nothing less than a rediscovery of himself and of others, a new grasp of the world of objects during the course of a game that became a ritual. The role of the object was equal to that of the live performer. Happenings attempted to smash the yoke of habit and the traditional perceptual framework imposed on us by our civilization. But in our super-technological times, one can well ask if the happening was not ultimately an anachronistic, almost desperate attempt to escape and rediscover a form of primitive ritual that would bind man to man, and gave him another vision of this world abandoned by the gods.

Whatever the judgment, the happening was a reality with as many diverse forms as

611. At the *Cafe au Go Go,* environment for a happening by Al Hansen, 1965. Phot. P. Moore. **612.** *Celestials,* happening by D. Higgins, Sunnyside Garden Ball Room and Arena, 1965. Phot. P. Moore. **613.** *Parisol 4 Marisol,* happening by Al Hansen, Gramercy Art Th., 1963. Phot. P. Moore. The search for a new kind of theatrical shock and audience participation.

613

614

614. A. Kaprow, *Happening,* New York, 1962. Phot. L. Shustak. **615.** T. Kantor, *Happening by the Sea,* staged by T. Kantor, Lazy, 1967. In this happening the audience finds itself surrounded by a "ready made object."

615

the social-cultural context permitting its birth (witness its variations in the U.S., Germany, France and Poland). Moreover, the happening cannot be overlooked because its roots are historic and grew out of the twin currents of our civilization: on the one hand, a theatricalization of life that is familiar to all periods of radical change, and on the other, a rapprochement between the spectator and art, such that the public finally participates in the creative process of the work.

In the theater the rapprochement meant progressively eliminating the gap between the audience and the dramatic action. The battle against the Italian stage did not start yesterday. From the moment the Renaissance perspective was cast in doubt, it was inevitable that a stage applying its principles would become obsolete. And once the proscenium arch had been suppressed, the search for new forms was underway, a search which has intensified during the past thirty years. It hardly matters that new theaters are still constructed in the familiar Italian style; since their architectures no longer fill the needs of contemporary theater, they are doomed.

The depth of this quest for new places and structures is quite evident. Think of the

616

616. J. Roustan and R. Bernard, *Baudelaire,* chor. M. Bejart, Grenoble, Maison de la Culture, Twentieth Century Ballet Company, 1967. Phot. Kayaert. **617.** *The Ninth Symphony* by L. van Beethoven, chor. M. Bejart, Brussels, Cirque Royal, Twentieth Century Ballet Company, 1964. Phot. Kayaert.

617

618

productions that have been mounted outside of the traditional theater, in churches, circuses and open places prepared for the occasion (the Cour d'Honneur of the Palace of the Popes in Avignon). Think of the increasing number of arena theaters, or of stages of more or less Elizabethan inspiration like those of Stratford in Canada, Chichester in England, or of the successful theaters-in-the-round in the United States. Think also of the transformable theaters, like the one at Mannheim which Piscator inaugurated with a production of Schiller's *Robbers,* or the Theatre des Amandiers at Nanterre, France, or those created in many American universities.

618. D. Heeley, *Henry V* by W. Shakespeare, dir. S. Burge, Stratford (Ontario), 1965. Phot. D. Spillane. Example of a modern "Elizabethan stage". **619.** E. Saarinen and J. Mielziner, maquette for the Repertory Theatre of the Lincoln Center for the Performing Arts, New York, 1965. Phot. Usis. **620.** View of the Arena Stage in Washington (opened in 1961) taken during a performance. **621.** P. Walter, *The Robbers* by F. Schiller, dir. E. Piscator, Mannheim, Nationaltheater, small transformable auditorium, 1957.

619

Abandoning the sacrosanct Italian stage has occasionally led to blasphemy or sacrilege. In staging *The Balcony* (by Jean Genet), Garcia had the illusionist theater serve completely different ends. He broke up a theater in Sao Paulo to install the spectators in a series of circular balconies so that they became voyeurs into the brothel imagined by Genet. Garcia also replaced the illusionist stage with a cylindrical volume in which a mobile platform rose and descended, the acting taking place on an immense spiral. Ronconi's production, *XX,* also derided the conventional theater. The audience, waiting to enter the Odeon, was soon engulfed in a three-dimensional labyrinth, a vast structure

620

621

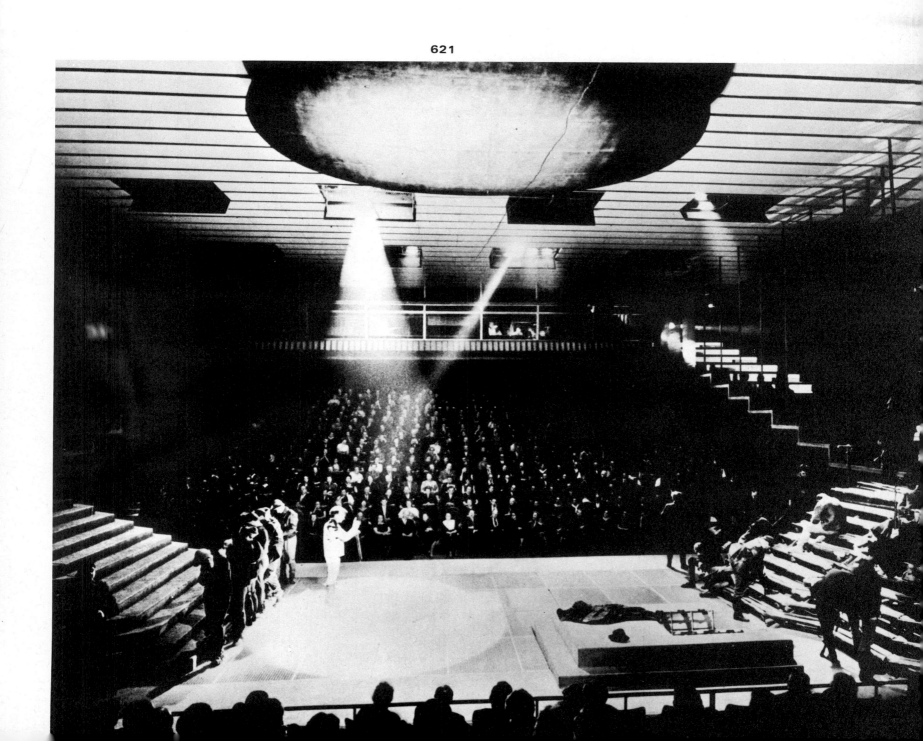

partitioned into many rooms that occupied the entire volume of the theater. And, going one step further, it seems that the spectator would not have been surprised to witness the Odeon burn up in a purifying fire of joy. These two productions (Artaud's influence was far from negligible here) testify to the search for new types of audience participation.

Contemporary directors are trying to overcome public passivity, to compel their audience to participate in what could be ritual, ceremony or festival. They try to encourage reactions, to change or at least touch people deeply. Some directors want to cast a spell, while others look for ways to appeal to the audience's critical intelligence. In both cases, the spectator is submerged into the action, if not required to participate.

There are times when artistic ideologies have induced similar aesthetics. Some critics have hastily grouped the works of the American Living Theater and those of the Polish director, Jerzy Grotowski, under the same banner. What do they have in common? The former is a little art theater, which little by little has become a community with anarchist goals; the director, Grotowski, on the other hand, has abandoned traditional ways in order to explore the actor's performance in his Institute for Research. Their respective scenographies show that their differences are greater than any parallels one might find.

At the risk of being too schematic, one could say that from *The Brig* (1963) to *Paradise Now* (1968), the Living Theater passed from naturalist sets to the abandonment of all scenographic forms other than those created by the positions and gestures of the actor, and from realistic costumes to blue-jeans to complete nudity.

The set for *The Brig* was a U.S. marine

622 a

622. a,b,c,d. W. Pereira Cardoso and V. Garcia, *The Balcony* by J. Genet, dir. V. Garcia, Sao Paulo, Ruth Escobar Th., 1970. An entirely rebuilt theater. Cylindrical auditorium in which the action took place on a circular platform that moved up and down; the audience seated on the circular balconies, became voyeurs into Genet's brothel.

622 b

622 c

622 d

prison which shocked the public because of the violence and merciless regularity of the unfolding situations. For *Mysteries and Smaller Pieces,* there were practically no sets (except for some wooden boxes that were used in the tableaux vivants). After the "plague" scene, the actors shifted into the theater, and the playing area remained off stage. In *Frankenstein,* Julian Beck erected a large, high tubular construction which was divided into fifteen compartments that recalled Traugott Muller's arrangement for *Hurrah, We Live!,* or Raffaelli's for *America.* Half-abstract, half-symbolic, the formal structure was hardly realistic; here again, certain sequences took place in the theater.

In *Antigone,* all decor disappeared. The space was organized as the actors moved about and created spatial relationships. When the actors shifted to the theater, the audience became more directly involved. Since the stage symbolized Thebes, and the auditorium, Argos, the audience participated as citizens from Argos. Whether the production was staged in a traditional theater, or in the open air, there was certainly a disintegration of traditional scenography.

With *Paradise Now* Julian Beck and Judith Malina took the final step. In the beginning the audience was surrounded on four sides by the playing area, but in the game of mutual participation, the audience soon invaded the stage. A total osmosis and inter-

623

623, 624. J. Beck, *Frankenstein,* conceived and staged by J. Malina and J. Beck, based on M. Shelly, Venice, Teatro La Perla, Living Theatre, 1965. **623.** Phot. G. Mantegna. **624.** Phot. J. Rouiller. **625.** *Mysteries and Smaller Pieces,* dir. J. Malina and J. Beck, Paris, American Center, Living Theatre, 1964. Phot. J. Rouiller.

624   **625**

penetration occurred when the actors, in turn, rushed into the theater.

It seemed as though the closed auditorium could no longer satisfy the spatial requirements of the Living Theater. During their last European tours, their performances took place in the streets, an excellent receptacle for their idealistic protests.

Grotowski does not look for the masses. He readily admits that he addresses himself to an elite audience, an audience who wants to engage in self-analysis, to be aroused during the course of the play, or to be part of a secular ritual, which is really the essence of every Grotowski production.

For *Cain* (1960), a frontal rapport was preserved, although the actors gradually moved into the central aisles and even made some incursions into the audience. With *Shakuntala* the following year, he utilized a central rectangular stage, on each side of which

626. *Paradise Now,* dir. J. Malina and J. Beck, Avignon, Carmelite Cloisters, Living Theatre, 1968. Phot. P. Moore.
627. *Paradise Now:* The Pentagon. Phot. M.C. Gaffier.

628. Plan of the scenic arrangements for three productions mounted by J. Grotowski in his Laboratory Theatre. From top to bottom: *Cain* based on Byron's text (Opole, 1960), *Shakuntala* based on Kalidasa (Opole, 1961), and *Forefather's Eve,* by Mickiewicz (Opole, 1963). The playing areas are in black. J. Gurawski, architect and author of most of the projects, played a very important role in choosing the proper spatial solutions at the Laboratory Theatre. Except for special mention, all of the documentation reproduced here comes from J. Grotowski's *Towards a Poor Theatre,* Odin Teatrets Forlag, Holstebro, 1968.

627

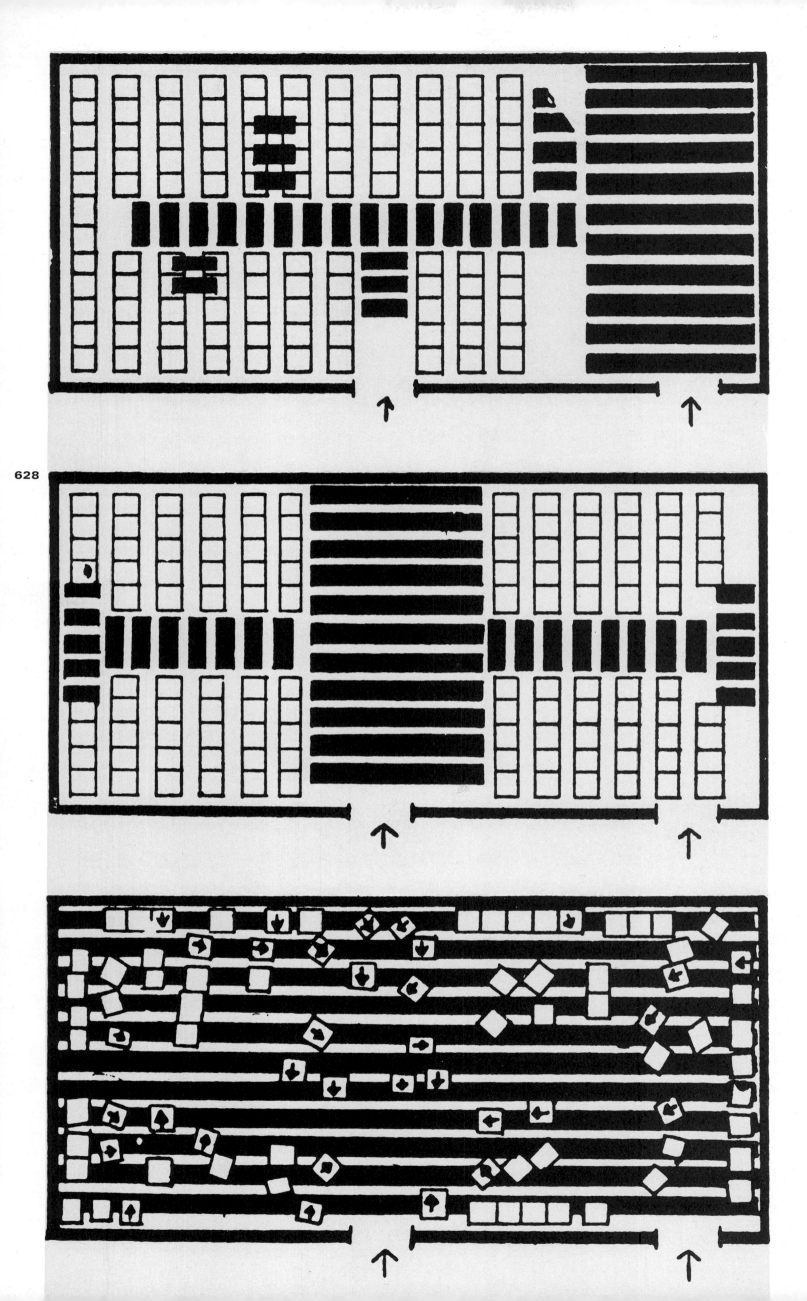

629

630

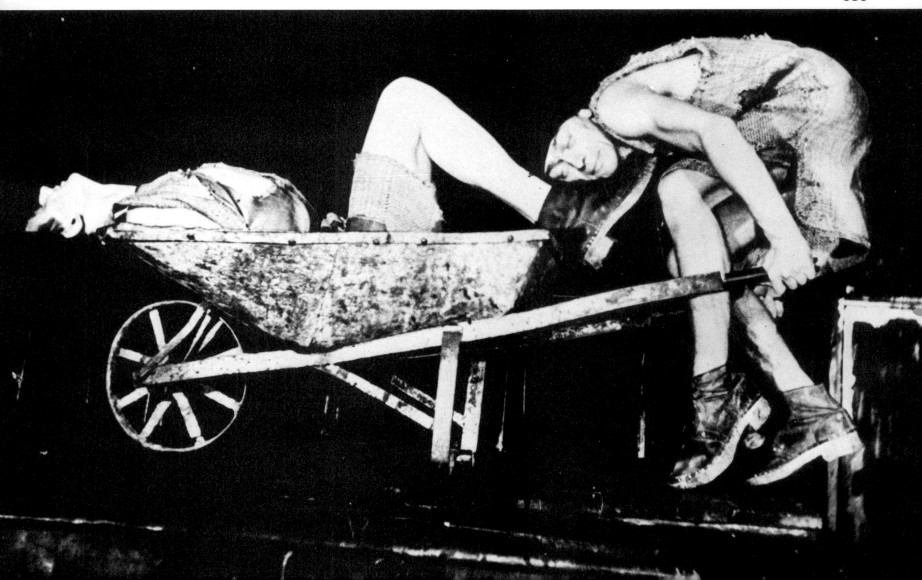

631

629. Outline of the arrangement for *Akropolis* by Wyspianski, dir. J. Grotowski and J. Szajna, Opole, Laboratory Th., 1962. On top: the beginning of the play. On bottom: the end. **630.** A. Jaholkowski and R. Cieslak in *Akropolis*, costumes by J. Szajna. Phot. Unpublished. **631.** Spatial solution for *Kordian*, based on Slowacki's text, dir. J. Grotowski, Opole, Laboratory Th., 1962. **632.** Spatial solution for *Faust* based on Marlowe's text, dir. J. Grotowski, Opole, Laboratory Th., 1963.

sat the audience. The actors also played behind the audience at various times. From these two productions we see that Grotowski, together with his scenographer J. Gurawski, tried to devise the right arrangement for each play, and a spatial staging that embraced both the public and the dramatic action. The scenographer's function was no longer to create a scenic place, but a specific physical rapport, which along with psychospiritual relationships, were meant to give the production its special dynamic power. "...We propose a rule of poverty," wrote Grotowski in *Towards A Poor Theater.* "We have practically renounced the stage. The only indispensable thing is an empty area where a space can be shaped for the audience and the actors, and in a different way for each new production so that the most diverse relationships are made possible. The actors can perform in the pathways formed between the spectators, much like chorus leaders of a community theater, leaders who enter directly in contact with the spectators, become their *emanation* and assign them a role (a passive one, the spectator-witness)."

632

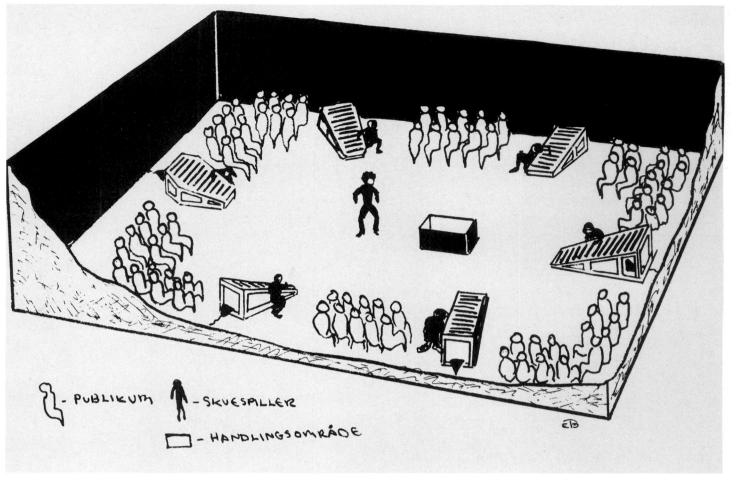

- PUBLIKUM   - SKUESPILLER
- HANDLINGSOMRÅDE

633

634

633, 634. *Kaspariana* based on Ole Sarvig's scenario, dir. E. Barba, Holstebro, Odin Teatrets, 1967. **633.** The scenic arrangement, archit. B. Nyberg. **634.** Pictures of the stage. Costumes and accessories were created collectively by all of the members of the troupe.

The above citation suggests the kind of arrangements for *Forefather's Eve* and *Kordian*. The latter took place in a mental asylum, and the audience sat on chairs and beds, in close touch with the actors. The following describes the spatial organization for *The Constant Prince*. "Conversely, the actors and spectators can be separated by placing them behind a partition, one so high that only their heads would be visible. And from that height, caught in this deforming perspective, they observe the actors as they would animals in a zoo. Like the public at a bullfight, or medical students observing an operation, or simply voyeurs, who, by their own indiscretions, cast the action in a murky light, transforming it into an infraction or moral fault." The task of the scenographer here is to organize the spectator's perspective.

In *Akropolis* there was virtually no contact with the dying souls who inhabited the concentration camp. Linked to the action by the roles assigned to them (the audience represented the already Dead), the actors' proximity does not bring about audience participation. *Akropolis* showed that physical rapprochement alone between the actor and the public is not enough to arouse, or the only means to achieve the latter's participation. Everything rather depends on the general conception of the play and on the interaction of its means of expression.

Today Grotowski's work surpasses theater. In Denmark, however, his disciple Barba has adopted similar spatial solutions: *Ornitofilene, Ferai* and *Kaspariana*.

It is also tempting to confront Grotowski with his compatriot, the painter Tadeusz Kantor, who has staged several interesting productions at the Theater Cricot 2, notably such original works as *The Water Hen* and *Lovelies and Dowdies*. Kantor certainly organizes the spatial association between the actor-spectator, dividing the area into zones for them, and so on, but the nature and the effects of the relationship differ from those sought by Grotowski. Moreover, Kantor the painter, is also revealed through Kantor, the director. The places and relative functions attributed to the actors and objects suggest he is a creator of packaged art and happenings. In *The Water Hen,* truth and illusion engage in constant battle; and art and life exist in an unstable equilibrium so that the play keeps shifting from theater to happening. "Naturally," says Kantor, *"The Water Hen* is not a happening, but I have been working with artistic elements that are very close to life. One more step, and you have life! .. Of course, this is not naturalism. One more step

and everything is destroyed, because then, there is no difference between art and life. The spectator no longer knows whether it is life or art. He feels uncertain and unreassured. In *The Water Hen* he wonders whether he himself is the actor ... which adds to the feeling of uncertainty and anxiety."

Each production thus affirms its unique characteristics. But aside from differences, all of them have one thing in common, which is that they belong to a major current of contemporary scenography. Without a doubt it is vitally important to have an inseparable relationship between the audience and the actor for each play, a rapport that is rarely frontal, and one in fact that can be changed during the course of the performance. Experiments in this direction include Arrabal's *Automobile Graveyard,* which was staged by Garcia in 1966 at the Dijon Festival. There have been others, and based on completely different ideologies which have played with the disintegration of the scenic space and the simultaneity of the dramatic action. *Orlando Furioso,* for example, created by Ronconi, or *1789* at the Theatre du Soleil.

Orlando Furioso, staged in various public places or in vast outdoor areas such as Les Halles (food market) of Paris, is certainly a case of a spatial explosion in which fixed scenography was totally impossible. The action unfolded in a large open space amidst the spectators. Rapidly moving wagons dodged the crowds (who were viewing events taking place in different areas) as the wagons were transported from one place to another. Some Italian hangings were employed at both ends of the rectangular space, but these were mere vestiges of a rejected theater. The elements of surprise and movement (of the mobile platforms, the audience) created constantly changing playing areas which caught the audience in the trap of a fluctuating scenography.

A very clever person can see the ideological ties between *Orlando Furioso* and *1789* or *1793* at the Theatre du Soleil. It requires, however, a still cleverer one to find parallels with Grotowski's works. The spatial solutions employed by all of them were not as dissimilar as one might have thought. *1789* was a festival of denunciation, the story of an incompleted revolution which was prevented by the bourgeoisie from attaining the "perfection of happiness." *1789* was designed for a large open space with the scenography of simply bare boards. It had all the elements of a fair. A network of platforms and flying bridges penetrated into the audience forming a rectangle, outside of which

635

635, 636. T. Kantor, *The Water Hen* by S.I. Witkiewicz, dir. T.
Kantor, Cricot Th. 2. **635.** Performance at Cracow, 1968. Phot.
Poplonski. **636.** Performance somewhere else. **637.** T. Kantor,
The Lovelies and the Dowdies by S.I. Witkiewicz, dir. T. Kantor,
Cracow, Cricot Th. 2, 1973. Phot. G.A. Oliver taken during the
performance at the Edinburg Festival of 1973.

636

637

638. N. de Arzadun and J. Monod, *The Tempest* based on
Shakespeare's text, dir. P. Brook, London, Round House, 1968.
Phot. B. Heyligers.

639

639-641. U. Bertacca (scenography) and E. Nannini (costume), *Orlando Furioso* based on Ariosto, dir. L. Ronconi, Rome, Teatro Libero, 1970. Photography taken during the performances in Paris which were given in Les Halles. **639.** View of the entire performance which unfolded in an open space. The players and the public mingled together. Phot. George. **640.** Duel on moving wagons. Phot. George. **641.** Flight. Phot. Pic.

640

641

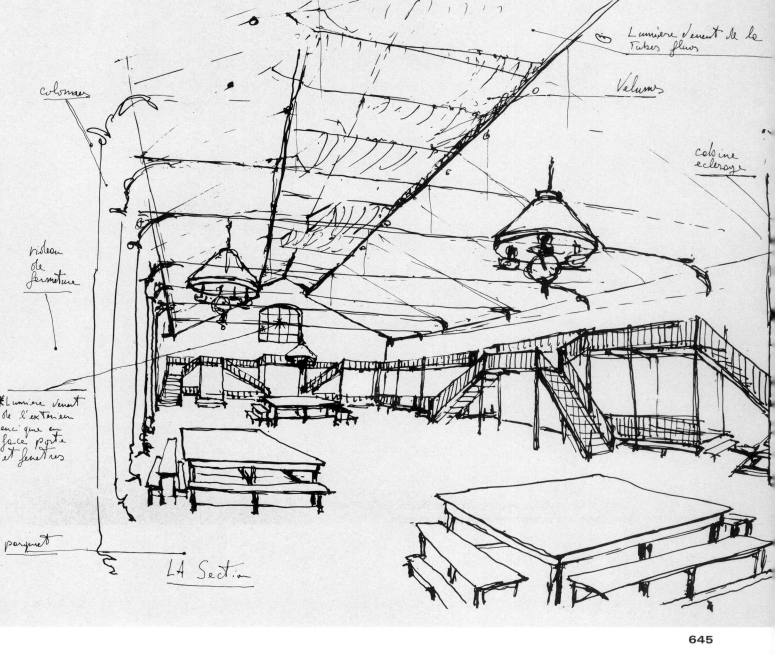

645

645-647. *1793,* collective creation by the Theatre du Soleil, dir. A. Mnouchkine, cartridge factory in Vincennes, 1972. **645.** General view of the disposition of the scenic action: a gallery, and three large table-platforms (sketch by R. Moscoso). **647.** Two photos of the stage which show the interaction between the public and the actors. Phot. M. Franck/Viva.

Bible, participating in peace marches or performing at the Salle Wagram, the Bread and Puppet Theater does not look for aesthetic flourishes, but manages to achieve a sophisticated and immediately tangible beauty. It is unquestionably a 'poor' theater, but it is also 'total' theater with an implicit scenography that employs the expressive power of puppets of all sizes and stresses language, mime and masks to give the play a general humanistic scope. This theater also knows how to use the most insignificant object. However, the object is ritualized in such a way as to conserve its lifelike impression, and the notion of "prop" never enters our minds. A simple strip of red scotch tape which the actor unrolls, breaks off and sticks on his clothing is sufficient to create the picture of a Buddhist priest committing suicide by burning himself alive.

646
647

648, 650. *The Cry of the People for Meat,* Bread and Puppet Theatre under the direction of P. Schumann, 1969. **648.** *Mother Earth and Uncle Fatso.* Phot. Tullmann and Werth. **650.** Another scene. Phot. Treatt.

648

649, 651. The Bread and Puppet Theatre participates in a peace demonstration on March 26, 1966 on Fifth Avenue in New York. **649.** Death masks. Phot. E. Finer Magnum. **651.** The animal (an airplane) attacks the women (Vietnamese). Phot. E. Finer Magnum.

649

650

651

652. Masks in *Fire,* production of the Bread and Puppet Theatre
under the direction of P. Schumann. Photography taken at the
Th. de la Commune in Aubervilliers in 1968.

THE DIFFICULTY OF CONCLUDING

During the course of this work, I have tried to focus on some of the most original creations of our century. Can one draw conclusions from them? The lack of historical perspective prevents us from making a decisive judgment; besides, the future remains unpredictable.

Two observations, however, are striking. First, that the Twenties tended towards the reign of "isms". From Expressionism to Constructivism there were many opposing currents with well defined styles and characteristics confronting each other. The variety today corresponds to a diversification that is accompanied by a disappearance of styles as such. Styles have become simply temporary means of expression at the disposition of the creative artists of the stage.

Secondly, for the first half-century "decorative" reforms played a considerable role in the effort to renovate the theater. The problem today seems different. Modern scenography has an artistic vocabulary at its disposal that answers the many questions posed by contemporary dramaturgies of a more traditional style. But, with the number of theories and new experiments taking place, the major problem at present is not so much an aesthetic one, but one of finding a rapport between the dramatic action and an audience who is ready to accept diverse forms of participation.

These are observations and clearly not conclusions. The very transformations of our civilization and the evolution of theater prevent us from drawing final conclusions. One might have believed during the Thirties that the aesthetic revolutions begun at the turn of the century were terminated, and that henceforth the problem would be one of constructive creation. Those revolutions, however, turn out to be only the first blows of the battering ram against an old tradition that started centuries ago. Since that time a basic questioning has been going on, sometimes wisely, sometimes violently, and it is not over yet. In the final analysis, it depends on the importance one attributes to the function of each art in a civilization in which new art forms are constantly emerging and being developed. It seems that whether we are the agents or the victims, we are hardly conscious of the "redistribution of cards" that is always taking place.

Selective Bibliography

This bibliography was compiled in 1973.

ARTICLES OF GENERAL INTEREST

Individual Works

A

ASLAN (Odette), *L'Art du theatre*, Paris, Seghers, 1963.

B

BABLET (Denis), *Esthetique generale du decor de theatre de 1870 a 1914*, Paris, Editions du Centre National de la Recherche Scientifique, 1965.

BANDINI (Baldo), VIAZZI (Glaudo), *Ragionamenti sulla scenografia*, Milan, 1945.

BAPST (Germain), *Essai sur l'histoire du theatre. La mise en scene, le decor, le costume, l'architecture, l'eclairage, l'hygiene*, Paris, Hacnette, 1893.

BATY (Gaston), *Rideau baisse*, Paris, Bordas, 1949.

BOLL (Andre), *Du decor de theatre. Ses tendances modernes*, Paris, E. Chiron, 1926.

C

CARTER (Huntly), *The New Spirit in the European Theatre 1914-1924*, London, Ernest Benn, 1925.

CHENEY (Sheldon), *The Art Theatre*, New York, A.A. Knopf, 1925.
Modern Art and the Theatre, Scarborough on Hudson, Sleepy Hollow Press, 1921.
The New Movement in the Theatre, New York, Mitchell Kennerley, 1914.
Stage Decoration, London, Chapman and Hall, 1928, New York, J. Day, 1928; New York, R. Blom, 1966.

COGNIAT (Raymond), *Decors de theatre*, Paris, Editions des Chroniques du jour, 1930.

D

DORT (Bernard), *Theatre public, 1953-1966*, Paris, Le Seuil, 1967.
Theatre reel. 1967-1970, Paris, Le Seuil, 1971.

E

Enciclopedia dello spettacolo, 9 volumes + 1 de mise a jour (1955-1965). Rome, Casa editrice Le Maschere, 1954-1966.

F

FISCHEL (Oskar), *Das moderne Buhenbild*, Berlin, E. Wasmuth, 1923.

FRETTE (Guido), *Decors de theatre*, Milan, G.G. Gorlich, s.d.

FUERST (Walter-Rene), *Du decor*, Paris, Editions de la Douce France, 1925.

FUERST (Walter-Rene) et HUME (Samuel J.), *XXth. Century Stage Decoration* by... with an introduction by Adolphe Appia, London, A.A. Knopf, 1928, 2 vol. (New edition, New York, Dover Publications, 1967.)

G

GORELIK (Mordecai), *New Theatres for Old*, New York, Samuel French, 1940.

GORI (Gino), *Scenografia*, Rome, Alberto Stock, 1927.

H

HAINAUX (Rene), YVES BONNAT, *Le Decor de theatre dans le monde depuis 1935,* texts and illustrations assembled by the national centers for the Institut International du Theatre; chosen and presented by Rene Hainaux with the technical advice of Yves-Bonnat, Brussels, Elsevier, 1956.
Le Decor de theatre dans le monde depuis 1950, texts and illustrations assembled by the national centers for the Institut International du Theatre; chosen and presented by Rene Hainaux with the technical advice of Yves-Bonnat, Brussels, Meddens, 1964.
Le Decor de theatre dans le monde depuis 1960. Scenography: texts and illustrations assembled by the national centers for the Institut International du Theatre; chosen and presented by Rene Hainaux with the technical advice of Yves-Bonnat, Brussels, Meddens, 1973.

K

KINDERMANN (Heinz), *Theatergeschichte Europas*, Salzburg, Otto Muller Verlag, Tome VIII, Naturalismus und Impressionismus (I. Teil), 1968; Tome IX, Naturalismus und Impressionismus (2. Teil), 1970.

KIRBY (Michael), *The Art of Time*, New York, E. Dutton, 1969.

KOMISARJEVSKY (Theodore), SIMONSON (Lee), *Settings and Costumes of the Modern Stage*, London, New York. The Studio Publications, 1933.

Kunst und Buhne, special number of *Das Kunstwerk,* Baden-Baden, Woldemar Klein Verlag, Bd. 41, 1953.

L

LAVER (James), *Drama, its Costume and Decor*, London, The Studio, 1951.

M

MACGOWAN (Kenneth), *The Theatre of Tomorrow*, New York, Boni and Liveright, 1921.

MACGOWAN (Kenneth), JONES (Robert Edmond), *Continental Stagecraft*, New York, Harcourt, Brace and Co. 1922 (New edition : New York, Benjamin Blom, 1964).

MOUSSINAC (Leon), *La Decoration theatrale*, Paris, Rieder, 1922.
Tendances nouvelles du theatre, Paris, A. Levy, 1931 (in english : *The New Movement in the Theatre,* London, B.T. Batsford, 1931 ; new edition, New York, Blom, 1961).

P

PIRCHAN (Emil), *Zweitausend Jahre Buhnenbild*, Vienna, Bellaria Verlag, 1949.

POLIERI (Jacques), *Spectacles. 50 ans de recherches*, texts and articles compiled by Jacques Polieri, no. 17 of *Aujourd'hui, Art et Architecture,* Boulogne-sur-Seine, 1958.
Scenographie nouvelle, numbers 42-43 of *Aujourd'hui. Art et Architecture,* Boulogne-sur-Seine, October 1963

POERTNER (Paul), *Experiment Theater*, Chronik und Dokumente, Zurich, Verlag Die Arche, 1960.

Q

QUEANT (Gilles), *Encyclopedie du theatre contemporain*, edited by Gilles Queant with the help of Frederic Towarnicki, art direction by Aline Elmayan. Vol. I : 1850-1914, Paris, Les Publications de France, 1957. Vol. II : 1914-1950, Paris, Olivier Perrin, 1959.

R

RISCHBIETER (Henning), *Buhne und bildende Kunst im XX. Jahrhundert*, herausgegeben von Henning Rischbieter, dokumentiert von Wolfgang Storch, Velber bei Hannover, Friedrich Verlag, 1968.

ROLLAND (Romain), *Le Theatre du Peuple. Essai d'esthetique d'un theatre nouveau*, Paris, Albin Michel, 1913.

ROUCHE (Jacques), *L'Art theatral moderne* Paris, Edouard Conely, 1910.

S

SCHUBERTH (Ottmar), *Das Buhnenbild*, Munich, G.D.W. Callwey, 1955.

SHERINGHAM (George), *Design in the Theatre*, commentary by George Sheringham and James Laver together with literary contributions by Edward Gordon Craig, Charles B. Cochran and Nigel Playfair, London, The Studio, 1927.

SIMONSON (Lee), *The Stage is Set*, New York, Harcourt, Brace and Co., 1932 (new edition : New York, Theatre Arts Books, 1963).
The Art of Scenic Design, New York, Harper, 1950.

SONREL (Pierre), *Traite de scenographie*, Paris, Odette Lieutier, 1943.

STRZELECKI (Zenobiusz), *Kierunki scenografii wspolczesnej*, Panstowowy Instytut wydawniczy, 1970.

V

VEINSTEIN (Andre), *Du Theatre Libre au Theatre Louis Jouvet. Les Theatres d'Art a travers leurs periodiques*, Paris, Librairie theatrale, 1955.

VIEFHAUS-MILDENBERGER (Marianne), *Film und Projektion auf der Buhne*, Emsdetten, Verlag Lechte, 1961.

W

WARRE (Michael), *Designing and Making Stage Scenery*, foreword by Peter Brook, London, Studio Vista, 1966.

WINDS (Adolf), *Geschichte der Regie*, Stuttgart, Berlin, Leipzig. Deutsche Verlagsanstalt, 1925.

Collective Works

Le Lieu theatral dans la societe moderne, studies compiled and presented by Denis Bablet and Jean Jacquot with the help of Marcel Oddon, Paris, Editions du Centre National de la Recherche Scientifique, 1963.

Les Voies de la creation theatrale, Paris, Editions du Centre National de la Recherche Scientifique :

Volume I (1970) :
Theatre Laboratoire. Wroclaw. Jerzy Grotowski. *Le Prince constant.* Odin Teatret. Holstebro. Eugenio Barba. *Kaspariana.* The Living Theatre. Julian Beck and Judith Malina. *The Brig, Frankenstein, Antigone, Paradise Now.* The Open Theatre. New York. Joseph Chaikin. J.-C. Van Itallie. *The Serpent.* Arrabal. Victor Garcia. *Le Cimetiere des voitures.* Odette Aslan, Christiane Aubert, J.-L. Bourbon-naud, Jean Jacquot, Serge Ouaknine, compiled and presented by Jean Jacquot.

Volume II (1970)
B. Brecht: *Mother Courage, The Resistible Rise of Arturo Ui.*
M. Frisch: *Andorra.*
P. Weiss: *The Investigation.*
A. Cesaire : *La Tragedie du Roi Christophe, Une Saison au Congo.*
J. Cabral de Melo Neto : *Mort et vie severine.*

Stagings by E. Axer, I. Bergman, G. de Bosio, B. Brecht, H. Buckwitz, E. Engel, G. Garran, K. Hirschfield, F. Kortner, P. Palitzsch, H.A. Perten, E. Piscator, V. Puecher, J.-M. Serreau, S. Siqueira, J. Vilar, M. Wekwerth.
Studies by O. Aslan, D. Bablet, J.-C. Francois, P. Ivernel, P. Laville, J. Lorang, M. Meyer, compiled and presented by Denis Bablet.

Volume III (1972) :
Jean Genet : *Les Paravents.*
Bertolt Brecht : *La Vie de Galilee.*
Eugene Schwarz : *Le Dragon.*
After John Reed : Les Dix jours qui ebranlerentle monde.
Stagings by B. Besson, R. Blin, P. Brook, P.V. Carlsson, P. Debauche, L. Epp, P. Giuranna, H. Lietzau, I. Liubimov, A. Vitz.
Studies by Cl. Amiard-Chevrel, O. Aslan, B. Dort, J. Jacquot, B. Picon-Vallin, compiled and presented by Denis Bablet et Jean Jacquot.

Principal Reviews Consulted

Buhnentechnische Rundschau, Berlin.

Interscena, Prague.

Theatre dans le monde, Brussels.

Travail theatral, Lausanne.

Tulane Drama Review, The Drama Review, New York.

Exhibitions (catalogues and documents) chronologically arranged

1900 REYNAUD (Charles), *Musee retrospectif de la classe 18, Theatre, a l'Exposition Universelle Internationale de 1900, a Paris,* Saint-Cloud, Imprimerie Belin Freres (1903).

1913 *Moderne Theaterkunst,* Mannheim, Kunsthalle.

1914 *Theaterkunstausstellung,* Zurich (texts by A. Altherr, A. Baur, A. Appia, F.E. Storck, E.G. Craig, etc.).

1922 *Internationale Theatertentoonstelling in het Stedelijk Museum te Amsterdam,* Amsterdam, 1922. Important publication on the occasion of this exhibition : *Wendingen,* an illustrated magazine of the arts of Architectura et Amicitia. The International Theater Exhibition in the Municipal Museum of Amsterdam, held in January and February 1922, Amsterdam, 1921.
International Theatre Exhibition Designs and models for the modern stage. London, Victoria and Albert Museum.

1924 *Internationale Ausstellung neuer Theatertechnik,* Vienna, Konzerthaus.

1925 *Exposition international des arts decoratifs et industriels modernes,* Paris.
Exposition internationale des arts decoratifs et industriels modernes, Paris. Rapport general de Paul Leon (vol. X, theater, photography and cinematography), Paris, Larousse, 1929.

1926 *International Theater Exposition,* New York, Steinway Building.

1927 *Deutsche Theater-Ausstellung,* Magdeburg.

1931 *Theaterkunstausstellung,* Zurich, Kunstgewerbeschule (texts by Carl Niessen, Oskar Schlemmer, Raymond Cogniat).
Das Problemtheater, Basle, Kunstgewerbemuseum (text by Carl Niessen).

1934 *Theatre Art International Exhibition,* New York, Museum of Modern Art.

1936 *Internationale Ausstellung fur Theaterkunst,* Gesellschaft der Freunde der National-Bibliothek, Vienna.

1955 *Europaische Theaterausstellung von der Antike bis zur Gegenwart,* Vienna, Kunstlerhaus.

1959 *Design for the Theatre 1934-1959,* New York, Sarah Lawrence College, Bronxville.

1963 *1 a Esposizione internazionale di scenografia contemporanea,* Naples.
Bild und Buhne, Wiesbaden, Stadt. Museum, Gemaldegalerie (texts by Lutsch, Clemens Weiler, Albert Schulze Vellinghausen, Shingo Endoh, Hann Trier).

1964 *Das Buhenbild nach 1945, eine Dokumentation,* Zurich, Kunstgewerbemuseum (texts by M. Buchmann, E. Billeter, Teo Otto, Rolf Badenhausen, Georges Schlocker, Rene Allio, Andrzej Wirth).
Beeldend experiment op de planken, Eindhoven (texts by J. Leering et D. Bablet).

1965 *Bild und Buhne. Art et theatre. Stage and Art,* Baden-Baden, Kunsthalle (texts by D. Mahlow, H.V. Kleist, E. Vietta, O. Schlemmer, T. Kantor, E. Vedova, A. Banach).

1967 *Premiere Quadriennale de Scenographie,* Prague.

1971 *Deuxieme Quadriennale de Scenographie,* Prague.
Die Buhne als Forum, Internationale Schauspielszene seit 1945, Berlin, Akademie der Kunste.

1973 *Die zwanziger Jahre, Kontraste eines Jahrzehnts,* Zurich, Kunstgewerbemuseum.

ARTICLES OF SPECIAL INTEREST ARRANGED ALPHABETICALLY BY SUBJECTS AND AUTHORS

A

ACQUART (Andre)
Exhibition catalog:
Cenarios e figurinos de Andre Acquart, Bulbenkian Foundation, Lisbon, June 1973.

ALTMAN (Nathan)
On Altman :
Etkind (M.), *Nathan Altman,* Moscow, Sovietski Khoudojnik, 1971.

ANTOINE (Andre)
Le Theatre Libre, Paris, Imprimerie Eugene Verneau, May. 1890.
"Causerie sur la mise en scene," in *La Revue de Paris,* 1 April 1903, pp. 596-612.
Mes souvenirs sur le Theatre Libre, Paris, Artheme Fayard, 1921.
Mes Souvenirs sur le Theatre Antoine et sur l'Odeon (Premiere direction), Paris, Grasset, 1928.

On Antoine :
Roussou (Matei), *Andre Antoine,* Paris, L'Arche. 1954.

APPEN (Karl von)
On Appen :
Dieckmann (Fredrich), *Karl von Appens Buhnenbilder am Berliner Ensemble,* Berlin, Henschel Verlag, 1971.

APPIA
Staging of Wagnerian Drama, Paris, Leon Chailley, 1895.
Music and Staging, Berne, Theater-Kultur Verlag, 1963.
The Work of Living Art, Geneva-Paris, Atar, 1921.

On Appia :
Volbach (Walther R.), *Adolphe Appia, Prophet of the Modern Theatre,* Middletown, Connecticut, Wesleyan University Press, 1968.

ARTAUD (Antonin)
Œuvres completes. Tome IV. Le theatre et son double. Le theatre de Seraphin. Les Cenci, Paris, Gallimard, 1964.

ART ET ACTION
Structures dramatiques, Paris, 1951.

AUSTRIA
Dietrich (Margret) et Kindermann (Heinz), *Dreihundert Jahre Oesterreichisches Buhnenbild,* Vienna, Institut fur Theaterwissenschaft an der Universitat Wien, 1959.
Catalog of an Exhibition :
Oesterreichische Buhnenbildner der Gegenwart, Innsbruck, 1968.
cf. Strnad (Oskar).

BAKST (Leon)
On Bakst :
Alexandre (Arsene), *L'Art decoratif de Leon Bakst.* Critical essay by Arsene Alexandre, notes on the ballet by Jean Cocteau, Paris, Maurice de Brunoff, 1913.
Levinson (Andre), *Histoire de Leon Bakst,* Paris, Henri Reynaud, 1924.

BALLA (Giacomo)
On Balla :
Fagiolo dell' Arco (Maurizio), *Balla : ricostruzione futurista dell' universo,* Rome, Mario Bulzoni, 1968.

BALLET
Amberg (George), *Art in Modern Ballet,* New York, Pantheon, 1946 : *Ballet in America, the Emergence of an American Art,* New York, Duell, Sloan and Pearce, 1949.
Beaumont (Cyrill W.), *Ballet Design Past and Present.* London, New York, The Studio, 1946.
Buckle (Richard), *Modern Ballet Design,* London, Adam and Charles Black, 1955.
Kochno (Boris), with the help of Maria Luz, *Le Ballet,* Paris, Hachette, 1954.
Lifar (Serge), *Traite de choregraphie,* Paris, Bordas, 1952.
Das Kunstwerk. Ballet und bildende Kunst, number of the review *Das Kunstwerk,* Krefeld - Baden-Baden, February, 1959.
cf. Ballets Russes, Ballets Suedois, Stravinsky (Igor).

BALLETS RUSSES
Works :
Cocteau (Jean), *Entre Picasso et Radiguet,* compiled and presented by Andre Fermigier, Paris, Hermann, 1967.
Gontcharova (Nathalie), Larionov (Michel), Vorms (Pierre), *Les Ballets russes. Serge de Diaghilew et la decoration theatrale,* Belves, Pierre Vorms, 1955.
Grigoriev (S.L.), *The Diaghilew Ballet (1909-1929),* London, Constable, 1953.
Kochno (Boris), *Diaghilev et les Ballets Russes,* Paris, Fayard, 1973.
Lifar (Serge), *Histoire du Ballet Russe depuis les origines jusqu'a nos jours,* Paris, Nagel, 1950; *Serge de Diaghilev,* Monaco, Editions du Rocher, 1954.
Propert (W.A.), *The Russian Ballet in Western Europe, 1909-1920,* London, John Lane, 1921.
Svetlov (Valerian), *Le Ballet contemporain,* work edited with the help of Leon Bakst, Paris, M. de Brunoff, 1912.
Recueil des plus beaux programmes des Ballets Russes, Paris, M. de Brunoff, 1924.
Revue musicale, special number on the Ballets Russes, Paris, 1930.

Catalog of an exhibition :
Exposition retrospective de maquettes, decors et costumes executes pour la Compagnie des Ballets Russes de Serge de Diaghilev du 14 au 28 octobre 1930, Galerie Billiet - Pierre Vorms, Paris, 1930.
Ballets Russes de Diaghilev. 1909-1929. Paris, Musee des Arts Decoratifs, 1939.
Buckle (Richard), *The Diaghilev Exhibition Catalogue,* London and Edinburgh, 1954.
Les Ballets Russes de Serge de Diaghilev, 1909-1929, Strasbourg, Ancienne Douane, 1969.
Diaghilev Ballet Material. Costumes, Costume Designs and Portraits, catalog of Sotheby auction (London) June 13, 1967.
Sergei Diaghilev, Boris Kniasseff, Max Reinhardt, catalog of Sotheby auction (London) December 15-16, 1969.
Costumes and Curtains from Diaghilev and De Basil Ballets, catalog of Sotheby auction (London) December 19, 1969.

Collections :
The Serge Lifar Collection of Ballet Set and Costume Designs, published on the occasion of the opening of Harkness House for Ballet Arts, New York City, November 1965, by the Wadsworth Atheneum, Hartford, Connecticut.

375

Lebel (Jean-Jacques), *Entretiens avec Julian Beck et Judith Malina*, Paris, Pierre Belfond, 1969.

LUGNE-POE

La Parade. I. Le sot du tremplin, Paris, Gallimard, 1930.
La Parade. II. Acrobaties. Paris, Gallimard, 1931.
Derniere Pirouette, Paris, Editions du Sagittaire, 1946.

On Lugne-Poe :

Robichez (Jacques), *Lugne-Poe*, Paris, L'Arche, 1955.

cf. Symbolism.

M

MALEVICH (Kazimir)

Catalog of an exhibition :

Malevich. Dessins, Paris, Galerie Jean Chauvelin, November 19-December 31, 1970.

MEINNINGER

Grube (Max), *Geschichte der Meininger*, Stuttgart, Berlin, Leipzig, Deutsche Verlagsanstalt, 1926.

MEYERHOLD (Vsevolod)

Stati, pisma, rietchi, bessiedi (articles, letters, lectures, conversations) vol. I and II, Moscow, Iskusstvo, 1968.
Le Theatre theatral, translated and presented by Nina Gourfinkel, Paris, Gallimard, 1963.
Ecrits sur le theatre, vol. I, translation, introduction and notes by Beatrice Picon-Vallin, Lausanne, La Cite, 1973.
Meyerhold on Theatre, translated and edited with a critical commentary by Edward Braun, London, Methuen and Cº, 1969.

On Meyerhold :

Gvosdev (A.A.), *Teatr imeni Vs. Meyerhold (1920-1926)* (Meyerhold's Theater 1920-1926), Leningrad, Academia, 1927.
Revizor v teatre imeni Vs. Meyerhold (Le Revizor au Theatre Meyerhold), texts by A.A. Gvosdev, E.I. Kaplan, I.A. Nazarenko, A.L. Slonimskov and V.N. Soloviev, Leningrad, Academia, 1927.
Vstretchi s Meyerholdom (Meetings with Meyerhold), collective work (Valentei, Markov, Rostotski, Fevralski, Tchouchkine), Moscow, V.T.O., 1967.
Roudnitski (K.), *Rejissoir Meyerhold* (Meyerhold, the director), Moscow, Nauka, 1969.
Volkov (Nikolai), *Meyerhold*, Moscow-Leningrad, Academia, 1929.
Fedorow (W.), "Der Maler und Konstrukteur im Theater" in *Russisches Theater*, special issue of *Das Neue Russland*, Berlin, number 3-4, 1925.

MIELZINER (Jo)

Designing for the Theatre, New York, Atheneum, 1965.

MINKS (Winifried)

Catalog of an exhibition :

Die neue Buhne, Stadtisches Museum, Leverkusen, October 20-November 26, 1967.

MOHOLY-NAGY (Laszlo)

On Moholy-Nagy :

Moholy-Nagy (Sibyl), *Moholy-Nagy, Experiment in Totality*, M.I.T. Press, Cambridge (U.S.A.) and London, 2nd edition, 1969.

Catalog of an exhibition :

Moholy-Nagy, Eindhoven, Stedelijk van Abbe-museum, January 20-March 6, 1967.

MOZART (Wolfgang Amadeus)

Catalog of an exhibition :

Mozart und das Theater, Ausstellung des Instituts fur Theaterwissenschaft der Universitat Koin zur Mozartwoche der deutschen Oper am Rhein, Dusseldorf, Duisburg, 1970.

N

NEHER (Caspar)

On Neher :

Caspar Neher, herausgegeben von Gottfried von Einem und Siegfried Melchinger, Velber bei Hannover, Friedrich Verlag, 1966.
Caspar Nehers Szenisches Werk. Ein Verzeichnis des Bestandes der Theatersammlung der Oesterreichischen Nationalbibliothek bearbeitet von Franz Hadamowsky, Vienna, Verlag Bruder Hollinek, 1972.

NIVINSKI (Ignat Ignatievitch)

On Vivinski :

Dokuvayeva (V.N.), *Ignat Ignatievitch Nivinski*, Moscow, Sovietski Khoudojnik, 1969.

O

OENSLAGER (Donald)

Scenery then and now, new edition, New York, Russell and Russell, 1966.

OTTO (Teo)

Meine Szene, Cologne, Kiepenheuer und Witsch, 1965.

P

PICASSO (Pablo)

On Picasso :

Cooper (Douglas), *Picasso theatre*, Paris, Editions Cercle d'Art, 1967.

Catalog of an exhibition :

Picasso et le theatre, exhibition at the Musee des Augustins, Toulouse, June 22-September 15, 1965.

PIGNON (Edouard)

On Pignon :

Parmelin (Helene), *Cinq peintres et le theatre. Decors et costumes de Leger, Coutaud, Gischia, Labisse, Pignon*, Paris, Cercle d'Art, 1956.

PIRCHAN (Emil)

On Pirchan :

Schepelmann-Rieder (Erika), *Emil Pirchan und das expressionistische Buhnenbild*, Vienna, Bergland Verlag, 1964.

PISCATOR (Erwin)

Le Theatre politique, Paris, L'Arche, 1962.
Schriften. 1. Das politische Theater. 2. Aufsatze, Reden, Gesprache, Berlin, Henschelverlag Kunst und Gessellschaft, 1968.

On Piscator :

Ley-Piscator (Maria), *The Piscator Experiment. The Political Theatre*, New York, James H. Heineman, 1967.

PITOEFF (Georges)

Notre theatre, texts and documents assembled by Jean de Rigault, Paris, Messages, 1949.

On Pitoeff :

Frank (Andre), *Georges Pitoeff*, Paris, L'Arche, 1958.

PLANCHON (Roger)

Copfermann (Emile), *Roger Planchon*, Lausanne, La Cite, 1969.
Itineraire de Roger Planchon, texts by J. Duvignaud, B. Dort, A. Gisselbrecht, R. Barthes, M. Vinaver, G. Dumur, P. Seller, R. Nataf, F. Kourilsky, Paris, L'Arche, 1970.
Le Travail au Theatre de la Cite, I. 1958-1959 Season, Paris, L'Arche, 1959.
Le Travail au Theatre de la Cite, II. 1959-1960 Season, Paris, L'Arche, 1960.

POEL (William)

Speaight (Robert), *William Poel and the Elizabethan Revival*, London, William Heinemann, 1954.

POLAND

Strzelecki (Zenobiusz), *Polska plastyka teatralna*, Warsaw, Panstwowy Instytut Wydawniczy, 1963 (3 volumes).

Catalog of an exhibition :

Wystawa scenografii, Warsaw, 1962.

cf Grotowski (Jerzy), Schiller (Leon), Szajna (Josef).

PRAMPOLINI (Enrico)

Scenotecnica, Milan, Hoepli, 1940.

On Prampolini :

Menna (Filiberto), *Enrico Prampolini*, Rome, De Luca, 1967.

Catalog of an exhibition :

E. Prampolini, Rome, Instituto italo-latino americano, January-February, 1974.

R

RABINOVICH (Isaac)

On Rabinovich :

Syrkina (F.Ia), *I. Rabinovich*, Leningrad, 1972.

REINHARDT (Max)

Carter (Huntly), *The Theatre of Max Reinhardt*, London, Frank and Cecil Palmer, 1914.
Niessen (Carl), *Max Reinhardt und seine Buhnenbildner*, Cologne, 1958.
Max Reinhardt. Sein Theater in Bildern, herausgegeben von der Max Reinhardt-Forschungsstatte Salzburg, Velber bei Hannover, Friedrich Verlag et Vienne, Oesterreichischer Bundesverlag, 1968.

Catalogs of exhibitions :

Max Reinhardt. Ausstellung in der Akademie der bildenden Kunste, Vienna, 1968.
Max Reinhardt und Shakespeare, Ausstellung der Deutschen Akademie der Kunste zu Berlin, s.d.

REINKING (Wilhelm)

Wilhelm Reinking. Verzeichnis meiner Arbeiten, Munich, Laokoon-Verlag, 1964.

ROMANIA

Scenografia romaneasca. Stage Design in Rumania. La Scenographie roumaine (the following have contributed to this work : Paul Bortnovschi, Liviu Ciulei, Jules Perahim, Eugen Schileru), Bucharest, Meridiane, 1965.

RUSSIA-U.S.S.R.

Carter (Huntly), *The New Theatre and Cinema of Soviet Russia*, New York, International Publishers, 1925; *The New Spirit in the Russian Theatre*, New York, Brentano's, 1929.
Evreinoff (Nicolas), *Le Theatre en Russie sovetique*, Paris, Les publications techniques artistiques, 1946.
Gourfinkel (Nina), *Theatre russe contemporain*, Paris, Editions Albert, 1930.
Gray (Camilla), *The Great Experiment : Russian Art 1863-1922*, London, Thames and Hudson, 1962.
Gregor (Joseph) et Futop-Miller (Rene), *Das Russische Theater, sein Wesen und seine Geschichte mit besonderer Berucksichtigung der Revolutionsperiod*, Zurich, Leipzig, Vienna, Amaltheaverlag, 1928.
Houghton (Norris), *Moscow Rehearsals*, New York, Harcourt, Brace and Co., 1936; *Return Engagement, A Postscript to "Moscow Rehearsals,"* New York, Holt, Rinehart and Winston, 1962.
Picon-Vallin (Beatrice), *Le Theatre juif sovietique pendant les annees vingt*, Lausanne, La Cite, 1973.
Pojarskaia (M.N.), *Rousskoe teatalno-decorat-sionnoe iskousstvo* (The Russian art of theater decoration), Moscow, Iskusstvo, 1970.
Ripellino (Angelo Maria), *Maiakovski et le theatre russe d'avant-garde*, Paris, L'Arche, 1965 ; *Il Trucco e l'anima. I maestri della regia nel teatro russo del novecento*, Turin, Einaudi, 1965.
Sayler (Oliver M.), *The Russian Theatre under the Revolution*, Boston, Little, Brown and Co., 1920.
Strijenova (T.), *Iz istoril sovietskova kostiouma* (History of Soviet costumes), Moscow, sovietski khoudojnik, 1972.
Mouzei imeni Bakhrouchina (The Bakhrushin Museum), Moscow, izobrazitelnoe iskusstvo, 1971.

Collective works :

Agitatsionno-massovoe iskousstvo pervykh liet Oktiabria (Materialy i issledovania) (The art of mass propaganda during the first few years after the October revolution). Moscow, Iskusstvo, 1971.

Istoria sovietskovo teatra - tom pervii (1917-1921) (History of Soviet theater Vol. I, 1917-1921), Leningrad, isdatelstvo khoudojestvennoi literaturi, 1933.

Khoudojniki teatra o svoiom tvortchestve (Painters in the theater on their work) Moscow, sovietski khoudojnik, 1973.

50 let sovietskovo iskousstva. Khoudojniki teatra (50 years of Soviet art. Painters in the theater) collective work (A.N. Chifrina and E.M. Kostina), Moscow, sovietski khoudojnik, 1969.

Das moskauer judische akademische Theater (Texts by E. Toller, J. Roth, A. Goldschmidt), Berlin, Die Schmiede, 1928.

Catalogs of exhibitions :

Katalog vystavski teatralno-decoratsionnova iskousstva (Catalog from the exhibition of scenographic arts), *1917-1935*, Leningrad, VTO, 1936.

Teatralno-decoratsionnoe iskousstvo v SSSR (1917-1927) The art of theatrical decor in the Soviet Union, 1917-1927, Leningrad, izdanie komiteta vystavki teatralno-decoratsionnovo iskousstva, 1927.

Russian Stage and Costume Designs for the Ballet, Opera and Theatre, a loan exhibition from the Lovanov-Rostovsky, Oenslager and Riabov collections. Touring exhibition organized by The International Exhibitions Foundation, 1967-1969 (U.S.A.).

Art in Revolution. Soviet Art and Design since 1917, London, Hayward Gallery, February 26-April 18, 1971.

Kunst in der Revolution. Architektur, Produktgesteltung, Malerei, Plastik, Agitation, Theater, Film in der Sowjetunion 1917-1932, Frankfurter Kunstverein, 1972.

Cf. Bakst (Leon), Benois (Alexandre), Chagall (Marc), Egorov (V.E.), Eisenstein (S.), Ereinoff (Nicolas), Expressionism, Exter (A.), Golovine (A.I.), Gontcharova (Nathalie), Larionov (Michel), Lissitzky (El), Malevich (Kazimir), Meyerhold (Vsevolod), Nivinski (I.I.), Ryndin (Vadim), Stanislavsky (Constantin) and the Moscow Art Theater, Tairov (Alexandre), Vakhtangov (E.B.).

RYNDIN (Vadim)

Khoudojnik i Teatr (The Painter and the theater), Moscow, Vserossilskoe Teatralnoe Obchtchestvo, 1966.

S

SCHLEMMER (Oskar)

Catalog of an exhibition :

Oskar Schlemmer und die abstrakte Buhne, Zurich, Kunstgewerbemuseum, June 18-August 27, 1961.

SCHILLER (Leon)

Pamietnik Teatralny, Warsaw, rok 1955, issue dedicated to Leon Schiller.

SHAKESPEARE (William)

Jacquot (Jean), *Shakespeare en France, mises en scene d'hier et d'aujourd'hui*, Paris, Le Temps, 1964.

Catalogs of exhibitions

Shakespeare und das deutsche Theater, Bochum (Stadtische Kunst-galerie), Heidelberg (Schloss), 1964.

Max Reinhardt und Shakespeare, Ausstellung der Deutsche Akademie der Kunste zu Berlin, s.d.

cf. Poel (William).

SIEVERT (Ludwig)

On Sievert :

Niessen (Carl), *Der Szeniker Ludwig Sievert*, Cologne, Greven und Berchtold, 1921.

Stahl (Leopold), *Ludwig Sievert. Lebendiges Theater*, Munich, F. Bruckmann Verlag, 1944.

Wagner (Ludwig), *Der Szeniker Ludwig Sievert*, Berlin, Buhnenvolksbundverlag, 1926.

STANISLAVSKY (Constantin) and the Moscow Art Theater.

By Stanislavsky :

An Actor Prepares, 1926.

La Construction du personnage, preface by Bernard Dort, Paris, Olivier Perrin, 1958.

My Life in Art, translated by J.J. Robbins, New York, Theatre Arts Books, 1948.

On Stanislavsky :

Moskovski Khoudojestvenni teatr. Tom pervi (1898-1917) Moscow Art Theater, Vol. I (1898-1917), collective work, Moscow, Gossoudarstvennoe izdatelstvo, izobrazitelnovo iskousstva, 1955).

Bassekhes (A.), *Khoudojniki na scene MKHAT* (Stage Designers of the Art Theater), Moscow, VTO, 1960.

Gourfinkel (Nina), *Constantin Stanislavski*, Paris, L'Arche, 1955.

STERN (Ernst)

Buhenbildner bei Max Reinhardt, Berlin, Henschelverlag, 1955.

STRAVINSKY (Igor)

Chroniques de ma vie, Paris, Denoel/Gonthier, 1962.

Catalog of an exhibition :

Stravinsky and the Theatre, a catalogue of decor and costume designs for stage productions of his works, 1910-1962, New York, The New York Public Library, 1963.

STRNAD (Oskar)

On Strnad :

Niedermoser (Otto), *Oskar Strnad 1879-1935*, Vienna, Bergland Verlag, 1965.

SVOBODA (Josef)

On Svoboda :

Bablet (Denis), *La scena e l'immagine. Saggio su Josef Svoboda*, Turin, Einaudi, 1970 ; *Svoboda*, La Cite, Lausanne, 1970.

Beriozkine (V.), *Teatr Josefa Svobody* (The Theater of Josef Svoboda), Moscow, Izobrazitelnoe iskousstvo, 1973.

Burian (Jarka), *The Scenography of Josef Svoboda*, Middletown, Connecticut, Wesleyan University Press, 1971.

Maresova (Sylva), *Josef Svoboda*, Prague, Divadelni Ustav, 1971.

SWEDEN

Bjurstrom (Per), *Teaterdekoration i Sverige*, Stockholm, Natur och Kultur, 1964.

cf. Ballets suedois.

SWITZERLAND

Vincent (Vincent), *Le Theatre du Jorat*, Paris and Neuchatel, Editions Victor Attinger, 1933.

Catalog of an exhibition :

Le decor du theatre suisse depuis Adolphe Appia, exhibition organized by Edmund Stadler, 1954.

cf. Appia (Adolphe).

SYMBOLISM

Fort (Paul), *Mes Memoires. Toute la vie d'un poete. 1872-1944*, Paris, Flammarion, 1944.

Knowles (Dorothy), *La Reaction idealiste au theatre depuis 1890*, Paris, Droz, 1934.

Robichez (Jacques), *Le Symbolisme au theatre. Lugne-Poe et les debuts de L'Œuvre*, Paris, L'Arche, 1957.

cf. Lugne-Poe.

SZAJINA (Josef)

On Szajna :

Madeyski (Jerzy) *Josef Szajna*, Cracow, Biuro wystaw artystycznych w Krakowie, 1970.

T

TAIROV (Alexandre)

Zapiski rejissiora, stati, bessiedi, rietchi, pisma (notes, articles, conversations, lectures, and letters by a designer), Moscow, VTO, 1970.

Das entfesselte Theater, Potsdam, Gustav Kiepenheuer Verlag, 1923 (new edition : Kiepenheuer und Witsch, 1964).

On Tairov :

Derjavine (K.), *Kniga o Kamernom teatre* (Book on the Kamerny Théater), Leningrad, gossoudarstvennoe izdatelstvo khoudojestvennaia literatura, 1934.

The Artist of the Kamerni Theater 1914-1934, forword by Abraham Efros, Moscow, 1935.

THEATER-IN-THE-ROUND

Jones (Margo), *Theatre-in-the-round*, New York, Rinehart and Co., 1951.

Villiers (Andre), *Le Theatre en rond*, Paris, Librairie theatrale, 1958.

THEATER, MUSICAL

Panofsky (Walter), *Protest in der Oper. Das provokative Musik-theater der zwanziger Jahre*, Munich, Laokoon Verlag, 1966.

Horowicz (Bronislaw), *Le Theatre d'opera. Histoire, realisations sceniques, possibilites*, Paris, Editions de Flore, 1946.

cf. Expressionnism, Mozart (Wolfgang Amadeus), Stravinsky (Igor).

TOTAL THEATER

Kirby (E.T.), *Total Theatre*, a critical anthology edited by ..., New York, E.P. Dutton, 1969.

"Total Theater", theme of the November-December, 1965 and the January-February, 1966 issues of the review *Theatre dans le monde*.

U   V

U.S.A.

Macgowan (Kenneth), *Footlights across America*, Harcourt, Brace, New York, 1929.

Sayler (Oliver M.), *Our American Theatre*, New York, Brentano's, 1923.

Theatre Arts Anthology, edited by R. Gilder, H.R. Isaacs, R.M. MacGregor, E. Reed, New York, Theatre Arts Books, 1950.

Art and Decoration. Stage Settings, special edition, New York, November 1930.

Catalog of an exhibition :

American Stage Designs, New York, Bourgeois Galleries, 1919.

cf. Bread and Puppet Theater, Fuller (Loie), Happenings, Jones (Robert Edmond), Living Theatre, Mielziner (Jo), Oenslager (Donald), Simonson (Lee), Theater-In-The-Round.

U.S.S.R.

cf. Russia-U.S.S.R.

VAKHTANGOV (Evgueni Bogrationovitch)

On Vakhtangov :

Gortchakov (Nikolai), *Vakhtangov metteur en scene*, Moscow, foreign language editions, s.d.

Zakhava (Boris), *Evgueni Vakhtangov et son ecole*, Moscow, editions du Progres, 1973.

VILAR (Jean) and the T.N.P.

By Vilar :

De la tradition theatrale, Paris, L'Arche, 1955.

On Vilar :

Serriere (Marie-Therese), *Le T.N.P. et nous*, Paris, Jose Corti, 1959.

Avignon. 20 ans de festival, Dedalus, 1967.

cf. Gischia (Leon), Pignon (Edouard).

W   Z

WAGNER (Wieland)

Richard Wagner und das neue Bayreuth herausgegeben von Vieland Wagner, Munich, Paul List Verlag, 1962.

On Wieland Wagner :

Herzfeld (Friedrich), *Neues Bayreuth*, Berlin, Rembrandt Verlag, 1960.

Lust (Claude), *Wieland Wagner et la survie du theatre lyrique*, Lausanne, La Cite, 1969.

ZOLA (Emile)

Le Naturalisme au theatre, Paris, G. Charpentier, 1881.

Index of names cited

The numbers in standard type refer to names cited in the text (page numbers). The numbers in bold type refer to names cited in the captions (illustration numbers).

ACKNOWLEDGEMENTS

for *Austria*	F. Tornquist, Graz.
	Mme D. Hinker, Mr. J. Mayerhofer and the Theatersammlung der oesterreichischen Nationalbibliothek, Vienna - The Bildarchiv der oesterreichischen Nationalbibliothek, Vienna.
for *Czechoslovakia*	Mmes E. Soukupova and J. Gabrielova, and the Prague Theater Institute - J. Hilmera and the Theater Section of the National Museum of Prague.
	The Burian Archives, Strahov.
for *East Germany*	The Berliner Ensemble-Archiv, East Berlin - The Bertolt Brecht-Archiv, East Berlin.
for *France*	Mme H.-G. Adam, Paris - Les heritiers de A. Barsacq - M. J. Chauvelin - Mme M.-H. Daste - M. J. Dupin - Mme Faurer - M. J.-P. Jouvet - Mme A. Larionov - M. J.-Cl. Marcade - Mme V. Pevsner - M. S. Pitoeff.
	Mlle M.-F. Christout, Mlle C. Giteau, Mme M. Herlin, et la Bibliotheque de l'Arsenal (Fonds Rondel, Collections Art et Action, G. Baty, J. Copeau, E.G. Craig, L. Jouvet, G. Pitoeff), Paris - Mme S. Chevalley et la Bibliotheque de la Comedie-Francaise, Paris - M. J. Robnard et l'Institut Suedois pour les Relations Culturelles avec l'Etranger, Paris.
	L'Association France-U.R.S.S., Paris - La Bibliotheque d'Art et d'Archeologie de l'Universite de Paris - La Bibliotheque de l'Union Centrale des Arts Decoratifs, Paris - La Collection Jean Vilar - Le Musee des Arts Decoratifs, Paris - Le Musee National d'Art Moderne, Paris.
	Les Editions Cercle d'Art, Paris - Les Editions Balland, Paris.
for *Great Britain*	J. Carr Doughty, London.
	G.W. Nash and the Victoria and Albert Museum, Theatre Section, London.
for *Holland*	The Stedelijk Museum, Amsterdam.
for *Italy*	Mme L. Balla, Rome - E. Bertonati (Galleria del Levante, Milan) - P. Marchi, Rome - G. Mattioli, Milan - A. Prampolini, Rome - Mr. G. Tintori and the Museo Teatrale alla Scala, Milan.
	La Galleria d'Arte l'Obelisco.
	Les Editions Fratelli Fabbri Editori, Milan.
for *Norway*	Munch Museet, Oslo.
for *Poland*	Z. Strzelecki, Warsaw.
	The Ministry of Culture and Art of the Peoples Republic of Poland, Warsaw - The Warsaw Theater Museum.
for *Sweden*	B. Hager and the Dance Museum, Stockholm.
	The Drottningholms Teatermuseum, Stockholm.
for *Switzerland*	G. Cramer, Mies - Mme L. Moholy, Zurich.
	Mme E. Billeter and the Kunstgewerbemuseum of Zurich - E. Stadler and the Appia Foundation, Collection Suisse du Theatre, Bibliotheque Nationale Suisse, Berne.
	La Galerie d'Art Moderne, Basle - L'Institut Jaques-Dalcroze, Geneva, The Kunstmuseum, Basle
for the *U.S.A.*	J. Mielziner, New York - Mme S. Moholy-Nagy, New York - D. Oenslager, New York - R. Pendleton, Middletown.
	F.J. Hunter and the Hoblitzelle Theatre Arts Library, The University of Texas at Austin - Busch-Reisinger Museum Harvard University - The Museum of Modern Art, New York - Wadsworth Atheneum Hartford - Yale University, Coll. Wickes.
	Theatre Arts Books, New York.
for the *U.S.S.R.*	State Central Theater Library of the U.S.S.R. Ministry of Culture, Moscow - Moscow Art Theater Museum.
	A. A. Bakhrushin State Central Theater Museum, Moscow - Leningrad State Theater Museum.

385

List of Abbreviations

Arch.	*Archives*
Bibl.	*Bibliotheque (Library)*
Chor.	*Choreography*
Part. Coll.	*Special Collection*
Doc.	*Document*
Ed.	*Edition*
Gal. Gall.	*Gallery*
Inst.	*Institute*
Msc.	*Mise en Scene*
Mus.	*Music*
Nat.	*National*
Phot.	*Photography*
Th.	*Theater*
Univ.	*University*

Ak.d. d. Kunste	*Academy of Art*
Berliner Ens. Arch.	*Archives of the Berliner Ensemble, East Berlin*
Bibl. Art et Arch. Paris,	*Library of Art and Archeology of the University of Paris*
Th. Lib. Moscow	*State Central Theatrical Library of the Ministry of Culture in the Soviet Union, Moscow*
Bildarchiv. Vienna	*Bildarchiv der oesterreichischen Nationalbibliothek, Vienna*
Appia Foundation, Berne	*Appia Foundation, Swiss Theatrical Collection, Swiss National Library, Berne*
Hoblitzelle Th. Arts Lib. The Univ. of Texas at Austin	*Hoblitzelle Theatre Arts Library, The University of Texas at Austin*
Inst. Th. Cologne	*Institut fur Theaterwissenschaft der Universitat Koln verbunden mit dem Theatermuseum*
Kunstgew, Mus. Zurich	*Kunstgewerbemuseum, Zurich*
Musee Nat. Art Mod. Paris	*Musee National d'Art Moderne, Paris*
Musee Arts Deco, Paris	*Musee des Arts Decoratifs, Paris*
Bakhrushin Mus, Moscow	*State Central Theatrical Museum Bakhrushin, Moscow*
Th. Mus. Leningrad	*State Theatrical Museum, Leningrad*
Th. Mus. Warsaw	*Theatrical Museum, Warsaw*
Sect. Th. Mus. Nat. Prague	*Theater Section of the National Museum in Prague*
R. Wagner Arch.	*Richard Wagner - Archiv. Bayreuth*
Theaterabt. St. U. Bibl. Frankfurt	*Theaterabteilung der Stadt- und Universitatsbibliothek, Frankfurt am Main*
Th. Inst. West Berlin	*Theaterwissenschaftliches Institut der Freien Universitat Berlin (West Berlin)*
Th. Mus. Munich	*Theatermuseum, Munich*
Th. Samm. Vienna	*Theatersammlung der oesterreichischen Nationalbibliothek, Vienna*
V. and A. Museum, London	*Victoria and Albert Museum, Theatre Section, London*
Yale Univ. Coll. Wickes	*Yale University Collection, from the Estate of Frances G. Wickes*

Table of Contents

This work was printed
in March, 1977
by Imprimerie Moderne du Lion - Paris

The composition was set
by JAD Computype - USA

The two original lithographs
of Joan Miro were printed
by Imprimerie Arte - Paris

88271   PN
2091
OVERSIZE   S8
B25

BABLET, DENIS
THE REVOLUTIONS OF STAGE
THE

DATE DUE	
JAN 19 1996	
GAYLORD	PRINTED IN U.S.A.